A DUKE
IN SHINING ARMOR

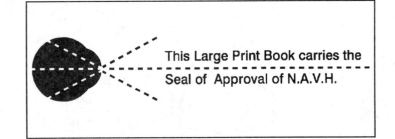

This Large Print Book carries the
Seal of Approval of N.A.V.H.

DIFFICULT DUKES

A DUKE IN SHINING ARMOR

LORETTA CHASE

THORNDIKE PRESS
A part of Gale, a Cengage Company

Farmington Hills, Mich • San Francisco • New York • Waterville, Maine
Meriden, Conn • Mason, Ohio • Chicago

Copyright © 2017 by Loretta Chase.
Difficult Dukes.
Thorndike Press, a part of Gale, a Cengage Company.

Thorndike Press® Large Print Romance.
The text of this Large Print edition is unabridged.
Other aspects of the book may vary from the original edition.
Set in 16 pt. Plantin.

LIBRARY OF CONGRESS CIP DATA ON FILE.
CATALOGUING IN PUBLICATION FOR THIS BOOK
IS AVAILABLE FROM THE LIBRARY OF CONGRESS

ISBN-13: 978-1-4328-5176-7 (hardcover)

Published in 2018 by arrangement with Avon, an imprint of HarperCollins Publishers

Printed in the United States of America
1 2 3 4 5 6 7 22 21 20 19 18

My cousin Valerie Kerxhalli, who has faced her own life challenge with all the courage, resourcefulness, grace, and good humor of a true heroine.

ACKNOWLEDGMENTS

Thanks to:

May Chen, my editor, who is able to read my mind when I can't, lift my spirits, and, generally, make me write a better book than I expect or hope to;

Nancy Yost, my agent, who takes care of business while inspiring, cheerleading, and coming up with terrific ideas I claim for my own;

Susan Holloway Scott, the other Nerdy History girl, my writerly confidante and bird of a feather, who shares my pain and laughter;

Bruce Hubbard, MD, who once again helped me navigate between the worlds of nineteenth- and twenty-first-century medicine;

Larry Abramoff, who built the footrest and saved my life (and possibly my writing career);

Gloria Abramoff, who said I could store

the footrest at their house (and possibly saved my marriage);

Cynthia, Vivian, and Kathy, my sisters, who've supported me from the get-go, in both writing and nonwriting matters, and haven't quit yet —

— with extra thanks to Cynthia, who's helped resolve more than one plot problem as we walk, stands by me at author events, and is always up for shopping;

Walter, my husband, who patiently brainstorms with me — *even though I didn't listen the last time* — takes me to wonderful places, and uses other masculine wiles to keep me from running away from the book.

All errors and poor judgment displayed here are, alas, my own.

PROLOGUE

London
Early morning of 11 June 1833

The Duke of Ashmont was not a very good duke — rather an awful one, actually. And so nobody could be in the least surprised to see him, drunk as an emperor — that was to say, ten times as drunk as a lord — staggering down the steps of Crockford's Club on the arm of one of his two best friends.

This one was Hugh Philemon Ancaster, seventh Duke of Ripley. Where Ashmont was fair-haired, blue-eyed, and angelic-looking, Ripley was dark. Unlike Ashmont, he did not appear to be spun of dreams and gossamer, and women did not follow his movements with the moonstruck expressions they accorded His Grace with the Angel Face.

On a good day, someone had said once, Ripley's face resembled that of a wolf who'd been in too many fights.

9

Furthermore, though his slightly older title ranked him a notch or two higher in precedence than Ashmont, Ripley was merely as drunk as a lord. He could still distinguish up from down. When, therefore, His Grace of Ashmont showed an inclination to stumble in the downhill direction, toward St. James's Palace, Ripley hauled him about.

"This way," he said. "Hackney stand up ahead."

"Right," Ashmont said. "Can't miss the wedding. Not this one. It's me doing it. Me and Olympia. Have to be there. Promised."

"You will be," Ripley said as he led his friend across the street. The wedding had been news to him, the choice of bride a shock: Lady Olympia Hightower, of all women. She was the last girl on earth he'd thought would marry Ashmont — or any of them, for that matter.

Not that Ripley knew her very well. Or at all. They'd been introduced, yes, years ago. That was in the days when respectable persons still introduced Ripley and his two friends to innocent girls. But those were not the kinds of girls the ducal trio wanted. Gently bred maidens were for marrying, and marriage was supposed to be years away, sometime in the dim, distant future.

Apparently, the future had arrived while Ripley wasn't looking.

First the Duke of Blackwood, the other of his two boon companions, had married Ripley's sister over a year ago, a few days before Ripley left for the Continent. Now Ashmont was doing it. Ripley had heard the happy news mere hours after his return to London yesterday.

No, he'd returned the day before, because today was yesterday now. He'd come to Crockford's because he wanted a decent meal, and Crockford's Ude was the next best thing to Ripley's own chef, Chardot, who'd come down with a foul cold sometime during the Channel crossing.

Chardot went with him everywhere because he was amply paid to do so, and Ripley liked his comfort. Having been forced, for no sane reason, to live like a pauper during his boyhood, he lived like a king now.

Ripley was debating with himself whether, on the whole, he'd better have stayed abroad, when four men spilled out of a narrow court, one crashing into Ashmont with force enough to dislodge him from Ripley's light grasp and push him into a shop front.

Ashmont bounced back with surprising energy. "You clumsy, bleeding, half-wit! I

11

have to get married, you bloody arsehole!" At the same moment, he drove his fist at the fellow's face.

One of the man's friends tried to butt in. With a sigh, Ripley grabbed him by the back of the collar. The fellow swung at him, obliging Ripley to knock him into the gutter.

What happened after that was what often happened when Ashmont was about: a lot of filthy language and filthy fighting, and men rushing out of the clubs, shouting bets, and a female or two screaming somewhere.

Then it was over. Their foes lay strewn about the pavement. Ripley didn't wait to count or identify them. He collected Ashmont from the railing he'd slumped against and trudged to the corner with him. He signaled, and the first in line of the hackneys plodded their way. He threw Ashmont into the decrepit coach and directed the driver to Ashmont House.

Servants waited up, as they were accustomed to do, for Ashmont. They bore him up the stairs to his bedroom and undressed and washed him without fuss. They were old hands at dealing with their master's little foibles.

After he'd seen His Grace safely tucked into bed, Ripley left.

He needed a bath, a nap, and a change of clothes.

He had a wedding to attend in a few hours.

CHAPTER 1

Newland House, Kensington
Late forenoon of 11 June 1833
If the bride *was* drunk — which she wasn't
— it was on account of celebrating.

In a very little while, Lady Olympia Hightower was going to make all of her family's
dreams come true. Hers, too, most of them.

She would become the Duchess of Ashmont.

Teetering on the brink of six and twenty,
she ought to thank her lucky stars she'd won
the heart . . . admiration . . . something . . .

. . . of one of England's three most notorious libertines, a trio of dukes known as
Their Dis-Graces.

She narrowed her eyes at the looking glass.

Behind gold-rimmed spectacles, eyes of a
can't-make-up-their-mind grey-blue-green
took a moment to focus on the grandeur
that was her. She. Whatever.

Elaborate side curls of a commonplace

brown framed her heart-shaped face. An intricate arrangement of plaits, topped by a great blossom of pleated lace adorned with orange blossoms, crowned her head. A blond lace veil cascaded over her bare shoulders, down over the full, lace-covered sleeves, and on past her waist.

She looked down at herself.

Four knots marched down to the V of the waistline. Below that swelled full skirts of brocaded silk.

A great waste of money, which would have been better spent on Eton for Clarence or a cornetcy for Andrew or *something* for one of the boys. Apart from his heir — Stephen, Lord Ludford — the Earl of Gonerby had five sons to support, a subject to which he'd given no thought whatsoever. His mind, unlike his daughter's, was not practical.

Thus, her present predicament. Which wasn't a predicament at all. So everybody said. There was nothing predicamental about being a duchess.

In any event, practicality had nothing to do with this bridal extravaganza. The money must be thrown away on Olympia, on a single dress, because, according to Aunt Lavinia, it was an investment in the future.

A duchess-to-be couldn't wear any old thing to her wedding. The bridal ensemble had to be expensive and fashionable, though not flamboyantly so, because a duchess-to-be ought to look expensively fashionable, though not flamboyantly so.

After the wedding was another matter entirely. A *duchess* could pour the entire contents of her jewel boxes over herself and never be overdressed.

With a few adjustments, a different arrangement on her head, and more diamonds or pearls or both, Olympia would wear the dress to the next Drawing Room, when her mother or perhaps Aunt Lavinia, the Marchioness of Newland, would present the new Duchess of Ashmont to the Queen.

That wasn't all that would happen after the wedding.

There was the wedding night, which, according to Mama, would not be unpleasant, although she'd been rather vague regarding details. But after the wedding night came the *marriage,* years and years of it. To Ashmont.

The about-to-be Duchess of Ashmont picked up the cup of brandy-laced tea Lady Newland had brought to steady bridal nerves. The cup was empty.

"Do not even think of bolting," her aunt had said when she delivered the doctored tea.

Certainly not. Too late for that, even if Olympia had been the sort of girl who backed down or ran away from anything, let alone the chance of a lifetime. She had six brothers. Being the second eldest child counted for nothing with boys. It was dominate or be dominated.

Some said she was rather too dominating, for a girl. But that wouldn't matter when she became a duchess.

She bent and retrieved from under the dressing table the flask of brandy she'd stolen from Stephen. She unstopped it, brought it to her mouth, and tipped in what she gauged as a thimbleful. She stopped it again, set it on the dressing table, and told herself she was doing the right thing.

What was the alternative? Humiliate the bridegroom, who'd done nothing — to Olympia, in any event — to deserve it? Disgrace her family? Face permanent social ruin? And all on account of what? The sick feeling in the pit of her stomach, which surely was nothing more than the usual wedding-day anxiety.

Only a lunatic would run away from becoming the bride of one of the kingdom's handsomest, richest, most powerful men, she told herself. That was to say, Ashmont could be powerful, if he'd bother, but he . . .

She lost her train of thought because somebody tapped at the door.

"Please," she said. "I'm praying."

She'd insisted on time alone. She needed to collect herself and prepare for this immense change in her life, she'd told her mother and aunt. They'd looked at each other, then left. Soon thereafter, Aunt Lavinia had returned with the doctored tea.

"Ten minutes, dear," came her mother's voice from the corridor.

Ten minutes already?

Olympia unstopped the flask again and took another sip.

Nearly six and twenty, she reminded herself. She'd never get an offer like this one, ever again. It was a miracle she'd got this one. And she'd known what she was doing when she said yes.

True, Lucius Wilmot Beckingham, the sixth Duke of Ashmont, was a bit of an ass, and so immature he made nine-year-old Clarence look like King Solomon. And yes, it went without saying that His Grace would be unfaithful.

But Ashmont was handsome, and he could charm a girl witless when he set his mind to it, and he'd definitely set his mind to charming her. He seemed to like her. And it wasn't as though any great shocks were in

19

store for her. His character was well known to anybody who read the gossipy parts of the fashionable periodicals.

The important thing was, he'd *asked*. And she was desperate.

"A duchess," she told the looking glass. "You can practically change the world, or at least part of it. It's as close as a woman can come to being a man, unless she becomes the queen — and no mere consort either, but queen in her own right. Even then . . . Oh, never mind. It's not going to happen to you, my girl."

Somewhere in Olympia's head or maybe her heart or her stomach, a snide little voice, exactly like her cousin Edwina's, said, "The Love of a Lifetime is never going to happen to you, either. No Prince Charming on his white charger will come for you. Not even a passionate lord. Or a shop clerk, for that matter."

She suffocated the voice, as she had wished, many times, to suffocate Cousin Edwina.

The Olympia who'd entertained fantasies of princes and passionate gentlemen had been a naive creature, head teeming with novel-fed romantic fantasies as she embarked on her first London Season.

For seven years, she'd been voted Most

Boring Girl of the Season. In seven years, she'd received not a single offer. That was to say, she'd received no offer any young lady in her right mind, no matter how desperate, would accept or, as had happened in the case of an elderly suitor, would be allowed to accept.

And so, when Ashmont had asked, what could she say?

She could say no, and face a future as an elderly spinster dependent on brothers who could barely support themselves and their own families. Or she could say yes and solve a great many problems at once. It was as simple as that. No point in making it complicated.

She took another sip of brandy. And another.

There came louder and more impatient tapping at the door.

"It's the right thing to do and I'm going to do it," she whispered to her reflection, "because *somebody* has to."

She took another swig.

"What the devil's keeping her?" Ashmont said.

The guests whispered busily. At every sound from outside the drawing room, heads turned to the door through which the

21

bride was to come.

No bride had made her entrance. It must be half an hour past the appointed time.

Ripley had gone out to inquire of the bride's mother whether Lady Olympia was ill. Lady Gonerby had looked bewildered and only shook her head. Her sister Lady Newland had explained.

"Something to do with the dress," Ripley said. "The aunt's gone up with a maid and a sewing case."

"A sewing case!"

"Something's come undone, I take it."

"What the devil do I care?" said Ashmont. "I'm going to undo it later, in any event."

"You know how women are," Ripley said.

"It isn't like Olympia to fuss over trifles."

"A wedding dress is not a trifle," Ripley said. "I ought to know. M'sister's cost more than that filly I had of Pershore."

His sister wasn't here. According to Blackwood, Alice had gone to Camberley Place, one of Ripley's properties, to look after their favorite aunt.

"This is boring," Ashmont said. "I hate these bloody rituals."

Lord Gonerby left the drawing room. He returned a moment later and said, jovially, "Apologies for the delay. Something to do with a troublesome hem or flounce or some such. I've sent for champagne. No sense in getting thirsty while the sewing needles are at work."

A moment later the butler entered with a brace of footmen, all bearing trays of glasses.

Ashmont drank one, then another and another, in rapid succession.

Ripley drank, too, but not much. This was partly because he hadn't yet recovered from last night's activities. He must be getting old, because he could have used another hour or more of sleep, after the extended bout of gambling and drinking followed by a street brawl followed by the too-familiar labor of getting Ashmont out of a melee and home and to bed.

The other reason he abstained was the job he'd undertaken.

Last night, at Crockford's, Ashmont had asked — or insisted, rather — that one of his two friends supervise today's proceedings.

"One of you has to make sure I get there on time, with the ring," he'd said. "And the license and such. Everybody thinks I'm going to bungle it. I *won't*."

"I've already done a wedding," Blackwood had said. "My own. I should like, this time, to look on, irresponsibly." Having shifted the job to Ripley, Blackwood had smiled and waved them on their way, suggesting they both go home and get some sleep.

If he knew more about Ashmont's urgent wish to be shackled, Blackwood hadn't said. Not that he'd had time to say much of anything. Last night, Ashmont had done all the talking, and his tale had knocked Ripley on his beam ends.

In the first place, Ashmont had acquired his betrothed fair and square, in the usual manner of wooing and asking. In other words, the bride wasn't pregnant. Second, and equally amazing, Ashmont had persuaded an attractive, eligible, and sane girl to accept his suit. Ripley would have bet a large sum that there didn't exist in all of England a gently bred maiden desperate enough to take on Ashmont — or whose family would let her, in the event his looks and charm got the better of her wits.

As he'd boasted in his infrequent letters, Almack's hostesses had barred him from their assemblies, the King had let His Grace know he wasn't welcome at the Royal Levees, and the majority of hostesses in London had cut him from their invitation lists. For a good-looking, solvent duke, these sorts of accomplishments took some doing.

However, it seemed that Ashmont's and Lady Olympia's paths had crossed near the

Clarendon Hotel some weeks ago. Somebody's ill-tempered dog, taking instant dislike to His Grace, had tried to tear his boot off. Ashmont, being well to go, as usual, had tripped as he tried to shake off the dog, and nearly tumbled into the street — into the path of an oncoming hackney cabriolet going at top speed, as they usually did.

"But there was an umbrella handle," he'd told Ripley. "It hooked about my arm, pulling me back. And in a moment I was stumbling back onto the pavement, trying to recover my balance. Meanwhile the dog was barking his head off. And she said, 'Hssst,' or something like that, and set the umbrella on the pavement, point down this time, with a sharp click. And do you know, the dog went quiet and skulked away!" Ashmont had laughed at the recollection. "And she said, 'Are you all right, duke?' And her maid was muttering something, trying to get her lady away from me, no doubt. I thought I was all right, but Olympia looked down and told me my boot was badly torn. I looked down. So it was. She said I couldn't walk about London like that — heaven only knew what would get into the boot and onto my foot, she said. And then, of all things, she said, 'My carriage will be here in a moment. We will take you home.' Which she did,

25

though her maid didn't like it one bit. Neither did the coachman or footman but there was nothing they could do. Lady Olympia Hightower! Can you credit it? I couldn't. How many times have we seen her at this do or that?"

Countless times, Ripley thought. A tallish girl, bespectacled, but not bad-looking. Good figure. No, make that very good. But she was a gently bred maiden, of very good family, and reputed to be bookish. She might as well have had the label Poison, with skull and crossbones, pasted over her fine bosom.

"She was kind," Ashmont had said. "Not in a simpering, sentimental girl way at all, but very matter-of-fact and calm, rather like a fellow. And I must say, I was quite taken with her. And it was no use, when I mentioned her to Uncle Fred later, his telling me I wasn't worthy of her or up to her brain level and other nay-sayings. 'That's up to her, isn't it?' I told him. Then I set about the wooing. It was uphill work, I tell you. But she said yes in the end, didn't she? And wasn't Lord Fred amazed when I told him. He even clapped me on the shoulder and said, 'So you had it in you, after all.' "

Ashmont had been elated to get the better of his manipulative uncle for once. However, as Ripley saw it, Lord Frederick Beckingham had seen an opportunity and made the most of it. Telling Ashmont he couldn't have or do something was a sure way to make him do it.

Not that it mattered, in the end, as long as Ashmont was pleased and the girl knew what she was getting into. Which she must do, if she was as intelligent as believed.

The problem was, the wedding didn't seem to be proceeding as smoothly as it ought, Ashmont was bored with waiting, and a bored Ashmont was a dangerous article.

Ripley glanced at his brother-in-law. Blackwood — dark, like Ripley, but sleeker and better-looking by far — raised one black eyebrow in inquiry. Ripley lifted his shoulders.

Blackwood made his unhurried way to them.

"Don't see what the fuss is about a hem," Ashmont said. "At the bottom, isn't it? Well, then."

"If she trips on it and falls on her face —"

"I'll catch 'er," Ashmont said.

Ripley looked at Blackwood.

They both looked at Ashmont. He was in his altitudes, beyond a doubt. He had all he could do to stand upright.

If the bride didn't appear soon, one of two things would happen: At best, the bridegroom would sink into a stupor and subside ungracefully to the floor. At worst, he'd pick a fight with somebody.

" 'Nuff o' this," Ashmont said. "I'm goin' t' get her."

He started for the door, and stumbled. Blackwood caught him by the shoulder. "Good idea," he said. "No point hanging about in here."

He caught Ripley's eye. Ripley took the other side, and they guided their friend out of the drawing room.

With the guests milling about the trays of champagne, they encountered only servants in the passage.

"Where?" Blackwood said.

"Downstairs," Ripley said.

"Not down," Ashmont said. "She's up. There." He pointed, his finger making unsteady curlicues in the air.

"Bad luck," Ripley said. "Bad luck to see the bride before the wedding."

"Was 'spectin' to see her *at* the weddin'," Ashmont said.

They led him toward the stairs, and then, not easily, down them.

"This way," Ripley said.

Though he'd been in Newland House

before, that was ages ago. He wasn't sure of the ground floor layout. In an old house of this kind he'd expect a breakfast or dining room and, possibly, a library. Not that the type of room mattered.

They needed to get Ashmont away from drink as well as anybody he might decide to quarrel with, which was more or less everybody.

He and Blackwood guided their friend toward a door standing at a safe distance from the main staircase. Ripley opened the door.

The first thing he saw was white, miles of it, as though a cloud had slid into what he was distantly aware was a library. But clouds didn't wear white satin slippers and clocked stockings, and did not stand upon a set of library steps.

"Oops," Blackwood said.

"Dammit, Olympia," Ashmont said. "What the devil are you about?" He tried to break away from his friends.

Ripley said, "Get him out of here."

"No, you don't, blast you," Ashmont said. "Got to talk to her. Can't botch this."

In his present state, this was exactly what he'd do.

Ripley gave Blackwood their patented What Do We Do Now? look.

"Bad luck," Blackwood told Ashmont. "Bad luck to see the bride before the wedding."

As he hauled the protesting Ashmont back into the corridor, he said over his shoulder to Ripley, "He put you in charge of wedding details. Do something."

"The ring," Ripley said. "The license. Ready money where required. Not the bride."

"Do something," Blackwood said.

Once more Ripley opened the door.

The library steps nearby held nobody. A sound drew his gaze to the windows. He saw a flurry of white. Ashmont's intended was struggling with the window latch.

Ripley crossed the room in a few easy strides.

"Funny thing," he said. "Aren't you supposed to be at a wedding?"

"Yes, I know," she said. "You might give the blushing bride some help. The latch is stuck."

He caught a whiff of brandy mingled with a flowery fragrance.

Though his brain wasn't at its sharpest at the moment, he could sum up the situation easily enough: drunken bride at window with the aim of getting out.

There was a problem here.

"Why?" he said.

"How should I know why it's stuck?" she said. "Do I look like a plumber to you? Or what-you-call-it. Glazier." She nodded. "Window person."

"Not being a window person, I may not be qualified to help with this sort of thing," he said.

"Rise above yourself," she said. "I'm the damsel in distress. And you —" She turned her head to look at him. She stared at the knot of his neckcloth, approximately at her eye level. Then her eyes narrowed and her gaze moved upward.

Behind the spectacles, her grey eyes were red-rimmed.

She'd been crying.

Obviously Ashmont had said or done something to upset her. Nothing new in that. His tongue often got well ahead of his brain. Not that any of them were gifted in the tact department.

"Plague take it," she said. "*You.* You're back."

"Ah, you noticed." He felt strangely pleased. But champagne usually had that effect, even in small doses.

"You're over six feet tall," she said, tipping her head back. "You're standing right in front of me. I'm shortsighted, not blind. Even without my spectacles I could hardly fail to recognize you, even at a more distant . . . distance. Which I prefer you were. At." She made a shooing motion. "Go away. I only want a breath of air. In . . . erm . . . Kensington Gardens."

"In your wedding dress," he said.

"I cannot take it off and put it back on again as though it were a cloak." She spoke with the extreme patience more usually applied to infants of slow understanding. "It's complicated."

"It's raining," he said with matching patience.

She turned her head and peered at the window. Rain droplets made wriggly trails down the glass.

She gave him a grandiose wave of dismissal. "Never mind — if you're going to fuss about every little thing." She turned back to the latch and recommenced trying to strangle it. This time it surrendered.

She pushed open the window. "Adieu," she said.

And climbed through, in a flutter of satin and lace.

Ripley stood for a moment, debating.

She wanted to go, and he deemed it unsporting to hold women against their will.

He could go back and tell Ashmont his bride was bolting.

He could go back and tell one of the men in her family.

She wasn't Ripley's problem.

She was Ashmont's problem.

True, Ashmont had put Ripley in charge of the wedding. True, Ashmont had seemed unusually concerned about getting it right. And true, Ripley had promised to take care of things: hold on to the ring, supply coins as needed, make sure Ashmont did what he was supposed to do.

Retrieving the bride wasn't in the agreement.

She oughtn't to need retrieving.

Just because she'd been drunk and crying . . .

"Damn," he said.

He climbed through the window.

Ripley spotted the cloud of white satin and lace an instant before she disappeared into a stand of tall shrubbery and trees.

He quickened his stride, glancing up at the house windows at the same time. No signs of anybody looking out. The wedding party had gathered on the other side of the house. That was all to the good. If he got her back speedily, they could patch up matters, and nobody the wiser.

A glance about him showed no sign of gardeners. The outdoor servants must be carousing with their fellows or taking shelter from the rain.

Ripley was aware of the rain, but it was no more than background. While conscious of its patter upon leaves and grass and footpaths, he concentrated on the bride, who moved at a smart pace, considering the miles of satin and lace and the ballooning sleeves and all the rest of it.

He didn't shout, because she wasn't running yet, at least not flat-out, and he didn't want to scare her into running or startle her into doing something even more ridiculous, though at the moment he couldn't guess what that could be.

She wasn't dressed for athletic feats — not that women ever were — and the place was something of an obstacle course. Newland House's gardens were thickly planted and mature. Some of the trees had waved their branches over Queen Anne. On slippery ground, wearing that rig, and more than a little inebriated, the bride was all too liable to get tangled in shrubbery or trip over her skirts or her own feet.

He was gaining steadily, in any event.

He was near enough to see her feet slide out from under her and her arms make windmills as she struggled for balance. He was a moment too late to catch her before she lost the battle and went down.

He grasped her under her arms and hauled her upright.

She twisted this way and that. Through several thousand layers of dress and under-garments, he felt her bottom make contact with his groin, which distracted him for a moment.

He was a man. *Exceptional bottom,* was his first thought.

Never mind, he told himself. *Do the job and get her back.*

"I beg your pardon," he said. "Did I make a mistake? Did you want me to leave you lying in the mud?"

"You're spoiling my sleeves!"

The rain beat down on his head.

His hat was in the house. He felt naked without it. More naked than if he were in fact naked.

He felt wet, too.

He let her go. "You've already spoiled the dress," he said. "Mud streaks and grass stains up the back. Looks as though you've been having a lovers' romp in the shrub-bery. Well, that will give everybody something to get excited about. It will certainly excite Ashmont. And since I'm the only male in your vicinity, I'm the one he'll call out. Then I'll get to tend his dueling wounds. Again."

"Punch him in the face," she said. "He'll hit back. Then he can't call you out, not being an injured party."

The long veil clung wetly to her head and shoulders. Her side curls were coming uncurled, and the headdress listed to one side.

Her face spasmed, and he thought she was about to let loose the waterworks, but she stiffened her jaw and lifted it.

"You can go now," she said. "I'm perfectly all right. I only want a moment to . . . erm . . . pray . . . on this . . . solemn occasion, which will change my life forever and for the better. So . . . au revoir."

He looked back toward the house.

What had Ashmont done? How bad or stupid was it? Was it better to let her go wherever she meant to go?

No, that wasn't part of the agreement. It wasn't Ripley's job to think. His job was to make sure his friend's wedding went off without a hitch. That meant retrieving the bride.

Ripley turned back to her, in time to see

her sprint away, into a path among a thick planting of rhododendrons. In an instant, they'd hidden her from view, except for a dot of white here and there.

She'd waited until his back was turned — well, his head — and decamped.

That was . . . enterprising of her.

All the same, she couldn't be let to go merrily on her way.

If she didn't want Ashmont, she'd have to fight it out with him in person.

After they'd had time to sober up, that is.

Ripley went after her.

Though the wedding party and guests had congregated in the vicinity of the champagne, at the west front of the house, the bride's eldest brother, Lord Ludford, was looking for his sister.

Newland House had been built in the early part of the seventeenth century and added to and updated since. The building, which sprawled over a large section of the land belonging to it, was a rabbit warren run amok. The families were close, their ladyships being sisters. Their numerous offspring had run tame in each other's houses, and everybody was as at home here as at home. Since Ashmont was impatient to get married, and Gonerby House was in the midst of renovations, their ladyships had agreed to have the wedding here.

They were afraid, Ludford suspected, that if Ashmont waited too long, he'd change his mind. Personally, Ludford would have preferred that. He deemed Ashmont unworthy of Olympia. If she'd run away, Ludford didn't blame her. On the contrary, that struck him as a wise decision. Also worrisome, however. Respectable girls like Olympia couldn't go off on their own. Appalling things could happen to them.

He hoped, instead, that she was hiding in the house.

Olympia, who'd sometimes spent weeks at a time here with her girl cousins, had a number of secret places to which she'd retreat to study one ancient tome or another, or memorize book sale catalogs. He assumed she'd done that today, though he had no idea why.

Like his father, Ludford was not a complicated thinker. When he'd noticed his flask had gone missing, he instantly suspected his younger brothers.

A good shaking, until the teeth rattled, was often enough to extract a confession. But this time, they'd seemed truly mystified. Little Clarence had seemed to know or suspect something, but whatever it was, he wouldn't say, and he was as stubborn as Olympia.

Ludford sought out Clarence now, in the nursery, to which he'd been banished after some games leading to broken champagne glasses. Andrew, his partner in crime, had been separated from him, to languish in the schoolroom.

Ludford flung open the nursery door. "You know something, brat," he said. "And you'd better own up, or I'll —"

He stopped, because Clarence turned away from the window he'd been looking out of, and his face was bright red.

Yes, he ought to be scared when Ludford burst in on him like that. That was the whole point. But Clarence jumped away from the window as though it had caught fire, and shouted, "No, I don't! No, I don't! And you can't make me!"

Ludford stormed to the window in time to catch a glimpse of white in the shrubbery and the Duke of Ripley moving toward it, not running, exactly, but not at his usual lazy pace, either.

Ludford raced out of the nursery.

On a moonlit night, Ripley would have enjoyed pursuing a merry widow along the garden path's twists and turns, with the tall shrubbery making the chase more challenging.

But this wasn't a moonlit night, and Lady Olympia Hightower wasn't a merry widow.

The flashes of white proceeded steadily and at surprising speed at a distance ahead of him.

As he plunged down yet another path, the white flares disappeared altogether. Then, through the pattering rain, he heard a faint clinking. He kept on, and the tangle of shrubbery gave way to a small clearing that led to an iron gate set in the tall wall.

A gate she was trying to wrestle open.

A few soggy strides brought him to her.

She paused in her labors and looked over her shoulder at him.

"Oh," she said. "You." She panted from her exertions, her bosom rising and falling. "The blasted thing's locked."

"Of course it's locked," he said. "Can't have the hoi polloi tramping through the garden and poaching the rhododendrons."

"Bother the rhododendrons! How is one to get out?"

"Perhaps one doesn't?" he suggested.

She shook her head. "We must find another way out."

"We?" he said. "No. You and I are not a *we.*"

She stiffened then, her eyes widening.

He heard it, too.

Voices, coming from what he guessed was the same route he'd traveled.

"Never mind," she said. "Too late. You have to help me over the wall."

"No," he said. "Can't do that."

"Yes, you can," she said. "Here you are, and what else do you have to do? Do be of use for once in your life and help me over the wall. And now would be a good time." She stamped her foot. "Now!"

Bits of her coiffure had come undone, and tendrils of wet brown hair stuck to her face. The thing on top of her head was now more on the side of her head, and stray rhododendron leaves and dead blooms had become trapped among the apple blossoms. Her veil had snaked around her neck. A smudge of dirt adorned the tip of her narrow nose.

"Over the wall," he said, playing for time.

"Yes, yes. I can't climb the ivy properly in this dress — and certainly not in these shoes. Hurry! Can't you hear them?"

He was trying to devise a delaying tactic, but his brain was slow to help. Then he heard a confusion of cries, and these called to mind baying hounds and angry mobs. At that moment, something in his mind shifted.

Since his Eton days, Ripley and his two

partners in crime had been eluding the forces of authority, along with irate farmers, clergymen, tradesmen, and, generally, all species of respectable persons, not to mention pimps, cutpurses, blacklegs, and others not so respectable.

"Hurry!" she said.

He laced his hands together and bent. She set one muddy, slippered foot on his hand, one dirty hand against the wall for balance, and boosted herself up. Then, with an ease that would have surprised him had he been capable of further surprise at this point, she climbed onto his shoulders and reached for the wall.

That, at least, was what he assumed she was doing.

The view he had — and a prime one it was, though brief — was of stockinged leg and garter. Then white satin and petticoats and the scent of a woman filled the world about his head. He barely retained the presence of mind to grasp her ankles to steady her.

"Up," she said. "It's still too high for me to get there. Up, up! Hurry!"

The voices neared.

Grasping her feet, he pushed her up, over his head. He felt her weight leave him as she found purchase at the top of the wall.

He saw the backs of her legs as she scrambled onto the top of the wall and into a sitting position. An instant later, she dropped out of sight.

The voices were very near now.

He hadn't stopped to think a moment ago and he didn't think now. As she disappeared over the wall, he caught hold of a tangle of ivy and climbed up and over.

He looked right, then left.

The cloud of white satin and lace was moving swiftly down Horton Street.

He ran after her.

CHAPTER 2

Ripley caught up with the bride in Kensington's High Street. She'd slowed her pace, but she didn't stop.

"Hackney," she said, nodding toward the hackney stand ahead. "Do you have any money?"

"First it was help over the wall," he said. "Now it's money."

"And here you are," she said. "Still. Again."

"Yes. Because —"

"I," she said, drawing out the single syllable. "Need. *Money.* For. The. *Hackney.*"

She waved at the vehicles and called, "Here!"

The driver of the first hackney cab in the line regarded her with interest but offered no sign of moving.

Why should he? She looked like a Bedlam escapee.

Not that Ripley didn't appear more than a

little eccentric himself, with no hat, gloves, or walking stick. Still, he was a duke, and one of England's most notorious and easily recognized noblemen.

Furthermore, here he was, as she'd said. Ashmont ought to be here but he wasn't, and somebody had to look after her. One did not let a gently bred young female roam on her own, especially a young female belonging to one of his stupid friends who couldn't hold on to her.

It was all well and good to be wild and reckless and not give a damn for Society. But when a fellow asked a girl to marry him, he oughtn't to give her any reason not to show up for the nuptials.

It was damned carelessness, was what it was. But Ashmont was spoiled, that was the trouble. He never had to exert himself with women.

Long past time he started.

Ripley clamped a hand on her shoulder. "Let's stop and think."

"I am thinking," she said. "What I'm thinking about is, where is the blasted hackney? Why don't they come?"

"Let's think about what you look like," he said. "You know. Wedding dress. Veil and all. Creates an odd impression, don't you think?"

"I don't care," she said.

"I daresay," he said. "But let's try to appear calmer and in our right minds."

"I am in my right mind." She clenched her hands. "I'm perfectly calm."

"Good. Very good. Now let's take this in steps. Where do you propose to go?"

She made a sweeping gesture. "Away."

"Away," he said.

She nodded, and the mound of hair and lace and whatnot shifted farther to the side of her head.

"Very well," he said. "It's a start."

He would simply have to do the thinking for both of them, a daunting prospect. He didn't like doing the thinking for himself.

He raised his hand and beckoned.

The first hackney coach lumbered out of line and toward them while she all but danced with impatience.

When the vehicle had drawn up alongside them, Ripley pulled the door open.

As she climbed onto the step, she struggled for balance and started to tip backward.

He gave her a light push forward, and she toppled into the straw on the coach floor. He watched her hoist herself up — bottom uppermost for a riveting moment — and fall onto the seat. She smoothed out her skirts, straightened her spectacles, and glared at him.

For some reason, his mood brightened.

"Where to, Yer Honor?" the driver said.

"Your *Grace*," she corrected. "Don't you recognize more than the usual lordly arrogance? Isn't it obvious he's a duke?"

Ripley's mood improved another degree.

If the driver heard her, he gave no sign.

"Battersea Bridge," said Ripley. He climbed into the coach.

The bridge lay a distance southward. This would give him time. To decide what he wished to do. But it wasn't too far to prevent his returning her in a reasonable amount of time, if that was what he decided.

The advantage was, Battersea Bridge wasn't the first place his friends would think to look.

"Or did you have a particular 'away' in mind?" he said.

"Don't talk," she said. "I'm thinking."

The coach rumbled into motion.

"That's odd," Ripley said. "Mind you, our communications have been brief, but from what I can see, thinking and you are two different countries. At war."

She shook her head and wagged a finger at him in the manner of the inebriated everywhere.

"That's not going to stop me talking," he

said. "If you must think, maybe you'd be so good as to think about explaining."

"Explaining what?"

He gestured at her dirty bridal attire and the coach's dirty interior. "This. The running away. Because I'm still rather muddled and not at all sure this is the best idea. I'm debating whether to tell the coachman to take us back."

"No," she said.

"But you can understand how tempting the idea is," he said.

"No," she said.

"Here's the thing," he said. "I've had rather a trying morning, you see."

"You!"

"Yes. It's not going the way it was supposed to."

"Join the club," she said.

"You see, I wasn't expecting to be traveling at a snail's pace in a dilapidated hackney coach to Battersea Bridge," he said. "Or any bridge. I feel reasonably certain I wasn't supposed to be helping a drunken bride who chooses the very last minute to flee her wedding."

"I am not drunk," she said. "And you're not the only one who's had a trying morning. If you don't want to help me, you're at liberty to stop the coach and disembark."

"I'm not at liberty," he said. "I'm the — the something. The bridegroom's special envoy. Or his keeper. For all I know, I'm the bridesmaid. The point is, he gave me the job, and maybe he has to take his chances of my bungling it. But one thing I do know is, you can't be let to gad about on your own. If you could, I should have gone back and got my hat. Or not. I might have simply gone back and left you to somebody else. But I couldn't, as I've explained, because of the job. No point in bringing the ring and the license and the money and all the rest when the bride's gone off who knows where."

Her gaze lifted to his head. "Your hair is wet."

He did not turn a wet hair. He was used to drunken non sequiturs. "Everything is wet," he said.

"Yes," she said.

"Don't worry," he said. "I won't melt."

"That's not something I'd worry about," she said. "The thing is . . ." She closed her eyes for a moment, but following a train of thought must have been too much for her because she opened them again and said, "When you drop me off at the bridge —"

"Another man, who had looked forward to a peaceful wedding ceremony and good

49

champagne and a fine wedding breakfast — the Newlands keep an excellent chef, you know," he said.

She regarded him stonily.

"That fellow," he went on, "missing the meal he'd looked forward to, and feeling a trifle short on sleep — that fellow might be tempted to drop you *off* the bridge. As in, into the river. But I —"

"Yes, you're the bridesmaid."

"I hardly ever drown women, was what I was going to say."

"I shall take a boat," she announced, as one might pronounce a fiat or a sentence of death. "To Aunt Delia. In Twickenham."

He blinked. "Remarkable. You have a plan."

"Yes. I only needed the mental stimulation of your stimulating company."

"Any chance of stimulating you into telling me what, exactly, you're running from?" he said. "Better yet, any chance of your changing your mind, like a good girl, and turning back? Any chance of something, oh, you know, bordering on reasonable?"

"The die is cast," she said in the fiat/death-sentence voice. "Be so good as to get this monstrosity off my head."

Because he wasn't nearly drunk enough — or at all, for he seemed to have gone extremely sober suddenly — it took him a moment to interpret the request. Command.

"Your hair?" he said. "Isn't it permanently attached?"

"Does this piece of architecture *look* permanently attached? It's sliding down and pulling the hair I do in fact own with it. It's most uncomfortable, and not like me at all. You can't make a sow's purse from a pig's ear. I tried to tell them, but nobody would l-listen."

"I believe you mean silk purse —"

She burst into tears.

Oh.

Tears threw some men into a panic.

Ripley wasn't one of them.

Had this weeping female been his sister, he'd let her bawl on his shoulder and spoil his coat and neckcloth and get rouge all over his handkerchief. Then he'd give her money and tell her to buy something.

If she'd been his mistress, he'd promise a ruby necklace or diamonds, depending on her tears' volume and velocity.

This weeping female wasn't like his sister or any of his mistresses or even his mother. This one belonged to a different species altogether. Among other things, she was Ash-

51

mont's betrothed. Ashmont had never had one of those before. This being a brand-new category of Situation with Weeping Female, Ripley needed a moment to determine his course of action.

The brisk approach, he decided.

"Brace up," he said. "You had mettle enough to go over the wall. You act like you've never run away before. It's not the end of the world."

"Yes, it *is*," she sobbed. "I've ruined everything. Clarence will never get to Eton, and Andrew won't get his cornetcy, and I shan't be able to do anybody any good at all, and I won't even have the *library*!"

Ripley had no idea what she was talking about and saw no point in tiring his brain, trying to get an idea. How often did women make sense? What were the odds of that happening now?

He said, in the encouraging manner of one addressing a jockey before a race, "The die isn't cast. You can turn back. Ashmont is so drunk, he'll believe anything we tell him. Then, tomorrow, he won't remember anything but the broad outlines. I'll tell him you got drunk accidentally and —"

"I'm not d-drunk."

"Believe me, I recognize the condition," he said. "You're more than tipsy. You couldn't even manage the coach step. Here's what we tell him. We say you accidentally drank brandy, thinking it was . . . hmm . . . what the devil could one mistake brandy for?"

"T-tea," she sobbed. "It was in the tea. At f-first."

"At first," he said.

She nodded. She fished out from one of her enormous sleeves a tiny, elaborate square of lace, took off her spectacles, and wiped her eyes and nose with the scrap of lace. She put the spectacles back on and gave the nosepiece a little poke with her finger to set it in place. "But I drank that. The rest was from Stephen's flask." She balled up the alleged handkerchief in her hand. "I purloined it last night. After Mama told me about the wedding night. That is to say, she more or less told me. Some aspects of the business are not at all clear. But I thought brandy would strengthen my resolve. For the Inevitable."

"She ought to have done a better job of telling you," Ripley said. "It's Ashmont, you know, not some inexperienced numskull."

"Yes, he's an *experienced* numskull," she said.

"In any event, it's nothing to be afraid of," he said. "People do it all the time. Consequences are hardly ever fatal."

"Consequences are babies," she said darkly. "I should have investigated the matter myself instead of relying upon Mama. I'm not sure she understands the connection. Between the conjugal act and babies. She has had them in excess. In her place, I should have stopped after three. Or after three boys. That's a good, safe number, isn't it?"

He didn't think it a good, safe idea for his mind to dwell on the conjugal act. It had been an unusually long time since he'd had a woman, and at present he wasn't in a position to do anything about it. His mind, though, being too easily swayed by the small brain below his waist, was all too eager to imagine how to repair the omission in short order.

He made himself concentrate on what she was saying. Fortunately, she'd moved on to another subject.

"I could not fathom why he asked *me*," she was saying. "I doubted he was desperate. You'd be surprised at how many girls will overlook a man's frailties when he's a duke. Or maybe you wouldn't be."

There might be many such girls, but they weren't the sort who'd make Ashmont a suitable duchess. For all his shortcomings, he had his pride — rather more than was good for him, in fact. Even in a drunken stupor he wouldn't marry a girl who wasn't attractive, wellborn, and in possession of all her faculties. He wouldn't choose one who was silly or boring or shrewish. He'd want, in short, perfection. Whether he deserved it was irrelevant.

"I told myself not to look a gift horse in the mouth," she said.

"What gift horse?" Ripley said. "He fancies you. Isn't that enough?"

She shook her head. "It doesn't make sense."

She must be *extremely* shortsighted. Had she not worn the Poison label, Ripley would have been all over her years ago. "It makes perfect sense," he said. "If you were a man, you'd see. As it is —"

"And then I went to the library today to look into the matter —"

"You waited until the wedding day," he said. "No, not merely the day, but the very moment when you were supposed to be saying 'I will.' " She'd waited until the moment when she'd become fully intoxicated, a condition she was, clearly, not used to.

"I tried not to think about it, but it *bothered* me," she said. "Did you ever try not to think about something?"

55

"I rarely have to try."

"You simply make it go away?"

"Yes."

"It's good to be a duke," she said.

"It is," he said.

It was far, far better than being a duke's son, in his and his friends' experiences. He wasn't sure theirs had been the three worst fathers in the British aristocracy, but they were definitely in the running for the prize.

"I can't do that," she said. "It's like trying to stop a gnat buzzing around my head. And things that don't make sense are the most stubborn gnats. But all I could find was a book on animal husbandry, and that was when, finally, I put two and two together. Or two and two and two and one. Seven of us, and only one girl. And they — whoever talked or tricked him into getting married — must have said to him, 'Why, there's Gonerby's girl. Can't ask for better breeding stock. Excellent odds of an heir and some extras in case of catastrophe.' "

"Knowing Ashmont, I find that theory highly improbable." Breeding would feature, naturally, because that was what often came of bedding, unless one exercised extreme caution. "You give him credit for more thought than he would ever put into it. You attracted his attention by being kind to him one day, as I understand it."

"Kind!" she said. "I could hardly let him get run over by a hackney cab."

"It was quick thinking, and showed a certain adeptness."

"I have six brothers! They're always falling into or out of this or that. I acted on instinct."

"He deemed it kind, especially your taking him home. In the course of the journey, it seems, he took a good, hard look at you, and you took his fancy. Since you're a gently bred girl, marriage is required." And this gently bred girl promised to lead Ashmont a more exciting life than he might have expected.

She shook her head. "I know there was something more. I am not the sort of woman men lose their heads over."

There was more, very likely. Ashmont probably would have forgotten all about the incident if not for Uncle Fred's underhanded methods. Ripley was not about to enlighten her in that regard, however. He could offer hints about how to manage Ashmont . . . but no. She was an intelligent girl. She'd catch on quickly.

"You'd be surprised," Ripley said.

"I am the sort they marry for practical purposes," she said. "To manage trouble-

some households. To take charge. To produce heirs and extras. When all else fails."

"Ashmont doesn't think that way."

She was looking out of the window. "But
you kn-know . . ." The tears began to trickle
down the side of her nose again. "We've had
our catastrophes, because there ought to
have been nine of us, and that was very hard
on Mama and Papa both. I did have my
doubts about how much comfort Ashmont
would be in such a case. And I knew what
else whoever it was would have told Ashmont. They would have s-said, 'No fear of a
cuckoo in the nest. No doubt whatsoever
nobody's ever t-touched h-her.' "

More sobbing.

Ripley tapped his knee with his index
finger. The sobbing continued.

This was not entirely comfortable.

"I see we've reached the maudlin stage,"
he said.

"Yes, I daresay you'd know." She rubbed
her face with the useless bit of lace. "Not
that I care what you call it, and I wasn't
expecting sympathy or even comprehen-
sion."

"I'm doing my best," he said. "But my
brain, you know."

"Yes, I know," she said. "Like his, more or
less — though *less* defies the imagination.

58

All the same, I thought I was ready to make the sacrifice — though I know most people would say it's preposterous to refer to becoming a duchess as a sacrifice."

"I would be one of those people," he said.

"I don't care what you say," she said.

"I'm devastated," he said.

"I don't know why I even try to explain," she said. "I'm sure he said everything he ought, and he can be alarmingly persuasive, and I did have my reasons for agreeing. I thought I was ready. But marriage is a Great Unknown. You think you know them, especially someone like him, who's been the talk of the town forever, but how can you? I know what you will say."

"I doubt it." He still had only the remotest idea what she was talking about.

"You will say, I ought to have asked him why he chose me — and don't say he fancies me, because nobody ever did."

He was sure a great many men must have fancied her. What he didn't understand was why nobody had claimed her by now. Not all men were like Their Dis-Graces. Any number actually wanted to get married, and spent a great deal of time and effort trying to find the right girl who'd have them.

He drew out his handkerchief and gave it to her. "Yes, well, he isn't like the other fellows," he said.

He looked out of the coach window. It was still raining.

Bridal nerves, he told himself. That's all this was, really.

He looked at her mud-streaked dress and the toes of her muddy slippers. He calculated the distance, via the river, to Twickenham and the time it would take, barring difficulties, which he knew better than to suppose wouldn't arise.

Taking everything into account, her plan was workable. He reckoned excellent odds of putting her safely into her aunt's hands in a matter of hours, well before nightfall. Her reputation would survive. In fact, running away from Ashmont might enhance it. As would Ashmont's running after her, which he was bound to do. Being possessive and obstinate, he'd do whatever was necessary to get her back. And Society would be thrilled to see a lady bring him to order at last. Assuredly Lord Frederick would enjoy that.

Accustomed to women of ill repute fawning over him, Ashmont had mucked up what ought to be the simplest business. He'd never had to make an effort, as Ripley and Blackwood so often did. True, none of them had much to do with respectable women, who were, evidently, rather more challenging. All the better. It was about bloody time a female made Luscious Lucius exert himself.

This one had made him work at the courtship, clearly. And the wedding. And she'd make him work at the marriage, too.

As to retrieving his bride, His Grace would need some guidance here and there, but that shouldn't be difficult.

Lady Olympia didn't seem to be completely opposed to marrying him. If not for the brandy, she might have gone through with it. But intoxicating liquors affected some people in this way: small matters inflated to prodigious size. And bacon-brained solutions seemed like brilliant ones.

Of all men, Ashmont knew how this could happen.

And wouldn't it be a laugh, watching him try to manage his bride — *this* bride?

"Your aunt's respectable, I trust," Ripley said. "Not eccentric or excessively dashing? Doesn't set fire to the pillows at odd moments? Carry on with footmen or grooms? In an obvious way, that is."

She wiped her eyes and nose. "She's somewhat dashing — at least Aunt Lavinia and Mama say so. Still, Aunt Delia is respectable enough to entertain the Queen on occasion."

"Then why didn't Auntie attend your wedding?"

"She suffered an indisposition that prevented her making the journey. That's what she wrote to Mama, at any rate. I'm not at all sure she wished to attend. She finds Newland House excessively noisy, with all the children coming and going. She feels the same about Gonerby House — which is even more chaotic at present, because of the renovations."

"But she will, in fact, be at home when we get there."

She nodded, and the headdress slipped farther. She winced. "You cannot expect me to answer prying questions while my hair is being torn out by the roots. Unless you enjoy employing the methods of the Inquisition. If you do not help me get this thing off my head — *this instant* — I cannot answer for the consequences."

"Is that supposed to be a threat?" he said. "Because you look so very much the opposite of threatening that I might die laughing."

She pushed her glasses back up the minuscule distance they'd slipped during the tear storm. She gave him a steady look, or as steady as her state of intoxication would allow.

"Never mind," she said. "If it's too complicated for you, I'll do it myself. But if things fly off and hit you in the face, you'll have only yourself to blame."

"That's what stopped you doing it yourself?" he said. "The chance of your coiffure exploding?"

"I haven't a mirror," she said. "I can't see the top of my head — or any of my head, for that matter. But never mind. Don't let me disturb you."

She reached up and started poking her fingers into the crownpiece. This set off various gyrations, which created intriguing movement in the areas directly above and below the dress's neckline. These brought to mind so-called Egyptian dancing girls he'd seen in a theater somewhere. Eventually, she managed to remove a single hairpin, which slipped through her fingers and into the straw. She muttered something.

A lost hairpin was no calamity. Her aunt would have heaps of them.

But the gyrations and visions of dancing girls reminded him of the way she'd squirmed when he picked her up from the mud — reminded his breeding organs, that is, and all too vividly, given the circumstances and the length of time since . . .

Right. He would address the matter of the recent months' celibacy later. This night, in fact. After the bridal complication was taken care of.

Ripley would leave her safely with her aunt. Given a nudge and a few broad hints, Ashmont would recover her.

It would all be a very good joke, the sort of thing Ashmont would appreciate, once he'd calmed somewhat. After all, he'd perpetrated plenty of jokes himself.

"I've decided to help," Ripley said. "I want to take a nap, and that's impossible while you're jumping about and swearing under your breath."

"I was not —"

"I do understand French, you know. To a point. All the bad words are well before that point."

Thanks to the rain and the windows' decades of accumulated grime, the coach was about as bright as the average tomb. All the same, Olympia could see the Duke of Ripley well enough. She could hardly miss him, when he took up most of the coach.

She was more aware than she wanted to be of his long legs stretched out, inches from hers.

She took her hands away from the head-piece and looked at him. Though his face was in shadow, she could make out the long, imperial nose and harsh angles of cheek and jaw. She knew his eyes were green.

That much she'd ascertained during her first Season, when they'd been introduced, and she'd felt so deeply uncomfortable. This was partly because he was so . . . overwhelming. She knew he wasn't any larger than Ashmont. All Their Dis-Graces were tall, athletic men. All, certainly, were not well-behaved. But Ripley's was the gaze that had made her feel as though she wasn't fully clothed. He was the one whose wolfish grin had left her tongue-tied.

But back then she'd been naive and unsure of herself.

Back then, the three dukes had been considered rather wild but highly eligible. They kept well clear of the Marriage Mart, though. Rarely were they to be seen near even the beautiful and far more popular young ladies.

This was why, when Olympia had seen him over the years, it was usually at a distance. Across a crowded ballroom. Riding or driving in Hyde Park. At a public event like a regatta or horse race. In the past year she hadn't seen him at all, because he'd been abroad.

As far as she could determine at present, he hadn't changed. He still had the sleepy gaze that made her feel prickly inside. It oughtn't to, since it told one nothing. People believed the eyes were windows to the soul. In his case, the shutters were closed. That was probably for the best.

Not that she was capable of gauging his mood even if he'd offered windows to his soul. Her brain at present was not trustworthy. When she tried to think, the thoughts danced away, out of reach.

Besides, the headdress made it hurt to think.

One thing at a time, she told herself. When they reached Battersea Bridge, she'd deal with the next thing, whatever it was. For now, all that mattered was getting *away*. From everybody.

"Move to the edge of the seat and lean toward me," Ripley said.

Between the coach's jolting and the brandy's effects, she wasn't at all sure she could keep her balance. She was not about to admit that to him. As it was, she felt sure he was laughing at her. But then, he was not renowned for being serious-minded. Furthermore, in all fairness, she hardly cut a dignified figure at the moment.

Most important, she needed the bridal monstrosity off her head. It felt as though she was wearing a clock tower.

She moved to the edge of the seat and leaned toward him.

Then she nearly leapt straight up from the seat, because his long fingers went into her hair, touching her scalp as they probed. The ruffles at his wrists tickled her face. She detected the scent of wet linen and something else — cologne or shaving soap, excessively masculine.

At that moment she remembered, with an inner repeat of the sensations she'd had at the time, his hands under her arms when he'd hauled her up out of the mud . . . the size of his hands and the way his powerful grasp felt . . . the size of *him* . . . and her back pressed to a torso like rock. Warm rock. Then those same long-fingered hands, linked for her to step on . . . then wrapped about her ankles.

Her brothers had helped her over walls and fences, but he wasn't her brother. He was the man who looked at a girl and made her feel she'd forgotten to put her clothes on. He was nothing remotely like a brother — and recalling Mama's incoherent explanation of what happened on the wedding night did not contribute to a state of serenity

67

at present.

Olympia wanted to jump out of her skin.

But no. She would *not* let herself think about what the Duke of Ripley might have seen when she stood on his shoulders. Merely thinking about thinking about it made her dizzy. Dizzier. And vastly uneasy.

"Stop wriggling," he said.

"I wasn't," she said.

"You're not holding still," he said. "I have to feel my way because there isn't light enough in here for me to see properly. I can't do it if you're moving."

"I can't help the coach's jolting," she said. "And I'm desperately uncomfortable." There was an understatement. She felt prickly all over. And hot. And confused.

"I'm working as fast as I can, but your maid or hairdresser has secreted the pins in the damnedest places. Is this thing *glued* together?"

"No, it's only a thousand pins and some pomatum."

"Hold out your hand and I'll give you the pins," he said. "We needn't save the bits and pieces of rhododendron, I trust? At the moment, you put me in mind of Ophelia after she fell into the water."

"The veil caught in everything," she said. Then she realized what he'd said. "You

68

know *Hamlet*?"

"I like Shakespeare's plays," he said. "Lots of violence and bawdy jokes."

No surprise there.

She held out her hand. His fingers brushed hers as he dropped some pins onto her palm, and the fleeting touch skittered along her skin. She wished she'd put on her gloves before she left. The trouble was, she would have had to return to her room to get them, and somebody was bound to be waiting there: Mama, Aunt Lavinia. Olympia would have been trapped. No turning back then.

Rightfully so. She should not have waited until the last possible moment to balk. She should not have balked. What was wrong with her?

She watched flower petals, some cherry red and others palest pink, drift down into the straw. Shiny bits of green leaves fluttered after them.

What had she done?

Never mind, never mind. One thing at a time.

She'd been wrong about the number of hairpins.

Ripley reckoned there must be at least *ten* thousand. Still, once he ascertained the pattern, he was able to get at them more efficiently. From her thick, shiny hair rose the fragrance of lavender, with a hint of rosemary. It was a shockingly chaste scent. He was used to the rich fragrances with which actresses, courtesans, and dashing ladies of the ton infused their pomatums.

He became aware of his head bending nearer. He drew it back.

Even done efficiently, the process was a long one, not merely of removing hairpins but also of disentangling the orange blossoms and intricate lace arrangement without, at the same time, disarranging her hair completely.

Bad enough for a woman to be running about in a bridal dress. In any dress, with her hair down, she'd be taken for a prostitute or a madwoman.

A lady did not let down her hair until she prepared for bed.

Loose hair meant loose woman.

This woman would be fair game for sport, in other words, of one kind or another.

Not for him, of course. He was the bloody bridesmaid.

He couldn't let her go anywhere without him.

Not that this was altogether bad. She was entertaining. And he was looking forward to helping her drive Ashmont frantic.

Yet Ripley did wish he had his hat.

The most wretched of paupers managed some sort of head-covering, however ragged. Small wonder that the Duke of Ripley, who regarded Society's rules as a joke book, squirmed inwardly because he was Out in Public without a Hat.

Best not to think about his naked head.

Useful as well not to dwell too much on the fragrance rising from her head and the way it conjured images of lazing in a sunlit Tuscan garden.

No Tuscan villa in the vicinity. No naughty contessas.

Only Ashmont's bride-to-be.

And this wasn't Tuscany or anything like Tuscany. This was London, raining as was its custom, while His Grace of Ripley sat playing lady's maid in a filthy hackney coach plodding toward Battersea Bridge.

It was a new experience, at any rate.

He managed to get the headdress separated from her head without too much screaming — hers or his. But it turned out that some of the plaits belonged to her, and the side curls had loosened, and in short, everything seemed to be coming down. He snatched hairpins from her outstretched palm and hastily got the dangling bits back up, not very elegantly, but up was up.

Then at last he dropped the crown and attached veil onto her lap and sat back.

She looked down at the mass of lace and orange blossoms in her lap.

"It's blond lace, so expensive," she said. "It's sure to fetch something at a pawnshop. More than enough to pay the waterman."

"I'm not taking your bridal veil to a pawnshop," he said.

"Did I ask you to? I'm perfectly capable —"

"Yesterday you might have been capable of many things," he said. "This isn't yesterday. This is today. You're inebriated. You're wearing a wedding dress. If you stir a step without me, you'll be assaulted. Whatever happens to you will be my fault, and there isn't a strong enough word for or enough words to put with *bored* to tell you how bored I am with duels."

She opened her mouth — to argue, no doubt. Then she closed it and turned her gaze downward again, to the dismantled headdress.

Second thoughts? He could work with that, although —

"Do you have enough money for the waterman?" she said. "After you pay the coachman? Yes, of course you're a duke, but in my experience, gentlemen don't carry a great deal of money with them."

He gazed at her for a time, at the dirt on her nose and the spots on her spectacles from tears or rain, and the bizarre arrangement he'd made of her hair.

Never since his unpleasant childhood had any woman asked whether he had enough money. For anything.

It was rather touching.

But it wasn't his job to be touched. His job was to manage matters to come out the right way.

Simple enough, really.

Get her to her aunt, make Ashmont retrieve her, and make everybody believe it was all a typical Their Dis-Graces practical joke.

"As it happens, I brought ready money for gratuities, bribes, and other odds and ends," he said. "Ashmont, obviously, was too . . . excited . . . about getting married to think of mundane matters."

"Excited," she said. "Is that what you call it? I would say he was extremely intoxicated when you three burst in upon me."

"And pot calls kettle black," he said.

The coach rumbled to a halt, as it had done numerous times on the interminable journey. Ripley looked out of the grimy window. Thanks to the scratches and dirt, the view might have been of anything. He pushed down the window. The rain had settled to a drizzle.

The coachman called out, "Battersea Bridge, Yer Grace."

"We can still turn back," Ripley said.

"No," she said.

CHAPTER 3

The voices Lady Olympia and the Duke of
Ripley had heard in the garden belonged to
her brothers, the youngest two of whom had
set out to thwart the eldest. The conspiracy
had proceeded as follows:

When Lord Ludford left the nursery,
Clarence shouted, "Drew, quick! Stop him!"

Andrew burst out of the schoolroom and
raced for the staircase, Clarence hot behind
their eldest brother.

"Let her go!" Clarence shouted. "You
leave her alone, you great bully!"

This was unfair to Ludford. Not only was
he no more of a bully than most older
brothers but he had as well, on countless
occasions, taken the blame and even the
punishment for his younger siblings' mis-
chief.

When Ludford turned to glare at Clarence, Andrew used the moment to dart to
the staircase ahead of them. He ran down

the stairs and into a passage and through a door and down one of the numerous back staircases that riddled the old house. Promising hell to pay, Ludford followed, or tried to.

Clarence, who chased Ludford down the main stairs, managed to get ahead of him on the first floor before sprinting for the servants' passage. Seeing guests near the drawing room doorway, and not wanting to call attention to himself and add to the gossip already in full spate, Ludford chose the path of discretion, and followed his younger brother.

They passed a few servants on the way to the ground floor, but nobody was startled. The servants were used to high-spirited children underfoot.

By the time Ludford reached the garden, Andrew was well in the lead, with Clarence not far behind.

"Look out, Olympia!" Andrew cried. "The hounds are in pursuit!"

Clarence carried on with the shouting, much in the same vein, as though dastardly foes hunted their sister, instead of her own older brother, who only wanted to know what was wrong.

Ludford's problem at present was that said sister had read too many romantic adventure books to the little ones in the nursery. Now they read them on their own, and created elaborate schemes involving bloodcurdling exploits and near-brushes with death among gallant knights, Vikings, pirates, highwaymen, and so forth.

It took Ludford a while to realize his brothers had led him in circles. He hadn't been in Newland House's garden in an age, while they'd been let loose there whenever the family visited.

By the time he reached the garden's back gate, he found the two young villains holding on to the lacy ironwork and looking out into the street beyond.

Ludford looked, too.

Neither his sister nor Ripley was in sight.

After directing several ugly oaths at his siblings, and heedless of the damage to his wedding day finery, Lord Ludford climbed over the wall and set off, at speed, down Horton Street.

"Not the steam vessel," Ripley said. "At the moment, the passengers are too busy shoving and cursing and trying to get aboard to care about anybody else. Once settled, though, they'll be looking for entertainment, and we'll be it, with you in the starring role."

He grasped Lady Olympia's hand and

pulled her toward the watermen congregated by the Battersea Bridge stairs.

His once-perfect neckcloth and his shirt's beautifully starched ruffles hung limp. Rain and mud spots adorned his coat and trousers. His shoes, never meant for hard use out-of-doors, bore scuffmarks and mud.

Still, he was not only a man but a duke, as well. What others thought didn't signify . . . though he did hate being hatless.

She wasn't a man and a duke.

Along with the rain-spotted, dirt-spattered, grass-stained wedding dress, mud-caked slippers, and torn and dirty bridal veil drooping over her arm, she was bareheaded. In spite of the pomatum, her damp hair was curling in a wild and wanton manner.

And there were her spectacles, perched on her narrow nose, looking so very serious amid all the shipwreck of bridal finery.

"Yes, of course," she said. She adjusted the spectacles, though these, so far as he could see, were perfectly straight. "This way we entertain only the men plying the oars. We can tell them we were on the way to the wedding when we were waylaid by highwaymen."

"We tell them nothing," he said. "It's their business to take us where we want to go and our business to pay the fare."

He eyed the vessels waiting along the shore, and settled on one of the four-oared wherries. Its watermen had rigged an awning as a rain shelter.

He led her toward it.

"But what if we're followed?" she said. "If we get the watermen's sympathies, they're less likely to betray us."

"I've found that money speaks louder than words," he said.

Betrayal didn't trouble him. Half the world recognized him, and people couldn't help noticing her, and people would talk. But as long as she was safe in Twickenham before nightfall, Ripley could manage the situation.

No, it wasn't the simplest prank he'd ever played. Too many elements out of his control, Ashmont being the main problem. He could be getting drunker, for all one knew. Or had already reached the unconscious stage. That increased the odds of her family being on their trail instead, a less amusing development.

Ripley didn't fancy listening to a lot of accusations and demands for explanations. He'd never seen any reason to explain himself to anybody, including himself.

They reached the boat and oarsmen he'd

decided on. Thanks to ready money and a ducal manner that did not invite questioning or hesitation, he settled business matters in short order.

Then he had to get her into the boat.

This ought not to have been difficult. The watermen's boats had a long, narrow prow, allowing passengers to climb aboard without getting wet.

Ripley had chosen a large vessel, meant for more than two passengers, and oarsmen who appeared to be the strongest and most trustworthy of those awaiting passengers.

She stared at the wherry and said, "Is that it?"

"The Lord Mayor's barge was otherwise engaged," he said. "My yacht is at Worthing, last I heard. This is the boat."

The two fellows looked on with interest. That they did so silently testified to the fee Ripley had offered for speed and silence. Thames watermen were not renowned for bashfulness.

"It seems very low in the water," she said.

"That's the way they're made," he said. "For stability and . . . Never mind. I can explain the science of boat building to you later. Just step into it, will you? And try not to fall off before you get to the seat. If you do, you're not likely to drown, because the water here isn't deep enough. But somebody will have to fish you out, and while I doubt I can get any wetter, I don't fancy wading into that muck."

He'd do it, of course. He would not let either of these two rough fellows put their hands on her.

"I feel dizzy," she said.

"Were you thinking of going back and having a pleasant lie-down?"

"No."

"Are you sure?"

If she wasn't sure, he'd take her back. He would say it was all one of Their Dis-Graces' famous jokes, and that would be that. No, it wouldn't be nearly as much fun as making Ashmont chase her to Twicken-ham. Still, even Ripley wouldn't knock her unconscious for the fun of carrying out a more elaborate prank.

"At this point it would be silly," she said.

"Right," he said. "And certainly, your be-ing here, now, instead of — let's say, at a wedding breakfast? That couldn't possibly — I'm only speculating — that doesn't strike you as imprudent?"

She peered up at him. "Do you think so? And you find nothing out of the way in your being here with me?"

"Perfectly in order," he said.

81

"Is it?"

"Didn't you tell me you were a damsel in distress?" he said. "I'm your knight in shining armor."

Her eyebrows went up.

"It makes for a change," he said.

"I should not call it a change," she said. "In your case I should call it . . ." Her eyebrows settled again and a glint of humor lit her eyes. "An apocalypse."

"Do you mean to get into the boat or shall I do what another, less knightly, very hungry fellow might do, and drop you off the bridge?" he said.

She looked up at the wooden bridge, which had stood, in defiance of the laws of physics, never mind aesthetics, for sixty years. It had been built at an awkward angle to the river's current, and boasted some eighteen narrowly spaced piers. Vessels crashed into it all the time. As more than one critic had noted, Battersea Bridge was built for the convenience of those going over the bridge, and the inconvenience of those going under it.

The only bridge on the Thames that could compete for awkwardness and stupidity was the next one upriver, at Putney.

"Or we could simply wait here," Ripley said. "If we wait long enough, Ashmont might come along to rescue you from me."

He glanced back at the crowd awaiting the steamboat. No signs of pursuit yet. But time was passing. How long had they traveled in the hackney? On horseback or in his own carriage, Ashmont could make better time — if (a) he was conscious and (b) he could put a clue or two together and (c) come to a fairly obvious conclusion.

Not terribly likely, in other words.

When Ripley brought his attention back to the bride, he found her watching him. Her eyes had turned blue.

"No," she said. "The die is cast. My fate is sealed. I'm not getting married today and that's that."

Very well. No turning back now. Good. No turning back promised to be more interesting, at the very least.

"Are you going to help me into the boat?" she said. "Or were you wishing to watch me fall into it?"

"Watching you fall into it would be more entertaining," he said. "The trouble is, it would amuse the watermen and bystanders as well, and we've already called enough attention to ourselves."

"I thought that was what you lived for," she said. "Calling attention to yourself. Or does that happen by accident? Because otherwise that would mean you thought about it and actually . . ." Her brow wrinkled. "Never mind. Best not to imagine what goes on in your head. At any rate, I can't think too hard because it's too hard. Is that a conundrum?"

"Don't imagine. Don't think. Just —"

"It does explain a great deal about the behavior of certain gentlemen who shall remain nameless. The effects of intoxicating spirits —"

"Get in the boat," he said.

He grasped her elbow and steered her to the prow. That was the easy part. After that came some stumbling and more French muttering and a prodigious amount of lacy veil fluttering about and skirts tangling with ducal legs and a couple of collisions between bride and groomsman. During these few minutes, he had the devil's own time not falling out of the boat, laughing, or, much worse, doing something unbridesmaidlike because, after all, he was not only a man but one who wasn't in the habit of behaving himself.

Eventually, however, he got her stowed on the seat under the ugly shelter.

The awning might have been used to collect fish or dredge the river. It certainly smelled like it. Her skirts swelled about him, and a gust of wind caught the veil and lifted it to tickle his face. He pushed it away at the same moment she pulled it away, and their fingers brushed.

She fidgeted and turned away to stare at the water.

His thoughts clung to the moments of her falling into and out of his arms while getting onto the boat. And to the scent of her hair.

Well, that was a bloody waste of thought.

As soon as this business was done, he'd find a merry widow or a courtesan and cure what ailed him.

He fixed his mind on hats.

He wished he had his, and wondered where he might get something remotely suitable in short order.

The boat pushed off at last, and all the odds and ends fretting his mind flew away on the river breeze.

At that moment, and not very greatly to his surprise, what the Duke of Ripley felt was relief.

Newland House
Lord Ludford found the Duke of Ashmont in the dining room bent over a large bowl. The Duke of Blackwood was pouring water over his head.

"Damn, that's cold," said Ashmont.

Blackwood paused.

"Don't stop," Ashmont said. "Got to get my head clear."

"Don't do it on account of the wedding," Ludford said. "Because it looks like there isn't going to be one. Olympia's made off with your friend."

Ashmont's blond head came up abruptly, splashing water on Blackwood, who calmly stepped back with a not-so-calm oath.

"What the devil?" said Ashmont.

"She's bolted, and Ripley's gone with her. They got into a hackney coach in the High Street but nobody could say where they were going."

Hackneys might backtrack or take a roundabout route to avoid roads commonly snarled with traffic. Without knowing the direction Ripley had given the driver, it was impossible to determine which way they were headed.

"I thought you'd know where he'd go," he said. "Or what he'd do."

Ashmont and Blackwood stared at him. Then at each other.

At that moment, a tall, fair-haired, middle-aged gentleman sauntered into the room. His fine, handsome features proclaimed him a Beckingham.

"Uncle Fred," Ashmont said. "Funny thing's happened."

Lord Frederick Beckingham raised an eyebrow. "So it would seem. You ought to be married by now."

Ludford explained what he'd recently witnessed.

Lord Frederick regarded his nephew. "This had better not be one of your jokes."

"Not mine," Ashmont said. "Ripley's."

"Obviously," Blackwood said. "As I was about to tell Ludford, it's nothing to worry about. They won't go far. They'll be gone only long enough to cause a fuss."

"Really?" said Lord Frederick. "I must confess it puzzles me vastly why Lady Olympia would go along with it."

"Yes, why would she?" Ludford said. "She thinks you three are worthless."

"She must think I'm worth something," Ashmont said. "She said yes, didn't she?"

"So you said," Lord Frederick said.

"But now she's bolted," Ludford said.

"She didn't bolt," Ashmont said. "Ripley sneaked away with her. He got her in on the joke, don't you see?"

"I thought you were the one who concocted the jokes," Ludford said.

"Not always," Blackwood said. "Ripley's come up with some fine ones. The question is, as Ludford has so intelligently asked, where would Ripley take her? It would have to be nearby. He wouldn't want to make . . . erm . . . complications."

"If he ruins my sister's reputation, I'll kill him," Ludford said. "That would be a complication, yes."

"You'll have to get in the line behind Ashmont," Blackwood said.

"Bloody right," Ashmont said. "I did all the work, wooing and such, and I should get the bride. That scurvy bastard. There he was, playing the innocent — and I asked him to look after things."

"You didn't ask," Blackwood said. "You told him."

"*You* told him," Ashmont said. "You said . . ." He paused, frowning. "I forget. But if he didn't want to do it, he should have said so, instead of stealing my bride."

"I can imagine a great many things," said Lord Frederick. "Ripley's stealing Lady Olympia isn't one of them."

"If he stole her, why was he chasing her through the garden?" Ludford said. "If he stole her, why wasn't he carrying her over his shoulder, that sort of thing?"

Ashmont's beautiful brow knit. "I'll confess, that does stump me."

"I daresay it does," said Lord Frederick.

"Rather than overwork your brain with this puzzler, I recommend you get her back, as soon as possible."

"In the meantime, what are we going to tell my parents?" said Ludford. "And the wedding guests?"

"I shall speak to your parents," said Lord Frederick. "I'll assure them that Ashmont has everything in hand, and will sort matters out. We'll tell the guests that Lady Olympia is unwell. Now if everybody would be so good, I should like to speak to my nephew."

The others filed out.

Lord Frederick said in a low voice, "What did you do?"

"I didn't do anything, dammit. I can't imagine what made her get the wind up. If she did. If it wasn't Ripley up to one of his tricks."

"I told you —"

"You didn't have to tell me, Uncle. I found her and I saw for myself. A splendid girl. Exactly what I wanted, and so I told you. And none of your unflattering remarks and prophecies of doom stopped me, did they?"

"I wish something I said could persuade you to reflect on your behavior."

"I didn't do anything!"

"I can only hope this is the case, and the matter is as minor as you seem to believe — because, if you lose this girl, Lucius, you may never get another chance," said Lord Frederick. "You may not think so now, but weeks or months or years hence, you will find yourself regretting —"

"I'm not going to regret anything. I'm going to get her back and I'll make everything right — whatever it is that's wrong — and the longer I spend with you, getting lectured at, the farther away she's getting."

"With Ripley."

"She's safe with him," Ashmont said.

"I hope so, for your sake."

"He's my friend," Ashmont said. "He's a scurvy devil, but he's my friend — and we'll have this all sorted out soon enough and it'll be a laugh, I'll wager anything."

By the time the boat left Battersea Bridge, the drizzle had thinned to mist. The riverside looked softer and some — not Ripley — might say it appeared more romantic. London seemed to be dissolving and reforming, and buildings that ought to be familiar loomed mysteriously. Or maybe the mystery was, they didn't look nearly as filthy as usual, thanks to the veil of mist.

Still, he had no trouble discerning the

ragged boys wading into the muddy river-bank, scavenging.

Not that London was so different, as to poverty and filth, from any other large city.

The truth was, he'd missed it.

He'd barely had a chance to alight in Town before he was off again, on a boat.

At present, that didn't seem such a bad idea.

For one thing, Ashmont's wedding day had turned out to be not as boring as expected. For another, Ripley had the bride, whom it hadn't occurred to him to steal. But now he had her, and the promise of an adventure, and they were on the river, away from everybody.

All he had to do was get her safely to Twickenham. By water it would take two or three hours. The journey by land was shorter in terms of distance, but clogged roads could make it slower.

"There's Battersea Church," she said. "Everything looks so different from this vantage point. I've only ever traveled the river in a steamboat or a yacht, never so close to the water as this."

As though her words had summoned it, a steamboat chugged by, churning up the waters. As he reached to steady her, the wash rocked the boat violently, and he nearly fell over. With a curse, he righted himself and grabbed her arm, which shrank at his touch — but no, that wasn't her arm. It was the puff inside her sleeve.

She didn't seem to notice. She was clutching the side of the boat. Her face was as white as the bridal dress.

By the time the wherry settled again, he'd got his breathing more or less even, though his heart pounded. If she'd fallen overboard . . .

But she hadn't. Nobody had.

"At least this won't be a boring river journey," he said.

"It's *very* different when one is low in the water," she said shakily.

"Don't sit so close to the edge," he said. "And do *not* get seasick."

She looked up at him. Her eyes seemed to have lost their color and turned grey, like the mist. "Now why has no one else ever thought of that? Simply commanding one not to be seasick. I'm sure it always works."

She spoke calmly, but she kept her hands fastened to the side of the boat.

"I've made a decision," he said. "I did wonder what Ashmont was about. But now it's clear he had the good fortune to find exactly what he needs."

The color washed back into her face. "I

don't care whether I'm what he needs. The question is whether he's what *I* need."

"He's a duke," he said. "That's all any woman needs."

One by one she loosened her fingers from the side of the boat. "I have told myself that at least a hundred times," she said. "How curious that it failed to quiet my trepidation."

"A pity you didn't drink more brandy," he said. "That might have done it. You got only as far as the reckless phase. A little more, and you might have reached the malleable and contented phase. Which reminds me: As to the casting-up-your-accounts phase —"

"I didn't know there were rules of intoxication," she said.

"Then listen to the voice of experience. If you mean to be sick in spite of my firm command, kindly do it over the side, but hold on. If you fall in, you'll drown in that rig, and I'll have a lot of boring explaining to do, instead of my simple yet cunning plan for salvaging this situation."

"You have a plan?"

"I've had several. One involved a detour to Portsmouth and a sea voyage."

"Ah, the clever running-away ruse," she said.

"I considered and discarded it," he said. "I've hardly come back. I haven't had time to recover from foreigners."

"I should like to meet some foreigners," she said. "I should like to meet nothing *but* foreigners."

"Then marry Ashmont and make him take you abroad," he said. He could picture her climbing the steps of the Boboli Gardens in Florence and looking out over the city. He wondered what color her eyes would turn when they first lit upon the palazzi overlooking Venice's canals. He could see her in a gondola, in the intimacy of an elegant, well-cushioned *felze* . . . and it was better not to imagine the sorts of things one could get up to in those tiny cabins.

"I've already thought of that," she said. "I've reviewed the advantages. Repeatedly. The library at his place in Nottinghamshire, I will admit, loomed large in my calculations. And in case I had overlooked any, Aunt Lavinia was more than happy to fill in the gaps. I should have everything I ever wanted, she said — though I would say it depends on what one wants. Not that I understand how he's managed not to be up to his ears in mortgages and debts. But you may be sure that Papa and Uncle Henry looked into those matters very closely. That is, Uncle Henry did. I don't believe Papa truly understands numbers, unless they're in the racing forms." She sighed. "Ashmont hasn't run through his inheritance. He's increased it." She put her hand to her head. "The world will think I'm deranged."

The world, if Ripley knew anything about it, would blame Ashmont. Hell, *Ripley* blamed Ashmont. He was a rich, beautiful duke. He'd been born charming, where others had to learn it the best they could. He ought to have swept her off her feet. She ought to have been dizzy with joy on her wedding day, not drowning her troubles in brandy.

Idiot.

"Second thoughts?" he said. "We can be back to Newland House in a jiffy."

"No, I have crossed the Rubicon. And look how far we've come." She pointed an unsteady finger. "There's Putney Bridge. I'd know it anywhere."

"Yes, there's quite a good —" He broke off. He'd been gone for more than a year. "Any earthquakes hereabouts lately?" he asked the watermen.

"No, Yer Grace," said one, while the other only stared at him.

"In that case, may one presume the White Lion at Putney still stands?" Ripley said.

95

"Still there, Yer Grace," the more talkative one said.

"We'll stop and eat at the White Lion," Ripley said. It would require their going into the High Street and would take longer than a riverside tavern, but one didn't take ladies to taverns.

Both men nodded, and began to redirect the boat toward the Putney side of the river.

"Stop?" she said. "We don't have time for you to corrupt innocent inn maids. I thought you were in a hurry to be rid of me."

"You can't expect me to travel with you all the way to Twickenham on an empty stomach," he said.

"Can I leave you here and continue on my own?" she said. "Because I'm not in the mood to corrupt innocent innkeepers today, and I should want something to do while you dally with serving maids."

"We're going to have something to eat," he said. "You and I. Or you can watch me eat."

"I thought you were in a hurry."

"It isn't dinner at Windsor Castle," he said. "We'll need no more time than what the mail coach gives passengers for dinner. You'd better eat. Less likely to get a headache that way. Voice of experience, remember?"

■ ■ ■ ■

Olympia couldn't remember when last she'd eaten. She couldn't remember a number of things. A great many articles were not in their usual places in her mind, and the world about her wasn't in its right place, either.

The duke hadn't made a wrong suggestion, she supposed. If the body wasn't nourished, the brain became weak. Furthermore — though she wouldn't admit it to him for worlds or diamond coronets — she believed she was somewhat intoxicated. That was the only reasonable explanation for the jumble of her mind.

Hers was supposed to be an orderly, practical mind. To a fault, some said. Well, everybody.

The one she had at present was chaotic and impractical.

She needed to eat. It wouldn't take long. They would be on their way, nourished and refreshed, and she would be able to think to the next step and beyond.

"I should like a sandwich," she said. "Do they have sandwiches?"

"I'm a duke," he said.

"Yes, of course they have sandwiches," she

said. If they didn't, they'd obtain them one way or another. It was good to be a duke, especially a large, intimidating one.

Not that she was intimidated. He was one of Their Dis-Graces and therefore rather an idiot. But he was a powerful idiot. And a man. And even on a boat meant for several passengers, he seemed to occupy all available space. He sat with his long legs stretched out, as though he lazed on a sofa in a Turkish harem. Her mind made a picture of him in a loose shirt and flowing trousers . . . then it drifted to what Mama had told her about the wedding night.

This was by no means a shocking revelation. Olympia had sneaked away with certain of her brothers one time, and watched a stallion mount a mare. It had seemed rather uncomfortable for the mare, and work for the stallion, but of course it would be different for people . . .

. . . and she did *not* want to think about such things when in proximity to this large, and not entirely civilized, man . . . or at all . . . and really, she was quite hungry.

The watermen pulled into the landing place. She watched impatiently as they stowed the oars. She would have leapt from the boat then, but Ripley grasped her elbow. Not hard. He didn't apply pressure. All the same, the light grasp kept her on the seat.

She wasn't sure how he did it but she suspected it had something to do with being a duke.

"Wait," he said. "Let them get out and hold the boat."

She waited, acutely conscious of the big hand clasping her lower arm, while the watermen took their time about disembarking, then more time to turn around and take hold of the narrow end of the boat to steady it.

"All right," Ripley said, releasing her. "Careful now."

"The boat is on dry land," she said. "Or damp land, to be precise."

"Not all of it," he said. "To be precise. The prow —"

"Yes, yes, I see." Hurriedly she collected her veil and rose. As she stepped toward the front of the boat, it rocked.

"Careful," Ripley said.

She turned back to him. "I can't stop the vessel from rocking," she said. "As you said, part of it is in the water, and water, being liquid —"

"Stay in the middle," he said.

"I *am* in the middle."

With a huff of exasperation, she turned away and started toward the front of the boat at the same moment he said, "No!"

The boat rocked jerkily. Then she was waving her arms for balance and Ripley was moving toward her, shouting. And there was his hand, which she tried to grasp, but it was a hairsbreadth out of reach. Then she was falling, and over she went, with a great, muddy splash.

He swore and swore again.

He climbed out of the boat, shoving away the watermen, who were moving toward her. He trudged into the muck to where she sat, looking very surprised, in a foot or so of murky water.

"You had to fall off the boat," he said.

"I didn't do it on purpose!" She tried to rise, but only contrived to slide backward into slightly deeper muck.

"I told you —"

"You shouldn't have distracted me."

"I was warning you."

"It is extremely annoying to be talked to as though one had no sense at all. No, don't trouble yourself," she added as he put out a hand for her to grab. "I am perfectly capable of climbing out of a foot of water unaided."

An audience was gathering. In another minute, gawkers would be pouring out of the riverside taverns.

"Take my hand," he said.

"I can take hold of the boat," she said.

He grabbed her hand, and started to pull her up, but she jerked free at the same moment, and his foot slipped, and down he went.

He heard laughter from the shore.

He looked at her.

She still had the curst veil tangled about one arm, and the hair arrangement he'd made was slipping downward. The fall had splashed muddy water on her face and spectacles. The latter were definitely crooked now.

He felt laughter welling, but then he realized he was sitting in water, and so was she, and she'd catch a lung fever if not worse.

He swore again and pulled himself up out of the water, set his feet solidly, and bent. He grasped her under the arms — how many times was that today? — and hauled her upright. The instant she was vertical, she tried to push him away, and stumbled toward the water again.

This time he pulled her hard against him. "Are you trying to drown yourself?" he said. "Because it would be wiser and certainly easier to jump off the bridge — in the *middle* of the river, you see, not at the shore."

She pushed at him. "Will you please get out of my way!"

She was wet and muddy and aromatic of river. He was aware of this. He was aware also of a supple, curving body pressed against his. His mind began to do what a man's mind does in such cases: It yielded to a stronger power, rather lower in the body.

"No," he said. With speech, even as little as that, a modicum of survival skill returned, and his mind produced an image of Ashmont waiting with the clergyman.

Ashmont's bride.

He'd chosen her and he deserved her. She was *perfect* for him.

While she was still pushing, Ripley shifted his weight and swung her up and into his arms, a wet, muddy mass of shrieking runaway bride.

The onlookers cheered. He was used to audiences. He nodded at them.

"Oh," she said. "You are ridiculous."

"Says the girl who landed on her arse in the river a moment ago."

She wasn't one of those so-called sylphs, who weighed nothing and looked as though a mild breeze would fracture them. She was a proper-sized female, with an excellent distribution of feminine assets. But he'd managed runaway horses and he'd hauled larger and far heavier friends out of taverns, brothels, boats, carriages, stables, and so forth. Furthermore, he was a man more physical than intellectual. It was no great feat to carry her up the mild incline and on into the High Street.

She talked or scolded or something the whole time.

He didn't know what she said because he didn't pay attention. He had to keep his mind from dwelling on what she weighed and what she was shaped like, because from there matters would proceed to his getting ideas in the tiny little head that liked to take charge when women were in close proximity.

He concentrated on the one thing he had to do.

He had to get her to Twickenham — alive, preferably — and make Ashmont go there and get her.

It couldn't be simpler, Ripley assured himself.

CHAPTER 4

As Olympia might have expected, everybody at the White Lion recognized the Duke of Ripley.

They would have recognized any of Their Dis-Graces.

Their images had been engraved in all the papers featuring gossip. They had appeared almost daily in London's favorite purveyor of scandal, *Foxe's Morning Spectacle,* and in caricatures in print shop windows.

There was no such thing, Olympia realized, as traveling discreetly with *him.*

Not that one could be discreet, wearing a ruined wedding dress and looking less like Ophelia and more like a drowned rat or the shipwreck the rat wasn't quick enough to escape.

There was no such thing, either, she thought, as getting His Grace to do anything other than what he wanted to do. In the matter of being allowed to stand on her own feet, for instance, she was obliged to wait until he was good and ready.

The truth was, she wasn't completely unhappy to be lifted out of the water and carried up the stairs past what seemed like hundreds of onlookers. While she would have held her head high — she was an earl's daughter, after all — she wasn't at all confident of being able to walk with anything like grace.

And while she'd rather not be quite so wet and muddy in a public hostelry, above all she did not want anybody to know she was drunk. That, she feared, was what the audience was bound to conclude if she attempted to walk on her own, dragging what felt like several tons of the Thames with her.

This was the first time since she was a little girl that a man had carried her in his arms. She didn't feel like a child, and it was nothing like being carried by one's father or uncle or grandfather. Awareness of his strength and size and the warmth of his body hammered at her senses. She wanted so badly to tuck her head into his chest.

It was the brandy, had to be. You'd think that having steamboat wash nearly overturn one into the Thames was enough to shock one back to sobriety. Apparently not.

He finally put her down in the hotel's

reception hall. Her legs trembling for no sensible reason, she listened while he demanded of the innkeeper two rooms, both with fires and hot water for washing, and dry clothes.

It took her mind a moment to settle down and make sense of what was going on.

Then, "Fires?" she said after the innkeeper had hurried away. "At this time of year?"

"Are you keen to develop a lung fever?" he said.

"By the time they get them going, we'll have washed and changed," she said. "That is, if they find clothes. How do you expect them to find clothes for us?"

"The same way I expect them to make up fires," he said. "How they do it is not my concern."

"I wonder nobody's tried to kill you before now," she said. "Do you do this sort of thing all the time?"

"No," he said. "You're the first bride who's kidnapped me. Naturally, though, they assume I made off with you, which suits our purposes."

"It doesn't suit mine," she said. "I can't —" She had been about to say *I can't afford to be made off with,* but that was absurd. To all intents and purposes she'd run away with the Duke of Ripley, and that was what the scandalmongers would say and the papers would publish, and there would be satirical prints of the event, drawn from the artists' imaginations. These would be lurid.

She told herself to look on the bright side. Never in her wildest fantasies had she ever imagined appearing in the print shop windows.

Never in anybody else's wildest fantasies, either. To her knowledge, nobody had ever been voted Most Boring Girl of the Season more times than Lady Olympia Hightower.

On the other hand, she'd embarrassed her family. Disgraced them. Disgraced herself. Made herself truly unmarriageable.

But no, she could not think about consequences or she'd go mad. As it was, her mind was on shaky ground.

One thing at a time.

A maidservant appeared to show them to their rooms.

Ripley followed Lady Olympia up the stairs, telling himself the bride-overboard scene was the sort of thing a fellow could expect to happen in the course of an adventure. Not that it was the sort of entertainment he'd expect to have with a respectable girl — but then, he hadn't had much experience with that type.

Happily, the setback had occurred early in the trip, near an inn he'd patronized time and again. True, he and his friends had behaved as badly here as they did elsewhere. True, also, that they always paid the damages.

The White Lion kept an account for him. This wasn't unusual in the case of a gentleman who frequently traveled the king's highway in search of excitement: boxing and wrestling matches, horse and boat races, and every sort of game on which one could bet.

What wasn't usual was the duke's agent's settling accounts — not on quarter days or twice yearly or annually or, in the grand tradition of the aristocracy, never at all — but *monthly.*

All accounts, paid in full, every single month.

This little eccentricity of his kept people quiet and made them cooperative. Instead of bolting the doors and windows and putting up Gone Fishing or Closed Until Further Notice signs when they heard he was coming, all the tradesmen flung open their doors and rushed out to greet him with open arms and, sometimes, their daughters.

It was good to be a duke, but best to be a

solvent one.

Money mended everything, usually.

It would soon mend the current problem, and Ripley would get Ashmont's bride to Twickenham in plenty of time.

She would not take a chill and develop pneumonia.

This was June, not November. The weather was mild, and she'd fallen into not two feet of water.

He became aware of water dripping on the stairs as she climbed them.

His mind came back to the present, and he realized she was wet to the skin. Her petticoats had to be soaked through. Otherwise, her skirts couldn't have plastered themselves to her bottom and thighs.

He recalled the way her body felt pressed to his, and the way she felt in his arms when he'd carried her up to the inn.

Of course he remembered. He was a man, and she was a shapely young woman.

And of course she was shapely. Ashmont wouldn't dream of wooing any other kind of female.

And since Ashmont had wooed and more or less won her, the shapeliness belonged to him. Which was as it should be. Beyond a doubt she was exactly what he needed. Lady Olympia would never let him walk all over her. She might walk all over him, which probably would be fun . . .

And let's not think about how much fun it would be, Ripley counseled himself when his imagination started to stray in that direction. *Not a useful train of thought at present.*

For the present, what he needed, first, was a thorough wash, and second, a hat — and they had better find something suitable. Third, he needed — as was perfectly reasonable and natural after months of unnatural abstinence — a shapely female who did not belong to one of his best friends. The first and second would be dealt with soon and the third this evening, he promised himself.

Meanwhile, being a man and by no means a saint, he did not tell himself to stop looking at Lady Olympia's muddy ankles.

Ripley waited until Lady Olympia was safely in her room with two of the inn's servants, Molly and Jane, on guard.

He'd taken them aside to tell them her ladyship had had a trying morning and was not as clearheaded as one could wish. Therefore he expected them to remain clearheaded and vigilant on her behalf.

They were to forestall any attempts by her ladyship to climb out of windows or make other sudden changes in travel plans. Their task was to get her clean and dry and fed and into fresh clothes. Under no circumstances were they to let her out of their sight. If by some bad chance she slipped away from them, they must tell him *instantly.* He would be next door.

Having addressed all contingencies, he waited until the door had closed behind the trio, then summoned the landlady.

"Send somebody to the dressmaker Mrs. Thorne," he said. "Make sure she understands that the lady had an accident and needs fresh clothing quickly, quickly. We haven't a moment to lose."

The landlady dashed away.

Then he folded his arms and leaned against the door frame of his room.

Another trick he'd learned through experience.

People performed their tasks more speedily when a large, intimidating nobleman stood waiting for them to do whatever he'd told them to do.

Servants bustled up with kindling and buckets of coals.

More servants followed, with pitchers of hot water.

Still, he waited. Time passed. His clothing stopped dripping and subsided to a sodden second skin.

He stepped out into the gallery overlooking the inn yard. He leaned against a supporting post and watched the activity below. In the humid air, his clothing gradually went from sodden to damp. He was growing increasingly bored and impatient when at last three women hurried into the yard. The most elegant of the three looked up anxiously at him.

He nodded.

She started up the stairs, the other two close behind, bearing large, muslin-wrapped parcels.

Then and only then did he enter his room.

In Olympia's large room, a fire blazed in the hearth.

In June.

Two immense pitchers, filled with hot water, arrived about the same moment the flames began to bounce over the coals.

Though the White Lion was a busy place, two of its overworked maidservants attended to one bedraggled lady.

Countless other servants — virtually all of those belonging to the inn and, very likely, its neighbors — ran about, attending to His Grace's whims.

Indeed, it was good to be a duke.

Or, more precisely — and Olympia was a

precise person, normally — if you were going to fall into a river in your wedding dress, it was good to be in a duke's company when it happened.

She was annoyed with herself for falling out of the boat.

She was annoyed with herself for letting him rattle her in any way.

She should not have been bandying words with him. What she should have done was watch what she was doing and where she was going and thereby get off the boat in a graceful manner.

But what she'd done instead was done and couldn't be undone. She'd behaved stupidly and ended up being carried by one of the most notorious peers in all of Great Britain along Putney's High Street, in front of the entire village population, watermen, coachmen, travelers, stray children and dogs — everybody, in short — and into the hotel.

She was hot all over, even inside her head.

She hoped that was simply the ridiculous fire — in June! — and the exertions of the maids, who scrubbed her from top to bottom. To distract her mind from imagining satirical prints of the recent episode, she turned her attention, as best she could, to the Next Step.

Though the brandy's effects seemed to

have dwindled and her mind was not as fuzzy as before, it took her a while to determine what the step ought to be.

What to say to Aunt Delia?

Good grief, where did one begin?

But Olympia would have to begin somewhere. Looking on the bright side, composing a satisfactory explanation — and there had to be one — would keep her mind fully and usefully occupied.

She worked on the problem while Molly and Jane rubbed her with warm towels, and helped her into a dressing gown. Olympia was still trying and discarding explanations when they sat her at a small dressing table and began combing out her hair.

They were patiently untangling knots when the dressmaker turned up.

Yes, an actual dressmaker, with a pair of seamstresses in tow, bearing what looked like a shopful of garments.

They all made deep curtseys. The most elegant of the group introduced herself as Mrs. Thorne while the two anonymous lesser beings untied their parcels and laid out clothing on the bed.

"How distressed we were to hear of your ladyship's accident!" said the dressmaker. "I should have made haste, in any event, to see what assistance I could render, even before I received His Grace's message. By a stroke of great good luck we had a few garments nearly ready, and two on the display. It is nothing, I assure your ladyship, to make alterations. We'll have your ladyship ready in no time at all, and I trust your ladyship will not be dissatisfied. We are not in London, precisely, but our patterns come from Paris, and I am sure my seamstresses — Oh, I do beg your ladyship's pardon. May I present Miss Ames and Miss Oxley. I believe you'll find them a match for any girls from London."

Olympia had often fought bitterly with her mother about her wardrobe, leaving dressmakers to negotiate. She could well imagine the hours seamstresses must spend hurrying to satisfy the whims of their overprivileged clientele. She rather doubted any seamstress could match London ones for stamina and resilience under extreme tension and, no doubt, abuse.

As to present company's level of skill: At the moment her main concern was wearing a dress not impregnated with mud. She didn't care if the stitches were crooked.

If she said so, though, she'd hurt the dressmaker's feelings.

She said, "Thank you for coming so quickly."

Ripley had snapped his fingers and ordered clothes, and here was the result.

One of the inn's servants must have run out into Putney and into Mrs. Thorne's dressmaking shop. And she had dropped everything to do His Grace's bidding.

It was not in the least strange, Olympia told herself. To be able to say a duke patronized one's establishment was a great coup. Most shopkeepers, especially in villages, would do what Mrs. Thorne had done.

But really, did he need to be spoiled more than he was already?

"I hope you weren't obliged to close your shop," Olympia said.

"Not at all, my lady," said Mrs. Thorne. "So good of your ladyship to think of it, but everything is in hand, and the shop will be looked after until we return. Not but what I wouldn't have hesitated to close it, if necessary. But if your ladyship will forgive the interruption — only a moment, please, if your ladyship would be so good as to stand, and we might take your size."

Olympia stood, and was instantly surrounded.

While the women held up this and that against her, she wondered whose garments they'd brought. Yes, one or two might have been display articles, although more usually a fashion print or a length of fabric, artfully draped, would appear in the shop window.

A modiste was unlikely to keep a supply of dresses ready, awaiting a customer. Garments were made to order.

On the other hand, when, for instance, certain customers who had large bank accounts and a reputation for paying promptly — or dukes — demanded something in a hurry, the dressmaker might alter clothing meant for another client.

Mrs. Thorne laid out a chemise and a corset.

They were shockingly beautiful, unlike anything Olympia had ever seen before. The chemise, of the finest linen, was embroidered with *colored* silk and trimmed with lace along the neckline and edges of the sleeves. The corset, of equally costly fabric, was even more scandalous. It was stitched in pink and black. Pink trim traced the sides of the busk. There was pink lacing for adjusting the bust line area, tied with tiny pink bows. Even the back lacing was pink!

Olympia had never worn — or seen, for that matter — anything but white undergarments in all her life.

She must have looked as astonished as she felt because Mrs. Thorne said quickly, "Some of our clientele are London ladies."

"Indeed," Olympia said. She wondered what sort of London ladies ordered underwear so excessively *French.*

She told herself it didn't matter.

She needed clean, dry clothing, and if the underthings seemed more suitable for a brothel, that wasn't surprising, considering who'd ordered them.

Her too-active mind envisioned a brothel, in the style of a Turkish harem. In it lolled women whose bodies matched those of Greek and Roman statues or perhaps women in Rubens's paintings. They lounged about on cushions and rugs in their lacy, colorfully embroidered underwear. Men like Ripley would saunter in and . . .

Best not to imagine that.

Better leave it to the satirists. No doubt they'd put Lord Gonerby's only daughter in a scarlet corset and petticoats.

Good grief, the look on Papa's face when he saw those pictures —

No, she would not think about that.

She would look on the bright side. There always was a bright side, though sometimes one had to look carefully indeed and use a magnifying glass or a microscope.

And the bright side was . . .

She'd lose the title of Most Boring Girl of the Season.

While she contemplated brothels and her new public character, the women got her out of the dressing gown and into chemise and drawers. They tied ribbons and arranged ruffles and smoothed fabric with as much care as if these underthings were made of silk and diamonds.

The corset straps needed adjustment, but Miss Oxley went to work, rapidly unstitching and re-stitching. Meanwhile Mrs. Thorne set Miss Ames to take in the petticoat.

Olympia was fascinated. In London, professional seamstresses were usually kept hidden in another part of the dressmaker's shop. When they did emerge from the workroom, it was to show an item of clothing or assist the dressmaker. She'd never seen them truly at work. The speed with which their needles flew, making the tiniest stitches, seemed superhuman to her.

She had always found books more interesting than needlework.

She hadn't more than a moment to observe, though, because they needed to finish dressing her. The maidservants helped her into stockings and tied garters, apologizing for hurrying her — "but His Grace said we must make haste, and he is so good, you know, we —"

"So good!" Olympia said.

"Oh, yes!" Molly said. "I'd be ashamed to disappoint him, I would."

"Good!" Olympia said. "This is the first I've heard of it. What's he done? Don't tell me he takes in wounded birds and nurses them back to health. Saves kittens from drowning, perchance? That must be it."

"But truly, my lady —"

"Good," she repeated. "Ripley. I vow, it hurts my head to put that adjective in his vicinity. The same goes for the other two nonsensical excuses for dukes. No, it's no use. I cannot wrap my wits about the idea."

The servants smiled and one of the seamstresses tittered. Mrs. Thorne glared at her, and the girl bent to her work.

"I know they say His Grace is wild, my lady, and he is," said Jane.

"Such goings-on," said Mrs. Thorne, shaking her head.

Yet Olympia caught a hint of an indulgent smile.

"But when my father fell ill, His Grace sent a doctor, you know," said Molly. "And paid the fee."

"And people may say what they like about Their Graces — and such doings as they get up to!" said Jane. "But whatever gets broke or burnt up or falls into the river, you know — or whoever — they do pay."

"The bed linens that time," said Molly. "Covered in blood, I vow. Still, we thought we could get it out —"

"Covered in blood?" Olympia said.

"The duels," said Miss Ames.

"Hush," said the dressmaker.

"His Grace did mention duels," Olympia said.

"Battersea Fields, you know," said Miss Ames. "Sometimes Putney Heath."

"But mostly the gentlemen come upriver some," said Jane. "To get patched up quiet-like."

"Not usually so bloody, though there was that one time —"

"The Duke of Ashmont —"

"When I saw the blood, I thought Lord Stewkley had shot his ear clean off!"

"But he'd only nicked his head, His Grace said, and how he laughed! Like it was nothing."

"And His Grace of Ripley said head wounds bleed like pigs —"

"They bleed like the very devil, is what His Grace said."

"Mind your tongue," said Mrs. Thorne.

"Not on my account," Olympia said. "I have six brothers."

"Boys will be boys, as we all know," said

Mrs. Thorne.

"More like boys will be little savages," said Olympia. "I'm not sure they ever become entirely civilized. Anyone who tries to shock me with the mad doings of boys will have their work cut out for them. Nothing seems to change much as they grow up, does it? I only marvel at their living long enough to grow up. What was the duel when Lord Stewkley almost blew off the Duke of Ashmont's ear?"

"That was a very long time ago," said Mrs. Thorne repressively as the others opened their mouths. "Nearly ten years, I believe."

"That long?" said Jane.

"In any case, they were young, hardly more than schoolboys," Mrs. Thorne said. "I'm sure nobody remembers what it was about. And I'm sure we have too much to do, to waste time gossiping about ancient history." She cast a warning look toward the other women.

The subject was dropped, and everybody concentrated on their work while Olympia digested recent information.

People tried to hush up duels because they were illegal, but it was nearly impossible to hush them up completely. Still, Olympia couldn't remember anything in particular regarding Ashmont and Lord Stewkley.

Hardly surprising. Their Dis-Graces had created so much scandal so often that extracting one — from a decade ago — would be like getting treacle out of a boy's hair.

The thought of treacle reminded Olympia she was hungry.

"I wonder if somebody would bring me a bite to eat," she said.

"Certainly, my lady," said Jane. She hurried out of the room.

The others installed Olympia in the naughty corset, made final adjustments, and laced her up. Then came the petticoat, which matched the other articles.

Then the dress, at last.

Olympia was vaguely conscious of a mass of pink silk and bows and lace, but by this time her mind was on food, and wishing the maid would hurry. A single piece of bread or cheese or a biscuit would do.

But no, Olympia had arrived with the Duke of Ripley, sainted in these parts, evidently, and the cook must be preparing turtle and lobsters and a fatted calf.

It wasn't until Mrs. Thorne draped a black mantelet over her shoulders that Olympia truly paid attention. She looked down at the bodice and skirt.

She pulled away from the women and

marched to the mirror.

They followed her and stood peering into the mirror around her reflection, a frame of smiling faces.

"Perfect!" said Mrs. Thorne.

"Perfect," her minions echoed.

"Perfect," Molly said breathlessly. "Oh, I never."

"I'll bet you never," Olympia said.

She straightened her spectacles, marched to the door, and pulled it open.

Distantly aware of the chorus of dismayed voices behind her, she continued her march to the room next to hers.

She didn't knock or stop to think. She pulled the door open, marched in, and slammed the door behind her.

"Is this one of your jokes?" she said. "Because . . ."

She found herself staring at the muscled back, taut bottom, and long, muscled legs of a man something over six feet tall, who stood, quite naked, in a large basin before the fire.

He went still, and Olympia ought to have turned her head — or better yet, marched out of the room with a semblance of dignity.

Evidently she wasn't yet fully in her right mind, because all she could think was how different an unclothed, fully grown man looked — in the flesh, literally — from a naked little boy.

The back of his neck and his shoulders and . . . muscle, miles of muscle. Good heavens, his arms. The arms that had carried her up from the river.

She'd seen marble statues of naked men. Who hadn't? She'd seen drawings. But he was alive, so very alive. As still as he stood, he was breathing, and she caught the faint motion of shoulder and back muscles. His skin wasn't marble or paper white but golden in the room's firelight. The amber light glinted on the dark hair along his arms and lower legs, and altogether it was — he was . . . nothing like a statue . . . and heat was swamping her and breathing was more difficult than it ought to be.

"I might have known," he said. He started to turn.

She started to turn, too, toward the door again, but her limbs refused to cooperate, and she failed to make a dignified exit before he reached for the towel draped over the nearby chair and wrapped it about him. Not completely. His broad shoulders, most of his back, and the lower part of his legs remained in view. He stepped out of the basin and stood, dripping, on the rug.

She lifted her chin and feigned a composure she by no means felt.

"You might have, indeed," she said. She told herself she was six and twenty, not a schoolroom miss by many years — seven long ones — and — and — what had made her burst in here?

The dress.

"It's *French*," she said.

"What?"

He turned, and now she was treated to the front view of strong neck, shoulders, and upper torso. Warmth rushed over her in waves and she felt her jaw start to drop.

Good heavens, he was . . . his physique . . . so . . . *athletic.* She was still recovering from the back view. The front . . . his collarbone . . . his chest . . .

Stop gawking, you ninny.

She made herself glare down at her attire, though in fact this was the most beautiful, most dashing day dress she'd ever worn.

"It's *French*," she said waving an only slightly shaky hand over the dress. "And I won't tell you what's underneath because you must already know, but I'll have you know I know exactly what it is."

"Undergarments?" he said. "Because it looks too —" He gestured with the hand not holding the towel. "Too much of a dress, in what can't possibly be your natural shape. With all that skirt swelling out, and the sleeves like wine barrels? Obviously what you're wearing underneath is a large stock of armature."

"The male mind is truly a wonder," she said. "That isn't the point."

"I knew there'd be a point," he said. "And modest fellow that I am, I didn't believe for a moment that you exploded into my presence with a wild longing to wash my back."

Heat swarmed over her face and her neck and other places that were not supposed to call attention to themselves.

"Brilliant thinking," she said. She fluttered the splendid mantelet draped about her shoulders. "It's this. Blond. *Black* blond. At the very least, suitable for a married woman — not but what I entertain great doubts as to whether any matron of my acquaintance wears black and pink embroidered under-things. And pink ribbons! I ask you."

His eyes became hooded, but she didn't need to see them. She felt his gaze going down and up and down and up.

Her skin prickled, the way it had done the first time she'd met him, only more so, though she was seven years older and had seen more than her share of rakes in action. Though never in action with her.

127

"If you're asking whether I can see your undergarments, the answer is no," he said, his voice a shade deeper than before. "And since I can't see them and you seem to be thoroughly covered — rather more thoroughly than before, I might add —"

"Never mind," she said. "I don't know what I was thinking, to think you'd understand. I shall make the best of it and tell myself at least I'm interesting, and after all, perhaps I'm far too hungry to think in an orderly fashion. I'm an orderly person, I'll have you know. And *boring.* I have never worn black blond in my life!"

She started to turn away, for the exit she should have made rather a while ago.

"About time you started, then," he said. "It suits you."

She turned back. "It doesn't suit me in the least. It's dashing. I'm not dashing."

"Could have fooled me," he said. "Bolting from your wedding and such. Climbing over the wall. Falling out of the boat. Whatever else one might say about you — and I'm not sure what to say, frankly — *boring* isn't on the list."

She waved a hand dismissively. "That isn't the real me. That is Olympia a trifling well to go."

He lifted one black eyebrow. "A trifling?"

"The point is, I am no longer slightly intoxicated —"

"More than slightly was my estimation, and I'm an expert, recollect."

"In any event, it was a stupid thing to do, and though I've racked my brains I cannot produce an intelligent or even intelligible excuse."

Panic wasn't a good excuse. True, not much time had passed between the courtship and her accepting the proposal and the wedding. True, she'd let herself be swept up in her mother's and aunt's excitement. Those weren't good excuses, either. Something had happened to her this morning, even before the brandy, else she wouldn't have drunk the brandy.

Maybe the brandy had propelled her, but in his company, the effects seemed to continue, even as the alcohol wore off.

No, in his company, the effects were getting worse.

She glanced down at the dress, and stifled a prickle of longing. "We'd better go back."

There was a pause, and she waited for the *I told you so.* Hadn't he asked her, several times, whether she was sure she wanted to continue? Hadn't he pointed out how easy it would be to return?

"We are bloody well not going back," he said.

CHAPTER 5

Though Ripley wore nothing but a towel, it would have taken a great deal more than near nudity to disconcert him. On the contrary, he would have paid a hundred pounds to catch the look on her face when she burst in on him. He'd been painfully tempted to turn, *sans* towel. He would have paid two hundred for her reaction to the frontal view.

Luckily he'd remembered in the nick of time that she was Ashmont's chosen one. Joke or not, a fellow didn't go about presenting his naked front to his best friend's bride-to-be.

In any event, the sight of a woman in a dashing dress, hair coming down, ranting at him while her bosom heaved up and down like a raging sea — and he fresh and clean in his birthday suit — was likely to trigger a lot of vain hopes in the sensitive fellow below his waist, aggravation Ripley could do without.

Equally important: In ordinary circumstances one could expect Ashmont to treat a scene like this as a great joke. These were not ordinary circumstances. While Ripley had no experience of strange encounters with friends' brides-to-be, he suspected even Ashmont might turn out to be a trifle tetchy when it came to his affianced bride seeing his best friend bare-arsed.

"That ship has sailed," he said. "We're not going back."

"Do not be nonsensical," she said. "You've asked me several times if I wouldn't rather —"

"That was before," he said. "But you've crossed the Tiber —"

"The Rubicon, you provoking man!"

"The die is cast," he said. "I'm taking you to your aunt, as we agreed, and you will stop changing your mind every five minutes."

"I do not change it every five minutes! I haven't changed it at all. Until now."

"We have a plan —"

"*You* have a plan, which all the world knows is never a good idea."

"I am quite dry now," he said. "Perhaps you would be so good as to spare my modesty and hand me the dressing gown."

"Where are the servants?" she said.

"Oughtn't you to have half a dozen of them running about to do your bidding?"

"Only minutes before you irrupted into this room," he said, "I sent them out to see what had become of the meal and clothing I had ordered *a good while ago.* Ye gods, even in one of his sulks, my chef Chardot can produce a feast in half the time they've been about it. There were a few other matters to be attended to, as well. It seems I sent them away not a minute too soon. One can't expect inn servants to hold their tongues, no matter how much one bribes or threatens. I doubt news of the present tableau will go down well with your family, and, as I believe I've mentioned, I'm bored with duels."

The dressmaker and maidservants would talk, but since they weren't eyewitnesses to this, he could use their gossip to advantage. He wasn't greatly concerned about Lady Olympia's blabbing, either. He counted the odds as slim she'd tell a lot of strangers she'd burst in on any man while he was bathing, let alone the infamous Duke of Ripley.

She colored. "All the more reason for us to return, sooner rather than later."

"No," he said. "The dressing gown? If your ladyship would be so good. Never

133

mind, I'll get it myself."

Chin jutting out, she marched to the bed, snatched up the dressing gown the servants had so reverently laid out there, marched back and, arm outstretched, held it out for him.

When he took the garment, she turned her back. "Now that my mind is clearer," she said, "the idea of leaving matters to you strikes me as an act of self-destruction."

He studied the back view.

Mrs. Thorne had chosen well. The black lace cape thing draped becomingly over her ladyship's shoulders, which were well shaped, neither too broad nor too narrow but neatly proportioned to the rest of her excellent proportions.

Indeed, she had a fine back. He'd noticed, more than once in the past, the way she carried herself, the hint of impatience in her walk that made a man want to slow her down and get her full attention. Maybe that's what had finally got to Ashmont: the challenge she offered — *I dare you to possess me.*

At present, the back was furiously straight and unyielding. Oh, she'd give Ashmont cause to pay attention.

But not yet.

Ripley couldn't return her to Ashmont

now. Well, he could, but that would make it too easy. His Grace with the Angel Face needed to make a *real* effort, more than his alleged wooing. By lucky accident, the man had found the perfect Duchess of Ashmont. But he wouldn't appreciate her as he ought to do if he didn't have to work harder for her.

"You cut me to the quick," Ripley said as he shrugged into the dressing gown. "I'm famous for my plans."

"I won't dispute the *famous* part," she said. "The newspapers like nothing better than to write about them. In detail. Let me see. There was the dinner party when you replaced all your dining and drawing room mirrors with distorting ones."

"A pity you didn't see it," he said. "It was a laugh, watching my guests reel from here to there, and not even drunk yet."

The mirrors had led several inebriated guests to cast up their accounts, but the fun was well worth replacing the carpet and several chairs. Ripley had laughed himself sick. As had his two friends.

"Then there was the dinner party you gave for stammerers and stutterers," she said.

"Can't take credit," he said. "That was Blackwood's idea. I did help him find them all and collect them in one place. No small

135

task, that one. But the conversation was worth it."

"It was cruel," she said.

"I'll have you know the guests thought it was hilarious," he said. "They were falling out of their chairs laughing, and the more they laughed, the harder it was for them to talk. A concept you won't understand — not talking."

"I don't doubt the wine helped."

"Of course. We never serve inferior wine."

"In any event, I am sober, and will not meekly do as the Duke of Ripley says merely because His Grace says it," she said. "In fact, the opposite course of action strikes me as far more rational."

"After all this, you're ready to go back with your head hanging and your tail drooping between your legs, the repentant runaway?" he said.

That wouldn't do at all. Ashmont needed her bold and defiant and, generally, difficult.

"It was very wrong, wrong in so many ways I get a headache trying to count them," she said.

"Headache is a known aftereffect of over-indulging in brandy," Ripley said.

"I've embarrassed my family," she said. "And while I know my so-called rejection won't hurt Ashmont, I have humiliated him publicly. His pride will be wounded, and that is an unkindness he's done nothing — to me — to deserve."

But it was such a good plan Ripley had devised.

A perfect plan. For Ashmont. For her.

And yet . . .

She was kind, Ashmont had said last night, his voice soft with wonder.

People weren't kind to Their Dis-Graces. People did what they were told or paid to do. People fawned or tried to seduce or gave the cut direct or put up with or lectured. It would not occur to anybody that a rakehell duke might want or appreciate kindness.

Ripley remembered last night — early this morning — Ashmont so cheerful, talking about getting married. Appointing Ripley to make sure all went well.

Stealing the bride — which is what it would be now, when she wanted to go back — was not, after all, making all go well.

"Very well," he said. "I'll take you back." But he'd drop a few hints on the return trip about the care and management of His Grace of Ashmont.

"Thank you," she said, and started for the door.

"But we're not taking the damned boat," he said to her back. Her fine, straight back.

She shrugged her equally fine shoulders and went out.

A short time later

Olympia sat, trying to eat a sandwich, while Molly and Jane arranged her hair. From where she sat, she could see her bridal dress and veil reflected in the dressing glass.

Her attendants had spread them out to dry in front of the fire. There the torn and dirty garments lay, like the corpses of her one chance to marry splendidly and rescue her brothers from their financially irresponsible parents.

She'd much rather not dwell on what she'd done this morning, but she wasn't a duke. Unlike Ripley, she couldn't make uncomfortable subjects leave her mind on command.

He had seemed to believe a second chance was possible, and he ought to know his way around scandal. On the other hand, none of the ducal trio fell into the World's Greatest Thinker category. And on the third hand — why not have a third one or a fourth, for that matter? — Ashmont was notoriously unpredictable. One had no idea when the next practical joke would happen, or the next fight. His title, looks, and charm had carried him until the past year or two, when

138

London's hostesses had had enough of his bad behavior and finally begun to drop him from their invitation lists.

Suppose he didn't give her a second chance?

Not that she was sure she wanted one . . . and then, to look on the bright side of his rejecting her, there was Lord Mends.

At this point he might seem to her parents a less monstrous candidate than before. If he was still willing to be a candidate. For all Olympia knew, he might have found another woman eager to be his librarian.

True, he was elderly and pedantic. True, Mama and Papa had been outraged to the point of hysteria at the idea of their one, precious daughter marrying a man nearly old enough to be her grandfather. If Olympia had truly loved him, she might have brought them round. But she only loved his books.

While her parents had declined his invitation to bring Olympia to see his library, she felt as though she knew it intimately, based on what she'd read and what he'd told her. Though he sadly admitted it couldn't compare to those of the late Dukes of Marlborough or Roxburghe, a catalogue he'd had privately printed had brought her close to swooning: the *Psalmorum Enchiridion,* in the beautiful binding by Clovis Eve for Marguerite De Valois, the works from Maioli's Library . . .

In any event, within days of her parents' rejecting Lord Mends, Olympia had had her fatal encounter with the Duke of Ashmont.

And now . . .

A fatal encounter with the Duke of Ripley's naked bottom. And other parts . . . and the realization that the Duke of Ashmont would have naked parts, too, and so would Lord Mends, and contemplating marital intimacy with either of the latter made her want to jump from her chair — and possibly out of the window.

At this moment, the door opened and the Duke of Ripley sauntered in.

She blocked all the other images from her mind and focused on where she was and who she was and him, because there he was and she could hardly see anything else.

"You're not done yet?" he said.

"No," she said. "And you're not to tell me to make haste. I and this army of women have been making all the haste that's humanly possible. It's hideously unfair of men, who haven't nearly as complicated a dressing process, to complain of the time required. Do you not recall all the time it took you to get that thing off my head?" She nodded at the corpse of the bridal crown and veil. "Do you think restoring a measure of sanity to my coiffure can be done in an instant?"

"I see we've reached the crosspatch stage."

That was putting it mildly.

"Is it at all possible, duke, or do I ask too much, for Your Grace to attempt to be a little — only a fraction of a fraction — less provoking?"

"Far too much," he said. "What do you think?" He made a sweeping gesture over his attire, which sharpened the image she couldn't banish from her mind, of what he looked like without any clothes on.

Studying him wasn't good for her, she was sure. She'd done it all too zealously a little while ago, and she wasn't sure she'd ever recover.

Eating seemed to have restored her to sobriety, though she couldn't be certain, not having a basis for comparison. With a somewhat clearer head, she felt even more strongly aware of the sheer *physical*-ness of him.

The stallion came into her mind, the one she'd watched cover the mare that time.

Stop it, stop it.

Be sensible, she told herself. *Look at the facts.* The simple fact was, it was hard to distance oneself from the physicality of a man when one sat looking up at him.

She lowered her gaze and from under her lashes surveyed him from head to toe: from the big shoulders stretching the black coat's seams, down over the pleated shirt and striped waistcoat, and down, quickly, over the white trousers to the scuffed black shoes. He carried a hat in his right hand.

She stared at the hat and tried to occupy her overactive mind with remembering the names of men's hats and trying to identify this one.

"Naturally it doesn't fit," he said. "Out of the question, given time constraints, though the tailor did the best he could. It's by no means the wool I would have chosen, and the linen is of mediocre quality."

She tried to pretend he was a shop mannequin. A strangely dressed one. "It's unexceptionable," she said. "I agree that nothing fits properly, but at least the trousers cover your ankles. And as long as you don't have to heave women in and out of boats or rivers, the coat seams should hold."

"But the pièce de résistance," he said. He approached, and the other women retreated.

He stopped at the horse dressing glass and set the hat on his head. He frowned and tilted it this way, then that, then tried it straight.

"Vile," he said. "I look like a bank clerk. But it was the only one that came close to fitting. How the devil do fellows buy these things ready-made?"

"You do not look like a bank clerk," she said. "If you wore a bargeman's cap you would not look like a bargeman. You look like a nobleman . . ." She thought. "In disguise. Not a very good disguise, admittedly." She gave a dismissive wave. "You'll do. You can wear anything and you'll remain tall, dark, and handsome —"

"Hand—"

"Men are deemed attractive when they're middle-aged and paunchy," she went on. "Men may go grey and sag with impunity. We women are allowed to look well until about age twenty at most. After that, we're crones."

The women about her protested.

"The lady is out of sorts," Ripley told them. "You've done a fine job. Her ladyship doesn't look nearly as crone-like as usual. Now, if you would all quit dawdling with the hair, we really must be away. Her ladyship is on fire to be off."

She was. The question was, *Where to?*

"Yes," she said.

■ ■ ■ ■

Handsome.

No one had ever accused Ripley of that before.

She must still be drunk. Not being used to drinking, she didn't get over it as quickly as a more experienced person. Furthermore, she was a gentlewoman, a maiden.

But the way she'd surveyed Ripley from under her lashes was not what one expected from innocent maidens. Who knew that a virginal bluestocking could employ a half-hidden gaze like that, or cause a man to simmer under it. Apparently, he had something to learn about bluestocking virgins.

He hadn't long to simmer. She turned her head slightly, and the firelight glinted off her spectacles, and then he couldn't see her eyes at all.

Not that he needed to, he told himself.

She'd seen quite enough of him and he didn't need to see anything more of her. Best not to, in present circumstances. Thanks to his monk-like existence of recent months, he was all too quick to heat.

He'd cure the ailment this very evening. As soon as he returned bride to bridegroom.

Along with the usual improper thoughts

natural to a nonvirtuous male, this was what passed through his mind as he waited, foot tapping, for the women to place a hat on Lady Olympia's head and tie the ribbons just so. When the hat ritual ended at last, and the bridal garments had been wrapped up in linen, he hustled her out of the room and, eventually, out of the hotel and into the inn yard where a post chaise waited.

"A post chaise!" she said.

"Did you think I'd buy a ticket for a mail coach?" he said. "At this hour?"

"Will it take us to Twickenham?" she said.

Ripley folded his arms, tipped his head to one side, and gazed at her. In the murky afternoon light, his eyes had darkened to the green of a cedar forest.

Olympia straightened her spectacles and put up her chin. "I've decided you made a telling point."

His green eyes narrowed.

"About going back with my tail between my legs," she said. "I am not a coward."

"I didn't think so," he said. "Undecided, possibly."

"I admit I was not thinking clearly," she said. "All the same, one might make a case for heeding one's instincts. I should like to speak to Aunt Delia before I return — if I

145

return. I believe she's the one best equipped to counsel me. Everybody else sees nothing but the headline, OLYMPIA, MARRIED AT LAST, TO A DUKE. I will tell you frankly the headline hung in my mind, too, to the detriment of clear thinking." She looked away.

So much had clouded her thinking. Her brothers' future. Her own.

Ashmont, too. Nobody had ever courted her so ardently. In fact, nobody had ever courted her at all, unless one counted Lord Mends's talking endlessly about his books. When Ashmont directed that earnest blue gaze at one, as though he saw nobody else in the world, and intensified the effect by casually mentioning his grandfather's vast collection of books, which she knew could easily compare with those of the Dukes of Roxburghe and Marlborough — well, it was impossible to keep a cool head.

As was not the case with Lord Mends, Olympia had seen for herself the duke's library at his place in Nottinghamshire. Her father had taken her with him to look at some horses. Ashmont had been away at school at the time. It was his uncle and guardian, Lord Frederick Beckingham, who'd kindly offered little Olympia — she couldn't have been more than twelve — a tour of the house. Once she'd seen the library, she wasn't interested in the rest of the house, much to the gentlemen's amusement.

"Twickenham," Ripley said, bringing her back to the present.

"Yes," she said.

He was silent for an exceedingly long time. She clenched her hands — not that she had a prayer of winning any fight with him — but as a signal she was prepared to fight, though she knew she'd been more than a little wayward.

She'd better not drink brandy, ever again.

"Very well," he said. "Get in the carriage."

She let out the breath she'd been holding and started toward the vehicle.

The postilion had put down the step and opened the door when a yelp of pain, then another, echoed through the courtyard.

Turning toward the sound, Olympia saw, near the yard's entrance, a wiry, red-faced man raise his whip at a cowering dog, a fine, brindled wolfhound or something like.

A red mist appeared before her eyes.

She forgot about Ripley. She forgot about Twickenham. She was moving before she thought about moving, marching briskly toward the scene, speaking as she bore down on her prey, her finger pointing at

147

him, then down at the ground. "You. Drop it. Now."

The villain froze. The dog sank onto its belly.

For a moment Ripley froze, too, dumbfounded.

"Now," said her ladyship. She was moving toward the whip-wielding fellow, not running, but moving swiftly and inexorably, like — like Ripley didn't know what. Something inexorable, as implacable as Fate. Which was absurd. She, in a hat with flowers springing up from the top, and a black lace cape fluttering about her shoulders, and ribbons streaming as she sailed along. A pastry confection, perhaps. Nemesis, hardly.

Yet every man in the courtyard paused at the tone of her voice. All of them, Ripley included, responded to that sound. It was simply the Voice of Command, though he wasn't sure he'd ever heard a woman employ it so effectively. His sister, perhaps. Or Aunt Julia.

Though the object of her displeasure looked as obstinate and belligerent as every other undersized blackleg and bully Ripley had ever known, and seemed to be drunk as well, the fellow brought his arm down. Otherwise, he didn't move, only stood, warily watching her ladyship's approach.

"I'll take that," she said. She held out her slender gloved hand.

"Meantersay," the brute began.

Lady Olympia didn't move, didn't utter a syllable, only stood with her hand out, waiting.

He gave her the whip.

Ripley would have let out a whoop, but instinct told him this was a delicate balance. Matters could turn dangerous in an instant. As Ripley moved nearer, as unobtrusively as was possible for a six-foot-plus man in fighting trim, the man spoke, and a cloud of alcoholic fumes floated outward.

"Meantersay, that's *my* dog, plague take him," he said. "And he cost me a bloody fortune, the miserable cur. Obedient, they said. Trained for — for hunting. Right. All my eye and Betty Martin."

"You struck a dumb animal," she said. "With a whip. How would you like it?" She raised the whip as though to strike.

The fellow put up a defensive arm. "Hoy! I wasn't —" He swayed and started to stumble, but righted himself at the last minute.

"I am painfully tempted to give you a taste," she said. "To help you remember, the next time. But that would be ill-bred."

She looked at the dog. "Come," she said. The dog rose.

"The devil!" the fellow said. "You can't — that's *my* dog!"

She made a slight beckoning gesture and the dog went to her.

"Sam!" his owner shouted. "You come here, or I'll —"

"You won't," said Lady Olympia. "You don't deserve to own a dog."

"You're not taking my dog! I'll have the law on you!" He looked about him. "Somebody fetch a constable. That's my dog, and when the stubborn cur don't do what I say, I teach him. Nobody else's bloody business."

The dog beater was shouting about robbers and interferers and constables and who knew what else. People emerged from the ground floor coffee room. Spectators spilled out onto the gallery overlooking the inn yard.

"Ahem," Ripley said.

Headed for the post chaise, canine at her side, Lady Olympia paused and looked up at him, surprised. "Oh," she said. "There you are."

"We're not taking the dog," he said.

"We can't leave him with that unspeakable person," she said. "Striking a dumb animal! With a whip! And it wasn't a light warning tap, or striking the ground to get the animal's attention. He made the dog cry out — you heard him — and this is a *lurcher.* They're stupendously quiet dogs."

Ripley could see what it was. A poacher's dog. A silent hunter. It stood close to her, by her hand, the one holding the whip. The animal trembled.

"They're stealing my dog!" the dog beater shouted. "Somebody stop them!"

"Don't be a bloody fool, Bullard," somebody called out. "It's His Grace of Ripley. A duke, you half-wit. He can do what he likes."

"He don't take my dog! After he lets his doxy do the dirty work for him. I want my dog!"

Ripley sighed. Of course. Always had to be some drunken blusterer in the vicinity, saying the wrong thing. Always had to be some jackass uttering words one couldn't let pass.

He turned back to Bullard and said, in the mild, amiable tone all who knew him would recognize as the Voice Of Death — or at least Of Serious Pain — "What did you say?"

Ripley spoke lazily, offhandedly.

All the same, the hairs on the back of Olympia's neck stood up and she sensed, with the certainty of a young woman who'd grown up surrounded by males, the stirrings of the inborn masculine need to kill other males.

Despite belonging to the opposite gender, she felt similar stirrings. She longed to thrust Ripley out of the way and lash the brute Bullard until he bawled like a baby. For the lurcher's sake, she made herself calm. Gently she rested her hand on the dog's head. He edged closer.

"You heard me!" the dog's owner said. "You and your fancy piece there, what goes around bullying fellows what's too mannerly to fight with women, and steals a man's property. You can't walk out with my dog, like you own the world."

"That's twice you've insulted the lady," Ripley said in the same mild tone.

"Lady! Her! And stole my whip, too!"

"That's thrice," Ripley said. "This is what I get for patience and forbearance. No more chances. You will address the lady as *my lady* and you will apologize. Now."

"Apologize? To *her*? I bloody well won't! I want my dog!"

Ripley hit him. It was shockingly swift, straight to the gut. Bullard folded over and crumpled to his knees.

"Apologize," Ripley said. "And make it quick. While these new gloves are far from ideal, I'd rather not get blood on them." He paused, waiting for Bullard to catch his breath.

"Took me off guard, you ugly buffer nabber," the drunkard gasped. He looked about him. "Everybody seen you do it."

Thanks to Mr. Grose's *Lexicon Balatronicum,* Olympia knew a buffer nabber was a dog stealer.

"It seems my warning went over your head," Ripley said. "Then I shall speak more plainly. If the next words out of your mouth are not 'I beg your pardon, my lady,' you'll oblige me to injure you severely."

"Try it!" Bullard put up his fists. "Try it, you filthy —" The rest comprised extremely bad words.

Ripley knocked his hands away, hard enough to unbalance him, but before the man could topple, the duke grabbed him, curling his big hands about the bully's throat and lifting him up off the ground. Clawing at the gloved hands, legs dangling, the man managed to choke out a stream of words Olympia had never actually heard uttered, though she recognized them from Mr. Grose's fascinating work.

The duke's calm, cool voice carried easily across the dead silence of the inn yard, "You will address the lady as *my lady,* and you will apologize, or I shall have to make your life unpleasant."

"Go ahead and kill me," the fool choked out. "You'll hang, and I'll see you in hell."

"Wouldn't dream of killing you," Ripley said. "Too quick. No fun in that. No, what I thought I'd do is start with breaking a few bones, then a few more, until there are too many for the surgeon to mend."

Bullard's face was turning purple, but he managed to gargle references to Ripley's penchant for unnatural acts with farm animals.

"What a tedious fellow you are," Ripley said. "Maybe I'll drop you and see what happens. I hope I don't accidently step on your head."

"Go ahead," the man croaked.

Ripley let go of him.

Bullard fell onto the cobblestones.

Olympia expected him to bounce up again. Some men didn't know when they were done for.

Apparently, hitting solid stone made an impression. Bullard clutched his throat but made no other movement. He lay where he'd been dropped, eyes open, staring up at the duke.

"Are you quite done?" Ripley said.

Bullard nodded.

"Then say you're sorry."

"Sorry," Bullard gasped.

"Not to me, you ridiculous person. To the lady."

"Sorry. My. Lady."

"Good. Now go away."

Bullard lurched to his feet. He called to the dog. Tail down, head down, the creature edged nearer to Olympia.

"No," Olympia said. "You've forfeited the dog."

"Sam's my property," Bullard cried hoarsely. "He goes with me!"

Olympia looked at Ripley.

"We are not taking the dog," he said.

"We can't leave him," she said. "He's hurt and terrified."

"That's my dog! I paid a bloody fortune for the mutinous cur! You've got no right!"

"You have no right to him," she said. "You threw it away when you struck a defenseless creature. You've lost him."

"Get in the carriage," Ripley said.

"I will not leave this animal to him," she said. "As soon as we're gone, he'll punish the dog for what you did to him."

"We are not taking the dog," Ripley said.

"Sam, come," Bullard snapped.

The dog looked at him and shivered.

"He's not going with that man," Olympia said.

"That's my bloody dog!"

"We are not taking the dog," Ripley told Olympia. "In case you failed to notice, this animal is not a Pekingese. He cannot sit in your lap. The post chaise holds two people, barely."

"He can ride in the boot," she said. "In the crate."

"Your wedding ensemble is in the crate," he said.

"The dog can use it for a cushion. It isn't as though I'll wear it again."

"That's my bloody dog! You're not taking my dog!"

"Stow it," Ripley told Bullard. "The lady and I are negotiating."

"You can't take my dog! He cost me —"

"You are an extremely tiresome man," Ripley said. He looked about the inn yard. "Somebody make him go away." He made a shooing motion in Bullard's direction.

"That's my bloody —"

Whatever else Bullard was going to say was cut off as two of the sturdier onlookers took hold of the brute and dragged him to a far corner of the yard.

Ripley turned back to Olympia. "If we take the dog, it's your dog," he said. "When I leave you at your aunt's, I leave him. Is that clear? Once we take him, there is no mind-changing, because I am not going to abandon him on the road or find him another home or adopt him. Do you understand?"

"Yes," she said, heart pounding. "Thank you for explaining it in simple terms, in case my girl brain was too small to grasp the implications."

"Good," he said.

He moved away to talk to Bullard, who was struggling with the men trying to hold him. A long debate followed, with Bullard's voice rising in outrage then gradually subsiding to a grumble.

Not long thereafter, a servant emerged from the inn with blankets. He carried them to the boot and arranged them over the parcel containing her neatly wrapped wedding ensemble.

"Will that do, or shall we hire a separate carriage for your new pet?" Ripley said. "And a footman or two to look after him, perchance?"

"That will do," Olympia said.

Ripley clicked his tongue and the lurcher looked at him, ears pricked. Ripley pointed to the crate. The dog jumped into it. He pushed the blankets with his paws and turned around a few times until all was arranged to his satisfaction. Then he settled down.

The dog had been well trained. Clearly the problem wasn't the animal's.

She glanced at Bullard, who stood, mouth open, looking from the dog to her to Ripley and back again.

"Get in the carriage," Ripley said. *"Now."*

Ripley watched her climb into the post chaise and settle into the seat in a flurry of lace and ribbons and bobbing flowers.

He gave one last glance about the courtyard to make sure Bullard wasn't about to rush out at them and make a pest of himself. More of a pest of himself.

Then Ripley went to the boot and examined the dog. He detected two welts, but saw no blood. The swine hadn't had time to get to serious whipping.

Ripley stroked the dog and made a few meaningless but comforting sounds, and the dog's trembling abated.

"You're one lucky fellow, I hope you realize," Ripley said. "Your timing was excellent."

The dog licked his gloved hand. "No

drooling." Ripley drew his hand away. "Even on these unspeakable gloves. And you are on no account to be sick on the way."

There.

He was better now.

Ashmont's duchess-to-be was alive and in one piece. Nobody had died. No blood had been shed, although Bullard would have many painful bruises as mementoes of the occasion.

In spite of agreeable thoughts like these, Ripley knew he would need some time to settle down after exerting so much self-control, to keep from beating Bullard to a bloody pulp.

Ripley took one last calming breath, left the dog, climbed into the carriage, and told the postilion to set out.

The vehicle had hardly begun to move and Ripley had hardly settled into the seat when Lady Olympia bounced up and threw her arms about him and said, "Oh, well done, indeed!"

Then she kissed him.

CHAPTER 6

She kissed him on the cheek because she was overwrought — or so Ripley's brain, had it been working, would have told him.

Had this organ of intellect been in operation, it would have told him to push her off and say something like, "Don't be ridiculous."

His brain wasn't working. He pulled her into his arms and kissed her on the lips, and not gently. He kissed her with all the anxiety, frustration, rage, and other annoying emotions he'd thought he'd finished with a moment ago. And with the simple lust he'd been fighting for what seemed like a very long time.

He felt her tense, and he was about to withdraw, but then her soft mouth was responding to his, and the taste of her was . . . different. Fresh and sweet and something else. He didn't know what it was and didn't care.

She had no idea how to kiss. He didn't care about that, either. Her mouth was soft and full and tasted good. In any case, he knew how to kiss, and he didn't doubt she was intelligent enough to catch on.

She melted into his arms and fit exactly as she ought to do, and for a moment he simply lost himself in the rush of excitement and relief and pleasure and other, more alien, feelings.

Then a dog barked, and the sound woke him from the mindless state he'd fallen into. He drew away — cautiously, because, his brain having belatedly begun normal operations, he knew he'd done something amazingly stupid. It made no sense to push her away when he was the one who'd turned an innocent peck on the cheek into something she'd never intended it to be.

"Damnation," he said. "Did nobody ever tell you not to get too close to men who've been fighting only a minute before?"

"You kissed me!" she said, eyes very wide and possibly blue at the moment, though it was hard to be sure in the coach's dim confines on a dim day.

"You kissed first," he said.

"On the cheek!"

"On the cheek, on the lips. All the same to me. Female, kiss. Male, excited. Do I have to explain simple facts of life to you?"

"Some, yes, it seems," she said. "I have six brothers, and I know about fighting. But I was — I don't know what happened. You saved the dog! And . . . and he — Bullard, I mean — he thought I was a demirep!"

"I believe he won't make that mistake again," Ripley said. He couldn't completely crush a prickling sense of frustration. It wasn't much of a kiss, when you came down to it. And it seemed to him there ought to have been a good bit more since now there would be a lot of talking to get through and — gad, how could he be so stupidly stupid? Ashmont's bride, of all women.

"No one's *ever* made that mistake," she said. "Who ever heard of a woman of ill repute in spectacles?"

"Why not?" he said. "They add an air of mystery."

She stared at him.

He let her stare. He was trying desperately to find a way out of whatever it was he'd got himself into.

"It's the dress," she said at last. "I told you. This ensemble was never meant for a spinster."

"You're not a spinster," he said. "You're a bride-to-be."

"Don't try to change the subject," she

said. "Whose clothes were these meant to be?"

"How in blazes should I know?"

"A courtesan's." She smoothed the skirt lovingly. "Or a dashing widow's. Mrs. Thorpe was certainly accommodating. From the way she spoke, I deduced she owed you a favor. Or a hundred."

"The favor wasn't my doing," he said. "It was my sister's."

Had Her Grace of Blackwood attended the wedding, as she ought to have done, Ripley could have enlisted her to help him retrieve Lady Olympia, and the runaway bride would not have got as far as the garden gate.

But no, Alice had to be thirty miles away from London with Aunt Julia, for some as-yet-unexplained reason.

Blackwood hadn't offered much information, but then, he and Ripley hadn't had much conversation, had they? Nearly all the talk had been Ashmont talking about getting married.

To the woman Ripley had kissed a moment ago in an excessively enthusiastic manner.

"You've met her, no doubt," he said. "She can be the damnedest — never mind. If you've met her, you know what she's like."

"Splendid raven tresses and green eyes," Lady Olympia said. "I was shocked when I heard she was to marry Blackwood. I'd thought she had more intelligence than that."

He'd thought so, too.

"You accepted Ashmont," he said.

"Your sister did not have five younger brothers to consider, or improvident parents, or a shrinking marriage portion, or being voted Most Boring Girl of the Season seven Seasons in a row," she said. "I was growing panicky. And so were my parents."

"You have a few good years left," he said. "I'm still puzzled about the boring part."

"You don't know me as I truly am," she said darkly. "I can prose on about first editions and Maioli's Library and early copperplate engravings until my listeners keel over in a dead faint. Worse, I have a System, inspired by the American president, Mr. Thomas Jefferson, who applied Bacon's table of science to the organization of books. My own method is rather more complex, and I can hold forth on the topic for about twenty times longer than listeners can bear to hear it."

He had been looking straight ahead at a not especially thrilling view — mainly of the postilion's back and the horses' posteriors.

Now he turned to look at her. She was gazing through the front window as well, a grim set to her mouth.

The mouth onto which he'd put his a very short time ago.

But it wasn't the first and wouldn't be the last mistake he'd ever made, he told himself. He and his friends had not won the title Their Dis-Graces for acts of virtue.

"Maybe you're the one who's bored," he said. "Maybe your brain's too large and lively for the company you keep. Good little girls. A lot of rules about every damned thing. Maybe you go on and on about the books because nobody understands you anyway, and at least it's fun to watch their eyes glaze over."

It wouldn't have occurred to him, in all these years, that she would have been bored. He'd assumed she was like other respectable girls, and she'd fit in. Now, having known her all of — what? Two hours? Three? — he was amazed she hadn't fallen into some kind of trouble long before now.

She blinked hard, and he saw a tear steal down her cheek. She brushed it away. "I don't doubt you speak from your own experience," she said. "It isn't hard to see boredom as a problem for you and bad behavior a perfect solution. But it's differ-

165

ent for women. We're supposed to be pleasing."

"Dress more daringly, and you'll please," he said. "Men are simple creatures, as I ought not to have to explain to a woman in possession of a surfeit of brothers. What you're wearing now, for instance. Shows off your figure. The black lace adds an air of mystery and danger —"

"I! Dangerous!"

"Didn't you see how relieved Bullard looked when he saw he had only me to fight, not you? Dress like a dangerous woman, and men won't notice what you say. They'll be too busy thinking improper thoughts."

"I can't believe I'm listening to the Duke of Ripley offer brotherly advice," she said.

"I do have experience in that line," he said. "I am a brother."

"Over whom his sister has influence, it appears," she said. "And this, in an as-yet-unexplained manner, has led to undying gratitude on the part of a Putney dressmaker."

"She wasn't always in Putney," he said, grateful for the return to the original subject. He wanted to hear more about Lady Olympia's System and he did not want her to cry because a lot of small-minded fools found her boring.

These thoughts were bothersome, and he preferred them out of his head.

The dressmaker was another matter entirely.

"Mrs. Thorne, under another name, was a successful London dressmaker before she married Mr. Kefton," he said. "She worked and he spent everything she made and then some. The bailiffs came and took away everything, lock, stock, and barrel. Kefton, courageous fellow, ran away. My sister, a loyal customer, told me the sad story and insisted I Do Something. To stop the nagging, I set up the dressmaker in Putney under the name Thorpe. The false name was necessary to foil the faithless spouse's creditors as well as the spouse, in case he came sneaking back."

"And now she does a booming trade in courtesans and merry widows?" Lady Olympia said.

"Let's say she's found a niche," he said.

"In other words, that's where you bring your mistresses," she said. "All three of you, I don't doubt. I can see the satirical prints now. My bosom will be falling out of my bodice, and bits of pink and black underthings will show, and my drawers —"

"Tell you what let's do," he said. "Let's stop talking about your underwear." An image had developed in his mind of her breasts escaping the dress's bodice. It was a perfectly normal thought for a man but thinking it was unwise at present. He put it as far back in his mind as he could — no easy feat when she sat next to him and there was her bodice, practically under his nose.

He made himself stare at the postilion's back, up and down, up and down, as the horses made what seemed to him excruciatingly slow progress out of Putney.

"Everybody will be talking about it," she said. "And imagining the worst."

"We'll be traveling for half an hour or more," he said. "After dragging unbalanced brides out of the Thames, insufficiently strangling bullies, and rescuing dogs, I should like a nap. Please exert your faculties to be less exciting. Much less exciting. More quietening."

She looked up at him. "You cannot be suggesting I explain my System for Library Organization."

"Exactly. Tell me all about it. In detail."

Their Dis-Graces were in the habit of mowing down whatever got in their way. Accustomed to this modus operandi, the world usually got out of the way as quickly as it could.

But one couldn't simply mow down one's future in-laws and wedding guests. The guests were easily subdued with buckets of champagne and a story about the bride having been taken ill. The future in-laws were another matter. Even with Lord Frederick's help, the company was not quickly appeased, especially Lord Ludford, who put the blame squarely on Ashmont.

Olympia was a good, sensible girl, Ludford said. She wouldn't run away unless she was tricked or driven to it. He wouldn't have people slandering her because His Dis-Grace didn't know how to treat a gently bred girl, who did him a *very great favor* in accepting him.

Luckily, Ashmont, for once, didn't start a fight. He was too impatient to be off to take much notice of anything anybody said.

Eventually the company was deceived and appeased to Lord Frederick's satisfaction. Then, Blackwood having had the forethought to order the horses brought round well before everybody had settled down, the two dukes set out.

They soon reached Kensington's High Street, though it wasn't soon enough for Ashmont, who spent the short journey cursing his uncle and everybody else for making mountains out of molehills and slowing him down.

Then, since one couldn't mow down possible sources of information, the dukes had first to fend off the hordes of boys who appeared out of nowhere and rushed toward them, offering to hold their horses.

"Looking for a bride," Ashmont said. "Anybody seen her? With a tallish fellow, dressed for a wedding?"

The boys looked at one another, then at him, faces blank.

Ashmont held up a coin. "Come now," he said. "A bride. In a veil and everything. Hard to miss. A shilling to the first lad who has something useful to tell me."

No response.

"They're as hard here as in London," he muttered to Blackwood as he took out another shilling. "There's two bob," Ashmont said more audibly. "For the clever lad who gives me information."

He saw one boy whisper to a smaller one, who was dressed in a curious costume. Under the grime, the smaller boy appeared to be fair, with an innocent-looking countenance. He shook his head at the larger one, who moved away.

Ashmont narrowed his eyes. "You, there," he said. "I can tell a ringleader from a furlong away."

All wide-eyed perplexity, the little one looked at the boys about him.

"Never mind them," Ashmont said. "I'm talking to you, old fellow. The jockey." For, upon further examination, he realized the boy was dressed in the tattered remains of what looked to be a racing costume. And the thing on his head was a yellow cap, two sizes too big.

"I fink His Nibs means you, Jonesy," one of the boys said.

"If I was a jockey, you fink I'd be wearing vis?" the boy said.

Blackwood, who was more adept in Cockney, translated. And since he was the linguist, he continued with the boy. "Come along and let's talk," he said.

"I don't know nuffink," said Jonesy.

And all the other boys said, "We don't know nuffink."

Blackwood turned his horse and rode a little away, but not before displaying a crown so that only Jonesy could see it. No more than a glimpse before Blackwood made it vanish.

The boy approached him and stood, arms folded. "Vat was pretty good."

"Owning the coin will be even better, I'll wager," said Blackwood. "But only if you tell me what you saw and heard when the toff and the bride were here."

"Maybe he was here and maybe he wasn't," the boy said. "But if he was, I fink I remember he give us a glistener."

A sovereign? Not impossible. While none of them were pinchpennies, Ripley was the most likely to give a lot of vagrant children an entire pound to keep mum.

"Then why aren't you out celebrating your riches?" Ripley said.

"On account of not wanting to get flicked." The boy made a gesture indicative of throat cutting. "I got it where it's safe."

If the boy had a coin of such value on him, he wouldn't be safe, even in Kensington. Not that he looked as though he belonged hereabouts. He had rather more of the city urchin and less of the rustic about him — which probably accounted for the other boys taking their lead from one so small. His age was anybody's guess.

Blackwood considered the shabby jockey costume. "It wouldn't be breaking your sacred oath if you *showed* me where they went. I don't have a sovereign on me at the moment, but I will take you up on my horse and trust you to show me the way, and give you the crown, as well."

He'd made the right offer. The boy's eyes

widened — startlingly blue — and filled with longing. Then he glanced back at his cohort and shook his head.

Blackwood reached down and yanked him up onto the saddle in front of him. Though the boy protested loudly, screaming about being kidnapped and murdered and such, he didn't put up much of a fight.

Blackwood carried him away and Ashmont followed, and a lot of boys as well, shouting as they ran after them. But the horses picked up speed, and after a time the boys gave up. When he decided it was safe, Blackwood slowed and said, "Well played, Jonesy. Now show us the way."

Something tickled Ripley's nose.

He opened his eyes.

Flowers bobbed against his face in time to the chaise's jolting.

They were attached to a hat. A lady's hat.

He came abruptly awake to discover Ashmont's future duchess in his arms. In spite of the jouncing chaise, she, too, had fallen asleep: deeply, judging by the steady rise and fall of her bosom.

Hardly surprising, he told himself, given the brandy, the day's events, and the likelihood she hadn't slept much the previous night, although for reasons altogether different from his.

Hardly surprising, either, for his arm to work itself around her shoulders. He'd been asleep, or dozing at the very least. A warm female body had settled close to his. Bringing it closer was instinctive.

Other instincts came into play now, and he was getting ideas in his head and elsewhere that would be all well and good in other circumstances. At present they were deuced inconvenient.

Still, he hated to wake her.

He remained as he was and looked out of the window. To keep his thoughts from wandering where they could only annoy him, he dragged into the front of his mind her curious System.

Instead of arranging books in the usual way — alphabetically or by size — she organized by subject, under broad headings like History, Philosophy, and Fine Arts. Within these broad categories were more specific ones. The last thing he remembered was her describing the difficulty of deciding whether one ought to break up into categories sets of books from a single collection, like that of Diane de Poitiers, for instance.

As he considered the pros and cons, bits and parts of a dream intruded: a woman falling off library steps into his arms . . . he, running madly through London streets, chasing a bridal dress that flew above his head like a kite . . . books tumbling out of windows as he ran.

His mind veering from books to dreams, he registered little of the view from the window until the chaise slowed and stopped. He blinked and took in the scene.

Richmond Bridge stretched ahead. They'd reached the tollgate.

His travel companion stirred, and tipped her head back to look at him. Her eyes widened and she jerked away.

"Too late to be shy now," he said. "We've slept together."

Olympia was sure she'd drooled on his neckcloth and developed sleep creases in her now-red face from pressing it into his lapel.

She had fallen asleep on one of Their Dis-Graces, and not the one she was supposed to marry. Furthermore, she had been far too comfortable tucked against his hard chest, with his muscled arm about her.

It was a very good thing no man had tried to lead her astray all these years, because it seemed as though she was all too likely to go.

She said, "I should not boast of it, if I were

you. You're hardly my first. Clarence would scream and scream during thunderstorms until he was allowed to crawl into bed with me."

"Now I'll know what to do the next time a thunderstorm strikes," he said. "Your hat's crooked."

She turned to the window, but the scratched glass offered more of Richmond and less of her own reflection at present.

"I can't see," she said. She turned back to him. "Please straighten it. My aunt will be curious how I came to be dressed this way as it is. I'd prefer not to appear disheveled."

"You'll arrive with a dirty wedding dress and veil wrapped up in linen and a new large dog. I doubt she'll fuss over a trifle like a crooked hat."

"Aunt Delia is extremely fashionable," she said. "She'll fuss a great deal more about the crooked hat than anything else."

He tugged the hat to one side. He stared at her face for a time, frowning, while she resisted the urge to look away, or shake him. Then he tried the other way. After repeating the procedure five times, he lifted his hands in a gesture of surrender.

"I don't think it matters," he said. "In any case, you can't possibly look a fraction as disheveled and mad as you did in your wedding dress."

The chaise passed through the tollgate. From this point on she'd have to pay attention. The postilion would need specific instructions to her aunt's villa.

She relayed the directions through Ripley. They were simple enough, and the distance wasn't great.

It was only after the chaise crossed the bridge that she remembered she hadn't yet composed her explanation. She swore under her breath.

"Now what?" he said.

"That wasn't meant to be heard," she said.

"I have exceptionally keen hearing on occasion," he said. "That is to say, when I'm paying attention. With you, a man must pay attention at all times. Had Ashmont paid sharper attention, for example, you wouldn't have run away. Had I paid sharper attention, you wouldn't have fallen out of the boat. But I've learned my lesson. I'll keep you under close scrutiny until I've deposited you safely with your aunt."

Ripley's *close scrutiny* was a dangerous article. He'd said things and looked at her in ways other men didn't, and the combination had started to make her think she wasn't altogether the young woman she'd always believed she was. She knew rakes were dangerous but she hadn't understood how subtle the danger could be. Her ideas about a great many subjects were threatening revolution. It was a good thing Aunt Delia was only a short distance away.

Yes, right. Focus on Aunt Delia. Not him.

"I don't know what to tell her," she said. "Nothing I compose sounds rational." At present, her idea about being bought for breeding, which had appeared so compelling when she was drunk, now struck her as ludicrous. And in her drunken idiocy, she had prattled about the subject to Ripley, of all people!

"If I were you, I wouldn't explain," he said.

"No, you mean if I were you," she said. "Men, especially of high rank, do as they please, and the rest of the world can like it or lump it."

"You're a woman of high rank," he said. "You can do as you please."

"Not unless I'm willing to sacrifice my reputation. Which I admit, I've already done."

"That can be mended," he said. "Do you know, I think it's a good thing we've had a little time together because you are in dire want of schooling."

"Indeed, what I desperately need is

schooling in — in whatever it is you're so expert in. How to be disreputable. Do you know, I believe even I can deduce how to do that."

"I believe you've already embarked on that path," he said. "Let us cast our minds over the last few hours, Lady Olympia, and —"

"I told you it was easy," she said. "Even I can do it." A little more time with him, and she'd be an expert.

"I wouldn't dream of arguing," he said. "Disreputability wants little effort and that little mainly pleasurable, which is one of its charms. But as to you — and if you would be so good as to let me say my little bit without interruption —"

"I wouldn't dream of interrupting."

"Thank you. If I may be more specific: The schooling you need is how to manage the world about you."

"Let me explain something to you," she said. "One's income can be managed, although this seems to be a feat beyond my parents' abilities. A library can be managed. The world cannot. Only a duke — and one of Their Dis-Graces — would suppose otherwise."

He dismissed this with a wave. "Picture the scene. You appear at the door, trailed by me and the dog, who, by the way, is clearly

179

not a Sam. Do give a moment to relieving the animal of that ridiculous name. Offer him something with dignity. Like . . . Cato. Cato will do."

"Thank you for letting me choose the dog's name."

"You were too slow," he said. "Now listen to me."

"Have I a choice?"

"I have experience with situations that seem to require explanations," he said. "Besides which, I have a sister." His gaze shifted to the front window. "And we don't have much time."

He ordered the postilion to stop the chaise. "Wait," he said, and climbed out.

She saw an alternative to waiting: running away. But that hadn't worked so well before, though it had felt so very good, and absolutely right, at the time.

Running away looked good to her now, when she was quite sober — a clear sign she'd spent far too much time with this man.

She waited and watched through the chaise's front window.

He went to the boot. Cato looked up eagerly at him. Ripley made a beckoning gesture and the dog sprang out. Ripley removed the large linen parcel, sent the dog back to his blanketed nest, climbed back into the carriage with the wedding corpse, and told the postilion to go on. The chaise rumbled into motion.

Ripley took off his gloves and began untying the parcel.

"I'm not wearing that," she said.

"I beg you will give me some credit," he said. "A very little will do. We need it for the scene."

"I like my aunt," she said. "I won't let you make her the butt of one of your practical jokes."

"It isn't a prank," he said. "It's a scene. A sort of dumb show-what-you-call-it."

"I have no idea what you call it."

"Like charades," he said. "But the other thing."

"A tableau?"

"That one. Wait."

She watched him undo the parcel, his long fingers so adept and graceful. She remembered those fingers in her hair.

She turned her gaze away, and her obnoxious mind promptly conjured a scene. More than a year ago it had happened. Maybe two years or more: Lady Nunsthorpe's ball. Known ironically as the Nun, according to Stephen, her ladyship clearly liked to live dangerously, for she'd invited all three of

Their Dis-Graces. During their dance, his hostess had been doing her best to seduce Ripley — not that Olympia supposed this demanded much effort. But she hadn't been able to look away. He'd moved with the power and grace of a thoroughbred, and she'd wondered what it felt like to dance with him.

The man standing in the basin had looked like a thoroughbred — splendidly proportioned, powerfully built. They could also be temperamental and dangerous, as her father had discovered at great expense.

Not that Papa ever learned from experience. She hoped she didn't take after him in that regard. But she'd never been tested before. Never been tempted . . .

Ripley's voice called her mind back from the treacherous place it was heading for.

"As I said before, you'll appear on your aunt's doorstep with your entourage," he said. "This will comprise one canine and one disreputable duke, who will be carrying the wedding dress and veil."

"Like a dead body," she said. The corpse of her family's hopes and dreams. The corpse of her brothers' futures. She was growing hysterical. *Stop it,* she told herself.

"Exactly. As soon as you see your aunt, you will fall into her arms, weeping."

It was simpler and cleverer than she'd expected. She could picture it easily. Presented with such a tableau, Aunt Delia wouldn't expect a coherent explanation. She'd see at once what a muddle Olympia had got herself into.

But.

"I can't weep on command," she said.

"Think of something heartbreaking, like saying goodbye to me forever."

If she had a sane segment of brain remaining, she'd jump up and down with delight and relief. Instead, she felt unhappy and panicky.

She looked at him. "It doesn't seem to be working," she said.

His black brows met over his nose. "How curious. That usually produces buckets of tears — until I produce the rubies or diamonds or whatever."

"I told you this dress was a problem," she said. "Because of it, you've confused me with one of your paramours. Weeping for jewelry is not, to my knowledge, the procedural method of a librarian."

"Well, then, imagine a library *on fire.* Imagine your favorite library in flames, books curling up into black ash. Imagine it's the library at Alexandria. Or . . . I know, the one belonging to what's-her-name

Potters —"

"Diane de Poitiers."

"And not in flames but sailing across the ocean to the American President Jefferson, who's bought every single volume."

"He's dead," she said.

"Doesn't signify. Picture the ship caught in a storm, and all those volumes sinking to the bottom of the Atlantic Ocean."

"Now I understand where the pranks come from," she said. "Yours is a lively imagination."

"It must be all the Shakespeare plays," he said. "Yet here I am, killing books by the thousands, and you remain strangely unmoved."

"My mind is analytical," she said. "To a fault."

"And to a point," he said. "Then something gives way and you run amok. Fascinating."

Had something given way? She had run amok. That much was indisputable. As to the rest . . .

"No one has ever called me that before," she said.

"Amok?"

"Fascinating. But you didn't mean *I* was fascinating. It was my errant behavior. When I reverted to my usual boring self, talking of my System, you fell asleep."

"I was not the only one, I noticed."

"I was tired," she said.

"As was I," he said. "Ashmont kept me up well past my bedtime."

"I don't see why you can't admit you were bored, as everybody always is."

"On the contrary, I was so excited, your books haunted my dreams," he said. "But we're running out of time. We need to solve the main problem. You need to sob on your aunt's bosom. How about this: Imagine every valuable library in England sold to pay debts, and they're all bought by *Americans.*" He opened his green eyes wide and made the kind of facial contortion actors did when feigning the throes of horror.

She swallowed laughter. Laughing would only encourage him and he'd already made himself more likable than was good for her.

"As long as the Americans take care of them," she said. "They might do better, actually."

"You had better think of a tragic scene in a book, then," he said. "You do actually read the things, yes? Not merely sort and catalog and put large books next to small ones in an unsightly manner? Or fondle them as precious objects?"

"I will admit to a degree of fondling. But

mainly those printed before 1550. In general, I read."

"Then think of a sad scene. If that doesn't work, we'll have to pin our hopes on your weeping with relief to be done with me when you throw yourself upon your aunt's mercy."

She suspected she wouldn't feel relieved when he was gone. Two or three hours or however long she'd spent with him, in one vehicle or another, was the most time she'd ever spent in close proximity to any man who wasn't a member of her immediate family. She was used to males, but not used to a Male, in the extreme sense he represented. He'd given her dangerous glimpses of a world forbidden to her.

There was no getting away from him and the atmosphere he created. He dominated the carriage's interior. She was keenly aware of every place her body touched his. In a post chaise, not touching was impossible. But he touched her mind, as well, that private place, and threw everything in it out of the neat order she'd so painstakingly created.

The things she'd done this day, so not like her.

But then this whole day had not been like her.

He'd fought a man for insulting her. Which had never happened in all her life, because men didn't notice her enough to insult her. And she'd been so excited, so happy, she'd kissed him.

She hadn't expected to get kissed back. She hadn't expected anything. She hadn't been thinking sensibly. Or at all.

But he'd kissed her back. Only more so, a great deal more so. *On the mouth.*

With only his lips he'd done things she didn't know could be done, such as making her feel the kiss in twenty different parts of her body but most especially in the pit of her belly.

Ashmont had kissed her when she'd said yes, and she'd believed it quite a nice kiss. Now she realized it had been *friendly.* She wouldn't have recognized this had she not experienced an alternative. What Ripley had done with his mouth wasn't friendly. It was something altogether different and stronger. Much stronger and definitely indecent.

She wished it had never happened because now she knew something she hadn't known before. And she wished it had gone on rather longer, because she'd hardly got a sense of what it was like and what she ought to do before it stopped.

Clearly, just being near him had corrupted

her mind. Either that or prolonged spinster-
hood had damaged it. Whatever the reason,
the Olympia of recent hours was a person
she hardly recognized.

She looked straight ahead. They were
nearing the gatekeeper's lodge.

The cowardly part of her wanted to leap
from the carriage and run to the house. If
she could get away from him and the heated
atmosphere he created, she could clear her
head.

But that was craven as well as silly. She
couldn't keep running away from difficulties.

Not to mention, she'd spoil the tableau.

His tableau. She, boring Lady Olympia
Hightower was letting the Duke of Ripley
fabricate one of his addlepated scenes, with
her in the starring role.

But after all the time she'd had to prepare
for meeting her aunt, after all her thinking
about it, Olympia hadn't produced a reasonable alternative or even an unreasonable
one.

"Ah, here's the gate," Ripley said. "And
here's the gatekeeper, come to inspect us. I
trust he knows you?"

"Yes, yes, of course," she said.

She watched Fawcett approach the vehicle.

Ripley put down the window. "Lady Olympia, come to visit Lady Pankridge," he said.

"Lady Pankridge?" the gatekeeper said.

"Is this not her residence?" Ripley said.

"Of course it is," Olympia said.

She leaned over him toward the gatekeeper. "You know me, Fawcett. I've come to see my aunt."

"Yes, my lady. Certainly I know your ladyship. But we wasn't looking to see your ladyship today." He glanced at Ripley, and his perplexed expression deepened.

It didn't take magical powers to understand what the gatekeeper was thinking. He knew this was Olympia's wedding day. All the world knew. And here she was with a gentleman whom Fawcett would surely know wasn't Ashmont. Villagers in Madagascar probably knew what Their Disgraces looked like — and would run if they saw them coming.

"I realize the visit is unexpected," Olympia said.

"Her ladyship would be happy to see your ladyship at any time," he said. "What I mean is, her ladyship isn't at home."

"But she was ill," Olympia said.

"Don't think so, my lady," said Fawcett. "But what I do know is, she isn't in."

Don't panic, Olympia told herself. "It's no great matter," she said. "I've come all this way. I'll wait for her to return."

"I beg your pardon, my lady," the gatekeeper said. "I ought to have said her ladyship won't be back today. Nor tomorrow nor the next day. I thought her ladyship had wrote to let you know why she wasn't coming to the wedding." He paused briefly and looked from her to Ripley, then quickly back to her, his face reddening. "All arranged weeks ago, and me told to expect them. Lord Clendower and his sister Lady Elspeth, that is. They came yesterday and took Lady Pankridge to Scotland with them. For the summer."

CHAPTER 7

The Dukes of Ashmont and Blackwood and the boy Jonesy sat on their horses, staring at Battersea Bridge.

True to his street-gang principles, Jonesy hadn't said a word, only gestured in the direction they were to go.

When they reached Battersea Bridge, he'd pointed at it, then held out his hand for the promised coin.

Though he now had it clutched in his grubby hand, he offered no sign of leaving his place on Blackwood's horse. Where he'd made himself quite comfortable, by the way, and Blackwood considerably less so, for the boy stood in dire need of a bath. Or, possibly, a scraping and sanding, for the grime seemed well-aged, and the accompanying aroma more than ripe.

At their arrival, the usual crowd of urchins swept toward them, offering to hold the horses. They engaged in a lively exchange of

191

insults with Jonesy before Ashmont started calling for information. The boys instantly didn't know nuffink and disappeared into their lairs.

Others in the vicinity were more helpful. A number of people had noticed, an hour or two earlier, the arrival of a large man, who looked like the Duke of Ripley and who accompanied a disheveled woman wearing a white dress and spectacles and carrying what looked like a lot of lace and flowers.

The pair had been observed getting into one of the wherries, but no one knew more of its destination than "upriver." Other watermen reported that the two who'd taken the bride and her companion had not yet returned.

"What the devil is Ripley about?" Ashmont said. "Upriver? Where's he taking her?"

"He can't be meaning to go far," Blackwood said. "Putney? The White Lion?"

"By boat? Why a boat to travel that short distance? The hackney would've taken them to Putney, and more discreetly."

"It doesn't seem they were trying to elude pursuit," Blackwood said. "They were not inconspicuous."

"I don't know what it means," Jonesy said.

"Inconspicuous means you'd never notice

them," Blackwood said. "So what do you think *not* inconspicuous means?"

"You could tell 'em from a mile away," the boy said. "On account of the wedding dress. And *him.*"

"Right."

Blackwood heard the ragamuffin repeat *inconspicuous* under his breath several times.

"The trouble is, everybody was too busy staring at Olympia to pay attention to where they were going," Ashmont said.

"You'd think Ripley would have left us a clue," Blackwood said.

"If he did, I'm hanged if I can make it out," Ashmont said. "Still, if he means to prove he's cleverer than I, he'd better think again."

"I doubt he thinks the first time," Blackwood said.

"We're going to have to follow by boat, curse him," Ashmont said.

"And stop at every stopping place along the way, to find out if they disembarked there?" Blackwood said.

"Good point. He'll be laughing himself sick, thinking of us following in that way."

"We could stop at the Swan," Blackwood said, nodding toward the inn that stood on the waterfront. "And wait for the watermen to come back. We could hire Jonesy to keep watch for us. He could nose about the neighborhood while he's at it. Unless he has any pressing engagements. Well, Jonesy?"

"I dunno," Jonesy said.

"Do you know what a pressing engagement is?" Blackwood said.

Jonesy nodded. "Like when ol' Truller couldn't meet us no more on account he had a pressin' 'gagement with a lag ship."

Thanks to time spent in low places, the two dukes knew that a lag ship was another word for a vessel used to transport convicts to Botany Bay, Pine Island, and other faraway lands.

"Would another crown clear your busy schedule?" Blackwood said.

"I fink so," Jonesy said. He dismounted with surprising agility, gave the horse a fond pat, and walked away.

Twickenham

Ripley and Lady Olympia looked at each other.

"I should have known," she said. "Aunt Delia wasn't ill, merely *indisposed* to go to London to be annoyed by my family when she had a better offer from Lord Clendower and his sister. I'll wager anything he'll offer for her again, and this time she'll say yes.

He amuses her, and she likes his sister —
and I must admit they're more entertaining
than a boring old wedding."

"Yours was not boring, as it turns out,"
Ripley said. This was, in fact, one of the
least boring days he'd spent in a very long
time. He wondered if he amused Lady
Olympia, and if she would like his sister,
once she got to know her.

"Too bad she's missed the excitement,"
Olympia said. "Meanwhile, so much for our
ingenious plan."

"Give me a moment," he said. "I'll think
of something."

"I'm not at all sure that's a good idea,"
she said. "Weren't you the one who had the
brilliant notion of placing false advertise-
ments in other's names? As a result, if I
recall correctly, seventy-five bagpipe players
descended upon Lord Eddingham's house
at midnight. On another occasion, ten wag-
onloads of elderly fish were delivered to
Lord Adderley's place. At yet another time,
one hundred twenty-five redheaded persons
turned up at dawn at Lady Igby's."

"That was a team effort," he said.

"I'm amazed nobody pays you back in
kind," she said.

"No imagination," he said. "I see you keep
abreast of our activities."

"One would have to be deaf, dumb, and blind not to know of them," she said. "For as long as I've been out in Society — and before that, I don't doubt — you three have been making spectacles of yourselves." She paused and gazed out of the window at the dog.

Ripley looked that way, too.

Cato had stood to survey his surroundings. The gatekeeper had retreated a distance from the lurcher, Ripley noticed.

"You did save the dog," she said.

"Had I a choice?" he said. "My being the knight in shining armor and all."

She bit her lip.

The lip he'd tasted. And it had tasted good.

And it was pointless to go any further with that thought.

"I'll confess, the prospect of playing a trick on Ashmont has its appeal," she said. "Although I'd vastly prefer playing one on all three of you. A dose of your own medicine."

"Early days yet," he said. "You'll get to it in time. Start small, with one of us. Then you can graduate. For now, the important thing is to get you to a reputable establishment before nightfall." And not give the men of her family any excuse for challenging anybody to duels. "You can't stay here or anywhere else on your own, that's certain. Any other aunts?"

"All the others as well as the great-aunts and so forth, came to the wedding," she said. "*Everybody* came. Except Aunt Delia."

"And Alice," he said.

She turned away from the window to look at him.

"According to Blackwood, my sister felt obliged to go to our place near Guildford," he said. "Something about Aunt Julia having one of her spells — though I'm not sure what that means, and Blackwood seemed to be equally in the dark. In any event, it's something over twenty miles from here."

"Twenty miles!"

"No great distance," he said. "A few hours. If we keep to a brisk clip, we'll arrive before nightfall. More important, Alice is there, and whatever one may say of her spouse, she's a respectable matron. No impropriety — or our world's fool notions of impropriety — in your staying with her."

"Your sister," she said. "I'm not at all sure that will do."

"You know her."

"Everybody knows her," Lady Olympia said. "Whether she knows me is another matter."

"Everybody knows you," he said. He'd had no trouble putting face and body to the name of Ashmont's betrothed. It dawned on him that he couldn't say the same of most of the other young ladies, including Alice's friends. But then, they weren't at all intriguing. They didn't secret themselves among the chaperons and elderly and bores of all ages. Also, none of them carried themselves in the way she did. The hint of impatience in her walk, that seemed like a dare.

"I'm famous for boring people to death, I know," she said. "That is not quite the same thing as being properly acquainted with somebody upon whom you propose to foist me."

"When Alice finds out you ran away from Ashmont, she'll welcome you with open arms," he said. "I hope she doesn't injure any unborn offspring when she falls down laughing at the sight of your bridal corpse."

He told Cato to lie down, and gave the postilion directions to Camberley Place.

There was no alternative.

Olympia needed a refuge of some kind, and the Duchess of Blackwood appeared to offer the only one within a reasonable distance.

Her Grace was not a complete stranger, though near enough.

They had not traveled in the same social circles. Among other things, the lady had lived abroad with her mother for several years. Then, too, though the beau monde was a small, incestuous world, there were groups within groups. The one to which Lady Alice Ancaster belonged comprised the most sought-after girls, and Olympia had, early on, found herself consigned to the opposite category.

There were pretty girls enough in Society, but not all pretty girls were popular. She still wasn't sure what the qualifications were. In her experience, a great many sought-after girls were not interesting to talk to or even agreeable. Though she liked gossip as well as the next person, she liked other topics, as well. However, the fashionable girls seemed to have only two topics: gossip and themselves. And it was no use her trying to start another topic. None of the others was interested in anything she had to say.

Neither were the gentlemen.

After her first Season, she began drifting further and further away, to the groups of elderly, intellectual, and otherwise unfashionable people.

Not that Lady Alice had ever been rude to her, as some girls were. She hadn't been part of Cousin Edwina's group, the ones who'd voted Olympia Most Boring Girl of the Season. Ripley's sister and Olympia had hardly exchanged more than a word or two. She knew a great deal less about the lady than about her disreputable brother.

All the same, Lady Alice had astonished even more *au courant* persons when she married the Duke of Blackwood.

"I didn't realize you had a place near Guildford," Olympia said.

"Belonged to my Uncle Charles," he said. "Alice and I and our friends spent a great deal of time there in our childhood. He left it to me, but it's Aunt Julia's for her lifetime. A ramshackle old house, in desperate need of modernizing, but one treads carefully in that regard."

She looked up at him. "I'm trying to picture you treading carefully. The image fails to come."

He laughed. "I rather dote on my dotty aunt."

"How dotty?" she said. "Does she set fire to the pillows at odd moments?"

He grinned at her.

She knew he was an easygoing man — easy morals, easily amused. All the same

200

she reacted to that grin as though it were a gift. He made her feel as though she'd accomplished something, when all she'd done was repeat what he'd said a few hours ago. It was the sort of simple joke she might have shared with her brothers, but it wasn't the same. This felt more intimate.

That was only charm, she told herself.

In spite of their titles and wealth, he and the other Dis-Graces would have been drummed out of the beau monde ages ago if they hadn't charmed so many women and won over so many men. His Majesty, being a sailor with a sailor's rough ways, had taken some time to reach the end of his tether. No doubt because they made him laugh.

"How dotty?" she repeated. "Does she keep monkeys? I draw the line at monkeys."

"No monkeys," he said. "No cats, because she's a bird lover. And after the last dog died, she's been reluctant to get another."

"Oh, dear." She looked out of the front window at Cato who sat, mouth open, tongue hanging out, taking in the passing scene and its scents.

"She likes dogs," he said. "It's only that she takes their demise hard. Don't fret. She and my sister will welcome Cato with open arms."

"If all is well," she said. "If your sister

201

didn't come to the wedding because of your aunt, I deduce that all is not well."

"That won't stop anybody welcoming Cato," he said. "A fine, well-behaved canine. Not the handsomest fellow, but good-looking enough and intelligent. If he had been one of those vile little yapping dogs, I should have dragged you away — by force, if necessary — and left him to his fate."

"In my experience, they become vile little yapping dogs because their owners spoil them," she said. "But nothing excuses beating an animal. You would have had an interesting time trying to drag me away, I promise you."

"Oh, I know I would," he said. "I get delicious chills, contemplating the prospect."

No one got delicious chills on Olympia's account, and she had no business having delicious chills at the thought of causing them in him.

She'd spent too much time with him, that was the trouble. More time than she'd ever spent in the company of any man not a relative. He was infecting her brain and turning it silly and hopeful and waking up old wishes and dreams.

Time to turn boring.

"Do you know what gives me delicious chills?" she said.

"Let me guess." He closed his eyes.

"I strongly doubt —"

"The *Æsopi Fabulae,* from Maioli's Library," he said.

She became aware of her jaw dropping, but not soon enough, because he chuckled.

"Uncle Charles was a great collector of books," he said. "I learned some things."

"He owned the *Æsopi Fabulae*?"

"From Maioli's Library. I paid attention to that one, you see, because it was *Aesop's Fables,* which is more entrancing to a little boy, as you might imagine, than bibles and codices."

"I should love to see it," she said. "Papa sold ours — or at least I think it was that book. He did not keep proper records — or any records — and my grandfather's papers are not quite in the order I should wish. I should have made much better progress in my cataloguing if we had not had to come to London every Season. Hope springs eternal in the parental heart, you see. And Papa is not skilled at calculating odds. If he had been, he wouldn't have needed to sell the *Aesop,* or any other valuable book."

"They don't always fetch as much as one would think," he said. "My uncle acquired some ancient works at little more than one pays for a half year of 'The Library of

Romance.' "

"This *one* you refer to," she said. "You speak generally, not specifically. In other words, *you* don't buy romances."

"But I do," he said. "Every month."

"For your sister."

"Why would I do that? She can buy her own. And now she can make Blackwood buy them. Besides, we don't like the same books. She prefers essays and other brain-taxing works. Her last letter mentioned Bulwer's *England and the English.* I grew sleepy merely reading the title and the author's name."

"And what doesn't make you sleepy is . . . ?"

"*Schinderhannes, the Robber of the Rhine.* Second volume coming August first. Victor Hugo's *The Slave-king.* Sixth volume, also on August first. Ripping good stories. I can hardly wait. The booksellers sent them to me while I was abroad, along with lists of coming publications. Smith, Elder, and Co., Cornhill, if you can ever tear yourself away from the Gutenbergs and such."

"I quite understand the sensational appeal of some of those books," she said.

"Do you?"

"Of course. It's a great thing to be swept away by a story."

"It is," he said.

"But do you not find some of them excessively sentimental or maudlin?"

"Yes, but I vastly admire the writer with the skill to bring tears to these jaded eyes, even when I know I ought to be laughing."

Her mind wrestled with the Duke of Ripley as a romance aficionado. "Well," she said, "this is an interesting side of you."

"I have many interesting sides," he said. "In fact, I'm a fascinating fellow."

He was turning out to be more fascinating than was good for her.

"I suppose you must be, to have got away with so much for so long," she said.

"A thriving dukedom helps," he said. "And a good mind for finance if not for high intellectual realms."

"I've often thought it would have been a good thing," she said slowly, "if Papa had a mind for finance. Yet in fairness to him, he's a doting husband and a kind and loving parent. There are worse things in life, much worse kinds of families."

"So there are," he said.

She caught a hint of something — a shift of mood, an emotion? Or maybe it was merely a pause before he went on, "But your library labors continue to intrigue me. You mentioned books being sold, yet you seem to have plenty to do." He settled back in the seat and stretched out his long legs. "Why do I suspect that's an exciting tale?"

"To me it is," she said. "Rather too exciting at times." So many narrow escapes from calamity. "To you, an altogether different matter."

"I'm a fellow of unplumbed depths," he said. "You must have realized that by now. I've astonished you more than once in our short acquaintance. I want to hear about the books."

"To help you sleep?"

He shrugged. "Does it matter? We've hours to while away."

Fifteen miles later

Indeed, Ashmont would have his hands full.

Lady Olympia Hightower was bookish, beyond question. But she was nothing like what *bookish* meant to Ripley. True, she seemed to have memorized most of the major book sales of the past twenty years, and she tended to forget her audience and slip into bibliophile jargon. But it wasn't merely collecting to her. Her relationship to the books was *passionate.* And the passion drove her to . . .

"Wickedness," he said. "You are a wicked, manipulative daughter."

"Some people need to be saved from themselves," she said. "Papa is truly good-hearted. He doesn't mean to destroy his precious inheritance."

Her paternal great-grandfather had bought the bulk of the collection. The present Earl of Gonerby, on the other hand, knew as much about a Grolier binding as the dog did. Before Lady Olympia was old enough to understand the collection's value, several precious items went for the sorts of prices Uncle Charles had paid occasionally.

"It would have been more wicked to educate him," she said. "He would have decimated the library in no time. He wouldn't go there merely when he needed ready money quickly. It would be a wholesale slaughter."

Unlike so many other debts, debts of honor — gambling debts, mainly — must be paid promptly. The library had been Gonerby's way to get hard cash in a hurry.

"Thanks to his lack of interest as well as knowledge, I've been able to save many important works," she said. "For instance, the Mazarin Bible printed by Gutenberg and Fust circa 1450 — the first production with movable types!"

Her voice throbbed with excitement. The glow in her face was nearly blinding.

"Ashmont will buy it for you," he said. And would receive in reward, beyond a doubt, a fine romp in bed or elsewhere.

Or Ripley could buy it as a wedding present and she would look at him with lustful blue-green-grey eyes and make Ashmont jealous of him, for once.

Do Luscious Lucius good, too.

"He will not get it for a farthing under two thousand pounds, if I have anything to say about it," she said. "Lord Mends would give a vital organ for it."

"Which organ, I wonder? If I'm thinking of the correct fellow — elderly, pear-shaped, and pedantic — wears wigs. That him?"

"Yes," she said.

"Not the freshest organs, I'd say," he said.

She drew her spectacles down slightly. Over them, she directed a look at him that reminded him of a tutor he'd once had.

"You're adorable when you look like that," he said. "Be sure to use it on Ashmont. He'll eat out of your hand."

She adjusted the spectacles and looked away. "You are simply bursting with marital advice," she said.

"I find this situation inspiring."

She gave a little huff, also charming.

"The *important* thing is, my father knows nothing about rare books," she said. "He simply snatches whichever impressive-looking one is handiest. Covered in gilt, for instance. We own quite a few of those. Costly books, but not rare. Too many copies printed, for instance. That sort of thing. When I can get them cheap, I buy them and put them on the shelves at his eye level."

He pictured her furtively adding garish books to the shelves. The picture was delicious. He laughed.

"Yes, I'm a liar and I cheat my own father," she said. "Only you would find that admirable."

"Ashmont will like it, too," he said. "I realize you agreed to marry him for mercenary reasons. With your family's strong encouragement." Add to that Lord Frederick manipulating behind the scenes, and what chance had she had? "All the same, he's not a bad fellow at heart or difficult to manage, if you know his quirks."

"What's happened is nobody's fault," she said. "No one forced me to consent. Nobody locked me in a dungeon and fed me stale bread and water. They were merely . . . excessively enthusiastic. In short, I knew what I was doing." She frowned down at her hands, neatly folded in her lap. "Or so I thought."

"Thing is, you're no more capable of marrying a tame fellow than my sister was. Speaking of Alice, I do believe we'll arrive before sundown, after all. We've made surprisingly good time, in spite of —"

He broke off as the offside horse reared, as though it meant to fly up into the nearby trees. The chaise gave an almighty jolt, throwing Lady Olympia forward. Ripley grabbed her before her head hit the front of the vehicle, and pulled her back.

"Plague take the fellow, how could he let — dammit to hell! Now the dog's off."

Olympia had been looking at him, and it was only out of the corner of her eye that she'd discerned the off horse shy at something. That set off a small earthquake, propelling her from the seat — and in the same instant, practically, Ripley pulled her back and half onto his lap. Hastily she wriggled off and into her place.

She couldn't tell what was going on, only that the postilion was struggling to bring the horses to order, and the chaise was slowing.

"What was it?" she said.

"I couldn't see," he said. "A bird. A squirrel. A rabbit. And the damn dog's gone after it. Cato!"

She turned her gaze to the boot. Empty.

Looking to the left, she saw, through an opening in the low hedges, the dog dart across a field. Above the clumps of trees dotting the field here and there, mounds of grey clouds moved restlessly.

Even before the chaise had fully stopped, Ripley wrestled the door open. He stepped down from the vehicle and marched to the edge of the road. "Cato!" he called.

Caught up in the chase, the dog kept running.

Olympia alit from the chaise and trotted to Ripley's side.

"He doesn't know his name," she said.

"I'll be damned if I'll call him Sam." Ripley put his fingers to his mouth and let out a piercing whistle.

The dog went on running, growing smaller and smaller as he raced across the field toward the trees beyond. He soared over a fence.

"Single-minded," Ripley said. "You wait here." He started across the field.

She jumped down from the post chaise. "I have no intention of waiting," she said. "He's my dog and my responsibility."

"Ten minutes," he said, walking briskly. "I'm not chasing him for hours. I give him ten minutes to come to his senses. Then we get back into the carriage and go on our

211

way." He glanced back. "Postboy's fooling with the leading rein, but the horses look to be all right and nothing seems to be broken. Ten minutes. No more. Then Cato may go to the devil."

She nodded. She hated to think of the dog running happily after its prey, then wandering through the night in an unfamiliar neighborhood, where vile men like Bullard could get hold of him. But if Cato had run away, that was that. They needed to reach Camberley Place before nightfall.

Ripley stomped on. "That is Satan's own dog. Did you see him leap?"

"I nearly expected to see him sprout wings," she said.

"There he is, and whatever else he is, he must be part greyhound."

Olympia looked where he pointed. The dog's chase had brought him somewhat nearer, but he was still in pursuit. Whatever the creature was, it was good at eluding predators. Cato was prodigious fast. In a straight run, he'd have caught his prey, but it ran erratically.

Ripley whistled again. The dog ignored him.

"He's having too much fun," she said.

"We'll have to break his concentration," Ripley said. He started into the field. "You go that way." He gestured to his left. "Make a lot of noise and wave your hands. Try to get his attention. I'll go the other way. With luck, we'll get him between us, and he'll want to play with us instead."

He walked briskly while he talked, and Olympia hurried to keep up.

"Cato!" she called "Time for dinner!"

"He just ate dinner!" Ripley shouted back.

When they'd stopped a few miles back, to change horses and postboys, Ripley had fed the dog, saying he looked famished.

As though dogs didn't always look famished.

"He's a dog," she said. "He won't remember."

"Dinner!" Ripley shouted. "Rabbits. Delicious rabbits!"

"Squirrels!" she called. "Foxes!"

"Badgers! Weasels! Beef, thick and bloody, the way you like it!"

They went on calling, and the lurcher went on running, in zigzags and in circles, sometimes coming nearer to them, and other times dashing farther away.

She put her fingers to her mouth and whistled. The dog paused and looked toward her.

She heard Ripley shout, and turned in time to see him fall forward to the ground.

■ ■ ■ ■

The Swan at Battersea Bridge, with its constant comings and goings, turned out to be the wise choice for waiting for information. Since various delays had cost time, the two dukes estimated they were about two hours behind their prey. This was sufficient, it turned out, for word of the Duke of Ripley's activities at the White Lion in Putney to travel, via watermen and others, back to them.

As they were about to set out, however, the boy Jonesy disappeared. Trying to track him down delayed their departure.

Street boys were useful, and clever ones like Jonesy could save a duke a lot of boring time questioning people when he could be in a tavern, drinking.

But Jonesy had vanished, and as usual, everybody "didn't know nuffink," and Blackwood and Ashmont set out on their own for the White Lion in Putney.

There they heard a great deal. Putney was abuzz with recent events, and the locals couldn't wait to tell their versions of the story.

What people were less helpful about was Ripley's destination.

"Plague take 'em, didn't anybody watch which way they went?" Ashmont demanded while the innkeeper and his wife debated whether the post chaise was headed to London or to Twickenham or another place entirely.

"Well, he's clever, you know, Your Grace, and it'd be like His Grace, wouldn't it, to seem to be going one way when he means to go another," said the landlord.

"He said Twickenham," said his wife. "Only a short journey out of the way, if he was going back to London. Whyn't he say Doncaster or Brighton if he meant to send them on a proper wild-goose chase?"

"I wonder if Twickenham is a clue," Blackwood said. "Otherwise, I can't think —"

"How the devil is one to think, famished and dying of thirst?" Ashmont said. "We should have eaten before, in Chelsea, instead of looking for that wretched boy."

"Some local authority harassed him, no doubt, and he took off," Blackwood said. "Or he found another pigeon to pluck. How much did we give him, altogether, I wonder? Maybe he's gone to buy himself a thoroughbred to race at Goodwood."

"To hell with the little ingrate," Ashmont said. Turning to the innkeeper, he said,

"Give us the Sun or the Star or one of them to sit in without yokels bothering us, and something to eat and drink. As quickly as you can — in case anybody has anything intelligent to say before next Wednesday about that scurvy, bride-stealing, thinks-he's-so-clever, so-called friend."

They adjourned to the private parlor called the Sun, where they assuaged their hunger and thirst if not Ashmont's frustration.

"Do you think he's gone back to London?" Ashmont said, after his tankard had been refilled for the third time.

"Yes," Blackwood said. "At any rate, it's what I'd do. Take her out of Town for a while, give everybody time to get into an uproar, then circle back and sneak her home."

"It's what I'd do, too." Ashmont frowned. "I don't understand why she went."

"I don't know," Blackwood said. "She doesn't seem the sort — that is, it's the kind of thing I'd expect from Alice, actually. And I did, too. Right up until the minister said we were man and wife, I was ready to find out it was all a joke, or hear her raise an objection — you know, when the minister asks if anybody knows any reason you shouldn't be shackled? There I was, waiting for her to say, 'I have a good reason. He's an idiot. Will that do?' In that way she does. And then — but she didn't." He shrugged.

After a moment, Ashmont said, "I think Olympia bolted."

"Well, why not?" Blackwood said.

"I don't know," Ashmont said. "But it's deuced aggravating."

"We are not matrimonial prizes," Blackwood said.

"That's what Uncle Fred said. He was right, too, curse him. I had to use the library on her. And even then I had to do a devil of a lot of talking."

"Well, then."

Ashmont slammed his tankard on the table, sloshing ale. "But Ripley didn't. He didn't do all the work. And now . . ." He considered. "No, wait. I told him to look after things. If she did bolt, and this wasn't his joke, he's looking after her. He'd better be looking after her. Because she's the one. I found her."

"It isn't as though she wasn't in plain sight, year after year."

"But we didn't see. Least I didn't. But then I did. And I wooed. So I get her. Not Ripley. If she bolted . . ." His jaw set. "Then I'll simply have to mend whatever it is needs mending and — and bring her round."

"You'll do it," Blackwood said.

"Need to find her first. What do you think? London?"

"I do think it's London," Blackwood said. "Very likely Gonerby House."

"Not the wedding house, then?" Ashmont said. "But no, probably not. Damned shame they had to have it in Kensington. Would have been harder for her to bolt from Gonerby House. Maybe I should have waited for the renovations to be done."

"You would have waited a year, maybe two. Because I promise you, they won't be done in less than a twelvemonth."

Ashmont shook his head. "No, why wait? Found her. Wooed her. She said yes. No point in — now what?"

The innkeeper's wife had entered the parlor. "It's Twickenham, Your Grace. The postboy's back and he says they changed at Twickenham. And they were going on to Guildford."

Ashmont looked at Blackwood. "What the devil?"

"Guildford," Blackwood repeated blankly. Then, "He's taking her to Camberley Place. To Alice." He laughed. "This should be interesting."

Ashmont bolted up from his chair. "Curse him. Now I've got to chase the numskull to

Guildford."

"Yes, and pry Lady Olympia away from my duchess and her aunt. That'll be fun, that will."

But Ashmont was already storming out, demanding his horse.

Moments later, as he was about to swing up into the saddle, a red-faced man ran out into the inn yard, yelling about a stolen dog.

Ashmont didn't care about the dog or anything the fellow had to say about the Duke of Ripley. He wasn't in the best mood, and he wanted to be off. But the man made an unpleasant observation about the lady who'd been with Ripley.

There was another delay while Ashmont tried to kill him.

CHAPTER 8

Ripley saw stars, then, as he opened his eyes, mud under his face.

He struggled to rise, and pain shot up his right leg.

He swore.

A cry made him lift his head, and he watched Lady Olympia run across the field to him, skirts flying, black lace fluttering.

With more effort than it should have taken, and sharp protests from his right side, he rolled over and pushed himself up into a sitting position.

His right foot throbbed, and that side of his body ached and stung in sympathy. Not pleasant. Not convenient. But not likely to kill him, either.

It's nothing, he told himself. *Get up.*

She crouched by his side. "Don't move," she said.

"I damned well will," he said. "In a moment. As soon as the stars stop whirling about my head. Stepped into a rabbit hole, is all. Probably belonging to the one leading Cato a merry chase." He put his weight on one arm and tried to get up. His leg wobbled and pain arced upward.

She set a gloved hand on his shoulder. "Don't."

Hearing the Voice of Command, he stilled, instinctively. Then he laughed at himself. So ridiculous. He'd heard her sharp whistle — pitched precisely to summon boys and dogs — and like any boy or dog, he'd stopped short and turned to her.

And tripped. And fallen on his face. In a muddy field.

"I'm all right," he said. "Fell down wrong."

"Do *not* move," she said. "Let me look."

"Nothing's broken," he said, more for his own benefit than hers. He would not allow any fractures. He hadn't time. "But my hat's over there, in the cow dung and —" He tried to rise, and won himself a pain parade up his leg. He sucked in air and let it out. "Damn."

"Right," she said. "Will you try to use some part of your grossly underworked brain and employ a dash of common sense? You've injured your foot."

"It got a jolt, I daresay, when I fell on my

face," he said. He couldn't have done more than wrench the ankle. It oughtn't to be making such a fuss.

"I daresay," she said. "Now, keep still, hold your tongue, and let me look. No, never mind. I know it's too much to tell you to hold your tongue. But you must keep still. The idea is to *not make it worse.*"

He could hear the *you dolt* she was thinking.

She was right. Had their situations been reversed, he'd have roared at her to keep still. The trouble was, he could hear a faint inner voice telling him he'd done real damage, and that voice was trying to throw him into a panic.

He told himself not to be a baby. He wasn't dead. No signs of blood anywhere. He was simply incapacitated. Somewhat. For the moment.

And not in the least worried.

"Look at my gloves," he said, holding out his hands. "Just look at them."

"You hate them anyway," she said.

"It's the principle, dammit." He supposed his face was dirtier than the gloves, but it had never been very pretty, and so, no great loss there. "And it's deuced undignified, falling on my face in a farmer's field."

"Yes, more dignified to fall on your face at

a party because you're inebriated," she said.

"Exactly," he said. "Drunk, you don't know you're undignified. Equally important, you feel no pain."

"Men," she said. She moved to his feet. "The right one?"

"Yes, nursey."

"On second thought, maybe I'll shoot you and put you out of your misery."

"Sadly, we have no weapons," he said. "I should have thought of that in Putney. Traveling without firearms is — oh."

She had grasped his foot. Gently.

All the same . . . not pain, exactly. More like . . . excitement.

Well, he was a man, and when a woman touched a man, he was likely to get excited, whether he needed to or not.

"Tell me when it hurts," she said. Carefully she moved his foot to the right, to the left, and in a circular motion, as she must have learned to do ages ago, having so many brothers and, as far as he could make out, loving but inattentive parents.

Perhaps he let out a small yelp.

His face heated. "It isn't broken," he said quickly. "I'd know." He wouldn't allow anything to be broken. "But it's sweet of you to fuss."

"I am greatly tempted to drop it. Hard.

On a rock."

"Too bad. Only mud and cow shit here-abouts." He glanced about him. "Possibly sheep shit, too. Can't say. I'm no agrarian."

She rose and set her hands on her hips and looked at him. "I can't leave you here, great as the temptation is."

"Actually, you could. The postilion knows the way."

He was perfectly capable of getting up, Ripley told himself. He would not have to crawl back to the chaise. He could move on one foot, more or less. He simply needed to stop whimpering to himself about a dash of excruciating pain.

He'd been in worse fixes than this. He'd been more badly damaged in fights and reckless riding episodes.

But at all those times he'd been drunk.

Never mind. Drunk or sober, he didn't have time to play the invalid.

He had to get back to London forthwith. He had to advise Ashmont and goad him if necessary. Ripley had to make sure no duels happened and nobody got maimed or killed over the wedding fiasco. Above all, he needed to get away from her and get an un-respectable woman into bed. Quickly.

"It's the shoes' fault," he said. "Can't go

tromping about fields in go-to-wedding shoes."

Little more than slippers, formal shoes didn't protect a fellow's feet against wet, let alone stepping into rabbit holes. But one couldn't get proper boots in short order in Putney or anywhere else. The inn servants had dried out and cleaned his wedding footwear as best they could.

"I'd better help you up," she said. "You must not put any weight on the right foot."

"I *know* that," he said. "Go back and tell the postilion you'll mind the horses, and send him to me."

"I could drag you back to the carriage by your good foot," she said.

"And spoil this beautiful coat, you insensitive female? Get the postilion."

She glanced back over her shoulder toward the post chaise. "He's still fussing with something. I wonder what frightened the off horse."

"The postboy let his attention wander," he said. "That or drunkenness is the usual reason for losing control of post horses. It's not as though the creatures have any spirit left in them. Will you kindly get him?"

"He's smaller than I am," she said.

"He's wirier. Just. Get. Him."

She smiled down at him. "No. I like seeing you somewhat helpless."

He smiled back at her. He liked seeing her standing above him, hands on her hips. Liked it very much. Wounded as he was, he'd have hooked his good leg about her ankle and brought her down on top of him . . . if she hadn't belonged to his stupid friend.

She planted her feet hip-width apart and held out her hand.

"If you try to help me up, you'll fall over," he said.

"Do try to think rationally," she said. "It's the same as using a chair or a tree stump. I'll provide support, so you won't put any weight on the foot."

"You can't take my weight," he said.

"That's what they all say."

"I can get up on my own," he said. "It's the going forward part that's going to be awkward. *Will* you get the postilion?"

"How I should like to knock you unconscious with a rock and drag you by one foot," she said. "Or an arm. Or your ears. But that could take a while." She looked up at the darkening sky. Her spectacles lost their sparkle, mirroring the gloomy view overhead. "And it looks like rain. Again."

He laughed. In spite of throbbing and dirt in his mouth and another set of ruined clothing.

Giving himself a push with one hand, and taking his weight onto his left foot, he propelled himself upright. Then he was glad indeed to have her handsome shoulders for support, because even the small amount of pressure on his right foot hurt like blazes. He managed not to do more than grunt, but he couldn't help grimacing.

"Use me like a crutch," she said. "It's all right. I'm not fragile. Quite strong, in fact, thanks to dragging library steps about and hauling books up and down — and some of them as heavy as a cow, thanks to the gilt."

She was stronger than he would have thought, in more ways than one. All the same, he hated making a crutch of her. He did it, though. No choice: one hop forward at a time on his left leg, with her as support for the right. Even so, he couldn't keep the right foot fully clear of the ground, and every time it made contact, pain vibrated from his ankle.

But the common sense part of his brain told him that if he tried to get back to the carriage on his own, on this uneven ground, he'd land on his face. And end up crawling. He doubted it was much more fun to crawl with a throbbing foot as to walk.

And so, wrapped tightly together, they

inched along the uneven ground. As they moved, her breast pressed against his arm and her hip against his upper thigh. The attendant sensations traveled easily to his groin, distracting him from the pain and thoughts like, *Now what do we do?*

Only another five miles or so to the house, he told himself. It wasn't going to be the most pleasurable experience, jolting along the rough country road of the last stretch, but he'd survive.

And then?

He'd think about *and thens* when the time came.

At long last, they reached the road, and he dared to look up from the ground ahead he needed to cover.

The lurcher stood in the chaise's open door.

"Woof!" he said.

Olympia caught the look in the dog's eye in the nick of time.

As Cato vaulted from the carriage, she hauled Ripley out of the way.

The dog failed, by a very narrow margin, to bowl them over. One would have thought he'd be fatigued after his chase. Instead he was excited and apparently quite proud of himself.

"Sit," Olympia ordered, and the dog sat, tail thumping.

"Where on earth did I get the idea you were well trained?" she said.

"Woof!"

"And silent?"

"Woof!"

She looked up at Ripley, whose face seemed paler than before.

"Sorry about that," she said. "But I saw in his eyes the urge to pounce on a human, and I couldn't be sure it wasn't you he chose to greet overenthusiastically."

"I saw it, too, the trickster, acting so meek and mild before," he said.

"I don't doubt he behaved so well before because he was cowed and shocked," she said. "But he's a dog, and seems to have forgotten. That tells me Bullard didn't have him for long. He'd be much more timid otherwise."

"Instead, he's reverted to his natural, obnoxiously exuberant personality," Ripley said.

After they'd contemplated the cheerfully innocent-looking Cato for a moment, he said, "You're tougher than you look."

"All those tomes, as I told you," she said.

She summoned the postilion. Pale and stammering, he apologized. He'd let his attention wander, as Ripley had said, and reacted too late as a consequence.

To his credit, the duke accepted the apology without berating the fellow further. It wasn't the postilion's fault, certainly, that Cato had decided to go hunting.

Then Olympia focused everybody's attention on getting her injured companion into the carriage. The process was awkward — a post chaise wasn't the roomiest vehicle — and it took a while to get him settled.

She doubted the result was very comfortable. He had to sit sideways, wedged into a corner. Propped up on the linen parcels, his injured foot rested awkwardly upon her knee.

"Your knee is going to ache after half a mile," he said.

"That's nothing to what your ankle will feel like," she said. "But we'll go at an easy pace."

"We'll go like the devil," he said. "The faster we get there, the better."

"You'll be screaming like a girl."

"I'm not a child. A bruised foot will not have me puking and shrieking."

"Grown men are worse than boys when it comes to pain," she said. "And if that ankle's as bad as I suspect — and we unequipped with strong spirits or even vinaigrette —"

"Vinaigrette! As though I were a swooning debutante!"

"Ah, there's a picture," she said. "The wicked Duke of Ripley swooning. But since I've nothing to revive you with, I must urge you to be brave. And if you must be sick —"

"As though I'd vomit on account of a few bruises."

"If you must be sick, do it out of the window."

Before the duke could retort, she told the postilion to keep the horses to a walk. She used the voice she normally employed when her brothers needed discipline. With Ripley, obviously, one must Dominate or Be Dominated.

The postilion appeared to listen to both of them, but he did not "spring 'em," as His Grace demanded.

Her mind at ease on that count, Olympia concentrated on keeping Ripley distracted from the acute discomfort she knew he was hiding. He did it well, but she was watching, and she noticed the way his mouth tightened when they traveled over bumpier sections of the road.

After they'd covered about a mile, he shifted position, as though he meant to put his foot down.

"You'd better keep it upraised," she said. "I realize it's an awkward position."

The seat held two people, with no room to spare, and his legs were long.

"It shouldn't rest on your knee," he said. "It's too heavy."

"I've layers of clothing to cushion my knee," she said. "But you might feel more comfortable if we take the shoe off."

"After the foot's been in a rabbit hole, in a farmer's wet field?"

"I have six brothers," she said. "My stomach is strong."

He gave a chuckle, a pained one, but that was enough. She'd amused him. He let her take the shoe off.

This was not as easy as it might have been. His swelling foot told her he'd either sprained the ankle or bruised it quite badly. Luckily, the shoes were soft, thin leather, not practical for tramping in fields but easier to get off than boots.

Though his stockinged foot smelled only of wet earth, she recoiled as though it had been a rotting carcass and held her nose and pretended to gag and carried on as though she would swoon. He thought this was hilarious.

Males never did grow up. Not that this

was always a problem. There were positive aspects of men being such simple creatures.

To look on the bright side, she wouldn't have much trouble keeping him entertained for the remaining few miles of their journey.

And that was very much for the best, because she needed to keep herself distracted, too. The intimacy of holding his large, stockinged foot upon her knee was almost painful.

A short time later

The duke had told Olympia that Camberley Place was a ramshackle old house.

She had pictured an old manor house set in a rustic landscape. The word *ramshackle* had conjured images of later additions tacked on, creating a rambling, picturesque structure.

She was completely wrong.

Camberley Place was an immense house dating to Tudor times. From the outside it didn't seem to have changed much since then.

Originally, though, it must have formed a quadrangle around the courtyard. The present structure opened into a pleasing U-shape, and it was delightfully, excessively decorated in terra-cotta and an abundance of painted glass.

While they weren't expected or invited, he was, after all, the master. The gatekeeper had ushered them in without hesitation or any hemming and hawing about the family not being at home.

By the time the post chaise drove into the courtyard, people — servants, it looked like — had clustered at the windows. A moment later, a tall, thin man, whose authoritative bearing told her he was the house steward, emerged from the entrance. His minions trailed behind him.

The house steward, whose name turned out to be Tewkes, behaved in the way any self-respecting chief of household staff ought to do: He didn't turn a hair at finding a common, dirty post chaise in the grand, ancient courtyard, but took it completely in his stride, without so much as an eyebrow twitch.

Then, when the servants ran up to open the carriage doors, and everybody got a glimpse of who was inside, there was a lot of bowing and scraping and underlings being ordered about.

When the footmen helped Ripley out of the post chaise, his jaw tightened and his face whitened a shade. While Olympia was sure he hadn't broken his ankle, she knew a sprained or wrenched ankle could be extremely painful, especially at first.

Luckily, Camberley Place had been built on level ground. He didn't have to climb a single step to go inside.

Leaving Tewkes to deal with the dog, the postilion, bridal corpses, discarded shoe, and everything else, Olympia followed Ripley and the two strong footmen he leaned on into a cavernous Great Hall. There she found the expected heavy oak paneling and arrangements of armaments on the walls. But she could admire these antiquities later, she told herself.

At present, she needed to prevent his worsening the injury.

At least he hadn't objected to the footmen helping him. The road, especially the last bit, before they reached the carriage drive, had been especially rough.

She wondered where to put him. Their hostess had not yet appeared.

She told herself not to panic. Since the ladies weren't expecting company, they might be anywhere. Visiting neighbors, for instance.

One thing at a time.

"Where to now?" she said.

"Library," Ripley said.

It wasn't the nearest room, but he insisted, without explaining. Not that he explained much of anything — such as letting anybody know why he couldn't walk on his own and wore only one shoe.

Beneath his ducal dignity to explain, of course. Everybody about him must try to assemble clues and work things out as best they could.

But she wasn't a duke, and she saw no point in letting the staff whisper and conjecture instead of knowing precisely what they were dealing with.

By the time the footmen had planted him on a sofa and propped up his foot on a cushion, Tewkes had returned.

To the steward she said, "His Grace appears to have sprained his ankle."

"Bruised," Ripley said.

"We'll see," she said as she bent to examine it. "But since I didn't shoot you in the foot or drop a large rock on it, and nobody here knows me, I'd rather not be under suspicion."

"Hardly the sort of thing to upset anybody here," he said. "Amuse them, rather." He looked up at the house steward. "Whether her ladyship did or didn't use violence against me, I need a restorative, Tewkes. Brandy. Large."

"Yes, Your Grace."

"And ice," she said. "As soon as possible.

Though it doesn't seem grossly swollen, it's certainly not as it should be. At best, the bruising is severe, and the quicker we deal with it, the better. I shall want bandages, as well. And vinegar. And a maidservant to assist me."

"And a physician, my lady?" Tewkes said.

"No quacks," Ripley said. "I only banged my ankle. I don't need any bones set and I won't be bled and purged for a little mishap in a rabbit hole. All I want now is a large glass of brandy."

Tewkes went out.

Olympia rose. "Where is your aunt?" she said.

"Somewhere about," he said.

"Are you sure?" she said.

"She hasn't left Camberley Place in three years," he said. "She hasn't been socially inclined since Uncle Charles died. She'll be somewhere about, but *somewhere* covers a considerable territory. We may have a wait before she appears."

She gazed at him accusingly. "She doesn't like company, and you brought me here —"

"It isn't quite like that," he said.

"Then what is it like?"

"I'm not sure," he said. "My mother and sister seem to understand. Alice says she's a ghost —"

"A *what*?"

"Figure of speech," he said. "You're not going to turn hysterical on me now, are you?"

"I might." She sat in a nearby chair and folded her hands. "This day feels as though it's gone on for weeks. I believe my nerves are wearing." For a moment she'd envisioned a deathly ill or dying auntie, and having to leave this house and seek yet another refuge. In that moment, she'd wished she'd stood before the minister the way she'd promised to do.

Was it only this morning?

She wanted to put her head in her hands and weep, but she couldn't. She had to see to Ripley's injury first, before he did anything to make it worse. Males had an appalling tendency to worsen their injuries because of a mystical belief that, if they said nothing was wrong, nothing was wrong, and they could do what they wanted.

"Nothing to fret about," he said. "Aunt Julia is a superior sort of relative."

Before Olympia could ask any more questions, Tewkes returned, with two footmen, a sturdy maid named Mary, the brandy, and the various other items Olympia had requested.

"Tewkes," Ripley said. "Where's my aunt?"

"At the mausoleum, Your Grace. Joseph has gone to inform her of your arrival."

"You heard him," Ripley told Olympia. "At the mausoleum. I told you she was somewhere about."

Well, then, Aunt Julia wasn't better.

Still, this was Camberley Place, and even haunted, it remained the refuge Ripley remembered: household in order, servants going about their business calmly, and everything looking clean, neat, and well cared-for. The antithesis, in short, of the home in which he'd endured too much of his boyhood.

He watched Lady Olympia direct the servants to bring a small table to the sofa. There she had Mary set out strips of cloth and bowls, a bucket of ice, another of water, and a small pitcher of the vinegar she'd ordered.

She had them move her chair closer to his foot.

Then she sent all of the servants except Mary out of the room.

When the door had closed behind them, Ripley said, "You didn't want a brace of footmen leaping to do your bidding?"

"Best not to let the men see you weep," she said. "And do try to keep the screaming down. I don't want them bursting in to the rescue and making things worse."

A titter escaped Mary.

"Do not be alarmed," he told the maid. "I shall sob quietly into my brandy." He took a sip — and then nearly choked because Lady Olympia drew up his trouser leg, and her hand — her bare hand — touched his skin for an instant, and it was as though she'd applied an electrical machine. He didn't leap from the sofa, but he must have twitched at least, because she looked up at him.

"Sorry," she said. "Is it tender?"

"Erm. No. Just . . . nothing. Thought of something."

"I shall do my best not to hurt you," she said. "But I fear the area is going to be very sensitive."

Several areas, actually.

"Don't worry," he said. "I've borne worse."

He told himself to relax and enjoy it. By the looks of things, this was as close to womanly attention as he'd get this night, but as he saw her hand move to his garter, he said, "I can do that."

"Really?" she said. "You know how to

untie your own garters?"

"And pull up my own stockings," he said.

And darn them, too, he could have added.

"Drink your brandy," she said. "It's better to leave this to me."

"I'm not sure it's proper," he said. "Not that I remember what is and what isn't."

"There's nothing to be afraid of," she said.

"Afraid!"

"I've done this any number of times. If it isn't one of the brothers, it's one of the cousins. Or their friends. You're safer with me than with most doctors."

"That I don't doubt," he said.

"Then be brave," she said. "I'm going to untie the garter. Try not to cry."

Gently, she untied the garter. His groin tightened.

She set the garter on the sofa. He stared at it and drank brandy.

She touched his stocking.

He swallowed a groan.

Slowly, gently, she peeled the stocking down his calf. The room grew hot and he tried to think of cold things. Like the mausoleum. And Ashmont. Yes, Ashmont, to whom she belonged. Ashmont, so cheerful, talking about getting married.

Slowly, gently, she drew the stocking down his foot.

Ripley's heart beat faster, and it was no good trying to stop what was happening inside him. He was a man, and a woman had her naked hands on his naked skin. A woman was touching him, undressing him. This was what he knew. The rest — he, trying to reason with himself and not be a damned fool — the rest was noise, like the noise of the London streets.

He drank.

She slid the stocking off his foot and gave it to Mary, and he was aware of his breath, coming so hard, it seemed to whoosh like a wind through the library.

She, innocent that she was, hadn't an inkling what she was doing to him.

He would have laughed if he could have mustered the breath for it.

She was so serious, concentrating fully on what she was doing.

He watched her work, her brow slightly furrowed above the spectacles, her lip caught between her teeth, as she made a mixture of ice water and vinegar. She soaked the cloth in it.

"It's going to be cold," she said. "Brace yourself."

Cold, yes. He needed cold.

She wrapped the icy bandage about his ankle. And he nearly jumped off the sofa.

And said a word even he knew one didn't utter in front of women.

"Yes, I know," she said. "But in a moment it'll feel better."

"Right," he gritted out. Then it did feel better, in more ways than she knew. The cold shock worked wonderfully, numbing not only his foot but the frustrating sensations of a moment before.

With Mary helping, she continued her work, wetting more strips of cloth, and wrapping them about his foot. He told himself his suffering was his own fault. He should have insisted one of the menservants attend to him.

But Lady Olympia was so dictatorial that the reasonable thing to do hadn't occurred to him.

And dictatorial, he told himself, was exactly what Ashmont needed.

And yes, maybe Ripley felt a qualm or two about a misspent life that had kept him away from such interesting girls. And yes, maybe he wouldn't altogether mind being wrestled into order by a tyrannical female in spectacles.

But mainly what he felt was balked in every direction. Her ministrations had got him all excited, with no way of relieving the excitement. He hadn't a prayer of dealing with his celibacy this night or of dealing with Ashmont. The chances of Ashmont running amok were very good. One could only hope he'd drunk himself unconscious before he could get into fights with members of her family.

Her voice dragged him out of the private hell he was constructing.

"I know that many medical persons recommend liniments or leeches or both," she was telling Mary. "But mariners rely on cold and wet. They will hold a sprained part under the pump when the ship is pumped out, morning and evening — and you know seamen are wanted to be fit and strong again as quickly as possible. A number of medical men urge similar treatment. At least it isn't wintertime. As the shock fades, the cooling sensation ought to be not entirely unpleasurable."

She looked up at him, her brow wrinkled in worry. "Have I made the bandages too tight?"

"No," he said.

"You're scowling," she said.

"Yes," he said. "I had a plan. I mentioned this, I believe. I would bring you here, then go back and deal with Ashmont and everybody else."

"You can't go anywhere," she said. "It's

essential to rest the foot, and keep it elevated."

"Drat you, Ripley, now what have you done?" came a familiar voice from the doorway. "Hardly back in England and in trouble already."

CHAPTER 9

Aunt Julia remained for a moment on the threshold, fists on her hips, wearing the grim expression that had cowed him when he was a child. Even now it made him uneasy.

She looked harmless enough, fair and sweet-faced and while above-average height, not impressively so. She had the knack, however, of appearing impressively above-average formidable. She'd stood up to his impossible father when few men would or could.

All the same, she seemed to Ripley a pale imitation of herself — the ghost Alice had written about — and that wasn't simply the somber grey dress, with its sensibly narrow but unfashionable sleeves.

Still scowling, she advanced upon him. She didn't box his ears as he expected, but ruffled his hair as though he were still a boy before turning her attention to Lady Olympia. "And this, I collect, is the lady who shot you?" Her brow knit. "Plague take you, Ripley, it's Ashmont's *bride.* What on earth were you thinking?"

"Excessively intelligent, my aunt," he said to Lady Olympia. "Knows everything about everybody. Did I mention that?"

"You never were good at pouring butter," said his aunt. "No subtlety."

"I daresay. Aunt, may I present Lady Olympia Hightower."

His aunt rolled her eyes. "No, you mayn't. I met Lady Olympia when she was presented at Court. I should know her anywhere, in any event. Yet I hoped against hope my eyes were playing tricks on me today. Silly of me. How I *wish* your uncle were here. Of all the stupid things you've ever done, this beats them all. By miles."

"Lady Olympia, it appears you are acquainted with Lady Charles Ancaster, my favorite aunt —"

"I disown you, as of this moment."

"Auntie Julia, don't be cross. Can't you see I'm wounded?"

His aunt gave him a look that would have shriveled a better man. Not being a better man, he bore it as he'd borne any number of disapproving looks, though her opinion counted for more than others' did.

"In fairness, Lady Charles," said Olympia, "I was the one who did the stupid thing, and the duke has been my knight in —"

"Don't say that," he said.

"The duke has been trying to save me from myself. He even tried to make me see reason."

Aunt Julia studied his companion for a moment. "Hugh tried to make you see reason? My nephew? This great, useless hulk of a fellow? Now that is something I should have liked to witness."

"I'm not entirely sure she did a stupid thing," Ripley said. "And when she wouldn't give it up, of course I went along."

"That goes without saying," said his aunt. "Then what? You drove her to violence?" She moved to examine his foot. "Neatly done, Lady Olympia. But had you not considered amputation?"

"Don't put ideas in her head," Ripley said. "I'll need all my limbs to clear up this business. Which I had intended to do this evening. The Fates, however, had other ideas."

"Fate, indeed. You weren't looking where you were going."

"I wasn't looking to step into a rabbit hole, I agree." He'd been looking at Lady Olympia in all her finery. So dashing and splendidly feminine — and whistling like a man.

"We were trying to catch a runaway dog who'd deceived us into believing he was properly trained," Lady Olympia said. "I advised Tewkes to have him taken to the stables. I didn't like to bring a strange canine into the house when I'm so uncertain about his manners."

"A runaway bride," said his aunt. "A runaway dog. An incapacitated nephew. It seems the evening's conversation won't be boring. Come, Lady Olympia. You must be longing for a respite from my nephew, not to mention wishing for the sorts of things a lady needs when she finds herself a stranger in a strange place, unsupplied with luggage, servants, or anything else necessary to her comfort."

"Our departure was hasty," Ripley said. "We hadn't time to —"

"Really, Hugh, I'm not completely in my dotage. You needn't point out the obvious. The servants will make up the bed in your uncle's study for you. If I catch you trying to climb the stairs, I'll shoot you."

She was bearing Lady Olympia away when he remembered. "Where's my sister got to, by the way?"

"Alice?"

"I've only the one, last I heard."

Aunt Julia shrugged. "She was here for a time, and I was glad to see her, but what is there for her to do in this gloomy place? I sent her with Georgiana to the Drakeleys' house party. I refer to my youngest daughter," she explained to Lady Olympia. Turning back to Ripley she said, "Alice won't be bored there. You know the Drakeley boys adore her."

"Excessively, I always thought," he said.

"That is her husband's problem," said his aunt. And out she went, taking Lady Olympia with her, and leaving Ripley to wonder why Alice hadn't gone back to London to her spouse, instead of in the other direction, where her beaux lurked.

After helping Olympia wash off the dust of travel, Lady Charles's maid, Pickard, had gone in search of something suitable for the guest to wear to dinner. This left the two ladies to enjoy in private the tea Lady Charles had ordered, "as a restorative after your trials."

Olympia had remembered her as soon as she saw her, but had not expected to be remembered among so many debutantes — from seven years ago, no less. Besides, Lady Charles had always traveled in diplomatic and political circles, whereas Mama and Papa gravitated to the sporting types. Their paths had rarely crossed.

The lady was about Mama's age and, like Mama, had not lost her looks. There the resemblance ended. Ripley's aunt was altogether different in manner. She had a fearless air and she was infinitely more organized and orderly. A strong woman, in character and confidence.

And sad, too.

The subdued grey dress would have told the tale, even if one failed to see the sorrow shadowing her hazel eyes.

It was so like Ripley's lack of consideration, Olympia thought, to bring a stranger here to intrude on the lady's grief.

"You'll wonder why I waste my breath scolding my nephew," Lady Charles said after she'd poured. "But somebody must, and fiercely, even though he won't heed. Since he had the wits to bring you here, however, one must admit he isn't entirely bereft of sense. Well, then. You are my first bolter. I did wonder how Ashmont won you over, a sensible girl like you. But there is Alice, wed to that blackguard Blackwood. Did *she* have the sense to abandon him at the altar? And so you see I am of two minds. I appreciate the feelings that drove you. On the other hand, my dear, this will be rather a muddle to sort out."

"Yes, I kn-know." Then, to her dismay, Olympia wept as she'd wanted to do before, in the library.

Lady Charles stood up quickly, and moved to give Olympia's shoulder a sympathetic squeeze as she said, *"Men,"* in exactly the tone to make Olympia laugh and sob at the same time, like a complete ninny or hysteric.

Her hostess had hardly sat down again before the ninny-hysteric was telling her story in all its not-making-much sense, although leaving out the parts about naked dukes and more-than-friendly kisses in post chaises.

"Ah, I was not aware that brandy came into it," said Lady Charles at the end. "That explains a good d-deal." Her lip trembled, and for a moment, Olympia thought she'd weep, too, perhaps reminded of her own wedding day.

Instead the lady laughed, and heartily, and while she did, the cloud that seemed to hang over her vanished, and the atmosphere lightened and brightened. At that moment Olympia understood, in her heart as well as her head, what made this aunt special to Ripley.

But the laughter subsided too soon, and

her hostess said, "The first thing we must do is set your parents' minds at ease."

"I should have sent a message myself, but at first all I could think of was getting away. And then I didn't know what to say. I've hardly known my own mind."

"As I said, the brandy explains a good deal. Then, too, we must keep in mind your traveling companion. Not the type to contribute to clear thinking." Lady Charles closed her eyes briefly, then, with a sigh, opened them. "Those three. Really. One makes allowances, given their fathers. But my dear, when a man reaches the age of nine and twenty, one would hope for maturity."

Olympia knew nothing about their fathers. None of them had been alive by the time she left the schoolroom. Though Lady Charles had made her very curious, it would be impertinent to seek details.

"All in all, I thought the duke took matters calmly and about as logically as he could, in the circumstances," she said. "My behavior was irrational. There I was, changing my mind constantly and falling into the river and stealing the dog — and he took everything in his stride."

"Of course he would," said her hostess. "It's nothing to what those three have done.

Stop berating yourself. When men do the sorts of things you did, everybody's amused."

"But I'm not a man! You know caricatures of me will hang in the print shop windows and my name — of all names — will feature in *Foxe's Morning Spectacle*. And nobody will say, 'Boys will be boys' — because I'm not a boy!"

"Indeed, it's most unfair," Lady Charles said. "But you leave it to me. I'll write to let your parents know Ripley brought you straight to me. It's best they think so. You may trust me to find a way of putting matters so as not to distress them. I've had a good deal of practice, I promise you. The letter will go out this night, express. They'll have it in a few hours and will sleep easy."

"I should like to think so, but I very much doubt it. How they'll face their friends, I cannot imagine — and how I wish I'd thought more of them before I climbed through the window."

"They'll get over it if you end up married to a duke," said Lady Charles. "All the world will get over it."

"That isn't likely at this point. The Duke of Ashmont —"

"Needs you," the lady said. "It's perfectly obvious."

254

"Not to me," Olympia said.

"That's because you don't understand him as well as some of us do," Lady Charles said. "I heard about your encounter near the Clarendon Hotel. The metaphor was obvious to me. Ashmont desperately needs to be pulled back from the brink. Like most men, he may have some idea he's unhappy, but like most men, he doesn't examine his feelings. As a result, he has no notion what the problem is. But some part of him must be weary of the life he lives and the chaos he creates." She paused. "I wondered if Ripley was weary — of Ashmont or of that life — and if that was what sent him abroad without his friends."

Neither man struck Olympia as weary with anything, but then, she didn't know them as well as this lady did.

"But that is neither here nor there," Lady Charles went on more briskly. "The point is, you weren't having any of Ashmont's nonsense, and that got his attention."

"He decided to marry me because I made him go home and change his boots?" Olympia said.

"Your manner made him take notice of you. After that . . ." The lady considered for a moment. "I strongly suspect that someone told him he hadn't a prayer of attaching you. That's what I would have done had Ashmont mentioned to me a girl I approved of. He's competitive to a fault. He'll soon realize he'll have to work to win your respect and love. And when he does —"

"*If.*" Olympia couldn't help interrupting. She'd managed five younger brothers. She couldn't look forward to playing nanny to a grown man.

"Not *if,*" said Lady Charles. "*When.* I know him as well as I know my nephew and the other idiot. Where one goes, there go the other two. They've been inseparable since they met at Eton. I should never have expected Ripley to go abroad without them, and stay for a full year. But as I said, it's possible he was tired of that manner of life. And I do think he must have matured — not much, to be sure — but enough to do what he could to . . . well, not make matters worse today."

Matters would have been better if Olympia had not seen him naked.

And if he had not kissed her in that not-friendly way.

But he was wild and had always been wild. A practical joker as well as a rake. The trouble was, she'd been exposed to more disreputability than she was used to, it had happened in the course of a few hours, and this had thrown her off balance.

When she wasn't drunk or off balance, she was a practical girl. This was why she'd agreed to marry the equally disreputable Ashmont in the first place. Nanny or not, his failings aside, if she got a second chance, she'd be a great fool not to take it, because, after this debacle, it would be her last chance, absolutely.

Had Aunt Delia been at home to take her in, the scandal would have been muted. Now Olympia's reputation must be in ruins. Ripley said otherwise, but he was a man — and a duke. He had no idea how quickly and harshly women could be judged. She'd traveled all day and into the evening in a closed vehicle with one of Their Dis-Graces. The world would soon get wind of the scenes enacted en route. She was descending into despair, horrific satirical prints filling her mind, when Lady Charles spoke.

"Listen to me," the lady said. "Don't underestimate Ashmont. It may take some time, but when he wins your respect and love, you'll be happy you married him. I speak from experience. Charles was not my first choice. I confess, in fact, that I married him in resignation, if not despair. But he was determined to make me happy, and the testimony to my happily married life is my unhappy widowhood. Still, time heals all wounds," she added more cheerfully. "Everybody says so, and I'm sure I'll come to my senses eventually. But we can talk more later, if you like. For now, I recommend you try to rest."

She went out, and a servant came in and collected the tea things.

Lady Charles had given Olympia a great deal to think about, as though she hadn't enough already. Her mind racing, she was sure she hadn't a prayer of resting. She began to pace the room, instead, trying to sort and catalogue everything that had happened to her today.

She didn't remember lying down, and was very surprised when Pickard woke her to dress for dinner.

Though he wore to dinner a set of his uncle's clothes, which didn't fit, Ripley carried it off, as he'd done with the garments he'd acquired in Putney. He looked ducal and upsettingly attractive.

After an argument, Olympia persuaded him to keep his foot up on a chair. He did this with a lot of grumbling. But after a while, he forgot about the indignity, stopped grumbling, and became entertaining.

He talked mainly about his travels on the

Continent, and he was a fine storyteller, like the writers of romance he was so fond of. He made both women laugh, again and again — and he looked so disarmingly mischievous and pleased with himself for accomplishing this.

This was good, because it took Olympia's mind off family and scandal and Ashmont. It was bad because she could have listened to him all night. When last had she wanted to listen to a man who wasn't talking about books? Why did it have to be him, of all men?

Still, she let herself enjoy the respite from inner turmoil. With servants going in and out of the dining room, private matters had to wait until after dinner.

They didn't wait long.

After dinner, Lady Charles and her guests adjourned to the library.

As soon as the servants had settled His Grace upon a sofa, finished fussing about this and that, and gone out, Lady Charles rounded on her nephew.

"Did you have any sort of plan?" she demanded. "Or did you come here expecting me to sort everything out?"

"It's complicated," Ripley said.

"Lady Olympia has told me — not *everything,* knowing you — but the relevant portions," said his aunt.

Face hot, Olympia left her chair and went to examine a set of books at eye level. Not that she saw what they were. She was too busy telling herself that Lady Charles couldn't possibly have imagined a naked duke scene as one of the parts of the journey her guest had failed to mention.

"My plan was to leave Lady Olympia safely with you and Alice," Ripley said. "I would then return to London and encourage Ashmont to try again."

"Really?" said Lady Charles. "Why would you suppose he'd remain quietly in London? That isn't like him at all. It's far more likely he's hunting you down."

"That's the complicated part," Ripley said. "He was already half-seas over when Lady Olympia and I set out. When he didn't catch up with us in Putney, I gambled that he'd kept drinking, and Blackwood would put him to bed, as we always do. Since Ashmont hasn't turned up yet, the odds seem to be in favor of that theory. Still, if he does turn up now, I'll deal with him. You may leave it to me."

Olympia turned away from the books. "Leave it to you! I'm the one who ran away. If he does come — which I very much doubt — I ought to be the one to deal with him."

"Not a bad idea. When he comes, attack first and make him defend himself," Ripley said.

"If he comes," she said.

"He'll come," Ripley said. "I merely laid odds he wouldn't arrive *today.* Still, we might allow for the possibility, remote as it is, of Blackwood sobering him up. In that case, and if Blackwood's with him, helping him put two and two together, he'll find us soon enough. We didn't exactly pass unnoticed. The problem is, I should have preferred to talk to him *before* he came here to carry off his bride."

"Since that is not going to happen, you'd better make an alternate plan," Lady Charles said. "If, for instance, those two scoundrels turn up at three o'clock in the morning."

"You assume he wants to carry me off," Olympia said. "If I were he, I'd come only to tell me good riddance. Actually, I wouldn't bother to come at all."

"He'll come," the aunt said with the same unshakable certainty as Ripley.

"It's only a matter of when," Ripley said. "You may have six brothers, Lady Olympia, but that doesn't make you an expert on

Ashmont. He's competitive to an extreme. As well as used to having his own way and getting what he wants."

"And which of you isn't?" Olympia said. "What male isn't? What about his masculine pride? I *deserted* him. In front of *everybody.*"

"You're looking at this the wrong way," he said. "You're a woman. His woman. His pride will tell him to vanquish whatever made you run away. What you need to keep in mind is, he can't resist a challenge."

Remembering what Lady Charles had said, Olympia looked from her hostess to him. "A challenge."

"Ashmont's always had it too easy with women," Lady Charles said. "This may have something to do with the kinds of women with whom he associates. But the fact remains."

"And so my appeal is that I'm difficult," Olympia said.

"And different," Ripley said. "You're nothing like what we're used to."

"Different and difficult," she said.

"Exactly."

Such irony, she thought. Being different and difficult was what had got her banished to the Wallflower, Chaperon, and Elderly Department. If only she'd known these qualities appealed to rakes — but no, it wouldn't have made any difference, because good girls kept their distance from men like Their Dis-Graces.

"It isn't exact at all," Lady Charles said. "Ashmont's a man. The first thing he notices is not her personality."

"Oh, that goes without saying," Ripley said.

Olympia couldn't think of what else men noticed first, apart from looks, which was perfectly obvious. Since they failed to notice hers, she clearly wasn't up to par. "No, it doesn't," she said.

Ripley rolled his eyes. "Use your head — the one with the big brain inside. If you weren't pretty and shapely, he wouldn't have courted you, challenge or no challenge."

He said it as though it were the most obvious thing in the world.

Pretty and shapely.

Right. That was why she had to fight the men off with a stick. Never.

Seven years. One offer, from an elderly scholar.

Pretty and shapely.

But only look at who said so: the Duke of Ripley, a famous libertine and ne'er-do-well. And here she was, going hot and fluttery, when everybody knew rakes were *completely* undiscriminating.

"What he won't want you for is your mind," Ripley said. "He won't realize you have one, and that's probably for the best. He'll think he's the clever one, and you can wrap him about your finger."

Lady Charles smiled. "Of that I haven't the slightest doubt. Listen to my nephew, Lady Olympia. He knows whereof he speaks."

Olympia gazed at His Grace, who half reclined on the sofa, like a pasha in the harem. Instead of a hookah, he held a glass of wine in his hand. He was swirling it, his dark head bent as he peered into it, as though he read her future there.

The thought came into her mind, and then it was too late, because she couldn't un-think it:

Ashmont isn't the one I want to wrap about my finger.

And that was when she realized, finally, how much trouble she was in.

The lady balked because you didn't woo her thoroughly. All I did was try to persuade her to come back. When she wouldn't, what else could I do but make sure she didn't get into trouble?

That, or something like it, summed up what Ripley had intended to tell his friend. He had a good deal of advice to supply as well, on the care and handling of Lady Olympia Hightower, though it would be no small labor, getting Ashmont to sit still long enough to pay attention.

First, he'd want to punch Ripley in the face.

Then Ashmont would want to sweep the bride off her feet.

The two likelihoods still held.

The trouble was, Ripley wasn't going to get to Ashmont ahead of time.

The trouble was, here was the intended bride, dressed fetchingly if not quite as dashingly as before. She wore a blue dress Ripley supposed had belonged to Georgiana or one of his other cousins, or perhaps even Alice. Not Aunt Julia's, though. These days her wardrobe ran to dull greys and browns and boasted little in the way of ornament.

This evening, Lady Olympia was as prettily ornamented as one of his French cook's fine pastries.

Though her neck and shoulders weren't bare, they might as well be, because the embroidered lace chemisette, being nearly transparent, could not hide the smoothness of her fine shoulders and the soft swell of her breasts above the dress's neckline. The maid had put her hair up in a fashionable style, with braided loops along the sides of her head and large twirls of hair on top, and ribbons twining through.

Ripley was a man. This meant that, even while he was trying to decide what could be done about Ashmont, he was thinking in greater detail about the process of undoing ribbons and letting the soft, thick, brown hair fall about her shoulders, and undoing the rest of her ensemble, bit by bit. He tried staring into his wine, as though an oracle lived there, but he was aware of her all the same.

He should never have had a taste, because a taste was never enough. He was a man always greedy for pleasure — of the table, of bed, of everything — and he was too much in the habit of getting what he wanted and too little in the habit of resisting temptation.

He reminded himself that this wasn't the usual temptation. He wasn't competing with Ashmont for an actress, ballet dancer, courtesan, or merry widow. Ripley wasn't allowed to compete this time — and this wasn't one of those tedious social rules he had no compunction about breaking. Ashmont was his friend and she was Ashmont's *betrothed.* Heaps of legal documents had been signed. Half the world had been invited to the wedding.

And Ashmont wanted to marry her. He'd made that more than clear.

He'd simply failed to persuade the bride she wanted to marry *him.*

"Ripley?" His aunt's voice jolted him back to the moment. "If you have no further marital advice for Lady Olympia, perhaps you'll turn your mind to preventing mayhem if your partners in crime come roaring to the house in the small hours of morning."

"You don't allow mayhem," he said.

"This is an exceptional circumstance," she said. "You've never made off with one of your friends' brides before."

"To be strictly accurate, I made off with the duke," Lady Olympia said.

"I went willingly," he said.

"No, you didn't," she said.

"Not at first," he said. "But you won me over by degrees."

He watched her color rise. She'd blushed before, when he mentioned her figure, and then of course he'd had to emphasize her shapeliness, in order to watch the blush deepen.

Well, what was he to do? She was pretty and shapely and she tasted good, and when sainthood was mentioned, his name would not come up.

"Ashmont will have to understand that," he said. "You ladies make much ado about nothing. It's quite simple: If he and Black-wood turn up in the middle of the night, the servants are not to let them in but to come and get me. If my friends grow ob-streperous in the meantime, set the dogs on them." His aunt might have given up on house pets, but every estate had men and dogs guarding the property. "Either way, I'll deal with them, as I've done a thousand times before. And, Auntie, if you don't mind being roused from your bed, you might glare at them as you do so beautifully."

"And I'm to do what?" Lady Olympia said. "Cower in my room?"

"Read a book," he said.

The look she sent him over her spectacles! It made a man want to pick her up and —

And nothing.

This was very bad. He'd better deal with Ashmont very soon.

"And speaking of dogs," he went on, "Ash-mont knows the house. In the event he proves sneakier than one expects, you might want Cato with you this night."

"Cato!" she said. "For all we know, he'll welcome intruders and lick their faces.

We've no indication he's a guard dog."

"He's a hunter," Ripley said. "You saved him from a shocking beating. He'll protect you."

Even from me.

Not that he'd do anything improper. Out of the question. She was Ashmont's betrothed. She was an innocent. There existed a few rules even Ripley didn't break. And so he would not make up excuses to check on her after she'd gone to bed.

Yes, he would very much like to see her in her nightdress. And out of her nightdress.

And what a bloody waste of fantasy!

No wonder he and his friends kept away from virgins and respectable matrons. Can't do this. Can't do that.

"I won't have that dog in the house until I know I can trust him," Lady Olympia said. "He should have come when called. We should not have had to chase him. If he'd behaved as he ought, you wouldn't have stepped into a rabbit hole. He'll remain in the stables or wherever they've put him until —" She broke off, frowning.

"Aye, there's the rub," Ripley said. "Until Ashmont comes and carries you off? Or your parents?"

"Nonsense," said Aunt Julia. "Lady Olympia will remain here for as long as she likes.

I've written to promise her parents I'll look after her, and I shall. She'll be perfectly safe, and nobody will carry off anybody. You, meanwhile, will manage your fool friends. Tomorrow we'll see about the dog. Lady Olympia, you need more rest than you think you do. Let's make an early night of it. If those two ridiculous men arrive this night, I'd rather be upstairs, where I can prepare myself for the encounter. With boiling oil, if necessary."

Once more she took Ashmont's bride away.

All for the best, Ripley told himself. He was doing too much thinking and he couldn't keep his waste-of-time thoughts in order. There was nobody nearby to cure the celibacy that made them so difficult to subdue, and he was incapable of going out to find a cure.

He glared at his damaged foot. How many days would this cost him?

And how was he to get through them without losing his mind?

The following morning

"He can't ride to London!" Olympia said. "He should not have come this far. He was not to put any weight on his foot. Everybody knew that!"

She had gone down to breakfast rather earlier than she was accustomed to, on account of being woken by a bad dream. In it, Ashmont had been pounding at the door, and Ripley and Cato had leapt through a window to knock him down. But while Ashmont and Ripley were fighting, Bullard had caught hold of the dog, and started whipping him.

Her conscience plaguing her about abandoning Cato in a strange place, she'd been unable to go back to sleep. Instead she'd made a quick breakfast before hurrying to the stables, where a groom informed her that His Grace had ridden out "a short while ago." He was headed to London.

"I'm sorry, your ladyship, but we didn't know His Grace wasn't to go," the groom said. "Even if we did, we'd have a job trying to stop His Grace doing what he wanted to do."

"That reckless man! I don't doubt he pulled off the bandages, as well. Not that they'd do much good if he meant to tramp about stables and ride to London. He would have been sorry, I promise, before an hour had passed. And by then it would be too late."

She stroked Cato's head and he licked her gloved hand. "Why didn't you stop him?"

she said. "It's a pity I hadn't time to train you to take the tail of his coat between your teeth. But no, he's a grown man, and if he wishes to behave in a self-destructive manner, wiser persons or canines can't stop him. We'll go for a walk, Cato, and see what your manners are like. And we shan't trouble our minds with the Duke of Ripley's determination to cripple himself."

This was the rational thing to do.

Let him go.

Deal instead with the dog who, bad manners or not, would be infinitely more manageable and far easier to train than a spoiled, reckless nobleman.

"Woof!" said Cato.

She looked down at the dog who returned her regard, eyes bright, tail up and wagging.

"Ah, but you are reputed to be a hunter, are you not?" she said. "Shall we see?"

To the groom she said, "I shall want a carriage."

She explained what she wanted it for.

Then she took off, at a run, for the house.

CHAPTER 10

This was not a mistake, Ripley told himself.

Another day in Lady Olympia Hightower's vicinity and he'd turn into a gibbering imbecile.

The way she'd looked at him when he said she was pretty and shapely . . . the way she'd colored and the light in her eyes. She'd gazed at him the way another woman would if he showered her with diamonds.

He'd told himself it was normal, enjoying her blushes. But it wasn't normal for the recollection to follow him to bed and haunt him. It wasn't normal to feel guilty and unhappy and angry with the world on account of a woman.

Celibacy couldn't be that poisonous. Something more was going on, which he was not going to think about. He wasn't going to think at all.

He was going to put her behind him and do what needed to be done. He was going

273

to do the right thing, because he was the bloody knight in shining armor. For every-goddamn-body.

Including Ashmont, who couldn't be sober for his own wedding, or pursue his own runaway bride, and was taking his own bloody time about finding them, though Ripley had done nothing to conceal himself, and half the world must have recognized him as he passed. Could one have left a clearer trail? Ought Ripley to have posted signs?

Meanwhile his ankle, which had seemed well enough this morning when he set out, had decided to make this morning more hellish than it already was.

Only two more miles or so to Cobham and the George Inn. He'd rest there.

No, he wouldn't. After traveling what? Six, seven miles? He ought to have covered twice the distance by now, ankle or no ankle.

But he was so bloody tired. Sick and tired.

He hadn't slept, thanks to her. The naughty dreams wouldn't have been a problem. He had them all the time. But those weren't the only kind. She'd appeared in her bridal rig, all virginal white, her face glowing, and he'd lifted her into his arms and carried her away from a furious Ash-mont. In another, she'd appeared in the wedding that hadn't happened, standing next to Ashmont but looking at Ripley through her veil, her eyes dark. He'd watched tears stream down her face, under the veil, until it was soaking wet, and her dress was wet, too. Then it was raining and they were on the boat and she fell into the river and it carried her away, out of reach, while he roared her name.

He'd awakened in a cold sweat.

After that he hadn't wanted to try to go back to sleep.

He'd waited until the first hints of daybreak, and pulled on some of his uncle's clothes. Why in blazes did Aunt Julia keep them? How was she to get better if she clung to . . . what she couldn't have anymore.

Stop it, he told himself.

He'd got away undetected. That was what mattered.

Not long after leaving Camberley Place, he'd stopped at the Talbot in Ripley, his namesake town. There he'd nursed a tankard to make up for the breakfast he'd missed. He shouldn't have stopped so soon or for so long. He'd wanted another tankard and another and he wanted to blame it on his peevish foot, but the fact was, he couldn't seem to pull himself together.

He'd wanted to turn back. Still wanted to.

Which he couldn't do. There was nothing for him there.

So here he was, plodding along at the kind of pace he supposed her Lord Mends preferred.

Why? Because her ladyship had taken so much pains with Ripley's curst ankle. Desperate as he was to get to London, he couldn't bring himself to undo her work. Not to mention, he couldn't appear crippled and weak when he met up with Ashmont.

So more torture: Every time the plaguey ankle gave one of its obnoxious twinges, Ripley remembered Olympia's hands on him, on his foot, and the businesslike way she'd looked after him, completely oblivious to his desperate state of arousal.

She was kind, Ashmont had said.

She had no idea what her brand of kindness did to men like them.

He glanced up. The sun, trying to break through leaden clouds, cast a sickly light. Oh, good. Just what he liked best: plodding along to London in a downpour.

Yes, you poor, sad martyr. Travel in the rain. As though you haven't done it time and again, at high speed.

But then he'd been drunk. Now he was all too sober. He should have drunk those additional tankards.

How much would he need to drink to wash her out of his brain?

Not too late to find out. He could hire a post chaise at the George. Then he could travel at better speed. He could drink a tankard or three while the stablemen made the chaise ready. And take a bottle with him in the carriage. With somebody else driving, he could drink himself blind.

Only two more miles, or not much more.

He'd no sooner thought it than the world about him darkened. Above, the clouds churned, turning black around the edges. A droplet splashed on the horse's head. He heard another strike his hat. His uncle's hat, rather. Though vastly superior in quality to the one he'd bought in Putney, it fit only a degree better.

More raindrops fell, faster and faster, pattering on leaves and scattering the road's dust.

Lovely.

Why the devil hadn't he stayed in Florence for one more blasted day?

He wouldn't be here now.

The wedding would have been a fait accompli.

Or not.

At any rate, the bride would have been somebody else's problem.

And he would never know what he'd missed.

His mount, untroubled by the rain, plodded on.

Ripley told himself to plod on. A little wet wouldn't kill him.

The rain beat down harder, and poured off the rim of his hat down his neck. Demons dug their daggers into his ankle.

He peered out from under his hat brim into the downpour.

On the near side stretched a common. No shelter there. Not many yards ahead on the right, though, at the edge of a tangle of bushes, stood a wooded area. He made his way there, and found a narrow track. He turned into it and rode on a short distance into the cluster of trees. They grew thick enough to keep off the worst of the deluge.

There he waited.

And waited.

His ankle throbbed. He needed a drink. He needed to fight with somebody.

He dismounted, his ankle acting as though he was trying to murder it.

"Go to hell," he told it. He found a stump and sat down, his leg outstretched.

You must keep it elevated, she'd said.

He remembered the way she'd held her nose and pretended to gag when she took off his shoe. He remembered the way she went after the bully.

He thought about her being married to Ashmont and felt sick.

He told himself not to think about it, but this time, he couldn't make it go away.

An eternity later, the rain began to abate.

He looked up through the dripping trees. The sky was lightening.

The horse tossed its head. Something rustled in the bushes.

Ripley looked that way.

"Woof!"

Cato trotted toward him, tongue hanging out.

"Good boy!" called a familiar voice.

Behind Cato, striding along the muddy path, came Nemesis.

"You stupid man!"

Oh, he was, because the sound of her voice made the skies turn blue and the sun burst out in golden glory and, in short, he came perilously close to weeping with relief.

He dragged his stiff body up from the stump. Yes, he was deranged. Perhaps she'd made him so. Still, he had manners, of a sort, where relevant, and she, after all, was a lady. A gentleman rose when a lady appeared, no matter who she belonged to and

279

how she plagued him.

"What on earth do you think you're doing?" he said.

"What does it look like?"

She wore what looked like one of Aunt Julia's dresses: Narrow-sleeved and of a dismal shade of brown, it fit completely wrong. While she and his aunt were nearly the same height, their shapes were different. The waist hung some inches below where he estimated Lady Olympia's navel to be, the shoulders didn't follow the perfect slope of hers, and the bodice was in places her breasts weren't. The hat, as somber as the dress, and topped by a single drooping feather, sat at a tipsy angle upon her head, the ribbons tied clumsily.

He felt as though he'd drunk exactly the right amount of fine champagne. He realized she'd made him feel that way from the moment she'd ordered him to help her with the window.

Making his expression surly, he glanced at the dog. "You hunted me down," he said. "With the dog. You are a dangerous woman."

She stood, hands on hips, eyeing him up and down. "Mad, perhaps, trying to save you from yourself. Sit, for heaven's sake!"

Cato sat. Ripley did not.

"The masculine mind is truly a wonder," she said. "Are you *trying* to cripple yourself? Have you any idea of the damage — the permanent damage — you might do?"

"No, I don't, because there won't be any. I've sprained parts before. I shouldn't have let you coddle me. Those sailors you were talking about? You think they get to loaf about the ship in between cold seawater treatments?"

"You're not a sailor. You're a spoiled, self-indulgent nobleman. If you're talking about recovering from boyhood injuries, remember that your boyhood passed *a long time ago.* Boys' limbs are still growing. They mend quickly. You're a grown man — all except the brain — and it's *different* for you."

"I'm not a fat old hypochondriac, either," he said. "You seem to have confused me with your Lord Mends."

She blinked once. "No, no, I can tell you apart easily," she said. "My Lord Mends wears a wig. You have more hair than wit."

"I never tried to pass myself off as a scholar," he said. Mends was, though. A highly regarded one, the pompous ass. "Because I won't meekly do what you think I ought, I'm brainless."

He wanted to meekly do whatever she

wanted him to do.

He needed to be shot. Preferably in the head, where it would do some good.

"Obstinate, too," she said. "Go ahead. Lean on the horse. Or the tree. It's killing you to stand upright — but you'll do it, by Jupiter, won't you, for no better reason than to prove whatever it is you have to prove."

He wanted to lean on her.

"I have nothing to prove," he said. "I had a plan, as I mentioned last night. I saw no reason to change it. I'm going to London."

"Saw no reason," she repeated, shaking her head. "How I wish I'd dosed you with laudanum." She looked at Cato. "It's exactly the same as talking to boys, which is like talking to a brick."

She took a deep breath, and let it out, which created mesmerizing movement in the bodice. He knew better than to tell himself not to look. He was a glutton for punishment.

Turning from Cato to Ripley she said, "I know it's a waste of breath, but both Reason and Conscience demand I point out a few simple pieces of common sense: One doesn't put weight on an injured limb. One keeps it elevated. One gives it time to recover."

"It had plenty of time," he said.

The calming breath hadn't worked, apparently, because her eyes flashed and her cheeks pinkened, and she cried, "Ten hours isn't time enough, you brick-brain!" She waved her fists in the air, and the motion made the dress go one way and her breasts another. "And hours riding about the countryside don't count, you great ox!"

She was delicious.

He hated Ashmont. Also himself.

It was long past time to make his exit.

"If you're quite done with the sermon, I'll be on my way," he said. He turned away to collect the reins.

"Go," she said. "Have it your way. I must have experienced a temporary derangement, thinking Reason and Conscience carried any weight with you. You're impossible, the lot of you. Hell-bent on self-destruction. I ought to know better, but no, I must come out on this wretched day to rescue you from your folly, because you did what you could to rescue me from mine. Rescue you — any of you — what a laugh. Well, it's but one more error of judgment. I apologize for interrupting your journey."

He heard a furious rustle of skirts and petticoats. He knew he ought to ignore it and get on the horse and get himself far away. But he'd always had a problem with *oughts.*

He turned in time to see her start away, head up, back ramrod straight. That back. The hint of impatience in her walk. More than a hint at present.

What a cur he was.

She'd looked after him. She'd done what she could to help him heal. And he — well, he was what he was. He couldn't change his character and he couldn't change the past. He couldn't make it come out that he'd been the one in front of the Clarendon Hotel that day.

"Dammit, Olympia." He limped after her.

She marched on. "I don't care what you do. You'll go lame. You'll never dance again. It's nothing to me."

"I can't stay there — at my aunt's!" he said to her back. "You don't understand. You'll never understand. I don't want you to understand."

That made no sense and he didn't care.

"You're right," she said. "I don't want to understand. It doesn't signify at all to me what you do. But I thank you for the lesson." She turned toward him in a storm of swooshing skirts. "If I get another chance with Ashmont, I'll know better than to take any notice of anything he does. I shall live a life of the mind, which is more than acceptable and worlds less aggravating than trying to *communicate* with any of you."

He grasped her arm. He was vaguely aware of Cato growling, but that was merely background noise to the foreground cacophony in his head. "I have to go away because —"

"I don't *care.*"

"Because," he said.

Because there she was, irate and smelling of rain and woodland and fresh things, her arm warm under his hand. She'd kept him up all night, and the too-brief taste of her still haunted him. He was a reckless blockhead, but that was who he was. And here she was. And they were alone. And he *wanted.*

That was as much as he knew, really, as he pulled her into his arms, muttering, "Because this."

He kissed her. And at the first touch of his lips to hers, the desire he'd been battling for what felt like eons won.

He kissed her in the way of a man who wants what he can't have and has to have it anyway, the way of a man who knows only when he's got it and needs to know nothing else. And with the first taste and feel of her mouth and the way her body felt, crushed to his, all the feelings that had been crashing this way and that, all wrong, turned right.

And when she grasped his shoulders and held on, something inside him, some taut part of himself, which seemed to have been waiting eternally, surrendered.

He cupped the back of her head, and kissed her more urgently, persuading. *Stay,* he urged with his mouth. With a sound like a sigh, she gave way, and the world tilted right again. Her lips parted to him and her body melted against his, and the warmth of it and the wave of turbulent pleasure made him stagger, his bad leg wobbling dangerously.

He didn't care about his foot or about pain or anything but her. He held her, and drank in the taste and feel of her as he sank backward, falling, until his back struck something hard and rough.

Up or down, it didn't matter, because this was what mattered: the shape of her and the way she fit against him and the wondrous rush of feeling. And above all the power of a kiss, ever-deepening as she followed his lead.

Ah, she did that well. She learned quickly, and demanded in the same way he did, until the first, pleasurable warmth swelled into a dark heat, burning up what little reasoning power remained in his brain.

Sensations, emotions, on the other hand, he had in plenty. They swamped the inner voice trying to remind him who she was and what was right and what was wrong. He dragged his hands down over her perfect shoulders and down her straight back to the fine curve of her bottom. That felt good. Perfect. He pulled her hard against his groin. That was better.

But she gasped and broke the kiss and wriggled. The spell broke, and he had no choice but to ease his strangling grip. Though this made only the smallest distance between them, it was enough. The world came back and his powers of thought returned, and his brain demanded to know what he was about. Had he lost his mind at last? Was he dead drunk? Concussed?

It didn't matter how much he wanted her. It didn't matter if she haunted his dreams and wouldn't let him sleep. It didn't matter if she charmed and intrigued him and he hated Ashmont for being the first to stop watching from a distance.

Still, Ripley didn't release her completely. If she'd pulled away more forcefully, he would have let her go — he hoped he would, at any rate — but she didn't. She only stood in the circle of his arms, looking up at him, spectacles askew.

"All right," she said, her voice thick. "Well." She shook her head. "But no." She pushed at him. Then he had no excuse not to let go. She stepped back, straightened her posture, straightened her dress, and adjusted her spectacles. "That was . . . educational."

Educational. Oh, it most assuredly was.

She, an innocent. She, his best friend's betrothed.

Ripley pushed away from the tree that had propped him up. He swore. He tore off his hat and hit the tree with it. He swore and swore until the space about him ought to have turned blue and the trees ought to have shriveled up. As it was, birds flew up from the branches and squirrels scolded and small, panicked creatures raced through the undergrowth.

"Ripley, for heaven's sake!"

He heard her, but his mind shouted more loudly.

Ashmont was his best friend. Since boyhood, since those miserable early days at Eton. They'd always stood up for one another, the three of them.

And Ripley . . .

He kicked the tree — with his left foot, not the damaged one, though that was pure luck because he wasn't thinking. But the jolt unbalanced him, and down he went.

Meanwhile at Camberley Place
"London?" Ashmont repeated.

He and Blackwood stood in Lady Charles Ancaster's drawing room. Ashmont sported a black eye. Neither gentleman's appearance was elegant. They appeared to have been run over by market wagons and, possibly, a herd of cattle.

"So it would seem," her ladyship said. She held out the note Ripley had left for her.

Ashmont took it and read, " 'Gone to London. R.' " He turned the note over. The other side was blank. "That's all?"

"He deemed it sufficient," she said.

Blackwood and Ashmont nodded. They rarely explained themselves, either.

It did not occur to them that Lady Charles, too, might leave a great deal unsaid, including highly pertinent information.

"London," Ashmont said. "We thought so, didn't we? Gone back to London, we said. Wild-goose chase. But then all the clues, you know."

"He did come here," Blackwood said. "Didn't go straight back to London. We weren't wrong."

"When you didn't appear last evening, we all assumed you'd remained in Town," Lady Charles said. "What a comedy of errors this has turned out to be."

"Dash it, did he think we wouldn't give chase?" Ashmont said. "Didn't he mean for us to do it?"

"On the contrary, we had been expecting you," Lady Charles said. "In fact, I should have thought you'd arrive before my nephew did or soon thereafter. His journey turned out more complicated than anticipated."

"Ours, too," Blackwood said, glancing at Ashmont. "We had an annoyance in Putney. Riot Act read. That sort of thing."

"Indeed," Lady Charles said. She put up her glass and studied his eye. "The bruise looks recent."

"That happened after the . . . erm . . . misunderstanding," Blackwood said. "He fell down some stairs."

"Something I ate didn't agree with me," Ashmont said. "Sick all night, or I would have come, dash it."

"Something you drank, most likely," Lady Charles said crisply. "A fine start to wedded bliss this is. I had hoped that even you could get married without making a muddle of it. And to such an admirable girl, too."

"I know she's admirable," Ashmont said.

"Saw it at once. Wondered why I didn't see it before. But wasn't thinking of marrying before, you see."

"Had you made your feelings clearer to her, she might not have run away," her ladyship said.

Ashmont frowned. "Yes. Didn't woo hard enough. So everybody tells me. But I did, you know. Told her all about the library, like Unc— that is, as I knew I ought — and she seemed pleased."

"We're not sure she did run, exactly," Blackwood said. "We suspect it was Ripley's joke."

"Do you, indeed?" said Lady Charles. "It puzzles me why a clever girl like Olympia would have gone along with him."

"That's what her brother said."

"Regardless of her motives, your behavior has not been calculated to please," said her ladyship. "You were too busy fighting and drinking yourself sick to hurry after her and coax her back."

"Extenuating circumstances," Blackwood said.

Lady Charles's expression chilled a degree further. "I shall not attempt to imagine what they were. I shall merely tell you that, in her place, I should have been greatly disappointed in my suitor." She made a dismissive gesture. "Go to London. But do not be amazed if she tells you to look elsewhere for a duchess. Perhaps that's for the best."

"I won't look elsewhere!" Ashmont said. "Whatever's wrong, I'll mend it. I said I'd marry her and I meant it. And I will. And Ripley may kiss my — my aunt."

He made an angry bow and started away.

But he paused, and must have thought better of his behavior, because he turned back, looking sheepish. "Beg your pardon, Lady Charles. Please forgive me. That was . . . Didn't mean to . . . Well, you know. Feelings." He gave her his most angelic smile.

"I recommend you learn how to express your feelings in a more intelligent and agreeable manner," she said. "Because if you don't look out, someone who can do that will steal her away. If that happens, you won't get her back."

"Yes, Lady Charles. I'll do better from now on."

He took a proper leave of her this time, and walked to the door.

Blackwood started to follow, then paused and said, "And Alice, by the way? Is she about?"

"Oh, Ripley, what have you done?"

A brown, hairy face loomed over Ripley's and a gigantic tongue approached. "Get off!" he pushed the dog away.

Ripley's ears rang. His foot was demanding to be amputated. Rain dripped from the trees onto his face.

Lady Olympia sank to her knees beside him. Her lips were swollen and her hat and spectacles were crooked.

I hate me, he thought.

"Dash it, Olympia! Don't kneel in the wet!"

"What about you?" she said. "It'll be a miracle if you haven't broken something."

"Nothing's broken," he said. "I'm not made of glass. I'm not delicate, plague take it." He raised himself onto his elbows. "Stop coddling me. You ought to punch me in the face. Do you see? Do you see what happens? This is why it's against the rules for unmarried ladies to be alone with men. We can't be trusted. Most of us, we get near an attractive female, and our minds fall straight into the gutter."

She sat back on her haunches. She adjusted her spectacles.

"Attractive?" she said. "Are you serious?"

Olympia's heart, which had not stopped pounding, now beat harder.

She still hadn't recovered from the kiss. She wasn't sure she'd ever recover. She didn't know a kiss could be like that. She wasn't sure *kiss* was the correct word.

Then he'd taken a fit. And then . . . *Attractive,* he'd said. Meaning her.

"I told you last night," he said. "Pretty and shapely. Did you forget?"

"No." How could she? "But you're a rake, and rakes are undiscriminating."

"When I'm drunk, maybe I'm less discriminating," he said. "I'm not drunk now, though I wish I were."

"I'm pedantic and boring," she said. "And I wear spectacles."

"Do you think that makes the least difference to a man?"

"Yes."

"Maybe in a crowded ballroom," he said. "But when one is alone with a shapely, pretty girl, one doesn't care about her spectacles — or anything else she's wearing." He tried to get up. Wincing, he raised himself to a sitting position. And swore.

She put her hand on his shoulder. "Stay," she said. "Let me get a servant to help you. It'll be easier on your foot."

He looked blank. "Servant," he said.

"I realize my behavior yesterday might lead a person to believe I'm a henwit," she said. "However, in the normal course of events, I am practical and sensible to a fault. I did not come to your rescue unaccompanied. I've brought the coachman, John, and the footman Tom, and we've come in your aunt's landau."

"Good of you," he said. "More comfortable traveling to London in the carriage."

"I daresay, but not today," she said.

"Olympia, I have to get to London."

"So you've said, more than once," she said. "Let's stop and think, shall we? Let's look at this in a logical manner."

He lay back, letting his bare head fall on the wet leaves and moss and whatever insects were making their way through the woodland debris. He gazed up through the trees at the gloomy heavens. Then he turned his green gaze to her. "Yes, let's," he said.

"It's more than twenty miles to London," she said. "Camberley Place lies scarcely a third of that distance from here. From where you lie, do the skies look promising of anything but more rain? In the circumstances, do you not agree that the practical thing to do is to return to Lady Charles, rest for a day or two, then go to London? In a carriage."

He closed his eyes for a long moment. Then, "Right." He sat up. "Mind ran amok for a moment. But of course. Obvious. I can hardly take the carriage and leave you here. Very well. Get Tom." He grimaced. "You ought to have brought him with you in the first place."

"I was trying to keep up with Cato," she said. "I wasn't thinking about the servants."

"Not thinking," he said. "Lot of that going about. Ashmont shouldn't have let you out of his sight for a moment. Asking for trouble. And surprise, surprise. Here we are."

"I don't understand," she said.

"He's my *friend*," he said.

It dawned on her at last, as it should have done moments ago, that his post-kiss frenzy was all about male honor. A gentleman, even one of Their Dis-Graces, didn't poach on his friend's preserve. Women were property, and in the eyes of the world she still belonged to Ashmont.

For a moment — for the shattering moment of that kiss — she'd thought Ripley felt something for her. But it was simply the male urge to conquer women. His urge had got the better of him, that was all. He'd spoken the plain truth. There was a reason unwed ladies weren't supposed to be alone with men.

She'd never believed a man would exercise

his urges on her, but it had happened. Now she truly understood, not simply in her brain, why the rule existed. If she hadn't been so startled to feel what she'd felt when he pulled her against him, and if she hadn't somehow brought to mind Mama's explanation of marital intimacy and what Olympia had seen that day with the horses, she would have been swept along in the storm of feelings. And ruined.

She almost giggled, it was so outlandish: Lady Olympia Hightower, debauched in a moment of passion. Then she almost wept, because the odds were so very good that this had been the only moment of passion she'd ever experience.

She told herself not to get hysterical — he seemed to be doing enough of that for the two of them — and said, "Calm down. Only think how you've broadened my education."

"That's Ashmont's job!"

"Let us look on the bright side."

"Bright side. Good God."

"When he discovers I'm not completely ignorant, he'll realize he's had *competition*," she said. "This, if I believe you and your aunt, will make him more eager to please me. He doesn't need to know who's responsible, and I shan't tell him." She made herself smile brightly. "Do you know, Ripley,

I believe I owe you thanks."

Lady Charles's sermon had given Ashmont food for thought. Some matters, which had appeared clear enough at the adventure's outset, had since grown murky. After briefly considering the problem, he realized what his trouble was: He was thirsty.

Accordingly, he and Blackwood stopped at the Talbot Inn. Had they not done this, they would have passed the landau on the road, going in the opposite direction. Had the roof of the landau not been put up against the rain, they would have seen their quarry, and their quarry would have seen them, and matters would have turned out altogether differently.

But that wasn't what happened. What happened was, idly looking out of the window, they saw a somewhat elderly landau traveling in the direction from which they'd come. Blackwood made a jocular remark about the carriage's sedate pace.

That was as much as they noticed because the rain started again, with a fury, and the view from the window became a blur. Turning away from it, Ashmont said, "What do you reckon? Ought I to storm the castle immediately when I get to London? Go straight to Gonerby House to win the lady fair and keep her won, this time? Lady C seemed to deplore my lack of derring-do."

"After the lady fair has traveled four or five hours, and scarcely had time to catch her breath, let alone rest from the journey?" Blackwood said. "Not to mention, do you suppose you'll make the best impression on her — you with the fresh stinker and wearing yesterday's clothes and, in short, not looking as pretty as usual?"

Ashmont gingerly touched his bruised eye. "Probably not," he said. "Tomorrow, then."

Chapter 11

"You let them go," Ripley said to his aunt. "They were here and you let them go."

They'd entered the Great Hall moments ago and learned of Ashmont and Blackwood's visit.

Ripley stood, bracing himself on the arm of a settee near the fireplace. He gazed up at the Elizabethan artifacts adorning the walls and wondered why the Fates had decided to torment him the instant he returned to England.

"You had better sit down," Aunt Julia said. "You're as white as a sheet."

"Do sit down," Olympia said. "Do try to be a trifle less stupidly obstinate."

Ripley sank onto the settee. He wanted to lie down. And be unconscious. His leg pained him, but not half so much as the thoughts crashing about in his head. He wasn't used to so much thinking. No wonder he felt so weary.

"I suspect you'll recover more quickly if you make use of your uncle's invalid chair," his aunt said.

"An invalid chair! Why not feed me pap as well?"

"Invalid chairs have footboards," Olympia said.

Ripley gazed up at the ceiling.

"To support the foot," she went on.

Visions appeared in his mind of fat, gouty invalids, rolling about in their chairs at Bath. How many satirical prints like that had he seen? And laughed at?

"If you let the injured foot rest in that way, duke, it will get better much more quickly."

"An invalid chair," he said. *Somebody shoot me now,* he thought.

"How art the mighty fallen," said his aunt.

He looked at her. "Very well, gloat. I've fallen, more than once. I feel like the devil. Lady Olympia was right. You were right. I should never have set out today. I should have been here when Ashmont and Blackwood arrived."

"But you weren't," said Aunt Julia. "And I acted as I deemed best. Perhaps I acted in anger, but it's done."

"Angry about what? Didn't you agree with me that Ashmont would come for Olympia?"

"I was displeased with his attitude, not to mention his appearance," his aunt said. "Neither was calculated to reassure an uneasy young lady. Instead, he seemed to be advertising his thoughtlessness, carelessness, and recklessness."

"Oh, he doesn't need to advertise," Olympia said. "I had no illusions, I promise you."

"You ought to have done," Aunt Julia said. "You ought to have had at least a few hopes and dreams on your wedding day. More important, he ought not to take you for granted. It did not seem to me today as though he'd studied to please you. Yet by now he must have realized that your disappearance was not a prank or a joke, and he has fences to mend."

"His Grace with the Angel Face must have looked very bad, indeed, to throw you into such a pother," Ripley said.

Had he been here, he might have thrown Ashmont across the room. What the devil was wrong with the man, making such a poor show when he might so easily have made a good one? Was he *trying* to drive Olympia further away? Or was he so conceited he thought he was always irresistible?

"He looked and smelled bad and acted worse," his aunt said. "I hauled him over the coals, and I hope I gave him something to think about. Most assuredly, he gave me something to think about. The pair of them did. I didn't like running the risk of their meeting Lady Olympia on the road and her having to fend for herself with that pair of blockheads. But she is a young woman of strong intelligence and will. And I did reckon long odds against the encounter. It seemed to me far more probable those two rakehells would make a detour to a race or a boxing match or wait out the rain in a tavern."

She turned to Olympia. "I've been out of touch for three years and more, ever since Charles fell ill. I always used to see Hugh and his friends as wild boys, and I made allowances, as I told you. But it dawned on me today that they're men, and it's well past time they took stock of themselves. In short, I cannot in good conscience hurry you back to your intended. You are welcome to stay as long as you like, my dear. When you wish to return to London, only say the word, and I shall accompany you."

She stalked out of the Great Hall, her footsteps echoing on the ancient oak floor.

Ashmont had come, after all, as Lady Charles and Ripley had insisted he would. Now he was gone.

A part of Olympia wanted to jump up and down with frustration. Another part wanted to jump up and down with joy.

This state of mind being unacceptable, she set about organizing and cataloguing her disorderly feelings about the two men in her life.

What Ashmont looked or smelled like or what his attitude was didn't especially trouble her. Lady Charles's comments in this regard were not revelatory. They were consistent with what Olympia had expected when she'd agreed to marry him.

She had no illusions. How could she have them? She'd been out in Society long enough, had heard and seen and read enough, to understand what manner of man he was. Still, no matter what he looked, smelled, or acted like, he was the *Duke* of Ashmont.

Had she stayed at Camberley Place today instead of chasing Ripley, she would have let Ashmont take her back to London and make her his duchess. What choice had she? If she'd returned with him, all her mad actions of yesterday wouldn't count anymore. Society would shrug off the excitement. It would merely be one more prank in Their Dis-Graces' lengthy repertoire. Above all, Mama and Papa and the boys wouldn't suffer for what Olympia had done.

But if she had stayed at Camberley Place, Ripley would have gone on to London and worsened his injury . . . and the kiss wouldn't have happened, and all she'd ever know of passion would be what her imagination painted. That, she now knew, fell far short of reality.

As Lady Charles made her irate exit, Olympia came back to the moment, and to the facts of her life: improvident parents and their unprovided-for sons.

Look on the bright side, she told herself.

The Duke of Ashmont still wanted to marry her, apparently.

She had experienced passion.

All she had to do now was try to keep Ashmont from changing his mind, although the evidence pointed to his being too obstinate and possessive to do so.

As to kissing Ripley, she would not let her conscience trouble her overmuch. Compared to what Ashmont had done over the past decade, and would no doubt continue to do after he was wed, her moment of passion was nothing. Except to her.

Besides, for all she knew — which, in this case, was nothing — any handsome, experienced young man could, under the right circumstances, arouse a similar ardor.

She hurried after her hostess. "Lady Charles, I do beg your pardon," she said. "I ought to have said —"

"My dear, after such trials, I wonder you can speak anything but gibberish," said the lady, slowing her pace. "Those three are the outside of enough. Wherever he and Blackwood stopped for the night, Ashmont might have had the servants clean his clothes. He ought to have shaved. Perhaps he assumed it would seem as though he was too eager to see you to bother with niceties of dress. However, if this were the case, one would think he'd have been too eager to see you to bother with fighting and drinking."

"So one would think, but men are not always logical."

They had reached the bottom of the staircase. Lady Charles stopped and patted Olympia's arm. "Make him work, my dear," the lady said. "Make him pay attention and make an effort. He needs more management than I had supposed, though I don't doubt you are capable."

Olympia had no choice but to be capable. She said, "In the circumstances, I should be a great fool not to accept your kind offer and remain where I am, at least for a day or two."

"Good. It will do him no harm to stew a

bit." Lady Charles started up the stairs.

"I know you know best about him," Olympia said.

"They were the sons I never had," the lady said. "Unfortunately, they weren't actually my sons, and I could exert only so much influence. I might as well tell you, since it's no great secret, though it happened so long ago that few remember. Ashmont's father fell into severe melancholia after his wife's death, and would have nothing to do with him. Blackwood's father was a rigid martinet who did nothing but find fault with him. Ripley's father suffered some sort of brain fever that left him irrational: He believed he was completely impoverished, and everybody was trying to steal from him. This house became their refuge. That is why I know them so well."

Olympia stood stock-still. "I didn't know."

Lady Charles paused and turned to her. "They all inherited too young. But they're grown men now, and I'm done making excuses. I understand that you acted on impulse. You felt panicky, I don't doubt." She smiled a little. "The brandy gave you a push, the dose of courage or recklessness or whatever it was you needed to act. Yet running away may have been the wisest thing you could have done. You need time to reflect and plan, away from the influence of your family and that stupid boy who wants to marry you. Camberley Place is the right place for calm reflection."

And this lady was the right guide, Olympia saw. Mama and the aunts were loving, but they did not have Lady Charles's intellect or her grasp of human nature.

In a few words, she'd given Olympia valuable insight. And eased her conscience a little.

"Thank you," Olympia said. "I do need to stay. And think. And I had better write some long-overdue letters. It's well past time the duke heard from me. I do believe, after all, it would be best we discuss matters directly with each other."

Lady Charles regarded her for a moment. "Yes, that would be best."

Ashmont House, London, that evening

The Duke of Ashmont had been dressing to go out when the two letters arrived, express, from Surrey.

Ripley's missive, typically, consisted of one line: *For God's sake, come and get her.*

The other was from Lady Olympia. Being thicker by several closely written pages, it was rather more daunting. This was Ashmont's second time reading it. He sat at his dressing table, clutching his head and disarranging the artfully windblown coiffure his valet had created.

The duke was debating whether to give the letter a third try or summon Blackwood for help when his valet hurried in and said, "Lord Frederick is here, Your Grace."

Ashmont bolted up from his chair and debated a quick exit via the window. "Tell him I'm not at home."

"Ah, but you are, Lucius," came his uncle's cheerful voice.

The valet quickly got out of the way of the voice's owner. When Lord Frederick made a small dismissive gesture, the servant went out of the room, gently closing the door after himself.

"I heard you'd returned," said his lordship.

Ashmont longingly eyed the decanter standing on a small table by the fireplace. The trouble was, if he poured himself a drink, he'd have to offer one to his uncle, and that would encourage him to stay.

"Only a few hours ago," he said. "You've wondrous good ears if you heard it already. I hardly knew it myself."

"You've returned without the future Duchess of Ashmont," said Uncle Fred.

"Erm . . . yes. As to that." Ashmont

glanced at the letter. "A trifle complicated. Comedy of errors, as Lady Charles said."

For an instant, Lord Frederick's customary composure disintegrated and a haunted look came into his blue eyes. But it was gone almost as soon as it had come, and he reverted to his usual unflappable self.

"You have been to Camberley Place," he said. He picked a bit of fluff from his coat sleeve.

Once Uncle Fred was there, he wasn't to be got rid of by any means until he was good and ready to go. Since he wouldn't be good and ready until he'd scraped Ashmont's brain clean, the duke briefly described the previous day's search for Ripley and Lady Olympia as well as today's visit to Lady Charles Ancaster.

As Ashmont came to the end of that part of the tale, he saw his uncle's attention shift to the dressing table, where the letter lay, its pages spread out, in plain view of all the world — or rather, of busybody, all-seeing, all-knowing uncles.

The duke moved casually to the dressing table to block his relative's view of the missive.

Too late.

"That looks like Lady Olympia's hand," his uncle said.

"Does it?"

"I should know it anywhere," Lord Frederick said. "Quite distinctive. We corresponded regarding a fifteenth-century volume. Boethius's *De Consolatione Philosophiae,* I believe it was. It would appear that she is speaking or, rather, writing to you. I take that as a promising sign."

"Erm, yes. The thing is, she's still at Camberley Place."

"So I deduced when I learned you'd received two letters, express, from Surrey," Lord Frederick said.

Ashmont didn't ask how or where his uncle learned it. Obviously, he had spies everywhere. More than likely, a few resided under Ashmont's roof. His uncle had been his guardian. Furthermore, the servants were afraid of him. Few outsiders would understand how this could be, for a milder-looking older gentleman with a more innocent countenance was not to be found in all of London or, possibly, all of Great Britain.

"Yes, it's rather complicated," Ashmont said. "You see . . ." He frowned. "That is, I think I've got the gist of it, but bless the girl, she uses a deuced lot of words."

"And, if it is not too private a matter, the gist of it is . . . ?"

"She was drunk," Ashmont said. "She'd taken brandy for her bridal nerves, you see. Only it didn't calm her, and so she bolted."

Lord Frederick's lip twitched. "Ah."

"Ripley tried to bring her back, but when she wouldn't be brought back, he made himself her bodyguard. Eventually he got her safe with his aunt, but because of her — Olympia, that is — he had an accident, and she feels —" He picked up the letter, turned over a page and read, tracing the lines with his finger, " 'obliged to stay at Camberley Place, to prevent his making his injury worse, his being a male and possessing a morbid aversion to good sense.' But don't you know, sir, Lady Charles didn't mention the accident. Odd, isn't it?"

The haunted look flickered briefly in his lordship's face, then vanished. "Not at all," he said. "Her ladyship can be inscrutable. A useful quality in managing her spouse, among others."

"Not the least use to me," Ashmont said. "But never mind all that. She — Olympia, I mean, offers to let me off the hook."

"Hmm."

"She says, 'No reasonable person would expect you to marry me now.' But I'm not reasonable, dammit!" Being unreasonable, he found himself too baffled and upset to care whether Lord Frederick stayed until Doomsday.

Ashmont marched to the decanter, filled two glasses, and handed one to his uncle.

"I don't mind telling you, I don't understand," the duke said. "Of all the damned things. If only we'd arrived later, or stayed longer, cold welcome or not, Olympia and I could have settled matters then and there." He drank. "Now I've got to go back to Camberley Place because Olympia thinks I care what anybody says. I said I'd marry her, didn't I? Does she think I'd go back on my word, because she had a fit of the blue devils or megrims or some such and ran?"

"In brief, it wasn't Ripley's joke, after all," said Uncle Fred thoughtfully.

"No, he only meant to unload her on a female relative, then come back and tell me where to collect her. But things kept going wrong. Then he went and broke his arm or something." He glanced down at the letter. "No, it was to do with his foot, but she uses words of twenty syllables to explain it. 'Incapacitated,' she says. And *he* says —"

"What Ripley says doesn't signify," said Lord Frederick. "You are not going to Camberley Place. This is a more delicate situation than you seem to recognize, which does not surprise me, considering the kinds of women with whom you usually associate. I cannot be surprised at your failing to know how to behave with a respectable girl."

"You said she'd never have me, but she said yes."

"And you didn't have the sense to hold on to her."

"I didn't let her go. She —"

"Have you any idea what you've got? Do you imagine women like that are everywhere, only waiting patiently for you to come to your senses? That young lady possesses the intelligence and strength of character to become a settling influence, which you badly need."

"Yes, I know she —"

"You think you know, but you don't. You are throwing away what promises to be your one and only chance of true happiness. Your father couldn't help what happened to your mother. But at least he had those years with her. You'll have *nothing*. You'll look back, years hence, and regret."

If this was the voice of experience speaking, Ashmont failed to hear it, in the same way he failed to notice the untypical emotion in that voice.

"Why does everybody blame me?" he said. "I wooed her, didn't I? You said I'd be wasting my time. She'd never have me, you said.

She was too intelligent, you said. But —"

"You couldn't get her to say 'I will,' could you?" said his uncle. "And if you think you're in no wise to blame, I invite you to take a look at yourself. Even bathed, shaved, and dressed in fresh clothes, you look villainous. Worse than a sailor after three days' shore leave. No, I do sailors a disservice."

"I was in a fight!"

"You're always in a fight. This time it shows. You can't simply explode upon a young woman who is, I don't doubt, in a highly agitated and confused state."

"I wasn't going to explode!"

"Take a long, hard look in the mirror, Lucius," said his uncle. "If she shied before, if she had doubts about your character or anxiety about your behavior, do you think she'll throw herself in your arms now?"

Ashmont clenched his hands.

"Do you mean to hit me?" his uncle said mildly.

"This is intolerable," Ashmont said. "You can't expect me to stay here, doing nothing."

"Learn to tolerate," Uncle Fred said. "I expect you to remain in London until you're more presentable in body and mind. I shall go and talk to her."

Ashmont unclenched his hands and

stalked to the window and looked out. "While I remain, so that every Tom, Dick, and Harry who fancies himself a humorist can twit me, asking where my bride's got to. And while the satirists draw my image with cuckold horns."

"You seem not to realize that you've been a joke for some time now."

Ashmont's face darkened, and he turned sharply away from the window.

"You can fight everybody who finds your antics amusing," his uncle said, "or you can show a little dignity and maturity for once, and laugh. If you can't devise an amusing retort to the mockers, ask Blackwood to compose one for you. But if you want to do something useful, write a letter to Lady Olympia, declining her offer to release you. Make it a *good* letter. On second thought, I had better dictate it."

Friday 14 June

The long-absent sun had finally deigned to send its beams through the windows of Camberley Place's east wing when the Duke of Ripley, swearing, maneuvered a mechanical chair out of the study and into the library.

Lord Charles had built the study along an outward-facing wall within the library, close to its southern end. Next to it, a narrow passage led to the staircase to the Long Gallery, directly above. Even with a part given over to the study, there remained a library extending some one hundred feet, nearly the full length of this wing of the house. It held a great many more obstacles, though, in the way of tables, chairs, footstools, and sets of steps than did the gallery above. Being above, however, the Long Gallery was barred to Ripley.

His feet rested on the raised footboard and his hands clutched the handles that extended from the chair's arms. Turning the handles — alone or together — moved the chair in various directions. The trick was remembering which combination of turns in which direction moved the chair which way.

After jerking himself about, right, left, and in a circle, he grasped both handles and turned both toward himself.

The chair shot backward, and he heard a little shriek behind him. Yanking the handles the other way, he darted forward. With a growl of frustration, he turned both handles right, and the chair turned right, and right again.

He heard footsteps approach.

"Perhaps, duke, you might wish to read

the instructions," said Lady Olympia.

He was aware of the hairs at the back of his neck rising at the sound of her voice. "No," he said. "If my grandmother could steer this thing, I certainly can."

She came closer and walked around him. "This doesn't look like any invalid chair I've ever seen."

"They were all the rage at one time," he said. "Don't know how many were made. Merlin's Mechanical Chair." He patted the worn handle. "Uncle Charles often talked about visiting Merlin's Mechanical Museum in Princes Street. He bought this for my grandmother."

She crouched to study the arrangement of metal rods connected to the wheels. "This is rather more intricate than what one usually sees."

She wore another of his aunt's dresses, plain and grey, except for the white neckerchief tied about her throat. The sleeves were narrow, boasting only a small pouf at the top of the arm. The bodice was equally severe. Like a coat, the thing buttoned from neck to hem. Though this one fit better than the one she'd worn yesterday, it didn't fit as it ought.

Her thick brown hair was better. It had been put up simply, with a few coils at the back of her head, and some curls framing her face.

He wanted to lean over to inhale the scent of her hair, the fresh scent he remembered too well. He sat straight and gazed straight ahead over the tops of his shoes.

"It's meant to allow the invalid more independence of movement," he said. "My grandmother took herself over lawn and gravel and every sort of surface. I believe there was some sort of joking theory about attaching a steam engine to it, to move individuals hither and yon without manual or animal labor. She'd still be racketing about in it, I daresay, if she hadn't succumbed to a vicious fever."

The same fever had, he'd been told, left his father a shockingly changed man. Though Ripley had been ten years old at the time, he barely remembered the person his father had been before, the witty, charming fellow his mother spoke of sometimes, the gentleman who'd won her heart. The miserable miser had crushed all happier memories.

"Uncle Charles must have been chagrined to have to use it himself," he said. "As I am chagrined. But there's no help for it. The ladies of this house scold me deaf and witless if I try to walk. And with my bad foot,

I'm not fast enough to outrun them."

She stood up and smoothed her skirts. "Such a tragic, tortured life you live."

"I never thought I'd see the day I'd be henpecked and rolling about in an invalid chair. But my time has come, it seems. I feel a touch of gout coming on. Maybe I'll wear a wig and false teeth."

She straightened her spectacles, though they were perfectly straight. "And so many have believed you'd never live long enough to suffer from gout or need a wig and false teeth."

"Did your ladyship only come here to mock my infirmity or had you another ulterior motive?"

She set her hands on her hips and surveyed the library. "Your aunt happened to mention that Lord Charles's more recent acquisitions were never entered in the library records. They're in a heap somewhere in this room. I offered to make myself useful."

Ripley turned the handles of the chair and it began to roll backward. "Down here."

"Do you have to do it the hard way?" she said.

"It's boring the other way."

"Or maybe you don't know how to make that thing go forward."

"Of course I do. Nothing to it." He turned the winches and the chair began to go in circles. He heard something thump onto the rug.

"For heavens' sake, Ripley, you're knocking books off — look out for the footstool!"

He dodged the footstool, but turned the handles too quickly, because the chair started to spin, and she cried, "Not the vase!" and jumped to catch it at the same time he spun the opposite way. She stumbled and fell across the chair . . . over his lap . . . vase in her hands and arse upward.

For one endless moment, neither of them moved. He was acutely aware of her body's warmth and the pomatum's scent rising from her hair. His head dipped downward and he inhaled, closing his eyes.

"It's heavy," came her muffled voice.

He lifted his head, cursing himself.

"If you can keep this thing perfectly still," she said, "I can set the vase down on the floor."

"I'm not sure about 'perfectly still,' " he said. His nether regions were alert to the female body in close proximity. He could feel her breast against his arm.

"Can you take it?" she said.

"What?"

"The vase. Can you take it from me?"

321

He reached cautiously with one hand. The chair rolled backward.

"Put on the brake," she said.

"I'm not sure it has a brake," he said.

"Don't be an idiot," she said. "Of course it does."

It was hard not to be an idiot when one had a shapely woman more or less in one's lap and one did not happen to be remotely saintlike.

"It's on your right," she said. "On the curving bit the arm's attached to. The smaller rod. You had to lift it to allow the chair to move."

"Ah, yes. Forgot." He pushed down the rod and locked the wheels.

She carefully set down the vase. This wasn't as easy as one would think. She had to shift her body from an awkward position to one not much less awkward. Though it would be wiser to look elsewhere — upward for instance — he wasn't wise. His gaze became riveted on her bottom, insufficiently hidden under a too-thin petticoat. Moving in an unbearably lascivious manner, it was mere inches from the hand holding the rod.

He gripped the rod more tightly.

She began to climb off him, cautiously turning to face away.

Too cautiously, because every small move

set off powerful sensations in his breeding parts, which cared nothing for friends, let alone propriety. All they cared about was the curving feminine body moving against his arms and chest and in his lap. His heart rate shot up and other sensations shot through him. His hand, gripping the rod so tightly, jerked it upward.

The chair began rolling, swiftly, toward the windows.

"Ripley, stop playing!"

"Stop wriggling."

"I'm trying to get off without hurting your foot. Or falling on my head. Stop the chair before we go through the window!"

He pulled on the handles and the chair spun rightward.

She was scrambling to get off him, and the chair kept moving because of her movement. "Stop it, Ripley."

"I can't get hold of the rod," he said. "Your skirt's in the way." Also her fine bottom, now resting against his stomach, was in the way of something. Clear thinking, absolutely.

She wriggled some more, and got herself awkwardly arranged with her bottom in his lap and her legs hanging over his knees. "Stop it so I can get off, will you?" she said.

He stopped the chair. He didn't want to.

He told himself to behave, but that went against years of doing the opposite. He looked down the long, obstacle-ridden library and something in his mind shifted.

As she cautiously began to get off his lap, he turned the handles.

The chair started moving again. She reached for the rod to stop the wheels, but his thigh was in her way. She grabbed his right hand, trying to turn the handle, but he held on, immovable.

She bit her lip. Her face was flushed and her breath was coming faster and her spectacles had tipped to one side.

He pulled the handles and the chair rolled forward.

She grabbed his arm. "Ripley!"

"After a false start, they're off, in good style!" he said. "Ripley in front, jockey Lady O holding on for dear life. But Chair and Other Chair follow close behind. Table inches up round the clump, but Ripley remains in the lead. The steed's speed is phenomenal!"

He went on as though shouting race proceedings to an eager crowd behind a peephole, while he turned both handles, and the chair rolled swiftly toward the southern end of the library.

"Ripley!"

He narrowly missed a footstool and rolled on. "Will Ripley crash into the chest King James I gave somebody who's been dead some hundreds of years? But no, clever Ripley misses by an inch, and now heads down the course to King Charles II's writing desk —"

"Left, you lunatic!" she cried. "Left!"

He made a sharp left, then more sharp turns, this way and that, going backward and in circles and zigzags, narrating all the while. He felt her back shaking against him, then it broke from her: a peal of laughter.

The world changed and brightened, and his heart lifted. He laughed, too.

"Here's a tricky turn," he said. "Will Ripley make it, or lose his footing — his wheeling — and pitch his rider onto the turf?"

"Left!" she ordered, laughing. "Sharp left. Now right. Faster, Ripley. Red Footstool is gaining on us. Watch out! Vase trying to break onto course. Don't be thrown off stride. That's the way! Faster, Ripley!" She pretended to whip his knees, and he laughed so hard he nearly toppled them both out of the chair.

On and on it went, up one side of the library, and down another, narrowly missing a king's ransom in ancient furnishings.

They never saw the door open or the face peering in. They didn't see the door close, quickly and quietly, as the mechanical chair rolled that way.

On and on the mad race went, until Ripley and his rider were both laughing too hard to do more. Then at last he let the chair roll to a stop among a tangled heap of rugs, not far from the books to which he'd meant to lead her.

"And here, at the finish line, the winner's trophy: a great heap of moldy old books," he said.

She looked over at the books piled on a large table, then up at him. Her face was flushed and her hair was coming undone.

"The brake," she said breathlessly. "Lock the wheels. As a jockey, I should be mortified to fall off my mount at the race's end."

He fumbled with the rod, unable to concentrate.

She grabbed his hand. "Really, it's not that complicated," she said.

He held her hand, his fingers closing around hers, then twining with hers. He drew her closer.

His breath came hard. His chest rose and fell. Hers, too. Her eyes were blue now, and bright as stars. Traces of laughter lingered in them, though her smile was fading. The sound of her laughter, that beautiful sound, echoed in his head.

"You win," he said. He bent his head and kissed her.

CHAPTER 12

The instant he'd taken her hand, Olympia knew what was coming. She could have escaped so easily. She didn't even try.

When he kissed her, she held tightly to his hand, pressed between them, against his chest. She could feel their hearts beating, so fast. Then he drew his hand away to cup her face while he kissed her, and she brought her arms up around his neck.

No thinking involved. Instinct. Need. That was enough. She answered the kiss the way he'd taught her and the way her heart urged her to do. He wrapped his arms about her, and her pounding heart felt so light, like a bird's, fluttering madly as it soared.

The kiss was wrong. A part of her knew this. But a stronger part of her knew she'd never find this feeling again. It would never again be like this. She was infatuated and foolish, yes. She knew that. She knew, too, that one had only one chance in a lifetime for a first infatuation. This was hers.

The kiss deepened instantly and, with the first full taste of him, reason and strength of will melted away, along with her muscles. She tasted the wickedness of his mouth and his tongue, and the wickedness raced through her like strong drink, stronger than the brandy that had set her on this path. It made her care for nothing but what she felt at this moment: the warmth of his body, the way he cradled her, the feel of his strong arms about her, the heat that was different from body warmth, and the pull of wanting more of whatever this was.

He gave her more, his hands moving over her shoulders and back, down her arms, as though he was discovering and memorizing her. He slid his mouth to her cheek and jaw and throat, making a trail of kisses, hot and sweet. She let out a little moan of pleasure and tried to follow his lead, touching, kissing. She heard the sound he made, deep in his throat, an animal sound that made her shiver. Then he was moving his hands all over her, over her breasts and waist and hips, and she grew hotly impatient.

No thinking, none at all. The mind couldn't swim against the flood of sensation. Thought ebbed to nothing while her body, her very being, came tautly alive. She moved under his touch instinctively, the way a cat or dog moved to be stroked and petted. No self-consciousness, because the pleasure and wanting and so many other feelings had all the power.

She was aware of his hand moving down along her leg. She heard the rustle of muslin and felt air touching her stocking where before her petticoat had touched it. She felt his hand, pulling up her dress, then resting on her knee for a moment before sliding over her stocking and up above her garter to her bare thigh. She trembled at the touch, at the intimacy of it. She knew this intimacy was wrong but she didn't care. She couldn't get enough of the feelings and the closeness. She wanted and wanted and didn't know what it was she wanted, beyond knowing she wanted him, and that the feeling, the wanting, was like starvation.

His hand, his hand. Warm, possessive, it slid over the bare flesh of her thigh. She tried to push herself closer, as though she could climb inside him, inside *it,* whatever this experience was, this wild race of feelings.

His hand stilled and his mouth came away from her neck and he said something she couldn't make out, his voice was so low and thick.

Then he said, more clearly, "Get off, dammit. I *told* you I can't be trusted."

Lady Olympia climbed off him, not in the most graceful manner. The chair wobbled a little, but the wheels had caught among the rugs and couldn't go far. That wasn't why she moved so awkwardly. Her lack of grace was Ripley's doing.

She was an innocent, and he'd taken advantage of her ignorance and got her stirred up. Not as badly as he'd stirred up himself, but enough to disorganize her immense brain, where he didn't doubt she kept everything neatly catalogued by subject.

Once she was on her feet, she shakily smoothed her skirt and pulled the dress's bodice fully round to the front. She straightened her spectacles and brushed distractedly at her hair with the back of her hand.

While she put herself to rights, he fought the urge to put her to not-rights.

I hate me, he thought. He concentrated on easing the chair out from the bunched-up rugs while he tried to calm himself.

"I don't care what my aunt says or what you say," he said. "The sooner you get back to London — or I do — the sooner we're separated, in other words, the better. I'm no

331

good at self-denial. I loathe it."

He'd given it up altogether after his father died. He'd practiced too much of it before then — though it wasn't exactly *self*-denial, when his mentally unbalanced father held the purse strings and all the other strings controlling his life.

She folded her hands at her waist and regarded him as she might have regarded a book whose category eluded her. "Do you not mean self-control?" she said.

"I mean I'm not good at not getting what I want. Which is deuced awkward, do you see — on account of your being *my best friend's bride-to-be*!"

She blinked. "It's awkward, I daresay."

"Whatever else Ashmont assigned me to do, it wasn't practicing for the wedding night."

"Probably not," she said.

"Definitely not," he said.

"Very well." Her color rose. "You seem to imply I'm what you want."

"Imply? Isn't it obvious?"

A pause.

"In that case, maybe you ought to be the one to marry me," she said.

For a moment, Ripley's mind felt like a clockwork mechanism after a spring had sprung loose.

"I need to marry a duke," she said. "That is to say, a man of rank with a large income. It would be the ideal solution."

Posture stiff, she explained: Her parents were loving spendthrifts who never thought about the future and the little they'd leave for their eldest son and heir, not to mention the nothing they'd leave for the five other boys. Meanwhile, her father wasted absurd sums of money on Seasons for her, with the ever-optimistic view of getting her married. Naturally, when Ashmont had offered for her, she had viewed him as a deus ex machina.

Ripley was still trying to digest her suggesting he marry her. The business about her family wasn't news. He'd already caught on to that, and once he'd spent some time with her, he'd understood that she couldn't have accepted Ashmont for romantic or ambitious reasons. All the same, her hard-headed view of her situation, combined with what amounted to a marriage proposal, had him at sea.

Collecting his wits, he said, "In short, being a solvent duke, I'd do as well as Ashmont."

"Or as badly. But I'm more used to you now."

Among other things, she must have grown

used to his taking advantage of every opportunity to debauch her. True, she hadn't discouraged him. True, she'd cooperated fully. Not that he of all men regarded this as a character flaw. On the contrary, he liked her enthusiasm. Very much. Ashmont would, too. What Ashmont wouldn't like was his best friend eliciting the enthusiasm.

"Have you been at the brandy again?" Ripley said. "Were you not listening? I can't steal my best friend's affianced bride. I can't seduce, bed, or wed her. It simply isn't done."

She adjusted her spectacles, though they didn't need adjusting. Her hair, yes, but he wasn't about to touch that with a barge pole. He eased the mechanical chair back. Out of arm's reach.

"Ah, yes, a gentleman's honor," she said. "But I'm not a gentleman. I need to be practical."

He didn't want her to be practical. He didn't feel practical in any way. He was still dizzy from what had passed between them. Not that it was so very much, really. A heated embrace and some naughtiness, true. But he'd only fondled, and hadn't really got to the good bits . . . and it was past time to stop thinking about that.

"The fact is, I'm not getting any younger,"

she was saying.

"Neither is Mends," he said.

"I didn't mention him," she said.

"I know he's in the back of your mind. Another practical solution, in case the ducal one doesn't work out."

"I do not understand why you keep bringing up Lord Mends," she said.

"I've seen him with you. The way he looks at you. It's disgusting, at his age." More than once in the past, Ripley had wanted to cross a ballroom, pick the fellow up, and put him out on the street, far away from her.

He realized now that, had Mends been a younger man, Ripley might have done something like it, but more violently. Why hadn't he ever crossed a ballroom to her? Had he assumed she'd always be there, waiting, until he was good and ready for a respectable girl?

He'd waited too long, and Ashmont had got there first, and there was nothing to be done.

"He's besotted with my cataloguing theories and the prospect of putting his library in order for free," she was saying.

"What you don't know about men would fill a library," he said. "Promise me you won't marry *him*. If I hear of such an atrocity in the works —"

"I trust I won't have to resort to Lord Mends, though I make no promises," she said. "At this point, it would be amazing if he still wanted me."

"It wouldn't be amazing at all."

Not that Ripley would ever let it happen. She would never have to resort to Mends or anybody else.

"If you say so. But first things first. Since you are too honorable, I shall make Ashmont marry me. In my letter, I did say he might consider himself released from our engagement but —"

"He won't." Curse him.

"I believe you're right," she said. "I was about to say that I believe he's too possessive and obstinate to give up. However, if it turns out he's entertaining doubts, I believe I can bring him round. Now that you've given me so much useful information about men, I have specific ideas as to how to go about it."

Yes, indeed. Ripley had given her heaps of ideas, curse him, too.

"He won't entertain doubts," he said tightly. "You don't understand at all. The night before the wedding? Ashmont could talk about nothing but you and getting married. Nobody else could get a word in edgeways. I've never seen him like that before, about a woman."

Her eyes, grey now, filled. She blinked hard. "Then it puzzles me," she said, her voice choked, "why he'd get so drunk on his wedding day."

Not to mention the night before.

"Maybe he was nervous," Ripley said. "Maybe you weren't the only one. But he wasn't the one who bolted, was he?"

She looked for a moment as though he'd struck her. He wished she'd strike him, preferably with one of the massive tomes near at hand.

Then her eyes sparked. She lifted her chin and said, "What had he to lose? When a woman weds, she becomes her husband's property. She's under his control. He has all the power. If he makes her wretched, what recourse has she? But Ashmont? You? Blackwood? A different story altogether. You three can go on doing what you did before you were wed, and no one will turn a hair. Marriage makes virtually no difference to men. For women, it can be the end of the world."

Power and control. Ripley knew what it was like to be the one who had neither. He knew what it was like to be at the mercy of an unpredictable man. For women, it was worse by far.

But Ashmont wasn't remotely like the late, mad, sixth Duke of Ripley.

"You'll be a duchess," Ripley said. "Dammit, Olympia, you can manage Ashmont. If you can make me forget my loyalties, do you imagine you can't do as you like with him?"

"But I don't —" She broke off, her brow knitting. Then she adjusted her spectacles. "You have a point."

"I should hope so."

"If you can lose control so easily, he can, too," she said. "More easily, I suspect, since all I've observed tells me he's quick to anger and fight, and the smallest thing will set him off. The quantity of alcohol he consumes may have something to do with that. Well, we'll see. I shall look for ways to channel his energies in more positive directions." She nodded. "Yes, that's promising. I knew there was a bright side. There always is." She beamed at him. "Thank you, Ripley."

He realized he was clutching the handles of the mechanical chair so tightly that the wheels were fighting the rod locking them. He loosened his grip.

"My pleasure," he said. "So glad I could be of service. I'll leave you to your books. I believe I'll take a roll through the garden."

■ ■ ■ ■

Olympia kept up the smile while she moved to the door to open it for him. She kept smiling while he maneuvered the chair out of the library and onto the graveled walkway. She closed the door.

Then and only then did her smile fade. Then and only then did her throat close up and her mouth tremble and her eyes fill. This time she let the tears fall. Not for long, though.

"Don't be maudlin," she told herself. She found her handkerchief and dried her eyes.

Self-pity was out of the question. She had no illusions when it came to men. She'd always known — after the first few Seasons, at any rate — that her marriage, if she could somehow get one, would not be a romantic one.

Even while knowing the odds were against her, she'd tried a moment ago for something more than a practical business arrangement. At least she'd tried.

But Ripley was right: Men cuckolded other men all the time, and Society shrugged, usually laughing at the cuckold.

Stealing one's best friend's affianced bride, though, was another kettle of fish.

Dishonorable. At least as bad as cheating at cards.

Furthermore, she didn't want to be the one who destroyed a lifelong friendship, one of the two true friendships Ashmont had. She didn't wish him ill. She didn't want to hurt him.

But he wasn't the one who bolted, was he?

She winced. She had run away. She'd acted unkindly. She was ashamed.

All the same, she couldn't make herself stop hoping for a different ending to her story.

"You ought to know better," she muttered. "You *know* what this is: You've become infatuated with a rake." The way thousands of other women did. Even clever ones. People wrote books and plays about it. They'd done so for centuries. She didn't doubt explorers would find hieroglyphs in Egypt telling the same story.

Very well. She'd succumbed. She'd simply have to un-succumb. She had one tried-and-true way to cope with life's setbacks.

She squared her shoulders and moved to the heap of books. She began to sort. History here. Philosophy here. Ah, and here was the dramatic poetry, Congreve and Dekker and Middleton and Schiller and Sheridan. And Shakespeare, of course, who had written of what she felt, as he'd written of the infinite variety of human feelings and behavior.

She took up a volume. *Romeo and Juliet.* Perfect example. Had she not found the story troublesome? Two very young persons, who could hardly know their own minds, believed they'd found the love of a lifetime. As a consequence they killed themselves in the most stupid manner.

True, Olympia was nearly six and twenty, not fourteen, but her experience of men, in a nonbrotherly way, was approximately that of a fourteen-year-old.

She set down the Shakespeare and took up another. *Don Quixote.* Several editions of that fine example of living in a delusion. At the top of another pile lay *The Castle of Otranto.* Ripley's cup of tea, she didn't doubt. Gigantic helmets falling from the sky and killing people, various nonsupernatural parties trying to kill one another, damsels in distress . . .

She quickly set down the book and let her gaze roam over the collection.

That was when she saw it. Three large volumes, vellum. For a moment, all she could do was stare.

"Here," she whispered. "*Recueil des Romans des Chevaliers de la Table Ronde.*

341

Here. At Camberley Place, of all places."

Reverently she turned pages. She'd read about this. It must be the set from the Duke of Devonshire's library sale, nearly fifteen years ago. Lord Mends had tried and failed to get it.

Beautiful. Hundreds of illustrations, in gold and color, of the *Tales of the Knights of the Round Table.*

Ripley's words intruded.

Didn't you tell me you were a damsel in distress? I'm your knight in shining armor.

She shut the book, but she couldn't shut out Ripley's voice or what she felt when he was near her, when he touched her.

She walked to the window.

Though the garden on the east front was rather a wilderness, she saw Ripley clearly. He'd stopped halfway down one of the paths, and he was looking away from the house. While she watched, Cato ran up to him, sniffed about, and tried to lick his foot. Ripley gestured at him. The dog backed off a pace and sat down beside the invalid chair, as good as gold, or pretending to be. A moment later, Lady Charles followed Cato to her nephew's side.

Olympia turned away from the window. Knights in shining armor belonged to the world of romances, a fairy-tale world. Lady

342

Olympia Hightower had to live in the here and now. If she must remember voices, she'd do better to remember the voice of wisdom: *Don't underestimate Ashmont . . . when he wins your respect and love, you'll be happy you married him.*

That was the voice of experience, reality, practicality. That was the voice a sensible and practical girl ought to heed.

"I will," Olympia said under her breath. "I will." She returned to Lord Charles's unrecorded books.

Ripley could still hear Olympia's laughter in his head. He still felt the curves and warmth of her body. He heard her say, *In that case, maybe you ought to be the one to marry me.*

Well, he couldn't, and it was pointless to suppose otherwise. She was Ashmont's. Any other man might try to lure her away. But not Ripley, because he was the bloody best friend. Because it was too late.

He was sinking into black gloom when he heard "Woof!" and Cato bounded at him.

"Down!" Ripley said, before the dog could jump on him. But the dog only trotted round him, sniffing. He spent a good deal of time sniffing about Ripley's lap . . . where Olympia had been. Then the dog tried to lick the injured foot. Ripley snapped his fingers. "Get off, you ridiculous beast."

The dog sat, eyeing the foot.

"He wants to play," came Ripley's aunt's voice from behind him. "But you've had your playing for the morning, it would seem."

"Have I?"

She clasped her hands behind her back and walked a few paces away, then came back. "You had better not be taking advantage of that young lady under my roof."

She'd seen or a servant had told tales. Ripley said nothing.

"I heard a commotion in the library," she said. "I trust to your honor that the fooling about came to nothing."

He didn't wince. The *fooling about* had come, more or less, to nothing, and that was for the best.

"For God's sake, Hugh, tell me whether I need to take the girl away."

He wanted Olympia gone. No, that wasn't true. He *needed* her gone.

The trouble was, she needed time away from everybody else — the family she was trying to rescue, yes, but Ashmont especially. She needed time to think and decide what was best and what was wise and what was right, not simply for her family but for her. No small challenge, trying to make things fit that didn't want to fit.

Ripley knew this. He knew, too, that one could find no better place, when one needed to come to terms with life's difficulties, than Camberley Place.

"It's complicated," he said.

"Life is complicated."

"Yes."

"I saw it wasn't simple, and it's become clearer to me how not simple it is," she said. "You — the three of you —" She broke off. "But never mind the other two. You're the one here and you're the one who needs to face matters. Some problems can't be bought off, nephew. Some need to be dealt with."

"Do they, really?" he said. "And what are you dealing with, hiding away here?"

She went still for a moment. Then she gave a short laugh. "Well done. Your sister tried it, but you're sharper."

"Than a serpent's tooth?"

"You've never been ungrateful," she said. "And you've never shied away from dueling with me. It's been rather a while, and I think my wits grow dull from the lack of worthy opponents. Not so dull, though, that I can't tell when I'm being deflected."

"Your wits are never dull," he said. "I wish

I'd been a fly on the wall when Ashmont and Blackwood came."

She shook her head. "Still deflecting. Very well. My girls are grown, managing their husbands and children. I'm not a girl anymore. I'm not a wife anymore. I'm not sure what I am. I have no direction, no purpose."

"That's why you're still here?" he said. "You need a bloody *purpose*?"

"Do you propose I be like you, with no aim, no purpose in life other than amusing myself?"

"If it's any comfort, Aunt, I'm not amused at the moment."

"And you can't run away." She smiled. "What a pity."

"And you've run away for three years." He smiled. "What a pity."

"No, dear, the pity is your losing the chance of a lifetime," she said.

"This isn't my chance," he said.

"Because Ashmont got there first? Because he's your friend?"

Ripley didn't answer. His aunt had seen a great deal too much. She always did.

"I wonder how you'll feel in a year's time," she said. "Or in five years' time, seeing a happiness that could have been yours. I wonder how much comfort your honor will be to you then."

Something in her tone made him think of his mother, and something she'd said about Aunt Julia, something surprising. A disappointment in love. His mind was in too much turmoil, though, and the vague memory roiled among other, more recent memories, and too many damn feelings. He was struggling to fish out the recollection — thinking about her was easier than thinking about himself, and he hated thinking anyway — when she turned her head toward the house, toward a sound she must have heard, which he hadn't.

Ripley turned his chair to face that way, expecting Olympia.

But it was only one of the footmen, hurrying to his mistress.

Her ladyship was wanted at the house, he said. Lord Frederick Beckingham had come.

His lordship had been quickly ushered into the drawing room and Lady Olympia summoned to join them.

The greetings had been cordial enough, though postures were tense.

While Ripley could understand Olympia's stiffness in the presence of her betrothed's uncle, and while Ripley himself wasn't entirely at ease, thanks to a decrepit conscience that decided now was the time to grow lively, the odd manner of the other two baffled him.

"I apologize for arriving without notice," Lord Frederick was saying, "and worse, coming to you in all my travel dust. But my nephew was in so great a state of agitation that I thought it best to waste no time. He is, in fact, so greatly agitated that I advised him to write instead of bursting upon you again, and to let me be his emissary."

In short, Uncle Fred had advised Ashmont to stay out of it and let his lordship do the talking. This was by no means a bad plan. Uncle Fred was a skilled courtier who somehow contrived to make himself equally welcome in both the King's company and that of the King's archenemy, his sister-in-law the Duchess of Kent. The mother of the Princess Victoria, present heir to the throne, loathed His Majesty. The feeling was mutual.

"Agitated?" said Aunt Julia. "Is that what you call it? What I saw yesterday was that Lucius had been drinking beyond what is good for him, as has seemed to be the case for some time now. He'd been in a fight — another pernicious habit — which I've little doubt he started, because he always does. And it is a laugh, I admit, your speaking of the dust of travel, knowing you've scarcely a speck upon you . . ."

She paused to give Lord Frederick a quick survey, and his blue eyes lit — but with anger or amusement or another emotion, Ripley couldn't tell.

"Naturally you had your valet with you," his aunt continued. "And you made sure to pause for a freshening up before driving the last mile or two." She took a seat, on the hardest chair in the room, and invited her guest to sit. Lord Frederick only moved to the fireplace, and stood with his back to it, as though this were the dead of winter and he needed his backside warmed.

Lady Olympia remained standing, too, near a window farthest from the others. Ripley wondered whether she'd try to escape by that method again.

"I wish I could say the same for your nephew," Aunt Julia went on. "Regrettably, he arrived in a state beyond disgusting, and which must be an insult to any lady, and most especially his affianced bride."

"Yes, well, that's one of the reasons I advised him to stay in London," Lord Frederick said, his usual imperturbable self but for the odd light in his eye. "Lucius truly was agitated, though, greatly so. The word I left out, I believe, was *disgusting.*"

The footman Joseph entered, bearing the tray of refreshments Aunt Julia had ordered while returning to the house.

Nobody said anything until the footman had gone out.

Olympia sipped and set her glass down on the table nearby.

Lord Frederick took a surprisingly long swallow. But then, he'd been traveling for several hours, the day was warm, and he was bound to be thirsty.

Aunt Julia, too, took more than her usual sip.

The thing Ripley had been trying to remember niggled in his mind, but it hung out of reach.

"Very nice," Lord Frederick said, nodding at his glass. "You always did keep a good cellar at Camberley Place as well as in London. But you have not been much in London of late."

"I haven't been to Town at all," Aunt Julia said. "I'm thinking of changing my ways, however."

A muscle in Uncle Fred's jaw twitched. He set his glass on the nearest table and said. "As fine a beverage as it is, Lady Charles, I must remember my mission. The urgent business that brings me here demands I keep my wits about me. I am charged with giving Lady Olympia a letter from my nephew."

From the interior of his far-from-travel-stained coat, Lord Frederick withdrew a surprisingly thick letter. Surprising in that, having come from Ashmont, it contained more than a single sheet of paper.

"With your permission, Lady Charles?" said Uncle Fred. "Or did you wish to read it first?"

"Certainly not. I am not Lady Olympia's mother. In any event, she is of age, and the letter is from her betrothed."

Lord Frederick nodded. He crossed to Lady Olympia. "I am to give this to you with the deepest apologies. Ashmont would have come himself had I not advised against it. He regrets making an exceedingly poor impression upon Lady Charles." He bowed in Aunt Julia's direction. "He did agree with me, eventually, that the best way to overcome the unfortunate impression was to resolve to respect a lady's sensibilities and not show himself until he's fit to be seen. In the meantime, he wishes to leave you in no doubt whatsoever about his feelings."

Lady Olympia took the letter from him. She seemed calm, but for the faint flush along her cheekbones. She adjusted her spectacles, though they couldn't be straighter, and opened the letter. She moved a little nearer to the window to read it, and Ripley found himself eyeing the latch, and wondering if it would offer the same difficulties as the one at Newland House . . . if she decided to make a run for it.

But why would she do that? She had nothing to run from. Ashmont was safe away in London and Uncle Fred, diabolical as he could be under the smooth surface of urbane good breeding, wasn't proposing to take her back with him.

Well, his lordship couldn't, could he? Aunt Julia must accompany her, or another respectable lady — or her mother. In any event, if Lady Olympia wanted to go back to London she would, and if she didn't she wouldn't, and none of it was up to Ripley, was it?

In that case, you could marry me.
How will you feel in a year, in five years?

Ripley was dimly aware of Lord Frederick moving to his aunt's side, and taking a chair nearby, and murmuring something, and Aunt Julia making some sort of answer. But that was the background, and they might as well have been the paintings hanging on the wall.

All Ripley truly saw was Olympia, her head bent over the letter, adjusting her spectacles from time to time. Her hair was not falling down, exactly, but it wasn't nearly as neat as it had been when she'd come into the library before . . . before . . . before . . .

Not so neat as before he'd kissed her and done more than he had any right to do, than was honorable to do though it was so little, not nearly enough . . .

You could marry me.

How will you feel . . .

At last Lady Olympia refolded the letter. The elders in the room must have been watching her without seeming to, because they fell silent.

She set the letter down on a table near the door.

She went out of the room.

CHAPTER 13

For what seemed like a lifetime, nobody said anything.

Ripley blinked, wondering if he'd dreamed what had happened. When he opened his eyes, he thought he might see Olympia reappear in his line of sight, still holding the letter, or looking up and straightening her spectacles before she spoke. But she was gone. He heard her quick footsteps retreating through the passageway leading to the Great Hall. He caught the sound of a door closing.

He started toward the doorway she'd gone out of, but Aunt Julia got in the way. The mechanical chair, not being as flexible as his body, prevented his squeezing by.

She snatched up the letter and unfolded it. "What on earth did he tell her?"

Lord Frederick moved to her, creating a larger obstacle in front of the doorway. "Only what he ought," he said.

"Only what he ought!" Aunt Julia echoed. "And what was that, pray tell, and how much do you know of it? Was this your work?"

"Will you get out of the way?" Ripley said. "I'm not interested in the letter. I need —"

" 'You suppose my sentiments have changed,' " Aunt Julia read, " 'and you are right in that, but not in the way you assume. My feelings for you have only grown stronger, as has my dismay at the prospect of losing you.' "

"I need to —" Ripley tried again, but his aunt went on reading, and while he tried to maneuver around her and Uncle Fred, he couldn't help hearing.

" '— destroyed my peace and obliged me to examine my behavior, as I admit I ought to have done long ago, before asking you to take the very great step of entrusting your life to my keeping. The past few days have caused me to think, and these thoughts have ranged over my faults and misdeeds. I understood these were more than trivial, else they would not have raised doubts and fears in your mind great enough to drive you to a desperate course of action. You write harshly of yourself, but my feelings toward you are far from harsh. I can only admire your courage and daring, and beg you to forgive me for causing you to take a risk that ought not to have been necessary.' "

Not Ashmont's style of writing but his sentiments, yes. Of this Ripley had no doubt, as he had no doubt of Uncle Fred's turning those sentiments into something rather more articulate than Ashmont's usual careless and all-but-incomprehensible style.

The night before the wedding . . . the things Ashmont had said about her. The soft, wondering way in which he'd said, *She was kind.*

But he'd said much more: about her grace and intelligence and liveliness and humor, and about her hiding her light under a bushel. How clever she was, and handsomer than others realized — as though spectacles could turn a pretty woman ugly. But it was all to the good, nobody realizing, because another fellow would have snatched her up by now.

Aunt Julia read on, and the letter grew more passionate and compelling, but Ripley, moving toward the door, barely heard above the noise in his brain, where a battle was going on between right and wrong, honor and desire, You Must Let Her Go and You Can't Let Her Go.

He heard his aunt say, "This is monstrous unfair, sir."

And Lord Frederick said, "To whom?"

That was the last Ripley heard as he wheeled himself through the passage and into the Great Hall, where he snapped at the footman Tom, who hastily opened the door for him.

"Which way did she go?" Ripley said.

Tom pointed. "Down the path to the right, Your Grace."

The path was gravel, not the easiest surface to negotiate in a mechanical chair, as Ripley had discovered earlier. But if his grandmother could do it, he could. This awareness made the experience no less frustrating. On foot — on two good feet, that is — he might have caught up with Olympia easily, though at the moment he couldn't see her. Still, she couldn't have gone far in the few minutes he'd been delayed.

He went on, and came to another set of pathways, these simply packed dirt. He spotted one of the gardeners not far away and called to him.

The man, one of the older staff — Hill, was his name — hurried to him, cap in hand. "Your Grace."

"The lady, Hill," Ripley said. "Which way did she go?"

Hill scratched his head and looked about

him, frowning. "Hard to say exactly, Your Grace, but she looked to be going southward, toward the river."

Ripley wheeled himself along the garden path, through twists and turns among plantings and statuary that reduced his view of his surroundings to what lay directly ahead, and then only a small distance ahead. At times, the world opened up, but it was a while before he finally spied her, a tiny figure in the distance.

As he left the large, formal gardens, the relatively flat landscape about the house's immediate environs gave way to the park's gently sloping ground. He caught a glimpse of her, moving in the direction of the fishing house where he and his friends and sister had spent so much of their time in years past.

Ripley made slow progress. Though he traveled slightly downhill now, the ground was rougher and more overgrown. Meanwhile, the bushes and trees along the twists and turns of the path blocked his view. Now and again he caught a glimpse of Olympia, not so tiny a figure as before, and he remembered the day in the Newlands' garden — was it only a few days ago? — when he'd followed the flashes of white through the shrubbery. Now it seemed to him as though he'd been chasing her for all his life.

He should have chased her before, years before. He'd known she was there, among the wallflowers and hens and feeble old men. He'd never wondered why. He'd taken it for granted she'd always be there. He'd never given it any thought. Had he somehow assumed it was for his convenience? Had he assumed she waited, like some lady in her castle, for him to come riding up, like the knight in a romance, to take her away? When he was good and ready?

"Thinking," Ripley muttered. "Stop it."

The vista opened up a moment later, and he saw her, closer now, within hailing distance. "Olympia!" he shouted.

She gave a start and turned.

"Go away!" she cried, and marched on, at no slow pace. He bumped along, twice into trees. The day, which had dawned relatively fair, had grown cloudy, and the warmth had become oppressive. His sweating hands slipped on the handles, causing the chair to veer off the path.

"Dammit, Olympia!"

"Go away!"

"I need to talk to you!"

"No!"

She stormed on.

He struggled with the chair, which more

and more objected to the terrain, the wheels not cooperating fully with the winches and rolling him into bushes. He bumped against small rocks, and the slope, gentle as it was, still drew him down faster while he fought to stay on the path.

She kept on, and it ought to have been easy enough to follow, but the path grew rougher still. Trees and shrubbery, which hadn't been cut back, apparently, for the past year or more, encroached. Apparently nobody had bothered, either, with clearing away the various pebbles and nuts and other debris that had rolled or washed into it.

Though the chair supposedly worked smoothly in any terrain, it hadn't been designed for wilderness travels. Ripley was trying to steer it while preventing its yielding to gravity and rolling headlong down to the river. To do this, he needed three hands. Having only the usual pair, he had his left hand on one winch and had to manage the right side with his right elbow while his right hand remained on the rod that stopped the wheels, which wasn't working as well as it might.

He was only about twenty yards behind his quarry when his cramped, sweating hand slipped from the brake handle. Before he could regain control, the chair rolled forward. He turned a handle to one side, to go off the path, where the undergrowth would slow him, but the chair bumped on a rock. The right handle came off in his hand, the chair wobbled sideways briefly, then bowled down the path, straight toward the water.

He looked at the useless handle in his hand.

He threw it aside.

He let go of the other handle.

He heard Olympia scream.

Horrified, Olympia watched the chair bump down to the path alongside the river then across it and over the riverbank, into the water. There it struck something, with a jolt hard enough to make Ripley's head snap back. The chair tipped over on its side.

She ran back the way she'd come and down into the water. It was shallow, but rocky. She splashed to where the chair lay.

A dark, dripping head came up. Ripley looked up at her and laughed.

Her heart, which seemed to have stopped altogether, sprang back into action so quickly it made her dizzy, and hot and cold at the same time.

She'd thought . . . she'd thought . . .

But no, there he was, the great blockhead, laughing. All in one piece. No blood. Not dead. She wanted to kill him.

"You reckless man!" she cried. "You could have broken your neck."

"You're wet," he said.

There was a low rumble in the distance. He tipped his head back and gazed at the sky. "And about to get wetter."

She looked up. The previously blue sky was swiftly shrinking behind the grey clouds massing above their heads. She heard another rumble, louder and nearer.

She grabbed the chair and turned it upright. Her hands shook. "Get up!" she said. "Get up!"

Using the chair for support, he hauled himself upright.

She was already wet. Getting wetter didn't worry her. But she didn't fancy standing in the open while a thunderstorm bore down on them.

"Sit," she said.

"It's broken, and you can't push me uphill in it, even this mild uphill," he said. "Not that I'm eager to get on that thing again. Look where it took me. There I was, minding my own business, when it decided it wanted a swim."

"You let go! I saw you!"

"I was tired of fighting with it."

"You could have broken your neck, your

thick skull!" She wished she didn't care what happened to him. She wished somebody, anybody else had followed her out of Newland House the other day — was it only three days? — and brought her back, before she could become infatuated with the wrong man.

"I didn't remember how rocky the riverbed is here," the Wrong Man said. "Farther downriver the bottom's smoother."

She was well aware of the rocky river bottom here. She didn't want to think about what might have happened. She wanted to be out of this river, where he'd nearly killed himself.

"Never mind." The rumbling grew louder. The churning clouds darkened the world about them. "We have to get back." She tried to push the chair up the riverbank, a job that turned out to be harder than it looked.

"What are you doing?" he said. "Leave it."

She kept pushing. She needed to fight something. It might as well be this curst piece of furniture.

He let out a sigh and joined her, each taking one corner of the chair's back. She hoped he was using it to support his bad ankle. Then she told herself he wasn't hers to worry about. He wasn't her problem. She had problems enough. She was going to have to teach herself to love another man because that man still wanted her, and she was a practical and sensible girl, and marrying him was the practical and sensible thing to do.

"The fishing house is around the next curve," he said, nodding that way. "Level ground, not uphill, and much nearer than the house."

She looked in the direction he'd indicated, then upward, in the direction she'd come from. She wasn't sure where the house was. She had no idea how far she'd walked, blindly, through the park. Ashmont's words had pained her, deeply, even though she knew those weren't his precise words. The letter sounded generally like him, though, and she'd wanted to run. Not that she had any idea where to run to. Not that she was at all clear about what she wanted to run from or saw, really, any point to running. If only she hadn't run in the first place.

She couldn't think about that now. The darkness was deepening while the thunder rolled toward them. Out of the corner of her eye she caught a flash.

She didn't argue when Ripley turned the chair in the direction of the fishing house.

■ ■ ■ ■

Ripley told her to run ahead, and he'd follow with the chair, but she wouldn't cooperate. If she left him to push the chair on his own, he would put too much weight on his bad foot, she said.

Luckily they had only a short distance to go. The fishing house had stood near the turn in the river for a hundred fifty years. At any rate, he hoped it still stood.

The storm steadily bore down on them, and as they reached the bend, lightning blasted the sky. Thunder followed rather too close in its wake. Raindrops plopped on the pathway, on the chair, on their heads.

He pushed the chair faster, ignoring the jolts up his leg when his right foot landed hard on an unexpected lump in the pathway. The grounds hereabouts needed attention, he thought, then pushed the thought aside for another time.

The landscape lay in deepening shadow. Thunder rolled while lightning flashed among the clouds.

As soon as they turned the bend, the house came into view.

In most people's opinion, it wasn't much of a fishing house. It looked nothing like the grand, multichambered and multistoried Classical, Gothic, and Chinese fishing temples of so many other great estates. This was merely a square stone structure, with a few temple-like architectural touches. An ancestor had built it sometime in the late 1600s. Unenlarged and unembellished since, it boasted a single room lit by windows on all four sides. A set of three shallow steps led to a narrow portico that sheltered the double doors.

As they hurried toward it, a blast of lightning lit the building. A moment later, thunder rolled over them.

Ripley left the chair at the bottom of the stairs and limped up the steps behind Olympia. As they reached the portico, the rain picked up its pace. He pulled the door handles. The doors didn't budge. Locked. Of course they would be.

"Never mind," she said. "We're sheltered from the worst of it, and very likely it'll pass through quickly."

"Don't think so," he said, glancing about him. "Doesn't look like that kind of storm. This one looks like it means to stay."

He left her and began limping round the side of the house, testing windows.

"Ripley!"

At the back, he found one with a broken latch.

"Found a way in," he called back. "Stay where you are."

He wrestled the window open, then went back to get the chair.

"You're going to stand on the chair while I hold it, and climb in through the window and unlock the door from the inside," he said.

He could think of a score of other women who'd look at him as though he was mad.

Olympia nodded.

She helped push the chair into place, and he let her, though he didn't need help. When he took hold of it, keeping it steady, she quickly climbed onto it then through the window in a flurry of skirts and petticoats and writhing limbs and a whirl of familiar scent. Though she wore his aunt's clothes, the scent he caught was of Olympia's skin and hair.

He remembered her climbing over the wall at the back of Newland House's garden. He remembered her dress and petticoats swirling about his face . . .

He shook off the recollection and moved back to the door and waited. And waited. The great drops of rain fell faster. Wind gusted.

"Do you mean to open the door?" he called. "Or were you wanting me to beat back the lightning with the chair?"

"It's dark," she called back. "I can't find the — oh, here it is."

The door opened, and Ripley dashed in.

"The chair," she said. "You left it —"

"Bother the chair." He looked about him. As his eyes adjusted to the dimness, he saw the tinderbox on the mantel, alongside the simple utensils the family always kept here: cooking pots, a few plates and cups, a pitcher and bowl. The table held a small basket of table linens. Wood had been stacked near the fireplace.

He made a fire. It gave him something to do while he tried to decide what to do. Or, more important, what to say.

He was aware of a taut silence within, while the world without went black with flashes of light and deep booms that rattled the old windows.

"Someone's been here," he said, as he watched the flames take hold. "Everything else about the park looks . . . not neglected exactly, but not well attended to. The firewood's been brought in recently, though. Must have been Alice's doing. We used to play here as children."

The three camp beds he and his two

friends had used were still here. Two were bare. One held bedding. Alice, clearly, had spent time here recently. Why? He hoped she wasn't having second thoughts about her marriage, because it was too bloody late. Not to mention he had enough complications in his life without adding Blackwood to the list.

The doors flew open to a blast of wet wind.

He and Olympia hurried to the doors and slammed them closed. He latched them, locking out the world. Holding reality at bay. For the moment.

She quickly stepped away, brushing the wet from her hands. "Look at you," she said. "You're soaked to the skin."

"It's summer," he said.

"It's not that warm," she said.

"We have a fire."

"The damp lingers in stone buildings," she said. "This one's practically on top of a river. You're not only wet but bruised. Your ankle will never get better, the way you abuse it."

"It's getting better," he said. "The way you fuss about it, a fellow might get the idea that you cared . . . about him."

For a long moment she stared at him.

"He might," he said.

"Might?" She marched to the fire, then to a window, then back to face him, hands on her hips. "*Might*? How thick can you be? I as good as proposed to you!"

"Yes, well, you shouldn't spring that sort of thing on a fellow without warning."

"I've all but ripped off my clothes and screamed, 'Take me now.' How much warning do you need?"

"That was rather too subtle for me," he said, "since you didn't actually take your clothes off. Then there's the thinking part. A large, complicated thinking part."

"It isn't that complicated," she said.

"Then let's say it's . . . fraught. That's a good word."

"It's a stupid word."

"You're going to make this difficult, aren't you?" he said.

"I'm not making anything difficult," she said. "I understand everything. Perfectly. Too, too well. Which means we need not go over the ground of friendship, loyalty, and honor once again. It makes me want to scream — and mine is not a nervous sensibility. I am not an excessively emotional sort of person. I'm practical and sensible. I know you haven't seen much of that side of me, but —"

"I've seen several sides of you," he said.

How will you feel in a year . . . in five years?
He knew how he'd feel. He felt it now.

"I've seen so many sides of you," he said. "Which means I understand, better than ever, why Ashmont won't let you go."

"Because he's possessive and obstinate."

"Is that what his letter sounded like to you? Because that wasn't what I heard. Mind you, I only caught parts of it — and that was against my will, but my aunt and his evil uncle were blocking the damned door while they argued about it. Otherwise I would have caught up with you sooner."

"You shouldn't have come after me. Not this time. Not the other day."

"No, it ought to have been Ashmont, but it wasn't."

"It wasn't Ashmont because he was too drunk — on his wedding day — the day you claim he was so thrilled about."

"Yes, well, he can be a bit of an ass at times."

"A bit! At times!"

"I'm not in a position to throw stones," he said. "The point is — the reason I came after you . . . this time —"

"He didn't even write the letter himself!" she said. "That is, he did put pen to paper, but those weren't his words. He doesn't write that way, let alone speak that way. And

371

there were hardly any inkblots. And it covered two sheets of paper, on both sides!"

"He makes the blots from stopping to think."

"He didn't have to think. Somebody else did that for him."

"Not exactly. The thing is, I'd rather not be defending him at the moment, but one must present the case fairly."

"I don't need anything presented. I'm not stupid."

"The letter shows how sincerely he wants you back," he said. He was going to be fair. He was going to be sporting. Honor and friendship demanded it. "For Ashmont to submit to the indignity of letting his uncle dictate a love letter — well, that shows feeling, I think. And though the words weren't Ashmont's, the sentiments were. I know. I heard him, on the night before he was to be married."

She folded her arms and her expression became stony. But her changeable eyes had turned grey, and he saw pain there.

About them, the storm threw fits. The world turned black, then bright white, then black again, while thunder underlined their words and their silences.

Inside was quiet, except for the fire's crackling, but the quiet was so heavy that

Ripley felt as though he walked through chest-deep mud.

Or maybe quicksand.

He thought, and picked his words carefully. "Is that why you bolted today? Because of the feelings Ashmont's uncle helped him put into words?"

"Yes." She unfolded her arms and paced to the fire, then to a window. "I wanted to cry. But when I got outside, away from everybody, I couldn't cry. And I couldn't go back and arrange the books to calm myself because everybody would find me, and then I would certainly cry. So I walked."

"If you don't want to marry him, don't marry him," he said.

"I don't want to. But I must. But I *can't*. How can I? How can I, when —"

A crash outside cut her off. The windows lit again. Another crash, with echoes.

As his eyes adjusted to the changing light, he saw that her pained expression was gone, as though the lightning had blasted it away. For a moment she seemed puzzled about something. Then she took a deep breath and let it out. He watched her bosom rise and fall. He told himself not to look there. He didn't listen, as usual.

"Never mind," she said. She unwrapped

the white neckerchief from around her throat.

He hadn't understood why she'd needed it in the first place, except as decoration for a very plain dress. And yes, it made sense to take it off. It had grown rather warm inside, with the windows closed and a fire blazing perhaps more fiercely than a damp day in June warranted. Because of thinking too hard and not paying proper attention to what he was doing, he'd made a great deal more fire than the small room needed.

Then she started unbuttoning her dress.

Ripley experienced the same sensation he'd felt a short while ago — a lifetime ago — in the library, when she'd set down the letter and walked out. He closed his eyes and opened them, but no, this wasn't a fantasy or a dream.

"What are you doing?" he said.

"I'm being unsubtle," she said.

The dress was made like a coat, buttoning from neck to hem. She was halfway down the bodice already, though there must be more than twenty very small buttons there. And another two or three thousand on the skirt.

While she went on unbuttoning with alarming efficiency, it took his mind a moment to make sense of *I'm being unsubtle.*

Then he remembered.

"Olympia," he said.

She went on unbuttoning, concentrating very hard on what she was doing, apparently, because she caught her bottom lip in her teeth and a small crease had appeared in her brow, directly above the nosepiece of her spectacles.

"Dammit, Olympia."

"Everybody says that," she muttered. " 'Dammit, Olympia.' Well, damn you back."

"Stop it."

"I think not. This situation is intolerable, and I don't see how it can get worse."

She'd got the dress unbuttoned to the waist. He could see her smooth throat, all of it. He caught a glimpse of skin farther down, and a sliver of white undergarments.

He told himself he was bigger and stronger, and could easily make her stop. But he couldn't. He'd have to touch her.

He could *not* touch her.

Not unless . . . until. Not *now.*

"It can get a great deal worse," he said. His voice had dropped an octave.

The storm went on, flashing and crashing about the little fishing house.

He swallowed. "Yes, well, maybe not such

a bad idea, after all. Your clothes are wet."

So were his. He was keeping them on.

She said nothing. She undid the belt and tossed it onto a chair.

The room grew oppressively hot.

She continued unbuttoning. She had to bend forward now to do so, and he could see the swell of her breasts above the chemise's simple neckline. And a lacy edging directly below the chemise. It was the edging of her corset. The one he'd bought her. Good God. Pink ribbons and lace and naughty stitching, around and over the — the — *there.* And *there* was ripe and full and creamy.

"Olympia," he said hoarsely.

She went on unbuttoning, and the front of the dress opened up, displaying the corset in all its delicious sinfulness and the neat waist it hugged . . . and the sweet curve tracing the fine swell of her hips.

Leave, he told himself. All he needed to do was open the door and walk out. A little thunderstorm wouldn't hurt him, and if it did, that was all to the good.

He tried to turn away, but she'd worked her way downward past her hips and was steadily, inexorably, opening the garment to her knees. He could see all of the corset and part of her petticoat, which was plain white, much plainer than the wicked corset, and couldn't have been a more innocent petticoat if a nun had been wearing it. But she wasn't a nun, and there was the naughty French corset . . . and her breasts, threatening to spill out of it.

He stood where he was, unable to move except for clenching and unclenching his hands, while his temperature climbed and his pulse rate with it. He stood, like the fool he was, watching as she unbuttoned, bending easily down, down to the very bottom of the dress. And when she'd undone the last button, she twisted and turned and wriggled her way out of the tight armholes and pulled the dress off, then tossed it onto a chair.

She looked up at him, her face pink, her eyes glittering, her soft mouth curved in a triumphant little smile.

She had every right to look triumphant. There she was, in all her shapely beauty and unpredictability. There she was, the spirited general of a girl who'd mowed down a bully. There she was, in a lot of white underthings and a naughty corset, the most deliciously irresistible thing he'd ever seen.

Ripley never resisted temptation. He hardly knew how.

He couldn't look away or run away or do the right thing. He'd never been a saint and he wasn't about to start now, of all times.

She said, "Is this too subtle for you?"

"No," he managed to choke out. "Dammit, Olympia."

Two limping strides closed the space between them. Two more brought her up against the wall.

Chapter 14

Olympia looked up at him. He was so near she could feel the heat of his body. His eyes had narrowed to dangerous green slits.

Her heart beat so fast she could hardly breathe, and a sensible and practical voice in her head said, *Run.*

But that was nonsensical advice, not to mention it came far too late. If running could have solved anything, she'd have run faster and farther, the day she'd left her drunken bridegroom waiting with the minister.

She'd called herself a damsel in distress, but she wasn't. Damsels in distress were always virtuous ladies in trouble through no fault of their own. She was in trouble she'd made for herself. No dragons. No evil sorcerers. No stage villains twirling their mustaches. No heartless parents or stepparents.

No, it was all Olympia, dammit.

And it was still Olympia, dammit, half-naked and looking up into Ripley's wicked wolf face, and smiling up at him while his green eyes sparked as hot as any dragon's flames.

A true damsel in distress would have at least tried to get away.

Escape was the last thing she wanted.

The scent of woodland clung to him, and the scents of a stormy summer day, the scents of wet wool and smoke. Under these and permeating them, she knew, though she couldn't quite catch it yet, was the scent of his skin. She inhaled deeply, the way the opium smoker draws in the drug he craves.

He started to say something, but as she inhaled, his gaze slid down, to her mouth, before lowering to her breasts, all too conspicuously displayed.

He caught the back of her head and bent his, and kissed her, hard. She kissed him back in the same way. No sweet maiden's kiss because she wasn't sweet, was she? She was Olympia, dammit, and she wanted more and more and more of what she'd only tasted before: sin and heat and wild feelings. The feelings she'd given up believing she'd ever experience.

She was aware, distantly, of rain drumming on the wooden roof and beating at the windows. She was aware, distantly, of the thrash and crash of the storm outside. But that was far away, as remote as a dream.

The center of the world was here, in the incorrect and unacceptable longing she was sick of fighting. This was what she'd wanted, very possibly from the moment he'd burst into the library with his friends. Whether it had started then or after or long before, he was what she wanted now.

She wanted to be crushed against his big body, his arms wrapped about her. She mightn't have known it before but she knew now that she'd been wanting to feel his chest rising and falling against hers, and to feel unmaidenly and unvirtuous excitement. She'd been waiting without knowing what she waited for until now: to feel heat coiling around and inside her. Like molten lava, it slithered over her skin and under it and into her brain. It melted and burnt up everything in its path: sensible and practical notions first of all. The world softened and hazed over and spun about her. She was lost and glad to be.

He wasn't the first man she would have chosen to lose her mind over. More like the last. But too bad for her. He was the one.

Just once.

Just this once.

Passion. This once, the man I want, even if it's wrong and ruinous.

He kissed her and kissed her and kissed her. Everywhere. Along the side of her face and her ear and behind her ear and along her neck. It was only his mouth upon her skin, so small a pressure to have so much power. But the touch of his mouth was enough to make her want more. It made her forget herself and all she'd ever been taught about right and wrong. Everything inside her that had seemed so sure and solid before — the mind and will of the practical and sensible Olympia — all gave way, surrendering to him and the power of his mouth, his touch, the scent of his skin, and the warmth and strength of his powerful body.

Oh, and his hands.

They moved over her while he kissed her throat, then the top of her breast. Animal sounds, little moans, spilled out of her.

And while he kissed her, she was aware — but distantly, as though it happened in another place — of his loosening her corset with smooth efficiency. In what seemed like no time at all she felt the ties giving way and the garment sliding from her. It was instinctive to grab it as it started to slip away. But his hands got in the way, and when he pushed the corset down and untied the tapes of her chemise with the same expertise, she forgot what she'd meant to do or why she'd wanted to do it.

He pulled the chemise down and then his bare hands were on her breasts . . . cupping and squeezing them . . .

A deep, sweet ache joined with a surge of happiness so sudden and powerful she could hardly stand up. She had wanted this, though she'd had no idea what *this* was and never could have imagined, no matter how wildly she imagined.

Then he put his mouth where his hands had been and suckled her. Heat shot deep into the pit of her belly. Her knees disappeared, and if he hadn't been holding her, she'd have slid to the floor.

"Oh," she said. "Oh." Her so-efficient brain could offer nothing more.

He had his arms fully about her now, and he lifted her off the floor and carried her a little ways. He set her down on something soft. He bent over her and gently unhooked her spectacles from behind her ears and set them . . . somewhere — she didn't care — because he started kissing her again, starting at her forehead.

He kissed her eyebrows and her eyes and her nose and her cheeks and her chin, and on from there. These kisses were fiercer than what had gone before, and they seemed to sear her skin and under her skin. They turned everything hot and hazy and dark.

He worked his way swiftly down, and she, squirming with pleasure and other, sharper feelings, tried to put her hands on his bare skin, too. She needed to kiss him in the way he kissed her, laying claim to as much of him as she could: *This is mine and this is mine and this is mine and this is mine.*

They were like two armies fighting for territory. But the fight was somehow the opposite of a fight. Whatever it was, it had to be done. She needed her hands on his skin and his on hers. She needed kisses, more of them, taken and given. And while she took as much as she could, she felt a loss of things that covered her — her clothes, yes, but something more. For years and years, she'd hidden her dreams and wants, and bit by bit, other parts of herself.

But from the moment she'd started unbuttoning her dress, she — whoever she was — had come out of her hiding place. She'd emerged from the world she'd tried to make safe and painless and had only made small and boring. With him, it was impossible to live in so small a place. With him, she couldn't play by the rules and didn't want to.

All she wanted was more and more and more of him and what he did to her. She tugged at his shirt, pushing it up, to put her hands on his chest, so warm and hard. She laughed inside, feeling triumph when he groaned, even while she ached, so deep. She felt triumphant and right, even when she couldn't stop crying out "Oh," and "Oh!" while she squirmed under him, impatient for something else, something more.

He said, "Olympia," his voice hoarse against her neck.

And she said, "Yes." And "Yes." And always, "Yes."

Yes, she said.

The *yes* thundered in Ripley's mind, as loud as the storm outside. Or maybe the single word was the storm.

He had, more or less, decided what he'd say to her.

But this wasn't what he'd meant to do.

Not yet, that is.

But the way she'd looked at him when she'd undone the buttons.

The way she'd *looked* — all luscious curves and white underthings and naughty pink ribbons.

He was a man, and not a virtuous one.

And so, when he should have said, *No, wait,* and then added something sensible and correct . . . he didn't.

Instead, he walked straight into trouble, the way he always did. He walked the few steps to Doing the Wrong Thing. Then she was in his arms, soft and willing and learning far too quickly how to make him delirious.

And now.

Yes, she said.

Yes, of course. What other choice was there?

He looked at her, lying on the cot in all her creamy softness and out-of-focus gaze and white and pink, and the only real thought in his mind was more instinct than thought, the feeling of the wolf when he's spotted his mate: *mine.*

And after all, he was a duke. Through his veins ran centuries of power and lordly compulsion to possess.

Yes, she said, and he moved his hand up over her leg, dragging her petticoat up as he went. He slid his hand over her knee and over her garter and up to the smooth skin of her thigh and up farther still, to the opening of her drawers and the silken place between her legs.

This was the time to call a halt. In a dark, distant part of his mind he knew this. But she only gave a small, surprised gasp, and then it was *Yes,* still, as she squirmed against his hand. And yes, she was wet and ready.

And no, he didn't think. Thinking wasn't a habit with him, and second thoughts were what other people had.

He stroked her, and felt her convulse around his fingers. That was what he wanted. This was as it should be. Yet it was more than he'd expected or ever experienced.

Her pleasure pulsed through him, like a summer storm, dark with flashes of light. She was the dark and the light, the danger and the excitement, and the sweetness, too. She was all he could see or feel or think: she, in his arms, under his hands, passionate and open and trusting and wild. She let out a little shriek, and a giggle.

He laughed, too, but mostly from shock.

Feelings. So strong.

He took his hand away and moved slightly away to get his bearings, and she said, "No, not yet!" She touched him, not meaning, he assumed, to touch where she did, where he was aching and rigid for her. But she did touch him there, and even in the dim light he saw her eyes widen. But instead of pulling her hand away, she left it there, and looked up at him, with the same little smile she'd offered before. A dare of a smile.

"Yes," she said.

He was lost, or maybe he'd been lost from the start, from the moment he'd seen her in a cloud of white and clocked stockings in the Newlands' library. Or long before that. Years ago. So much wasted time.

In a moment his trouser buttons were undone, and in another he was poised between her legs, and almost in the same instant he was pushing into her. She gave a choked cry at the intrusion, and he paused, though he thought he'd die. But it was only a heartbeat or two or a thousand furious ones before he felt her ease about him.

Then, "Oh!" she said. "Good heav— oh, my goodness, how — no, don't stop. Oh, Ripley! Oh, my goodness! I'm going to faint."

She didn't faint, and neither did he. He went slowly at first. Though it promised to kill him, he gave her time to grow accustomed and learn, but she learned so quickly and gave so easily of herself that he grew dizzy with the joy of her openhearted ardor.

He seemed to plunge deep, deep underwater, into a hidden place of happiness. He was the knowing one, the experienced one, but in all her innocence and eagerness to learn, she took him where he'd never been before. He looked at her and marveled, even while he thrust deep inside her, and felt her close about him, holding him inside her. It was only a moment before he was in charge again, supposedly in charge, and leading the lovers' dance he thought he knew so well.

But with her, this wasn't the dance he knew. It was altogether different. He had no words, no coherent thoughts, but the feeling was there, filling him, fulfilling him.

The new feeling was there, as he felt the last pleasure shake her and as her body pulsed about him. It was there as he was swept upward, to his own peak of pleasure. And it was there as he drifted down again, to the world, as their bodies began to quiet, and as his mind came back and he knew, first, that she was his. Second, that there was no going back. And third, he was in the worst trouble of his life.

Ripley became aware again of the storm whirling and crashing around the old fishing lodge, though not so violently as before.

He squeezed in beside Olympia on the narrow cot and drew her into his arms. He rested his chin on her head. Mingled with the scent of the dying fire and their lovemaking was her own scent, as fresh as this patch of woodland where he'd played in his boyhood. He thought how little the present moment resembled that young boy's notions of knights in shining armor and damsels in distress and the dragons a knight faced on a damsel's account. What he couldn't have foreseen was that the dragon, in his case, was a friendship he'd believed — and had good reason to believe — more precious to him than anything else.

Ashmont, his friend.

Ripley had betrayed him.

Ripley was a disgrace and had been for years, but this had to be the worst thing he'd done in his life.

Yet it seemed to him the best thing he'd ever done.

He said, "You've done it now. Have to marry me."

"Yes."

"No bolting."

"No."

She tucked her head into the hollow of his shoulder. He could feel her breath on his skin. He didn't want to move. He didn't want this moment to end. He needed time for it to sink in and make sense.

They didn't have time.

"We have to do it at once," he said. "Not a minute to lose. We have to leave here and be on our way to London before Uncle Fred knows we're gone. Matters are complicated enough without our having to deal with him."

She drew away from him and sat up. Her hair, dark honey with golden glints where the firelight caught it, was falling down, into her eyes and over her shoulders. Her breasts spilled out of the top of her chemise. The corset sagged at her waist. He reached up and clasped one perfect breast.

"Well, maybe not this very minute," he said gruffly.

He drew her down and kissed her breast and the hollow of her throat. He kissed her on the mouth, and she parted her lips to him instantly. The kiss deepened, the hot inner storm rolled through him, and he lost the will to fight it. In an instant his heart was racing again, and he was coiled about her, moving his hands over the smooth curves of her body.

A moment ago he'd been cooling. He'd started to become capable of thought. Now all he wanted was more of her. He kissed her throat and her neck and made trails of kisses over her breasts. He grasped her bottom and pulled her against him.

She giggled and said, thickly, "Maybe not this very minute."

They hadn't time for languid lovemaking, and this time he used no finesse. He cupped her most womanly part and stroked her. He did little more before she was moving against his hand, wet and willing. In another moment he was inside her again and her legs were wrapped around his hips and there was nothing in his mind but her and the way it felt to be joined with her and the shock of it: to feel so deeply, to feel so much happiness.

A soft pressure enclosed him, and he felt her muscles contract, drawing him in, holding him. The wonderful madness returned. The world went away and nothing remained but the way she felt and the way they felt together. It was new, still new, and a wonder to him.

He was inside her, trying to make it last, not wanting it to end.

Not yet. Not yet.

But it was like the maddest of races, fast, fast, too fast. The peak came too soon and there was no resisting or slowing it. It came to him in a burst of joy. And then he was tumbling, tumbling down into a quiet place.

■ ■ ■ ■

This time it took longer for Ripley's breathing to slow and his mind to uncloud.

He didn't want it to uncloud. He didn't want to think. He wanted to wallow in the thousand and one delights of Olympia.

He couldn't wallow.

He needed to be calm, to think. To plan.

Ashmont. What to do about him. If anything could be done.

If not, it was going to be very bad.

"It's a good thing I knew nothing about what this was like," she said shakily. "I'd have been ruined in my first Season."

And if Ripley had had any idea, all those years ago when he'd first met her, he would have ruined her in short order. So much wasted time. But no. If he'd ruined her years ago, he wouldn't have realized what he'd found.

Two days ago he hadn't realized. All while he'd pursued her and tried to get her back to the wedding, Ripley had told himself that she was perfect for *Ashmont.*

Blind, blind, blind.

"It's only this way with me," he said.

Just as it's only this way with you.

The realization was simply there, where it

hadn't been moments ago. He'd thought at first that what he'd felt for her was simple, if powerful, lust, the result of too long a time of celibacy. He'd realized, but not until yesterday, that it wasn't simple at all. Now there wasn't the smallest question in his mind. It had to be her. Nobody else, ever.

"I promise to make up for those lost years," he went on. "Would much rather start now, making up for lost opportunities. The trouble is, I've already started when it's not a good time."

Could there be a worse time? Not much more than forty-eight hours after she was supposed to marry his best friend — to whom she was still, technically, engaged. Who was going to hate him. And try his best to kill him. And whom nobody would blame for doing so.

No time to fret about that now. One thing at a time.

Look after Olympia first. "I'm going to get up," he said. "Some things to attend to. But you stay."

She murmured an answer he took to be affirmative.

Gently he released her and sat up. He felt shaky. Had he eaten anything this morning? He couldn't remember. It didn't matter.

He stood, and was surprised at the twinge,

until he remembered the bad ankle. Still, it was only a twinge. He found a handkerchief and quickly cleaned himself. He saw no blood. Nothing obvious, at any rate, in the firelight on a gloomy day. He'd been too impatient — really, a schoolboy would have shown more consideration. Still, he hadn't hurt her as much as he'd feared. She hadn't screamed or wept. That was good. Mindlessly he pulled up his trousers and tucked in his shirt. He buttoned the trousers.

"Stay here for a minute," he said. "I'll be back straightaway."

He grabbed a small pitcher from the collection of utensils on the mantel and went out.

It was still raining, though less fiercely than before. Not that it mattered. As it was, he had to cover only a short distance to the river, and trees sheltered most of the way. He filled the pitcher and limped back to the fishing house.

When he opened the door, she still lay where he'd left her. She was staring at the ceiling, but her gaze quickly shifted to him.

"No time to clean up properly," he said. "But there are some linens — it looks as though Alice camped here recently — and the water's clean." While he talked, he set the pitcher down within easy reach. He collected a few cloths from the basket of linens and lay them over the top of the pitcher.

She sat up, blushing, and the blush spread all over her neck and down, over her breasts. Swallowing a groan, he reached over her to retrieve the spectacles from the window ledge. He gave them to her, then busied himself with putting out the fire while his mind reviewed the perfection of her skin and the way she was round in all the right places.

What a miracle it was that nobody had caught her ages ago.

I'm boring and pedantic, she'd told him.

That was completely wrong, but he was glad that everybody had believed it. And he supposed he was glad it had taken him so long to discover she wasn't like the other respectable girls. Now at least he was old enough to appreciate how special she was.

But it would have helped if it hadn't taken him *quite* so long.

He turned back to her. She was pulling the tapes of her chemise closed. She tied them and started to reassemble her corset.

"I'd better help," he said.

She slid off the cot and stood. "It's easier standing up," she said. "Although I doubt it makes any difference to you. Even my maid can't get my corset undone as quickly as you did."

"Practice," he said. "Though I'm better at getting them off than on." Not that one needed to get corsets off so very often. Furtive couplings rarely involved much undressing, and he'd always rather liked furtive couplings. For the danger. "At any rate, I can do it more easily than you can."

He had only loosened the corset string enough to get at her breasts, and so it was mainly a matter of tightening it again and tying it. He picked up her dress and helped her into it.

He looked at the long parade of buttons and remembered her unbuttoning them, and the look she'd given him when she'd finished, and he wanted to pull the dress off again and throw it down and toss her back onto the cot.

But no.

Death awaited.

Not certain death, but it was a definite and well-earned possibility.

"You do the top," he said. "I'll do the bottom."

He knelt and started buttoning.

Her knees, very much to Olympia's surprise, managed to hold her upright.

Her breathing had returned to something

397

like normal.

As to the rest of her, she'd never be the same.

No wonder Mama had been so inarticulate.

She looked down at his dark head. She wanted to drag her fingers through his hair and kneel on the floor with him and kiss him and . . .

. . . make him do it again. And again.

You have to marry me now, he'd said.

Well, of course. She could hardly go back to . . .

"Ashmont," she said.

"Wrong name," Ripley said, looking up. "It's the shock. Got you confused. I'm Ripley. The other Dis-Grace. The one you're going to marry. And no bolting this time."

"No, I mean that Ashmont —"

"He's not going to be pleased about this development, no."

She hadn't thought this through properly. She hadn't thought at all. Now she remembered. All the fights. The duels. One in which, apparently, Ashmont had nearly had his ear blown off. It might have been his head. But now . . . What had Ripley said, the other day, in the garden? Something about a lovers' romp, and *since I'm the only one in your vicinity, I'm the one he'll call out.*

She was still engaged to Ashmont. Thanks to cowardice, she hadn't broken it off. A short time ago she'd lost her virginity to his best friend. She wanted to dash her head against the wall. So stupid. So *reckless.* She wasn't even drunk! What was wrong with her?

She said calmly, "You're his friend. Ashmont won't call you out. He can't."

"Right. Nothing to worry about. I'll punch him in the face and he'll punch back and then he can't be the injured party. I'm not sure that plan will work now."

"In that case, I'd better be the one to tell him," she said. "He can't call me out."

Ripley returned to buttoning. "You can tell him whatever you like. It won't make any difference. He's my friend and I've betrayed his trust. Oh, and there's the humiliation, too."

"I betrayed him," she said. "I didn't break off with him as I ought to have done. I hedged my bets."

"You did nothing of the kind."

"I did. I left it to him, knowing he's too stubborn to let me go."

He was halfway up the skirt. "You're a woman," he said. "You don't have the luxury of doing the decent thing or the honorable thing. As you pointed out a little while ago in the library, marriage is different for women than for men. You did the intelligent thing."

"The practical and sensible thing," she said.

"That, too. Since you couldn't be sure you'd get through my thick skull, you very wisely decided not to burn your bridges. Also, I'll wager anything you were too subtle and tactful in that letter. You didn't want to hurt his feelings. I don't understand why people are so shy about hurting his feelings. Must have something to do with the lost puppy look he gets. I can't manage it. Tried. Look like a gargoyle." He'd reached the waist of her dress.

"I wanted to be kind," she said. "It wasn't his fault."

"Kind." Ripley stood. "He isn't that fragile, and yes, it was." He found the belt and gave it to her.

She quickly wrapped it about her waist and closed it. "It's very good of you to defend me. That bodes well for a marriage. Still, it doesn't matter if he is or isn't fragile or whose fault it was. You don't know how hard I've tried. To do what was right. To be a good girl. To be pleasing."

"Yes, well, you're not a good girl," he said.

She sucked in her breath.

"Good girls don't get drunk and run away on their wedding day," he went on. "Good girls don't take off their clothes in front of wicked men. Good girls don't taunt those men into tumbling them. Good girls don't make the men wish they'd thought to do it years ago. Good girls are boring. You won the awards for boring because you were trying to be a good girl. You're not. You're a bad girl, and if you'd been a boy, you might have been one of my best friends. I'm glad you're not a boy. Now, can we stop talking and thinking and get out of here? We haven't a minute to lose."

Meanwhile in the drawing room of Camberley Place

Lord Frederick stood at the window, looking out. "The storm's let up. They ought to be back by now." He turned back to Lady Charles. "I don't like this."

She refilled her glass. "It isn't up to you."

"It has to be up to somebody."

"Ashmont isn't a child. It's time he took responsibility for his life. You can't protect him forever."

"And you?" he said. "You kept Ashmont's fiancée from him when he came here."

"I did nothing of the sort. She wasn't here at the time."

"You didn't tell him the whole truth. Whom were *you* protecting?"

"Olympia. From marrying the wrong man. Because the right one was too slow-witted to see what was under his nose."

There was a short, taut pause. Something passed between them. Unseen, unspoken. But felt.

Neither of them acknowledged it. They were both old hands at concealment.

If something flickered in her ladyship's eyes, it might have been a trick of the light. If a faint red tinged his lordship's cheekbones, it was from the same cause.

He said, coolly enough, "And you thought you'd give him a little time, and he'd come to his senses."

"Yes."

"And what if it takes years?"

The words *as it did me* might have hung in the short silence. Or maybe not.

Lady Charles laughed and said, "Until it's too late? In that case, I shall comfort myself with the knowledge that I tried."

"You put your oar in, you mean."

If only someone had done so then . . .

"Habit," she said. "I've been doing it for most of his life. You and I have that much in common."

"Yes, and I'm too old to break the habit

402

now," he said. "This is the last, best chance that wretched nephew of mine has. I won't see him make the same mistake . . . so many others do."

"If he doesn't make mistakes, how will he learn?"

"That's a chance I'm not going to take. I've waited long enough, I think. For all I know, they've gone."

"Why would they go?" she said. "All they've done is take shelter from the storm, separately or individually. You're jumping to conclusions. That isn't like you."

"You don't know what I'm like," he said. "But we both know what Ripley's like. And I have a good idea what he's going to do."

What I should have done when I had the chance.

"It doesn't matter," she said. "You're too late to change anything. You were too late before you came."

"We'll see." He bowed. "I bid you good day, my lady."

She didn't curtsey in turn but moved swiftly to the doorway and stood, blocking his way. She smiled. "Ah, no, not quite yet, sir."

"Woof!" said Cato, behind her.

CHAPTER 15

As they made their way to the stables, Ripley was more aware of the infernal ankle than he had leisure to be. He was cursing it in his mind when he saw Olympia move off the path and pick up a stout branch.

She held it out to him. "Walking stick," she said. "Use it."

"I don't need a bloody crutch."

"Is it possible, or do I ask too much, for you to set aside your manly pride for a moment and approach the matter in a calm and logical fashion?"

"I'm perfectly calm," he lied.

"Let's take this in steps, then," she said, much in the same way he'd talked to her when she was drunk. "We are proceeding as quickly as possible to the stables because we have to get to London, you told me, as soon as possible."

"To get married as soon as possible." He mimicked her patient tone. "To do this, we need a special license. Which means I must pay a visit to Doctors' Commons. And hope they don't keep me there for hours while the word goes round the place that the Duke of Ripley is frantic to marry Lady Olympia Hightower, and the Archbishop of Canterbury himself summons me to *explain.* Because, you see, he might remember that he recently granted the Duke of Ashmont a special license to marry the same lady."

"I understand," she said. "What I should like is for you not to break your neck before we're married. Because, you see, if you die, you can't marry me, and then I shall be in rather a pickle, don't you think?"

"A pickle?" He laughed.

"I had a good idea how babies were made," she said, and he stopped laughing. "Thanks to you, I now know precisely how human beings make them. I don't know what the odds are of our having started one. I do know that the practical and sensible thing to do is to be married to its father before it's born."

It was like a kick in the gut. Yet he had no business to be startled. He knew how babies were made. He should have had the courtesy to withdraw, a courtesy he'd extended how many times to other women?

"I won't break my neck," he said, face hot.

She held out the stick. She wore a look he recognized.

It was the same look she'd worn in the courtyard at the White Lion in Putney. With the blusterer who refused to back down from a ridiculous position.

Ripley took the stick and used it.

When they got to the stables, he did the practical and sensible thing and ordered the landau instead of the curricle. This meant an eternity of waiting for the horses to be put in harness and everything inspected and the coachman, John, to ensconce himself upon his throne.

But the shock she'd administered cleared Ripley's mind wonderfully.

Only a reckless halfwit would travel with Olympia in a small sporting vehicle, when the weather was changing every minute. A curricle's hood wasn't enough to fully keep out the wet. And the wet and the bumps of the less luxurious vehicle would make her fret about his ankle and his needing a comfortable seat on which to rest it. He'd be suicidally foolish not to give the ankle as much rest as possible, considering what lay ahead. More important, in the landau, with the hood closed, he'd enjoy the added benefit of four or five hours' privacy with Olympia while somebody else drove.

Though it took forever, they did set out at last, unhindered.

Lord Frederick's horse hadn't yet been sent for. He must still be busy quarreling with Aunt Julia, which meant there was a reasonable chance of his not traveling too close behind them. An encounter would be awkward, and Ripley was in no mood to explain matters to Ashmont's manipulative go-between. It had to be face-to-face, friend to false, traitorous friend.

Ripley had told the stable men to keep mum and not answer questions until they were asked. With luck, word wouldn't travel from the stables back to the house too soon. With luck, nobody would start asking soon. With luck, it'd be assumed he and Olympia had, either separately or together, taken shelter from the storm. Since the skies hadn't cleared, it might be a while before anybody decided to come looking for them.

In order not to trust entirely to luck, though, he told the stable men to take their time about sending Lord Frederick's horse to him.

Luck was with them for the journey, at any rate.

Though it rained from time to time, the thunderstorm didn't seem to follow them.

They reached London before nightfall.

Then it was on to Gonerby House.

Where they encountered a mob of family, including the Newlands, all swarming in within minutes of Olympia and Ripley's entering the vestibule.

After the first cries had died down somewhat, the swarm bore the travelers into the drawing room, where an odor of fresh paint prevailed and a set of steps blocked a door. Renovations still ongoing, in other words.

There the uproar began to swell again.

Ripley said, "Enough."

He was a duke. The tide of noise receded.

"Thank you for the thrilling welcome," he said. "Thing is, not helpful to talk to everybody, all at once. Only Lord Gonerby. Ah, and Lord Newland. Your counsel would be appreciated." Unlike his brother-in-law, the Marquess of Newland kept both feet planted firmly on the ground. "If we three might adjourn to another room. A matter of business."

All about Ripley, eyes widened. Gazes went from him to Olympia and back again. Confusion reigned for a moment. Then the two older ladies, at least, seemed to begin to form a picture in their heads. Judging by their expressions, they found the picture perplexing.

"Your study, Lord Gonerby?" Ripley said. "The library? Not here, in other words. Gentlemen's business to see to. As soon as is convenient."

"Yes, yes," Lord Gonerby said. "But —"

"Papa, the duke is famished," Olympia said. "We've been on the road for several hours, with only the shortest stops. Moreover, as I mentioned in my letter, he is injured. It would be a good thing if he could put his foot up. Perhaps the *buts* could wait until you take him to a quiet room and he's been given some refreshment and allowed to rest his ankle."

It wasn't the Voice of Command she'd used on the bully at the White Lion. Nonetheless, it was a voice that got things done and had a remarkable subduing effect on the listeners.

Ripley had grown up in a very small family, and he'd spent the bulk of his youth at school, away from his parents and sister, or in the peace of Camberley Place. He wasn't used to so much . . . family. Voices. Chaos. At Gonerby House, everybody had something to say. Even the little boys.

He realized Olympia must have had to do this for most of her life: create order where there was chaos. No wonder she put books in categories and subcategories. Books were easier than people.

Still, it could be done with people. To a point. As she'd demonstrated.

If Lord Frederick had goaded Ashmont into courting her, Ripley had no trouble seeing why. What other girl had a prayer of managing him?

Lord Frederick was not going to be happy about the change of bridegroom. The marriage had better take place before he got wind of it.

Fortunately, Newland took over from his rather vague brother-in-law, and in very short order, considering the state of the house, which seemed to be half coming down and half going up, the three men were in Gonerby's study.

Ripley ignored the chair offered him. He braced himself on the mantelpiece. Aware of the long night ahead, and what lay ahead, he went straight to the point. "Lady Olympia and I wish to be wed."

"To each other?" Gonerby said.

"To each other, sir, yes."

"Erm . . . but she's engaged to the Duke of Ashmont. Supposed to be married the other day."

"Yes, that was the other day and this is today. Her ladyship has changed her mind.

That is a lady's prerogative. We wish to be wed."

"And the Duke of Ashmont?" Newland said. "Is he aware of this change of plans?"

"He will be."

"In that case, perhaps we should wait until such time —"

"Since it's quite impossible for him to marry Lady Olympia — she being unwilling to marry *him* — and since we are rather in a hurry, it would be best we have the settlements drawn up as soon as possible," Ripley said. "I'll send my solicitors to you tomorrow."

After he had them make certain changes to his will.

"The wedding will take place no later than tomorrow evening," he added.

"Tomorrow," Lord Gonerby repeated. "Well, this is all very gratifying to be sure. Two suitors for my Olympia. Not that I'm surprised. She —"

"Is incomparable, and any number of men would wish to be suitors," Ripley said. "However, as far as Lady Olympia is concerned, there is only one, and that would be me. She ran away from Ashmont. I caught her. She didn't object to being caught. In fact, she's keen to marry. Me. Not Ashmont. I trust this is clear."

411

Judging by Lord Gonerby's expression, nothing was clear to him.

His brother-in-law was another matter. His grim expression told Ripley that the marquess had put two and two together — for instance, Ashmont + Ashmont's temper = duel — and quickly understood what the hurry was about.

Gonerby began, "Well, I am not at all sure that we ought —"

"Quite clear, duke," Newland said firmly. "Olympia was to have been married a few days ago," he told his brother-in-law. "The more quickly matters are resolved, the more quickly scandalous rumors will dissipate." Before giving Gonerby a chance to respond, he went on, "Since time seems to be of the essence, one assumes that settlements like those arranged with the Duke of Ashmont will be acceptable."

"That will make a starting point," Ripley said. He paid his lawyers well to fuss over details. "However, I mean to have my solicitors add a few conditions, to do with the Gonerby Hall library. I doubt you'll find them onerous. And now, gentlemen, I must be off."

A servant appeared then, with a tray of food and drink.

Ripley left the other two men to refresh

themselves.

He found Olympia pacing in the corridor.

"I thought you'd be with your mother, deciding what to wear to the wedding," he said.

"I don't care what I wear," she said. "And I strongly doubt you will."

"Something easy to get off," he said. "Without a lot of buttons, preferably." The image appeared in his mind of Olympia unbuttoning the endless line of buttons . . . the look on her face when she was done. "On second thought, lots of buttons. Hundreds of them." But, no, he couldn't think about buttons now. He needed to keep his head clear. "You're right. I don't care what you wear. Apart from the wedding ring."

"The thing is, I should like there to *be* a wedding," she said.

"There will be."

"And a marriage," she said.

Ah, well, that was a horse of a different color.

Olympia knew that facial expression. She'd seen it at one time or another on every male in her family.

Ripley was going to be a man.

Of course he was. He was a man.

She hid her despair, reminded herself it

413

was Dominate or Be Dominated, and said, firmly, "I know it's absurd to ask you not to do anything foolish or reckless. Not to mention, you'd be another man altogether if you weren't foolish and reckless. But I will ask you — no, I will tell you — that you are to give Ashmont this note from me."

She held out the note. The neat folds had become somewhat crumpled as she paced, waiting for Ripley to emerge from Papa's study. She'd suspected he'd try to slip out without saying goodbye.

He looked at it.

"Ripley."

He shook his head. "I'm going to see him tonight," he said. "I'll tell him, face-to-face. What I won't do is hide behind your skirts."

She didn't roll her eyes. She didn't grab him by the throat and shake him. She didn't draw back her hand.

She looked at him in the way she'd look at one of her brothers when he was being stubbornly wrongheaded.

He sighed and took the note.

"You are not to burn it," she said.

"Wouldn't dream of it."

"Or destroy it in any way. You will give it to Ashmont."

"Olympia, we discussed this."

What they had done was argue, for a good

part of the way to London. Then he'd given up arguing and started kissing, and from there, matters had taken an enlightening turn.

"It was not a discussion," she said. "You told me it wasn't my responsibility to write notes. You're the man and you would deal with your friend, one man to another. But you were wrong, and if you hadn't used unfair tactics —"

"All's fair in love and war."

Love.

Neither of them had uttered the word. She was still operating under the assumption of infatuation, possibly fatal infatuation. But then, he mightn't be using the word *love* in the strict sense.

"That's a handy phrase," she said. "Useful but not strictly true. The fact is, I broke my promise to Ashmont. A betrothal, after all, is a sacred promise. In times past —"

"Don't really have time for splitting historical and legal hairs, you know. A great deal to do and not much time to do it in."

"Ashmont *deserves* an apology," she said. "From me. I was wrong to invite him to release me from the engagement instead of telling him it was over and I wouldn't marry him. I was wrong to run away, instead of showing some backbone — or my true

415

colors — and telling him I didn't want to marry him."

"But if you hadn't done all those things, you'd be a good girl," Ripley said.

She was still getting used to the idea of being a bad girl. At first, it had been a dreadful shock. Now, a great deal that hadn't used to make sense about her life had begun to make excellent sense.

"Men can behave badly yet still do the honorable thing and apologize," she said. "I can be a bad girl and do the honorable thing, too. Which I've done. In the note. Which you will give to Ashmont."

"You're presuming he'll be sober enough to read it."

She wanted to cry. She wouldn't let herself.

"I don't know," she said. "I don't know if it will do any good. All I know is, I owe it to him." She paused, and told herself again she would not cry. "And I don't want you to fight."

She managed to get it out without her voice breaking.

"For all we know, he'll wipe his brow in relief, clap me on the shoulder and say, 'Better you than me,' " Ripley said.

"If he has any sense, he will."

"None of us has any sense, m'dear. You

know that."

"Oh, Ripley!" She flung her arms about his neck. "You are not to fight him," she said, her cheek against his chest. "I won't have it. You tried to do the right thing. I made it impossible."

"I'm glad you did," he said. He lifted her chin and kissed her. It wasn't gentle or kindly or even affectionate. It was strong and determined and it ran roughshod over her qualms and shame. She answered fiercely, and melted against him.

Then it was over, and he was drawing away.

"Well, then, what fellow wouldn't want to come running back for more of that?" he said, with a crooked smile that made her heart ache. "Or, in my case, limping back. Go argue with your mother about your second wedding dress, and leave the rest of this to me. It'll all come out right, I promise."

As he made his way home, it occurred to the Duke of Ripley that it had been a very long time since anybody fussed and fretted about his wellbeing.

He remembered Olympia's asking, on the way to Battersea Bridge, whether he had enough money for the watermen.

Well, she had brothers. A horde of them. Fussing came naturally to her. As did ordering males about. It would be a great thing if he spent the rest of his life being fussed over and disobeying orders.

It would be a great thing if his didn't turn out to be a very short life.

Once home, he ordered a light dinner and wrote several notes, which he sent servants to deliver to his solicitors and others. He turned himself over to his valet, bathed, and shaved. He changed into undergarments, waistcoat, and trousers, and shrugged into a dressing gown.

He ate in his private apartment rather than the dining room, doing what justice he could to the brilliant meal Chardot had prepared for him on short notice. For the first time since his Spartan boyhood, Ripley had no appetite. However, he had to be practical and sensible. A man couldn't think properly on an empty stomach. He needed to think and act carefully — a mode of behavior he wasn't used to.

Still, no matter how much thinking he did or how carefully he acted, in a short while, he'd have to deal with a man who did neither.

Which meant that this might be one of the Duke of Ripley's last meals, if not the last. Whether it was or it wasn't, he'd do his best to appreciate it. That was the practical and sensible thing to do, if he wanted to avoid antagonizing the best chef in London.

He pictured Olympia sitting at his right hand at the dining table, and one of Chardot's feasts spread out before them. He smiled and he ate, though he tasted nothing.

He returned to his dressing room, completed his toilette for the evening, chose his sturdiest walking stick, and went out.

Too late.

Thanks to Lady Charles's harassing questions and his own disinclination to lay violent hands upon a woman, no matter how severe the provocation, it took Lord Frederick far too long to leave Camberley Place. When he did finally ride out through the gate, he might have had half a wish to ride back again and continue the dispute. This unusual — for him — indecisiveness could have contributed to his slow progress thereafter.

There was the rain, too.

It beat on him from time to time as he rode back to the inn where he'd paused this morning to make himself presentable, and it beat upon his carriage as it traveled back to London.

Nonetheless, he did return, and it was all for naught. By the time he reached Gonerby House, Ripley had been and gone. All Lord Frederick could do was say he'd stopped to make sure Lady Olympia had arrived safely. Then he was treated to the happy news and obliged to pretend he had no objections and required no apologies. It wasn't, he'd told them with a smile, as though Ripley had stolen a lady from *him.*

He saw no way to mend matters now. Calling on Ashmont would be a waste of time. True, terrible things might happen. In Ashmont's case, that was practically a foregone conclusion. Yet terrible things happened all the time. Men, even including Lord Frederick himself, made mistakes that changed their lives forever. Lady Charles had said it wasn't up to him. Not that he agreed with her. But for the moment, vexed as he was, he felt disinclined to keep helping a young man who was determined to ruin his life. It was possible, in fact, that Lord Frederick ought to have kept out of it in the first place. Had he not interfered, his nephew might have forgotten the lady's existence by the next day.

But she was perfect for him, Lord Frederick thought. She might have saved him.

Maybe Ashmont had gone too far to be saved.

And maybe Lord Frederick might as well have stayed at Camberley Place and let Lady Charles aggravate him. She at least wasn't a drunken oaf of a nephew. Beyond question she was pleasanter to look at.

Not long before midnight, Ripley ran Ashmont to ground at Crockford's.

It seemed like an age since Ripley had walked out of the gambling club in the small hours of morning. It seemed like an age since Ashmont had appointed him guardian of the wedding.

Not even three days.

He found Ashmont in the hazard room with Blackwood.

One glance told Ripley that, early as it was, Ashmont was three sheets in the wind.

So much for hoping to find him in a relatively rational state.

"Ripley, you dog! There you are at last!" Ashmont pushed away from the table and rose. "About bloody damned time. I've been bored witless."

"Your Grace, your winnings," the croupier said.

"Spread 'em round, spread 'em round," Ashmont said. "Let the other fellows have a chance."

Ashmont cheerfully followed Ripley into the corridor, Blackwood bringing up the rear.

When they were clear of the room, and not within eavesdropping range, Ripley said, "I've come to take you home."

"Ha ha. Do I look as bad as that? But I'm well. Looks worse than it is. Only waiting, you know. Got Olympia back safe and sound? Or still with your aunt? Uncle Fred made a devil of a fuss. Said I wasn't fit to see her."

His skin was grey and drawn. His eyes were bloodshot, ringed with deep shadows.

"Not looking your best," Ripley said. "A trifle fatigued, perhaps? Let's go back to your house, where we can talk without shouting to be heard above everybody else."

Behind Ashmont's back, Blackwood lifted an eyebrow.

"My house?" Ashmont laughed. "Too early to put me to bed. Still on my legs, can't you see? But what's the news? Did she answer my letter? Did she send the answer with you?"

"She did," Ripley said. "I thought, though, you'd rather read it in a less public place."

Ashmont glanced about him, belatedly taking in the groups of men passing by, pretending not to be watching and trying to listen to Their Dis-Graces. When it came to gossip, men easily matched women.

"Oh, them," he said, and his mood darkened abruptly, as often happened. "Damned right. Not here."

He walked on unsteadily, Ripley on one side and Blackwood following. Ashmont went on talking as they made their way through the club. "Everybody laughing behind my back. Nobody dares say a word to my face. Think I'm deaf, dumb, and blind. As though I'd never hear about what they write in White's betting book. Odds against me and in favor of guess who? No, don't try. You'll never guess. *Mends.* Do you believe it? Sixty if he's a day. And everybody knows those aren't his own teeth. The ones in his drooling mouth came off the fields of Waterloo, off some poor sod got himself killed defending King and country. That's not a fraction of the entertainment. *Foxe's Morning Spectacle* pillory me over half the paper, every day, and in the extra editions."

"Must say, they've outdone themselves," Blackwood said.

"No girl in her right mind would have me, they say," Ashmont went on. "Satirical prints, with me as a drooling ogre, and Olympia running for her life. Not that they've the bollocks to print my initials, let alone my name. No 'D of blank' for them. It's 'an infamous peer,' and 'a notorious nobleman' and a 'titled libertine.' As though I'd waste my time suing the smug black-guards. And last night —"

He broke off as a group of men passed nearby.

"Ripley, you had your own annoyances, I understand," Blackwood said, before Ashmont could continue with his grievances. "A fuss of some kind at the White Lion."

"Over a dog," Ripley said. He outlined the excitement in Putney while they collected their hats and made their way out of the hubbub of Crockford's and into the hubbub of St. James's Street.

Mist shrouded the street.

At the bottom of the stairs Ashmont stopped. "She went after the brute," he said with a laugh. "I didn't know."

"Well, he wouldn't say, would he?" Ripley said. "She demanded the whip. And *he gave it to her.*"

His friends laughed.

"Knew she was well above the common run of females," Ashmont said. "Obvious, once I spent five minutes with her. But I taught him a lesson."

"The one I administered was insufficient?"

Ripley said.

"The brute accosted us, ranting about the dog," Blackwood said. "Now I see why he was so incensed. A girl got the better of him."

"Made remarks about Olympia," Ashmont said. "Couldn't let 'em pass."

"Thus the stinker," Ripley said.

Ashmont touched his bruised eye. "No, that was later. Fell down some stairs. But I'm not the only one damaged in the cause of Olympia, I hear. Ankle, she wrote." Unsteadily, he bent over to stare at Ripley's ankle. The wrong one. Then he swayed upright again and eyed the walking stick.

"A sprain," Ripley said. "No great matter, but the women made a fuss, and when I tried to get away . . . Ah, but it's a long story. I'll tell you when we find some quiet."

London's streets were noisy most of the time, and the St. James's neighborhood, shortly before midnight, was no exception. Men on horseback, carriages rattling on their way to this rout or that ball, pedestrians talking loudly, to be heard above the clatter of hooves and wheels on the paving stones.

He was aware of passengers staring at them through the windows of passing vehicles. He was aware of men gathering at

425

Crockford's windows as well, anticipating some kind of excitement, as usually happened when Their Dis-Graces were in the vicinity. Before long, word would magically reach White's, across the street, as it so often did, and the famous bow window would frame another sea of faces.

Raindrops began to fall, spitting here and there, casually, as though it were an afterthought.

Looking away from the windows, Ripley found Ashmont staring at him, eyes narrowed.

"What are you looking at?" Ashmont said.

"Bloody audience," Ripley said.

Ashmont looked about. "Jeering and mocking behind my back. Think I don't know."

The rain came down harder.

"Let's get a hackney," Ripley said.

"Good idea," Blackwood said. "The damn rain's back."

"To hell with them," Ashmont said. "To hell with the rain. Let me have the letter."

Yes, of course. Had to be now. "Now?" Ripley said. "You're going to read Lady Olympia's letter in the dark? In the rain? With all these idiots looking on and speculating what's in it?"

"Can we at least get out of the wet?"

Blackwood said. "And go somewhere we can get a drink? You're not going to be reading love letters in the middle of the street, are you?"

Oh, but Ashmont would.

Ripley must have been mad to promise Olympia he'd deliver the letter, when there wasn't the slightest assurance one could get Ashmont to read it in a rational state of mind — or even in private, like a normal person. "Get a hackney if you're afraid of melting in a drizzle," Ashmont said. "I want the letter."

Of course. It had to be like this. A public street, in the rain, with an audience. Because that was the way Ashmont was. Unpredictable. Volcanic. Always so bloody damned *exciting.*

"Rain's one thing," Ripley said. "But I want to get out of the street, out of the uproar, and to a place where I'm not the night's entertainment."

"Give me the bloody letter!"

"Can we get out of the blasted rain?" Blackwood said.

"You get out of the rain," Ashmont said. "Get a hackney. Give me *the bloody, goddamned letter*!"

"Christ. Give it to him, Ripley."

Ripley withdrew Olympia's letter from his

coat and held it out to his friend. Ashmont took it and walked to the nearest lamppost. He unfolded the letter and read, squinting. Rain fell on the paper, blurring the lines of ink.

There weren't many, not by Olympia's standards, at any rate.

After what felt like an eternity, Ashmont looked up at Ripley. "Is this a joke?"

"I don't know what's in it," Ripley said.

"You know," Ashmont said, his voice low and hard. "You bloody well know."

"I know it's no joke. Very much not. She was upset when she wrote it."

"Upset? *Upset?* That's what you call it? And you had the bollocks to look me in the face and smile and tell stories, knowing —"

"I didn't plan to deal with this in bloody St. James's Street! I came to take you home and —"

"What the devil?" Blackwood said. He grabbed the note from Ashmont and read it. "For God's sake. *Ripley.*"

"You bastard," Ashmont said. "You swine. You traitorous, lying sack of shit! I *trusted* you."

He launched himself at Ripley, knocking him back against the stone fence in front of Crockford's.

Ripley bounded back and went for him.

428

Men started pouring out of the clubs.

Ashmont swung and Ripley dodged. Swearing, Ashmont tried to grab him by the throat. Ripley blocked him.

Before Ripley could throw him into the street, Blackwood pulled Ashmont away. "Not here, damn you both."

Yes, here. Now. All Ripley knew was rage. It was all he could do not to tear Ashmont from Blackwood's grip and pound him senseless.

"Here will do," Ashmont snarled. "Here in the street, where everyone can see what a swinish, cheating, craven snake he is, my so-called friend."

"Swinish! Who was the one too bloody drunk to go after his own —"

"Not here, blast you," Blackwood said, keeping his voice low. "Do you want her name dragged through the mud, along with yours?"

That got through. Barely. Ripley made himself unclench his hands. Ashmont shook his head. "No, not here. You know where, then. And when. Dawn. Pistols for two and breakfast for one, Ripley. I'll see you at dawn tomorrow. Putney Heath."

"No, you won't," Blackwood said. "Pull yourself together. Ripley's no saint. None of us are saints. You would have done the same."

"To my *friend*?" Ashmont said.

Friend. No, that was over, dead. Deeds done that couldn't be undone. Words uttered that couldn't be unsaid: *Cheating. Craven.* Words and acts churning in a mad, consuming rage, blinding, mind-crushing. Yet *she* was there, too. Somewhere in the murderous turmoil was Olympia . . . the expression she'd worn before Ripley left her today. And somewhere in the roiling fury, he remembered he was at fault.

He'd debauched the woman Ashmont wanted to marry.

Only one thing, Ripley understood, would make it right between them. Only one, irrevocable thing. Olympia wouldn't understand. She couldn't. She was a woman.

Sorry, my dear girl.

To Blackwood, Ashmont said, "You'll act for me."

"I damned well won't," Blackwood said. "He's my brother-in-law, remember? Alice would get wind of it. You know she would. And she'd kill me. As it is — but no. Find another way to settle this. I won't stand by and watch you two shoot each other."

"Then go to hell," Ashmont said. "I'll send someone to you, Ripley."

"I supposed you would," Ripley said. "But

I won't fight you tomorrow. I'm getting married."

Ashmont's head went back as though Ripley had hit him, as Ripley still wanted to do, in spite of everything, because his friend was a bloody damned fool and a wreck, and he needed to be knocked on his arse.

Ashmont started for him, but Blackwood pulled him back. "Leave it," he said. "Use your head. They have to marry now. Quiet the scandal. Everybody saw them together, and you were too late. It's over, my boy. Let it go."

"No," Ashmont said. "It isn't over."

There was no way it could be over. What had happened was all too public. Ashmont's pride couldn't bear it. He wanted to kill Ripley, and he had good reason. Ripley had stolen the girl, cheated his friend, and made the friend a laughingstock.

Only one way to wipe the slate clean. Only one way Ashmont could hold his head up again.

Pistols at dawn.

"I know," Ripley said. "But not until after tomorrow." Leaning on his stick, he limped away, up to Piccadilly.

Behind him he heard Ashmont shout, "What are you lot looking at? Go to the devil!"

CHAPTER 16

The following day

The rain-streaked letter lay open on the Duke of Ashmont's dressing table.

He had his hand wrapped about the stem of a wineglass. His fair hair, through which he'd dragged his fingers repeatedly, stood on end.

He read, for the tenth or twentieth time:

Dear Duke,

This is the letter I should have written the last time, had I not been too great a coward. The best way I can think of to put it right now is to put it plain: I cannot marry you.

I am so very sorry for treating you so unkindly and unfairly. It was wrong of me to promise I would marry you in the first place, when my heart wasn't as fully yours as it ought to be. It was wrong again not to break off cleanly after I ran away. It is not your fault that I did not know my own heart. I never meant to give it to Ripley, and I know the last thing he wanted was to steal it from me, but it's his now.

You deserve a responsible and dutiful lady who could live up to the honor you wish to bestow. Regrettably, my character is headstrong, ill-behaved, and selfish. I beg you not to blame Ripley for what has happened. He tried to keep your friendship first in his mind and heart. He tried to do what was right, but he came up against my unruly nature. He was the one I wanted to be with, and when he tried to get away, I prevented him.

It's so clear now — as it ought to have been before — that I could never make you happy. Though I wish I had realized this before I caused you distress, it cheers me to know I have spared you, though you may not appreciate that at present. And knowing I've done you a favor gives me the courage — or perhaps the better word is audacity — to ask you to do me the very great kindness of giving Ripley and me your blessing. He is your friend, still, and he loves you dearly,

I know. Please do not let my poor judgment destroy an old and true friendship. With best wishes for your happiness,

Believe me yours,

Very sincerely,

Olympia

"Blessing," he muttered. "Wants my blessing. She's got bigger bollocks than any of 'em. Dammit, Olympia, I *can't.*"

Blackwood stormed into the room. "Have you taken leave of your senses at last? You can't truly propose to fight Ripley. The lady doesn't want you. Leave it at that and don't be a bloody fool."

"Who let you in?"

"Am I barred? Have you added me to the traitors list, too?"

Ashmont drank. "Leave me alone. It's nothing to do with you."

"I'm your friend, you jackass."

"Not friend enough to second me."

"Instead you chose that blackguard Morris? I saw him as he left the house, and he told me."

The Earl of Bartham's son had jumped at the chance to act as Ashmont's second, no doubt hoping to replace Ripley in Ashmont's affections, such as they were.

"He's done good work," Ashmont said.

"Four letters exchanged and everything settled." He folded up Olympia's letter. "Dawn tomorrow. Putney Heath."

"You hope to make her a widow the day after the wedding? Do you think she'll fancy you after that? What is wrong with you?"

"They'll never stop laughing at me if I don't." Ashmont refilled his glass. "They'll be telling the story for years. I won't be a joke." He drank.

"Why do you care, suddenly, what any-body thinks or says about you?"

"This is different. Between Ripley and me. I trusted him. Completely. He made a fool of me. Lied to me. 'Come and get her,' he wrote. Next thing I know, he's back in London, planning a wedding. His."

"You never gave him a chance to explain."

"Ripley doesn't explain."

Blackwood shook his head. "Why did I come? Why did I think I could reason with you?"

"Because you're afraid of your wife?"

A dangerous silence ensued.

Then Blackwood laughed. "I see. You want to fight me, too. You want to fight everybody. Sorry I can't oblige. I've a wedding to at-tend. At seven o'clock. St. George's, Han-over Square. For some reason, Ripley wanted to be married in church."

435

He threw a note onto Ashmont's dressing table. "Your invitation. That's what I came for, hoping to find you less of an ass. I know it's little use, but I'll say it anyway: If you've a grain of sense left, you'll attend. You'll laugh and treat it like a joke and you'll wish them well."

He went out.

Ashmont crumpled the invitation without opening it, and threw it into the empty grate.

The gossip columns of the afternoon papers reported a fight between the Dukes of Ashmont and Ripley in St. James's Street. None of the witnesses having ventured near enough soon enough, little of the exchange of words could be recounted, though everybody understood the cause to be His Grace of R's disappearing from Newland House with His Grace of A's bride on the wedding day.

However, since Their Dis-Graces had been known to resort to fisticuffs before when competing for women, and since the three dukes had left Crockford's in a friendly mood, most people assumed His Grace of A, being in his cups as usual, had simply taken offense at something His Grace of R had said once they were out of the club. This, at any rate, was what Blackwood had told some of the bystanders.

If any gentlemen suspected that the moment of fisticuffs had not settled matters, they were unlikely to make public statements to that effect.

Duels being illegal, they were kept strictly quiet. Otherwise the police would get wind of them and turn up to spoil everything.

In any case, the world believed even Ashmont wasn't hotheaded enough to pursue the matter in a fight to the death with his best friend.

Ripley let them believe it. He almost let himself believe it as he went about obtaining a special license and deciding what to wear to his wedding.

It was a quiet affair.

The group attending was a great deal smaller than the one at Lady Olympia's first wedding attempt. This time the observers comprised mainly the Newlands and Gonerbys, their offspring, and a small assortment of other relatives.

For his own side, Ripley had a very small representation.

On the way to London yesterday, he'd sent a message to Aunt Julia. But that was simply to inform her. He didn't expect her to race to London for his wedding. He'd written to Alice as well, for the same reason. He knew she couldn't possibly arrive in time.

Blackwood was here, though. To Ripley's surprise, he'd offered to stand up with him.

"Imagine what Alice would say if I didn't," Blackwood had said.

"Women don't understand these things," Ripley had said. "Men and honor."

"I don't think Ashmont understands, actually," Blackwood said. "Think I do, though."

Ripley made do with that cryptic remark. He hadn't time or inclination to think too deeply about Blackwood's ideas of women, marriage, or whatever it was. He was glad to have his friend at his side.

The only possible fly in the ointment was the chance of Lord Frederick Beckingham's turning up — say, about the time the minister was saying, "If any man can show just cause why they might not lawfully be joined together, let him now speak." In that case, the odds were good His Lordship would not "hereafter forever hold his peace."

But the ceremony got under way, and if Uncle Fred had secreted himself somewhere in the church, he did not suddenly appear like an avenging angel. Not that this was his style. His style was indirect and wily, i.e., the opposite of his nephew's.

And so the minister passed that dangerous area, and went on to the *Wilt thou* part.

Ripley looked into his bride's radiant face and said, "I will."

At that moment, all the troubles of recent days, recent hours, went away, and the world stilled. For the first time since he'd begun his journey with her, he felt at peace. It was as though he'd run a long and desperate race and won.

Everything seemed so clear and inevitable and right as he took her hand and recited his vows. And when she took his hand and recited hers.

And when at last Ripley put the ring on her finger, something shifted in his mind. It shifted the world, as well.

He was a hard, reckless man whom harsh experience had taught to scorn sentiment. All the same, his heart swelled. With feelings. Too many, and too unexpected to name. Whatever they were, they were too strong to withstand. Moisture gathered in his eyes. He met her gaze — so blue now behind her spectacles — and saw tears there as well, quickly blinked away before she smiled up at him and filled the church with sunshine.

He loved her. It was as simple as that. It was as immense as that.

The rest of the ceremony was a haze of bewildering happiness. The others were background. They might have been paintings or trees or clouds. He saw her, and that was all he really saw: the daring girl who'd led him a wild chase . . . the girl he'd raced with in his invalid chair . . . the girl he'd wheeled after through the park of Camberley Place . . . and made love to, madly and stupidly, in his favorite place in the world.

She'd lead him a merry dance, and he'd like it.

Ripley had thought it was Ashmont who'd like it, that she was perfect for Ashmont.

So blind. It was Ripley who liked it, couldn't resist it, couldn't resist her, this spirited, passionate, loving girl who was his now. For always.

For as long as we both shall live.

But he was too happy to dwell on that thought.

He had now, basking in the sunlight of Olympia's smile.

He had now, enjoying the mixture of joy and confusion in the onlookers' faces.

All the same, as they were leaving the church, he did glance about him at the small group of attendees. He looked up into the gallery, too.

Ashmont wasn't here.

Later that night

Ripley House's library was nothing like the long canyon of books at Camberley Place. It wasn't like the elaborate, two-story library that Olympia's father pillaged from time to time.

But it was more beautiful than either, she thought. It told her the man who built it hadn't done it for show or simply to house his vast collection. A man who truly loved reading had created a temple to literature. It was a haven, too, as a temple ought to be.

More furniture crowded this room than the library at Camberley Place. Comfortable furniture, meant for the sort of person who wanted to be lost in a book for hours on end. And though it wasn't a hundred feet long, it supplied volumes enough to be lost in for a lifetime. Bookcases covered the walls up to the top of the doors. Above the bookcases ranged stucco-framed portraits of English literature's greatest men.

She stood in the middle of the room, hands clasped over her bosom as she turned slowly, drinking it in. "Oh, Ripley," she said. "If I'd known you had such a beautiful library, I should have knocked Lady Nunsthorpe out of the way and dragged you behind the curtains and kissed you until you begged for mercy."

"The Nun?" He strolled to one of the bookshelves that filled the walls on either side of the fireplace. "What's she got to do with anything?"

"A party. You danced with her." She shrugged. "Some years ago."

He turned to face her and leaned against the bookcase, arms folded. "And you remember?"

"You made a strong impression."

"Good. As long as the impression increases your desire to kiss me. Now would be a good time."

"You were the one who put a stop to the kissing in the carriage," she said. " 'Not here,' you said. 'Too many clothes.' "

Though it wasn't as simple as the one of Lady Charles's that Olympia had worn to her lovely ruination, today's bridal dress wasn't nearly as elaborate as the one for the first wedding. It was white, yes. That part was easy. White dresses being fashionable, she had several in her trousseau. This, however, lacked the elaborate bows and cascades of lace of the original bridal ensemble. Under her mother's and aunt's supervision, two of the more skilled maids had fashioned a veil from segments of one of last year's court ensembles.

The most elaborate part of her attire, the

veil had ended up on the carriage seat during the drive home, before Ripley called a halt to the kissing and fondling.

"It's our wedding night," he said. "A hasty coupling in the carriage wasn't what I had in mind."

Her skin went prickly. "What had you in mind, Your Grace?"

"I thought I'd weaken your resistance first, *duchess*."

She was still getting used to that form of address. She wasn't sure she'd ever get used to the way he said it, his voice so low and suggestive. "As though I have any," she said.

"You don't know," he said. "You don't know what I have in mind. I'm a notorious libertine, recollect. Done shocking things. Will continue to do them."

She wondered what could be more shocking than what they'd done in the fishing house. And what had happened in the landau, en route to London.

But what had occurred in the vehicle hadn't been quite so . . . so . . . *fulfilling*. It had been more naughty than anything else, she supposed, though she was hardly qualified to judge, and no, she wouldn't have minded continuing to the logical conclusion. But Ripley had said the coachman would know, and that wouldn't do at all, and so she'd settled for tucking herself into Ripley's arms. Where she fell asleep, and woke, and fell asleep again.

In any case, it seemed her education was about to be broadened.

"The difference is, I shall do it all with *you,*" he went on. "Promised, didn't I? 'Forsaking all other, keep thee only unto her.'"

"I promised, too," she said.

"So you did. Time to make a beginning, madam. With the kissing. I placed myself here, in front of a number of rare tomes — some possibly worm-eaten — to make myself more alluring to you."

"Oh, Ripley." She crossed to him and put the palm of her hand against his cheek.

"My plan seems to be working." He turned his face to kiss the palm of her hand. Then his tongue was there, making little circles in the palm of her hand. Tingling shocks went up and down her backbone and spread out from there.

Then he released her hand to cup her face, as gently as though he held a bird in his hands.

"Blue," he said. "Your eyes are blue at this moment. I like your eyes in all their colors."

"My shortsighted eyes."

"You saw me well enough," he said. "You

saw something in me you deemed worth having."

"I saw you standing naked in a basin," she said. "I'm not sure I was capable of deeming anything after that."

He laughed and kissed her, but not as he'd done before, in the carriage, with so much pent-up . . . passion. Certainly it had felt like passion. It must have been. It was the same powerful feeling that had crushed her brain in the fishing house.

They had that. Desire. They gave each other pleasure.

Now she found something more. He kissed her this time with a tenderness so shocking, it left her trembling inside.

It made her heart ache, too.

She answered tenderly, sliding her hands up to clasp his arms, so powerful, yet so gentle. She'd watched him lift a man straight up off the ground. She'd seen the leashed violence in him.

Not a tame man.

But he could be tender. To her.

She remembered the way he'd smiled down at her as they said their vows. Seeing it through the mist of her tears, she'd felt that, whatever wrong they'd done, it had somehow come out to something that had to be right.

She kissed him, following his lead, learning how a kiss could be passionate yet tender and how the feel of his mouth and the taste of him could make a powerful blend of emotions, as though her insides were laughing and crying at the same time.

When he drew back, she was still dizzy, and she said, "There is more to this business of kissing than I could have supposed."

"There's more to kissing you than I could have supposed," he said. "It's a good thing I've had some practice."

"More than your fair share is my estimate," she said.

"Ah, but all the rest is for you, *duchess,*" he said. His green eyes wore their sleepy wolf look. "Every wicked idea . . . every devilish plan . . ." His voice lowered to a whisper. "Ah, the things I'm imagining . . . Probably not legal."

She looked up into his eyes and, though she still couldn't read them, quite, saw something that warmed and excited her. "I suppose it's too late to run away now."

"Definitely too late."

"I've made my bed," she said. "And now I must —"

"Yes. Bed. Better idea this night. We'll save the library for later."

He offered his hand. She took it. His long

fingers closed about hers. His hand was warm but it was more than simple physical warmth. She felt it wrap about her heart.

And she thought, *I am in a very bad way.*

And, *I'm glad,* she thought as he led her out of the library.

Better to feel like this, to feel so strongly, and to have hope.

She went with him up the magnificent grand staircase and up farther still, to the second floor where the private apartments lay.

And of all the tumultuous feelings, the one she didn't feel was the smallest urge to run away.

Ripley gave her time to prepare. She would bathe and her maid would pamper her, as was right.

This bedding must not be rushed. Her deflowering, passionate as it was, and as gentle as he was able to make it, had not been what it ought to have been. He needed to make amends this night.

He needed time, as well.

He had a letter to write to her.

He'd be gone in the morning, long before she awoke.

Usually, he scrawled his letters in haste, and his patience for the process rarely extended past a single page. He wouldn't let himself make an exception this time. He was no poet. In any case, length could only lead to excessive sentiment, and the last thing he wanted was to be mawkish.

No, the last thing he wanted was for the letter to be necessary. It would be a particularly unamusing irony if the Duke of Ripley should finally find what he'd been missing for all his adult life, then not live to enjoy it.

In that case, he had nobody to blame but himself.

He hadn't played fair, with Olympia or with Ashmont.

He took out the messages he'd received from Ashmont. They were politely worded, as etiquette dictated. Ashmont had received and sent enough missives of this kind to write them without having to tax his mind about it, and even he wouldn't stoop to rudeness, let alone abuse, in a letter of challenge.

It was one of the things a gentleman, even one of Their Dis-Graces, didn't do. Like cheat at cards . . . or despoil his friend's affianced bride.

With Blackwood wisely refusing to second either of them, Ripley had enlisted Lord Pershore, from whom he'd bought more than one fine horse, and whose discretion he could trust. He'd answered Ashmont's letter of challenge with matching politeness.

The seconds had met and attempted to prevent the duel. As Ripley had expected, they failed. There was no other way to wipe away the public humiliation. No apology Ripley could honestly offer would suffice.

He was sorry he'd wronged his friend. He was sorry he'd cheated. He wasn't sorry for taking Olympia away from Ashmont. Ripley would have been truly, irreparably sorry if he hadn't.

The meeting having been set for six o'clock tomorrow morning, Ripley had arranged for the post chaise to take him and Pershore to the dueling ground. He'd contacted his medical man, who'd meet them there. Everything was in order.

Nothing remained but to write what might or might not be the only letter he ever wrote to his . . .

Wife.

He shook his head, to shake off the feelings threatening to overpower him.

He dipped the pen in the inkwell.

My dearest girl, he began.

In great London houses, the rooms on the ground and first floors were magnificent, made for show. Those on the upper stories tended to be far less so, since few but the family and servants saw them.

This wasn't the case at Ripley House. Occupying nearly a full wing overlooking the extensive garden, the duchess's apartments were as spacious and sumptuously furnished as the public rooms. Though the furnishings weren't modern — some were ancient and valuable — all were in perfect order, clean and lovingly cared for.

Olympia had bathed and changed in comfort. Her maid, Jenkins, who'd come with her from Gonerby House, was in such a state of ecstasy that she came dangerously close to smiling.

Naturally Jenkins had assumed, as anybody would, that Olympia's running away from her wedding would turn her into a social outcast. This would have left the lady's maid to choose between remaining loyal to her mistress or looking out for her own future and finding another employer. If the family was in a scandal, so were the staff. Even the most loyal servants might find such a situation intolerable.

And that was one more in the long list of consequences Olympia hadn't considered when she fled her first wedding.

Yet if she hadn't fled, she wouldn't be here in Ripley House, sitting at her dressing table, wondering what her husband had in store for her this night, and Jenkins wouldn't be so happily fussing about her mistress's hair and the precise arrangement of her dressing gown's falling collar.

A deep masculine voice dispersed all thoughts of hair and bedtime attire.

"That will do, Jenkins," Ripley said.

Face red, Jenkins set down the hairbrush and hurried out of the room.

The reason for the red face became apparent as Olympia turned away from the dressing table toward the door. Ripley wore a dressing gown with, by the looks of it, nothing underneath. His strong neck was bare, and the narrow V of the robe's opening revealed golden skin bearing a fine dusting of dark hair. Her gaze slid down over the dressing gown. Embroidered dark green satin with a purple lining, it was as opulent as the rest of the house.

Her husband, clearly, liked his creature comforts. He would have fit in nicely with the pashas of the Turkish Empire. As he'd said, self-denial was not his favorite thing.

This was a man who loved luxury and self-indulgence and not playing by the rules.

She wondered which rules he planned to break this night.

A tremor went through her, but whether

it was nervousness or anticipation she couldn't say.

"I came in the nick of time," he said. "Jenkins had nearly tamed your hair, and I like it untidy. The way it was when I dismantled your wedding veil. The first one, I mean."

"Oh, Ripley." She started to get up. She wanted to throw herself in his arms. She didn't know why she felt so desperate to do it, but she did.

"No, stay a moment," he said. "I want to spoil your hair a little . . . and then despoil other parts."

She sat again, and stared into the looking glass on the dressing table. She was still Olympia, the same unremarkable-looking lady she'd been a few days ago when she'd gazed into a mirror at her bridal splendor. But she wasn't the same inside. She'd lived a lifetime in a few days. A lifetime with one man, she realized. Hours and hours, in the course of which she seemed to have fallen irretrievably in love.

He came to her, and untied the neat braid Jenkins had made. Then his long fingers went through her hair, loosening the plaits. She was aware of his hands in a way she hadn't been aware of her maid's. She was aware of his nearness and the warmth of his powerful body.

She wanted to turn away from the dressing table and make him pull her up into his arms.

She said, "It's dawned on me that you and I have spent more time together than most couples do before they're wed. And so we must know each other rather better than most."

"I know you rather better than I ought to, on our wedding night," he said. "But that's my fault, for being so impatient. You ought to have had a proper introduction. I'll give it to you belatedly."

"We aren't proper people," she said. "Why should our wedding night be like other couples'? And since when do you care about *oughts*?"

"Since you." He moved to kneel beside her.

He took her left hand and looked at it for a moment, where her wedding ring seemed to glow on her finger. He kissed the back of her hand. "Your wedding night ought to be special. Perfect."

"That is exceedingly kind and thoughtful of you," she said. "But bear in mind, if it isn't perfect, you can try again. And again. Practice, you know."

He laughed, but she caught an odd note

in his laughter that made her look up quickly, into his eyes. They were shuttered. All she saw was the sleepy wolf.

He bent his head over her hand again and kissed her knuckles and her fingertips. He turned her hand over and kissed the palm of her hand and her wrist. He took her other hand and did the same. This time, when he kissed the palm of her hand, she moved it to curl her knuckles under his chin. She lifted his chin and looked at him but all she saw was affection . . . and wicked promise, yes.

He smiled and took her hand away and kissed her chin, her cheek, and the top of her cheekbone. Then his mouth covered hers and the light caress went deep in an instant. It was gentle and it wasn't. It was like the summer storm they'd shared, but this time it didn't feel so much like a war. This time, it was a claiming of each other and a joining of two wild spirits.

She hadn't realized how wild hers was until she ran away with him, and she'd felt herself come alive without realizing what the feeling was. She hadn't realized how hemmed-in and pent-up she'd been until he told her she was a bad girl.

She hadn't realized how much she'd stifled herself, though now she saw so clearly why. She couldn't behave as her nature inclined her to do. Young ladies couldn't misbehave as young gentlemen did. Young ladies couldn't sow their wild oats. If they did, they'd be ruined, and bring shame on their families. Young ladies had to follow the rules.

With him, those rules no longer applied.

Free, finally, she came alive now, drinking in his kiss like a healing potion. Her body warmed, and the warmth entered and soothed her heart, too. Her too-busy mind quieted and softened.

It was like drinking too much brandy, but better, so much better.

Still kissing her, he lifted her up from the chair and carried her out of the dressing room and into the bedroom to the side of the bed, where he set her on her feet.

"I want to see you," he said. "All of you. And worship you with my body, as I promised to do in church."

"I want to see you, too," she said. "Whenever you appeared at an event, I watched you. It was easy to do without attracting notice, because everybody watched the three of you, to see what outrage you'd commit next." The words spilled out of her, indiscreet, but they needed to be let out. "The whole time, though, I was watching *you* — the way you moved, the way you danced. I wanted to be the dashing lady you danced with. I didn't even realize I was watching in that way or thinking those things or why. Or, if I did know, I refused to admit it to myself."

"I watched you, too," he said. "And I thought it was a bloody shame you were respectable."

"But I'm not," she said.

"I know that now," he said. "It only took — what was it — six, seven years since you made your debut? How thick can a fellow be?"

"Fortunately, I still have some good years left," she said.

"True." He slid his fingers through her hair, so gently that she trembled.

He kissed her forehead and the tip of her nose. He unhooked her spectacles and set them on the bedside table.

"I won't be able to see you properly," she said.

"I'll stay close," he said.

Her robe de chambre had no buttons or hooks. A tasseled cord at the waist was all that closed it. He untied the cord and the robe fell open. Underneath she wore a white, embroidered muslin nightdress. He brought his hands to her face and caressed her cheeks and her neck. He slid his hands to her shoulders. He bent and kissed her neck, her shoulders, and the hollow of her throat. Her skin vibrated with pleasure but she ached, too, with the sweetness of it, of being touched by him, kissed by him.

He untied the ribbon at the neckline and slipped the nightdress down past her shoulders. She was acutely aware of the night air on her skin.

He slid his fingers down from her neck to her breasts, pushing the neckline lower as he went, until her breasts were fully exposed to him. But she was a bad girl, and didn't feel shy or modest at all. Besides, he'd seen her already, in the fishing house. She wanted him to look at her the way he'd done then, as though she were the most beautiful creature he'd ever seen.

His face changed and she saw the look she remembered. She caught a glimpse of something else as well, something unexpected. Pain?

But he bent his head, then his mouth was on her, his lips trailing over her breast, the lightest of caresses. Light as it was, she felt it deep within her, tugging at her heart and lower down, yes, and now she recognized the feeling, the wanting.

She wanted him, and she understood

she'd waited years for him, without hope because she hadn't dared to understand herself. She'd made herself what she ought to be, and it was like a dress that didn't fit. No wonder her tiresome cousin mocked her.

Then he took the bud of her breast into his mouth and suckled and she forgot the past, her cousin, relatives, everything. She grasped his arms and held on, letting the sensations wash over her and through her, and she felt drunk, so beautifully drunk.

She'd learned to believe that no man would want her, truly want her, as she was.

He wanted her.

He teased and suckled the other breast, and worked his way down, drawing her nightdress down as he went and teasing her skin with his mouth and his too-adept hands. He licked her navel, making swirls with his tongue, and she let out a wild little cry.

He went lower still, and the nightdress slid down over her hips to the rug.

Then he put his mouth *there,* between her legs, and her body tightened. Spasms went through her, of heat and delight and a growing need.

"Oh," she gasped. "Oh, my goodness. Oh, *Ripley.*"

He didn't stop, and the feelings built to

an intensity all but unbearable. She dragged her hands through his hair and her body pulsed and pulsed, out of her control, until a fierce sensation racked her, and she let go of him, and slumped.

He grasped her waist and lifted her up and onto the bed.

While she caught her breath and tried to find her mind, he threw off his dressing gown.

Then she was short of breath again. For a moment she simply lay there, gazing at him while her heart thumped and her breath came in gulps.

Then she slid up onto the pillows and drank in her fill. He was her husband. She could look. And the front view was as beautiful as the back view had been, that day he'd stood naked in the basin.

She hadn't seen much of him in the fishing house. They'd kept most of their clothes on. Now . . .

His skin was bronze in the candlelight and perhaps from the sun of Italy, where he'd been so recently. The light glinting over the fine dusting of hair seemed to feather it with gold. Powerful shoulders and muscled arms and chest and belly — he was as beautiful and hard and solid as a Greek or Roman statue. With a difference. She'd seen classical statues, not all with fig leaves. She'd seen pictures in books. He was . . .

"Good heavens," she said in a stricken voice she barely recognized as hers.

He looked down to where his manly organ swelled . . . rather dauntingly.

"This is what happens," he said, "when a man is mad for his wife. But don't worry. Hardly ever fatal, as I might have mentioned some days ago."

She laughed. "Oh, Ripley, you say the most romantic things."

"Wish I could," he said. "In my case, best to let actions speak louder."

He climbed onto the bed and knelt over her.

"But you like words," he said. "I'll give you some. You're wonderful."

She felt tears prick her eyes.

"You were wonderful drunk and running away," he said. "You were wonderful, issuing commands. Telling me to help you over the wall and ordering me about and giving me the devil's own time trying to manage you. I wish I had starting chasing after you years ago. So much fun I missed."

"We'll make up for it," she said shakily. With a knuckle she rubbed her eye.

"No crying," he said.

"I'm not," she said. "I'm only . . . It's very

460

emotional. Conjugal relations."

"When it's done right, yes."

"When it's with the right one." She managed a smile. "Or when it's with the right wrong one." She put up her arms. "Kiss me," she said.

"As my lady commands." He bent and let her arms curl round his shoulders, and he kissed her. This time it wasn't so gentle. The tenderness was there, but fiercer and darker. It was like passing through a spring mist into a summer storm.

This time she touched him, too, exploring and learning the shape and feel of him the way he'd learned her. She ranged kisses over his shoulders and his arms, and moved her hands over as much of him as she could reach. And when she felt his sex pressed against her, she grasped his buttocks, and she heard his choked laugh as he stroked her in the place between her legs where he'd kissed her and done the lewdest, most delicious things, and where she ached for him now. Then at last, he pushed into her, and made a sound like a groan and a laugh combined.

This time her body gave way to him so easily. Then feeling was everything: the sense of joining and completion and the happiness of it. She was aware of heat and the scent of his skin and the mingled scent of their bodies but, above all, of the extraordinary feel of him inside her. She lifted her legs and wrapped them about him and he plunged deeper and she cried out: no words, merely sounds, of surprise and pleasure.

This time it went on for so much longer than it had done in that feverish time in the fishing house. This time they made love, unhurried, because of course they had all the time in the world. Lovemaking was all the dances with him she'd missed, but a great deal more: deeply intimate, skin to skin, hot and so joyous. She moved with him, following the rhythm he set — slow at first, then building and building, like a mad waltz, until she was spun away up into the heavens. Then she was a star, alight, and exploding with happiness. Then smaller explosions, and finally, she was drifting in the night sky, drifting downward, until she fell safely into his waiting arms.

CHAPTER 17

It wasn't enough.

It was all Ripley had.

He held her tightly, because this might be the last night he ever held her.

He said, "Now, that was more like it."

"I see," said his duchess. "These conjugal relations are not quite perfect unless the lady faints."

"Or screams. Preferably both."

She turned slightly in his arms to look up at him. "No wonder I could find nothing in the books at Newland House. No wonder Mama became unintelligible."

"Oh, there are books," he said. "I have an extensive collection of licentious works. Some are quite antique, though nothing to compare to the 1450 Mazarin Bible with movable types."

"The *first* with movable types," she corrected.

He laughed. "I am also the proud owner

of a generous selection of naughty prints, including a fine set of obscene works by Thomas Rowlandson. Where would you file naughty books, by the way, in your system?"

"Natural philosophy," she said. "Or in one of the categories of literature, depending."

He narrowed his eyes at her. "It seems you're not entirely innocent in that regard. I should have realized."

"Boccaccio," she said. "Ovid. Chaucer. But when one knows nothing, these sorts of works don't mean much. Now I shall study them with more knowledgeable eyes."

"If you'd ever come upon *The School of Venus,* you would have understood better. From the time of King Charles II, I believe. It describes, in frank detail, the sorts of things couples get up to. With illustrations."

Her eyes widened. He couldn't be sure what color they were at present, in the flickering candlelight. "Does it, indeed? That sounds like what I was looking for, when I was searching for information in my uncle's library. But I hardly knew where to look."

"If he has such books, doubtless he keeps them hidden," Ripley said. "As must your father."

"I'm not sure Papa knows what's in his library," she said. "And since it's coming to

464

us, he'll never find out. I hope you've thought of where to put them."

In exchange for a generous financial arrangement, the collection of the Earl of Gonerby's library was to be one of the items Olympia brought to the marriage. This was one of the conditions Ripley had added to the marriage settlements.

"You can put the books wherever you like," Ripley said. "We can enlarge the library here or move them to the house in Lincolnshire. Or one of the other houses. You may choose to shift volumes wherever you like. There's some worthless stuff, too, you'll want to cull. Plenty for you to do, though I'm not sure I can offer as much in that way as Mends could."

She pushed herself up onto one elbow. "I was not meaning to spend all of my time as your librarian, duke."

"I'm relieved to hear it. Because I have fantasies." He thought of all he'd missed in not having a wife. But no, it couldn't have been the same with any wife. It had to be Olympia. And it had to be now. The wrong time, the wrong circumstances . . . Never mind. No mawkishness. He had *now*.

"Well, if I must spend most of my time in bed —"

"A bed is not strictly required," he said.

"If I am to spend most of my time engaging in conjugal relations, it's good to know you have a lively imagination. Fantasies."

He grinned. "I do, my dear. Shocking ones. I imagine you as my hostess —"

"Your *hostess*?"

"I see you giving London's grandest balls and its most tantalizing dinner parties," he said. "I imagine driving you through the park and riding with you. I can picture the dashing ensembles you'll wear as a leader of fashion."

"I'm shocked, indeed."

"A bachelor duke is one thing," he said. "A married duke, however, has social obligations. And I do like to entertain, as you're well aware. But henceforth, my soirees will be the talk of the town for entirely different reasons. Imagine the jaws dropping when the beau monde reads in *Foxe's Morning Spectacle* of our entertaining the King and Queen."

"I can see the gentlemen in the clubs, falling out of their chairs in shock," she said. "Frankly, I should have fallen out of bed if you weren't in the way."

She leaned over and drew her fingers through his hair.

Her touch, her touch.

Her voice.

The feel of her skin and the warm curves of her body and the way she smiled and frowned and laughed. The way she looked at him, as though he were the whole world. Why had he waited for so long? Why had he been so stupid and blind?

"And shall we dance together, at last?" she said softly.

"We shall dance," he said.

He thought of all the promises he might break, so unwillingly, depending on what tomorrow brought. He added, "In fact, let's start now."

"We'll pretend to dance, you mean," she said.

"No." He sat up and kissed the top of her head. And her nose.

Then he climbed down from the bed. He found her nightdress and crooked his finger at her.

"It would be naughtier to dance au naturel," he said. "But that would be asking too much of my paltry self-denial skills."

She slid down from the bed and he tossed the nightgown over her head. Laughing, she pushed her arms through the sleeves and tied the ribbon.

He pulled on his dressing gown and tied the sash.

"You stand by the fireplace," he said.

"Pretend to be talking to your precious Mends, and be as pedantic as you can."

"I need my spectacles," she said. She snatched them up from the bedside table, put them on, and walked to the fireplace in the same way she might walk across a room at a ball. That beckoning hint of impatience. The Queen of Sheba must have walked like that. And Cleopatra.

She made her face very grave and began talking to one of the mantel ornaments. It was a porcelain gentleman wearing the dress of Ripley's grandfather's time, who sat at a desk, writing a letter. "I believe you are mistaken, Lord Mends. It's my understanding that the Antonio di Siena *Monte Santo di Dio,* with the three rare engravings by Baldini, from designs by Sandro Botticelli, is judged the earliest Book with Copperplates."

Ripley strode across the room to her. His right ankle gave a twinge, but he refused to let himself limp.

"Lady Olympia," he said, "I've come to claim my dance."

She looked up at him with a little frown of annoyance. "I don't recollect your asking, duke, nor my consenting."

"I didn't ask. This is the dance I want. And I *am* a duke, recollect."

From under lowered eyelids she regarded him up and down and up again, and he was aware of his temperature climbing. That look. Those eyes.

"So you are," she said. She sighed and turned to the porcelain gentleman. "I beg your pardon, Lord Mends, but as you see, he's a duke, and you know how *they* are."

Ripley took her hand and led her out to the center of the room. He bowed. She curtsied. He began to hum a waltz from Rossini's *La Gazza Ladra,* and swept her into his arms, and they danced.

His bad ankle protested from time to time, but halfheartedly. Nothing more than a small ache.

He ignored it, and they danced as easily and naturally together as they'd made love. As easily as they'd run away together.

He wished he'd danced with her before.

So many lost opportunities.

But they danced now, barefoot, whirling round her bedchamber while he hummed the music, and now and again sang a remembered Italian phrase here and there — probably the wrong phrase in the wrong place, but no matter. They danced from one end of the large room to the other. They danced into the dressing room and out again, Olympia giggling. They danced into the boudoir and round it, and out again into the bedroom. He didn't want it to end, but the night was short, too short, in summer, and he hadn't much time left.

At last he brought it to an end. He promenaded with her round the room, as though it were a ballroom, but instead of bringing her back to the gentleman on the mantelpiece, Ripley led her to the bed.

He bowed.

She curtsied.

They laughed, rather breathlessly.

He cupped her face. "I love you madly," he said.

"I love you madly," she said.

His heart beat hard again, and not from the waltzing. He thought it would burst from his chest. He thought he might weep. But he couldn't indulge. She wasn't to suspect and he wouldn't be maudlin. He had a dragon to slay, that was all. It was no reason to spoil this night for her, their first night as a married couple.

He said, "Good. Now that's settled . . ."

He quickly untied the sash of his dressing gown, shrugged it off, and threw it aside. She untied the ribbon of her nightdress and pulled it over her head.

He picked her up and lifted her onto the bed.

He made love to her again, as sweetly and tenderly as he knew how.

This time they slept afterward.

But the knowledge of what the coming day held never left him. It ticked steadily inside, like a clock, and he was awake when the sky began to lighten. She was still sound asleep, and scarcely stirred when he gently drew away from her.

Her breathing continued steady as he slipped out of the bed and found his dressing gown. He took out from a pocket the note he'd written and left it on the bedside table. Noiselessly he made his way through the passage joining their apartments and into his own rooms.

His valet, Snow, one of the handful of people aware of the morning's appointment, brought him coffee and a biscuit.

Ripley drank the coffee and ate the biscuit. He wanted neither. But he'd done this before. One needed coffee and something light to eat. One had to be awake, alert, and above all, not shaky with hunger or fatigue.

He dressed in black. The wise duelist always wore dark colors, to make himself a more difficult target, especially on a typically overcast London morning.

At the appointed time, he went out of the house with Snow. They walked out into

South Audley Street and on into Stanhope Street, thence into Park Lane where a post chaise waited. Pershore was inside. Leaving Snow to follow in another vehicle, Ripley climbed in.

The post chaise set out for Putney Heath.

Olympia was dancing at Almack's.

In the gallery, Weippert's band played a waltz from Rossini's *La Gazza Ladra.* She danced, in her nightdress, with Ripley. He was dressed like a Turkish pasha, mustachioed and wearing a jeweled and plumed turban, puffy trousers, and slippers that curled at the toes. They were the only ones dancing. Everybody else watched and pointed, laughing. Then somebody shouted, "Stop them! Stop them! They're getting away!"

The scene changed, and she and Ripley were running across Battersea Bridge, chased by an immense dog whose long fangs dripped foam. They vaulted into a hackney coach, slamming the door. The dog flung himself against it, barking furiously. Inside they found Ashmont, who held a pistol. While Olympia watched, unable to speak or move, he raised the weapon and aimed it at Ripley's heart. Outside the coach, the dog clawed at the door, howling like a demon. Ashmont pulled the trigger.

Olympia awoke, her heart pounding as though she truly had been running from demons and found herself trapped with a murderous former fiancé.

For a moment she couldn't shake off the dream, and didn't know where she was. Then, she realized the room wasn't dark but filled with the pearly light of early morning. Her gaze took in the costly bed hangings, and she remembered.

She closed her eyes. Last night. Ripley, so passionate and so tender. It was like a dream, like the fantasies of her girlhood. He'd made her feel like a princess in a story. He'd made her wedding night perfect, as he'd promised. He . . .

. . . wasn't here.

She sat up, chilled. She could see he wasn't there, but she put her hand out to touch the pillow where his head had rested. The pillow was cold.

Yes, of course married couples had separate bedrooms. They shared a bed only for lovemaking. Of course. But did they separate on their wedding night?

He'd been so affectionate.

I love you madly.

She hadn't dreamt that.

She hadn't dreamt the barefoot dancing,

or Ripley humming a waltz as he whirled her through her rooms. She hadn't dreamt the lovemaking. Her body ached in places where it wasn't used to aching. She hadn't dreamt falling asleep in his arms.

All that was real. This was, too. Good grief, what a ninny she was! For all she knew, he'd only gone out to use the water closet. And if he'd gone to his rooms, maybe he'd only wanted to let her sleep undisturbed . . . which was perfectly normal and reasonable and even thoughtful. If not for the bad dream, she'd still be sleeping.

Set back from the busy streets on all sides, and with its extensive garden, the main part of Ripley House received more sunlight than many London town houses did. Though the sun rose at four o'clock at this time of year, and though it didn't shine very brightly this morning, the angle of light and the quietness of the household told her she'd awakened hours earlier than she usually did. Her wedding night had extended long past midnight, she was sure.

If she didn't want to look haggard, she ought to go back to sleep.

She remained as she was, sitting upright, staring at the mantelpiece, where the porcelain gentleman she'd pretended was Lord Mends sat at his little writing desk.

She told herself nothing was wrong.

Something was wrong.

She pushed to the edge of the bed and was about to climb down when she saw the folded piece of heavy paper on the bedside table.

My dearest girl,

By the time you read this, matters will be settled, for good or ill. You'll be furious, I know, and call me a hundred synonyms for *idiot*. Believe me, could I behave in a more intelligent manner, I would. But my brain, you know. "Like his, more or less, though *less* defies the imagination." You said that to me on Tuesday. Do you remember? I remember so clearly. I hear you saying it, your changeable eyes slightly unfocused, due to brandy, and I find myself grinning like a simpleton.

Had it been possible to avoid this morning's imbecility, I vow I would have done it. However, I could not offer my friend the satisfaction he required. I regret betraying his trust. I regret the mortification he's endured. For these I could apologize. But I don't regret falling over head and ears in love with you. For all I know, I did this years ago, but was too stupid to realize it. At any rate, I know it now, and I refuse to apologize for failing to return you to him. When I think how close I came to doing so, and let myself imagine you as his wife instead of mine — but no. Let's not imagine it. You're mine, and I saved myself by the skin of my teeth.

Losing a friendship is certainly not too high a price to pay, when I would willingly lose my life for you. Not that I intend to, mind! But if things go badly for me, you must always remember that I regret nothing but any pain this day's events may cause you. You must always believe that I would not give back a single minute of the last four days, for any consideration. You must always believe I love you, dearly, dearly.

Believe me, dear Olympia,
my dear duchess,
Your adoring idiot,
Ripley

"You *idiot*!" Olympia cried.

She climbed down from the bed and rang for a servant. When nobody appeared instantly, she ran across the room, flung open the door, and shouted at the footman dozing in the corridor, "When did he leave?"

The footman Joseph stumbled up from his chair, blinking. "I beg Your Grace's pardon?"

"The duke," she said. "When did he leave?"

Joseph's eyes darted back and forth, as though he expected to see Ripley pop out from under one of the corridor's pier tables. "I don't know, Your Grace."

"Find out," she said. "And have somebody rouse my maid and Wrenson. Now." Wrenson was the house steward. It was his business to know everything about everybody at every minute.

Joseph looked panicked.

"Now," she said. "Wrenson will know if anybody does. But if he doesn't, or pretends not to know, you must make the porter tell you. And tell him I want a hackney cab — not a coach — waiting at the door in ten minutes. I don't care if you wake all the household. We've not a moment to lose."

She'd adopted the tone of voice she'd learned would quell males of all ages and ranks. The footman took off at a run.

She hurried back into her room and into the dressing room. She flung open wardrobe drawers and yanked out articles at random. "Jenkins!" she called. "Where the devil are you? How am I to find anything? Jenkins!

For heaven's sake, make haste!"

She was pulling dresses out of the drawers, and throwing them on the floor with their wrappings, when Jenkins hurried in, still tying her dressing gown, nightcap askew.

The maid's eyes widened as she took in the destruction her mistress had wrought.

"I need something I can put on quickly," Olympia said. "No bright colors." If she wore bright colors they'd see her coming from afar, and she might be a fatal distraction. "Ten minutes, no more — and even then I might be too late."

"Your Grace?"

"I'll explain later. We haven't time now." Olympia looked out of the dressing room's window. "We have a prayer of getting there before it's too late. They wouldn't start before six o'clock in summer. What time is it, Jenkins?"

"Close to half-past four, Your Grace."

"Time enough," Olympia said. "But I must be dressed in ten minutes — and that hackney had better be at the door."

"Your Grace, you know it is impossible —"

"Make it possible, Jenkins. This is a matter of life and death. I'll go in my chemise, if you can't dress me quickly enough."

The prospect of Her Grace of Ripley appearing in public in her chemise electrified Jenkins into doing the impossible.

It took a quarter hour, but Olympia had reckoned on twenty minutes at the very minimum for both the hackney and her attire. Jenkins had managed to dress both her mistress and herself in what amounted to no time because she insisted on joining Olympia, and Olympia said she wouldn't wait for her.

And so the Duchess of Ripley and her lady's maid left the house in good time — or as good as was humanly possible — perhaps not more than half an hour behind her husband, according to the porter.

The seconds would have to mark out and measure the ground, Olympia explained to Jenkins as the hackney made its way through the London streets. This could take time, because each second would want to place his man in the best position. A last-minute attempt to reconcile the combatants was possible, certainly. Though the meeting was likely appointed for six — the usual time in summer — it might be as late as seven. Either way, the actual fighting couldn't start until all the formalities had been gone through and everything had been checked and agreed upon.

Olympia kept her mind on the technicalities of the duel, so as not to dwell on the actualities of pistols firing deadly balls at two great blockheads who were supposed to be the best of friends.

Fortunately for her nerves, her hackney made good progress. Since Ripley House stood not far from Park Lane, they traveled the wider streets of the metropolis. The market wagons were making their way into London, but Olympia's hackney reached Hyde Park Corner without hindrance. Before long it was rolling upon the Fulham Road, headed for Putney Heath.

On the way to the place of meeting, Pershore offered Ripley a bottle of soda water dosed with a small amount of brandy.

Ripley took it with a laugh. "Ah, the bracing-up."

"You may not need it," said Pershore. "I do."

"Whether needed or not, it's an agreeable stimulant at this hour." Ripley drank. "I should have liked another hour or more of sleep." With his wife in his arms. But at least he'd had his wedding and his wedding night. And such a wedding night it had been!

"A duel on the day after your wedding,"

Pershore said. "That was ill done of Ashmont."

"He deems it ill done of me to have married his bride."

"If he'd waited longer, his temper would have cooled."

"Then what?" Ripley said. "He's the talk of London, which is nothing new, except that this time he's wounded in a man's tenderest part, his pride. He needs the meeting — and I confess I do, too. We've no other way to put the matter to rest." They had to fight. Otherwise there would always be bad blood between them. No other remedy but for one or both of them to put a bullet in the other.

Barbaric, Olympia would call it. But men were barbaric.

If the seconds had found a way to reconcile them, Ripley would have been amazed as well as glad. The task, as he'd supposed, had turned out to be impossible. Since they hadn't succeeded in making peace, he needed to focus on fighting and winning.

He couldn't go into this halfheartedly. Ashmont wouldn't.

Ripley couldn't dwell on his long history with Ashmont and Blackwood or the way they had saved one another at various times, but especially when they were three deeply unhappy boys during those first miserable days at Eton. It was like fighting one's own brother. But one couldn't think that way.

This was an affair of honor.

Honor demanded Ripley do his best to kill his friend and his friend do his best to kill him.

They reached Putney Heath in plenty of time. They arranged for the post chaise to wait in a sheltered place nearby, where the wounded or dead could be quickly taken. The post chaise also needed to be where it wasn't likely to attract the attention of Metropolitan Police on the lookout for exactly this sort of illegal early morning encounter.

After taking out the pistol case, Pershore and Ripley walked the short distance to the agreed-upon spot.

They arrived first, as Ripley had hoped to do.

He coolly strolled about the dueling ground, as though he'd merely come ahead of the other guests for a party. His ankle still wasn't altogether happy, but he refused to limp or lean on his walking stick.

The surgeon and Ripley's valet, who'd arrived shortly after Ripley and his second, left him to his solitude and kept out of Pershore's way. The latter was looking for obstacles to the line of sight when Ashmont and his second, Morris, emerged from one of the footpaths, surgeon and servant trailing behind.

Olympia's hackney stopped at the Putney Bridge tollgate, where it seemed to take forever to pay the toll and another forever for the gate to open. They clattered over the crazy old bridge and into the High Street, past the White Lion.

Her mind painted images: she, falling into the water . . . Ripley carrying her to the inn, while the onlookers hooted and cheered . . . the dressmaker and her minions and their naughty corset . . . Ripley standing naked in a basin . . . the scene with Bullard in the courtyard . . .

So much, in a single day, and the time they'd spent in Putney was only a part of that unforgettable day.

It could not be over so soon.

They could not have found each other only for it to end now.

It could not end with his falling dead in a muddy field on a summer morning, the day after their wedding.

"I'll kill you," she muttered. "You can't do this to me, Ripley."

"Your Grace?"

"What time is it?" Olympia said.

The last effort at reconciliation failed, as it was bound to do.

His face a mask, Ripley strode calmly to his station and looked hard at Ashmont, who appeared as cold and calm as Ripley.

Pershore gave Ripley his pistol.

Ripley's dueling pistols were always kept in pristine condition. The insides of the barrels held not an iota of rust. Locks and hair triggers were in order. Ripley knew to a nicety the throw of his pistols. Nonetheless, he'd checked them early this morning before leaving his house, and he and Pershore had checked them again when they were loaded. They were properly charged. He had no worries about misfires or other such accidents.

He, Blackwood, and Ashmont had been practicing since they were boys, and not simply shooting at targets. Using a rather complicated "dummy" operated by wires, which discharged a pistol — sans ball, of course — at them as soon as they shot, had taught them to be cool under fire. It was a skill Blackwood's exacting father had impressed upon them. Though the previous Duke of Blackwood had abhorred duels, he understood there were times when they couldn't be avoided. This being the case, a man ought to know how to carry it off properly.

Having seconded Ashmont in all too many affairs of honor, Ripley was as familiar with his ways as with his own. He didn't underestimate him, drunk or sober. Today, he appeared sober. Even he wouldn't be such a fool as to stay up all night drinking before a duel.

Ripley positioned himself sideways and exactly in line with his opponent, pistol in his right hand, the muzzle pointing straight down. He stamped his feet, to anchor himself firmly on the ground. He stood ramrod straight and raised his right arm, keeping his gaze, not on Ashmont, but on one of the buttons of his coat. He knew Ashmont was doing the same: choosing a small object to aim at, and concentrating on that.

They knew each other too well. They'd done this too many times, though this was the first time they'd aimed at each other.

The chances of their killing each other were exceedingly good.

Sorry, Olympia.

But that was the only moment of sentiment Ripley allowed himself. There was no place for emotion on the dueling ground.

The seconds retired to a safe distance

behind the duelists.

The surgeons took position not many feet behind them.

The servants moved back, behind the surgeons.

Ripley cocked his pistol and raised it.

All his mind, his being, was focused on hitting Ashmont. He knew Ashmont was doing the same, shutting out every other thought, every regret, every memory.

"Ready, gentlemen?"

"Ready," said Ripley and Ashmont at the same time.

When Olympia glimpsed the post chaise, nearly hidden among the trees, she made the hackney driver stop, and she was pushing down the ancient window, reaching for the door handle before the coach had quite stopped altogether.

She leapt into the road and ran toward the post chaise, Jenkins behind her.

"Where?" she said to the postilion. "Where are they?"

"Dunno," he said.

"You do know. They're —"

She broke off, hearing voices.

"Best not go in there all wild, missus," said the postilion. "Dunno what you'll get in the middle of. They been there a good while yet."

He was right. She had no idea what had happened, and the last thing she wanted was to make a distraction and be the cause of somebody getting killed by accident.

As opposed to getting killed on purpose, damn them.

But, oh, please let them still be fussing about ground and distance.

She made her way as quietly as she could along the path the men must have taken . . . and came to a sudden, shocked stop as the clearing opened up before her.

They were already in place, raising their pistols.

It was like the nightmare, where she'd been frozen, unable to move or speak. Now she didn't dare. She could only remain perfectly still, hoping Ripley hadn't noticed her out of the corner of his eye. It was too late to stop him. She mustn't distract him and throw off his aim.

All this went through her mind in no time but seemed like an eternity while she stared helplessly at the tableau: Ripley's hand holding the pistol pointed at his friend. Ashmont's pistol pointing at Ripley. Both men standing so rigid. From where she stood, they seemed to be made of stone.

A voice called out, "Ready, gentlemen?"

At the same moment, the two men said, "Ready," while she covered her mouth and held back the scream inside her: *Nooooooo!*

She saw the handkerchief fall. So slowly it seemed to fall, hanging in the air and fluttering down, down, down. Two blasts rent the morning's quiet, one an instant after the other.

In the same endless moment she saw Ripley's arm go up, his pistol firing into the air. Birds exploded, screeching, from the trees while she watched helplessly as he spun and fell to the ground.

Chapter 18

Olympia remained immobile, unable to believe what her eyes told her.

The world was so quiet, but for the birds, still squawking.

Numb, she watched Ashmont give his pistol to a man nearby and run to Ripley. Another man was moving that way, but Ashmont pushed him aside.

She moved then, on stiff muscles.

She saw Ashmont kneel on the ground and lift Ripley's head up. Something dark spread over the side of his face and down his neck.

She saw Ripley's body convulse. Ashmont's body shook, too, as he bent over his friend.

The numbness broke, and she ran across the clearing.

She flung herself at Ashmont, shoving him so hard, he fell over.

"Get away from him!" she cried. "Leave

him alone!"

She knelt beside her husband, whose body, on its side, was in spasms. Blood. So much blood. She wanted to be sick.

She was aware of another man there, opening a black bag, but he was simply there, like the indignant birds. Noise. Background.

She became aware of another sound, too, completely discordant.

It took a moment to recognize what it was.

Laughter. Great, rolling guffaws. She looked down at her husband's blood-streaked head. He was curled up, laughing.

She looked over at Ashmont, who'd rolled onto his knees. He was holding his stomach and laughing, too.

"I hate you!" she cried. "I hate you both."

She fisted her hands and pounded Ripley's arm. "You idiot! What is wrong with you?" She hit him and hit him. She was crying and she hated it, but she couldn't stop.

Finally Ripley grabbed her hand. "It's all right," he gasped.

"It isn't," she said. "Nothing is right. Look at you. What's wrong with you?"

Ripley was grinning. Blood trickled over his face.

"Ripley!"

"S-sorry, m'dear." He let out a snort. Ashmont made the same sound.

"I hate you both so much," Olympia said.

"If Your Grace would be so good as to allow me to examine His Grace," said the man with the black bag.

She moved aside. She drew up her knees and folded her arms on them. She rested her forehead on her arms and tried to catch her breath. Her heart wouldn't stop pounding.

"Dammit, Olympia," Ripley said. "You were supposed to be sleeping."

She looked up. "Don't speak to me."

He sat up, wincing as he did so. He put his hand up to his head. "That stings, rather." He took away his hand. It was sticky with blood. Blood oozed from the side of his head and covered half his face.

She put her head back down on her forearms again.

"We'll have it mended in a jiffy, Your Grace," said the man with the black bag. "Grazed the scalp. I believe Her Grace requires sal volatile."

"No," Olympia said. "I never faint." How many times had she seen younger brothers bleeding? They were always falling out of windows or trees or into lakes or onto rocks. Or fighting. But this was different. "It seems he's not dead."

"Apparently not," Ripley said. "Don't feel dead."

She turned away. She was furious and terrified at the same time. He laughed, but he would, while he had breath in his body. The surgeon made it out to be minor, but of course he would. Men made light of the most ghastly things and fell into a desperate state over trivia.

But there was so much blood. She remembered the way Ripley had acted about his sprained ankle. Men deemed it beneath them to be injured. They pretended they weren't. They'd pretend at death's door.

She edged away. She didn't need to hover while the surgeon attended to her dolt of a husband. Ripley wasn't at death's door. She was merely overwrought. Her hands were shaking. She glared at them.

"Yes, best to let the surgeon get on with it," Ashmont said. "Don't want the bastard to bleed to death from a trifling hole in the head."

"Trifling?" Ripley said. "Dammit, you almost killed me. What in blazes were you thinking?"

"You deloped!" Ashmont said. "You were supposed to shoot *at* me, you cheating bastard."

"Cheating?" Ripley said. "What did you

think I'd do? You almost killed me, you half-wit."

"What's wrong with you?" Ashmont said. "You didn't even *try* to kill me."

"Did you think I would?"

"Why not?"

While this went on, the surgeon went on calmly with his work. For once in her life, Olympia did not feel inclined to watch. At any rate, she had an idea what needed to be done. She would have cleaned the place and applied pressure to stop the bleeding. If it was as minor as the surgeon said, the bleeding would stop relatively soon. How long, she didn't know.

But none of the men were at all concerned. She would have sensed tension, even if they didn't show it. She sensed . . . relief?

Men.

"A hole in the head," she muttered. "Are we quite sure it wasn't already there?"

The surgeon threw her a faint smile. "The ball nicked His Grace's ear very slightly and grazed the scalp. It seems a great deal worse than it is because head wounds bleed profusely." He'd begun bandaging Ripley's head. "The wound is not mortal, I'm glad to say. Very nice. Very clean."

"He'll live?" she said.

493

"If you let me," Ripley said.

"You!" she said. "I'm not speaking to you." She glared at Ashmont. "Or you."

"I?" Ashmont said. "He was supposed to shoot *at* me. He didn't even shoot in my general direction."

"I couldn't shoot my best friend," Ripley said. "I told myself I could, but I couldn't."

"I was counting on you to shoot!" Ashmont said. "I would have missed you by a hair. But you put your curst arm up and spoiled my aim, damn you to hell."

"How was I to know?"

"What else could I do?"

Olympia looked from one to the other in disbelief. "Do not tell me this was all for show."

"Honor," Ripley said.

"Honor," Ashmont said.

"His," Ripley said. "Mine." He studied Ashmont's face for a moment, then looked at her. "Yours, too, duchess."

"Yours especially," Ashmont said.

She stared at him. "I! As though I'd want such folly committed in my name."

"Dammit, Olympia," Ashmont said. "I couldn't let you go without a fight."

"A *serious* fight," Ripley said. "Punch in the face was insufficient."

"It would have looked better if you'd actually shot at me," Ashmont told him.

"I daresay."

"Looked better!" Olympia couldn't believe her ears. She ought to. She had six brothers.

And exactly as her brothers would do, the two men regarded her with deeply puzzled expressions.

The surgeon quietly collected his bag and left.

Ripley said, "But don't you see? If Ashmont didn't fight over you, it would look as though he didn't think you were worth it."

"But you are," Ashmont said. "Had to fight."

"Heaven grant me strength." Olympia threw up her hands and walked away.

Ripley and Ashmont watched her leave. She walked with more than a hint of impatience this time.

Ashmont said, "Can't expect women to understand. You do, though."

"Yes. Took me a moment. A bit complicated."

"I daresay."

"Give us a hand up, will you?"

Ashmont helped him up. "I did rather want to kill you," he said. "Or wound you severely, at the very least. So I thought, at any rate."

"I know. Why didn't you?"

Why. Ripley had asked for an explanation, which one didn't do.

Ashmont's brow knit, and a long moment passed before he smiled again, crookedly, this time, and gave a shrug. "The letter she wrote. It was . . . kind."

His blue gaze returned to Olympia, storming toward the footpath. "You'd better go after her. Awkward if she bolts. Again."

He laughed and walked away to join the men who'd come with him.

Ripley went after his wife.

He found her waiting by the post chaise. Arms folded, she watched him approach. He took care not to limp. His head ached and stung, but he was not about to admit that.

"I suppose I'll have to change the bandages," she said. "And apply ice."

"Certainly not," he said. "Snow will do it. Do you want to hurt his feelings?"

She looked at his valet. "You will return to Ripley House with Jenkins. The duke and I shall travel in the post chaise."

Snow started to follow her orders — as men seemed unable to help doing — but caught himself and looked to Ripley.

496

"As Her Grace says," Ripley said. "Means to ring a peal over me, I don't doubt. Go, go. It won't be your first journey in a hackney, and Jenkins won't bite you. At least not very hard. Odds of infection quite small, I'd say."

Snow went away.

Pershore had had sense enough to make himself scarce.

If Ripley had been Pershore, and seen Olympia coming at him, he would have run, too.

Ripley helped Olympia into the carriage, then climbed in beside her.

Silence and a decided frostiness of atmosphere reigned until they neared the Green Man public house, at the crest of Putney Hill.

"We can stop, if you like," she said. "I know it's traditional, after a duel."

Ah. Thaw seemed to be in progress.

"Not today," he said. "Had a small bracer before. Brandy and soda water. That's traditional, too."

"I wish I'd known," she said. "That's what I could have taken before the wedding. The first wedding. Brandy is well enough. Tea is well enough. But together, they're not delicious. I'm glad to know you required a bracer. That shows some degree of sensibility."

"I wasn't insensible," he said. "But I wasn't afraid of Ashmont. Knew there was a chance he'd hit me. Still, the odds are small, you know, of fatality. One in fourteen. Merely one in six chances of being wounded."

She looked at him over her spectacles. "Merely."

"You're the practical and sensible one," he said. "Let's look at this practically and sensibly. Let us divide a duelist's body into nine parts. If a man's positioned himself properly, the ball won't kill him unless he's hit in one of three of those parts."

"Positioned himself properly. And that would be, say, in the next village?"

"Thing is, you don't face your man full front. That's ridiculous. But if you stand as we did, the chances against getting hit are five to one, and three to one against one of those hits doing for you."

"The chances are not nil, I notice."

"My dear girl, what do you reckon the chances were of your getting killed racing to Putney in a hackney cabriolet? Those so-called drivers think they're jockeys at Goodwood. The cabs are death traps. You know as well as I do they throw passengers into the road all the time. I'm the one ought to be furious with you for taking such chances, but I'm not, because I'm a forgiving fellow, and I know you did it out of worry for me. Which wouldn't have happened if you'd slept as you were supposed to. Didn't I tire you enough last night?"

Her eyes widened. "Was that why you did . . . all that? To wear me out?"

"Plague take it, do you think I'm as calculating as all that? All I wanted was you, and to make the most of our wedding night, and to make sure you never forgot it. I fully planned on not getting killed. But one does have to allow for the possibility, small as the odds may be."

She regarded his bandaged head for a moment. "I suppose, if we must look at the matter logically, you demonstrate the odds. An inch or so would have made a vast difference."

"I'd prefer the ball had whizzed an inch *past* the ear," he said. "This was a hair too close."

"Literally."

"All the same, one must give Ashmont credit. He judged about as nicely as is possible to do. We're all shockingly good shots. Blackwood's father saw to it. Drilled and drilled Blackwood. Naturally, we couldn't let him be better, so we drilled and drilled, too. But no matter how good you are, you can't predict what the other fellow will do. Can't know what he's thinking, even if you've known him this age and he's like a brother. I spoiled Ashmont's cunning plan. Stupid of me. Didn't mean to. Meant to shoot properly. But there you are."

In the end, when all was said and done, he'd wronged a friend who was like a brother to him, and the only honorable thing to do was shoot into the air. Ripley wasn't even sure he'd thought it out at the time. It was the work of an instant. He'd meant to aim at Ashmont, then he didn't.

"Oh, Ripley," she said.

The atmosphere had warmed, beyond a doubt.

"Come here," he said. He didn't wait for her to come, but pulled her into his arms and onto his lap. "That's better."

She rested her head against his shoulder. "That was the worst, worst, worst minute or two or however long it was, of my whole life."

"Sorry."

"But you thought I'd be asleep, and you assumed you'd get home, alive, before I woke and read your letter. You didn't mean to make the worst moment of my life happen the day after my wedding. My real wedding."

"It was deuced unsporting of you to wake so early."

"I had a bad dream." She told him about it.

"Me in a turban? Fancy that."

She leaned back to look up at him. "The bandage looks rather like a turban. I don't believe in omens, but I do believe I might have sensed something. With so many brothers, one develops an acute sense when they're up to no good. You're going to have the very devil of a headache, I hope you realize."

It hurt already, and his nerves could have used a brandy, without soda. Two or three brandies. But she was in his arms, and it looked as though he was forgiven, and he wanted to get home and let her make a fuss over him while he pretended he didn't want her fussing.

"I do realize. Went through this once with Ashmont. Long time ago."

"Was this the time when he nearly lost his ear?" she said. "The duel with Lord Stewkley?"

He stared at her. "You know about that?"

She tucked her head back against his shoulder. "I only know there was a duel.

Ten or more years ago, according to Mrs. Thorne. The seamstresses were talking about it, but she wouldn't let them go into detail."

"A boyish prank," Ripley said. "Stewkley didn't see it that way."

"He's a good deal older than you are," she said. "What you did must have been dreadful, for him to fight a young man barely out of school."

"He said we'd insulted his wife, and he fought Ashmont because the prank was Ashmont's idea and he made sure to take credit."

"That was Ashmont's first duel?"

"Yes. Not but what he hadn't been waiting for his chance, as we all did, wanting to prove ourselves, as young fellows do. The quarrel certainly livened up a dull gathering. Some sort of fete, as I recall. There were what-you-call-ems."

"I have no idea what you call them."

"Charades or tableaux or whatever they are. Unspeakably boring. We were to do ancient ruins. Ashmont picked Fountains Abbey. He had a large basin brought in and set on the floor. And we all three made fountains into it."

She gazed at him for a moment. Then her eyes turned very blue and sparkled like stars. And she laughed. And laughed.

That wonderful sound. She made him forget his hurting head. She made him forget his heartache, too, at the prospect of causing her sorrow. She made him forget all the other feelings he'd pushed away, in order to do what had to be done.

He undid her bonnet and took it off. He buried his face in her hair and inhaled the simple scent he liked so much.

He held her, and they didn't talk a great deal for the rest of the way, but at intervals she'd laugh. She said, "I'll never be able to say 'Fountains Abbey' again without going off into whoops."

He grinned down at her, like the doting imbecile he was.

There were, he decided, many, many fine advantages to marrying a bad girl.

The Duke of Ripley hadn't been married a week before he gave a party. Well before the bandages came off, he was closeted with his wife, planning. As he'd told her, he liked to entertain. In the usual way of things, by this time he would have organized some sort of gathering to celebrate his return from the Continent.

One difference for this event was, he'd acquired a hostess: a duchess, in fact.

Another difference was the guests: not a lot of men bent on carousing and curious about the next Their Dis-Graces prank, but a large segment of the beau monde.

Olympia's cousin Edwina attended, looking very cross. But she wouldn't have missed it for the world. This was the case for most invitees. In fact, machinations had gone on behind the scenes, to obtain the coveted invitations. It was the event of the Season: Dreadful Duke Weds Runaway Bride in Scandalous Circumstances.

If the great world had been surprised at the Duke of Blackwood's marriage to Lady Alice Ancaster a year ago, it was thoroughly confounded by this match.

"But she's so boring!" Cousin Edwina said to one of her friends as they watched the couple dance.

The duchess was looking up, saying something to the duke, which caused them both to laugh.

"He doesn't think so," said the friend.

As everybody had hoped, there was further excitement not long thereafter.

When the Duke of Ashmont led his hostess out to dance, the room grew hushed, the atmosphere tense.

"You had to choose a waltz," Olympia said,

as Ashmont swept her into the dance.

"Looks better that way," he said. "More exciting. There's Ripley looking daggers at me while I swoop down and carry off in my arms his wife, who happens to be my former bride."

"You three are masters of show," she said.

"It's fun, getting everybody into an uproar," he said. "Always has been. Breaks up the boredom."

They danced for a while before he spoke again. "After all these years of my upsetting hostess's plans and turning their balls and routs and fetes upside down, they think it served me right to have my wedding go to pieces. Poetic justice, they say. Maybe they're not wrong."

"I'm sorry," she said. "About ruining your wedding." She giggled. "But not really."

He looked at her. "But you wrote —"

"Oh, I meant it. Then."

After a short time, his handsome face broke into one of the smiles that must have undone countless women. "You wrote, asking me to forgive him, but I had to go and shoot him anyway. I did have to, you know."

"So you both claimed. To show I was worth fighting for."

"That, yes," he said. "But there's more. Complicated, as Ripley said. If I hadn't shot him, you'd be truly sorry. You'd feel guilty about what you did and sorry for me, because I would have been so noble and self-sacrificing. What an appalling prospect! Good thing, then, I shot him."

"I should not call it a good thing, but you did spare me a great deal of penitence."

"And myself a sick-making stain on my otherwise black reputation."

"If you'd hurt him a whit more than you did, I should have made you a great deal more than sick," she said.

"I know," he said. "Do you know, when you pushed me off him the other day, that was the first time a woman ever knocked me over?"

"I sincerely hope it won't be the last."

"Wicked girl," he said.

"Yes," she said, and laughed.

He laughed, too. And if he felt regrets, and if they went deep, he put them in a place where they couldn't bother him.

Ripley, dancing with his sister, was looking in the same direction as most of his guests: at Ashmont, laughing with the Duchess of Ripley.

"You do have the devil's own luck," Alice said. "Had you come home from the Continent one day later —"

"Don't say that. You'll give me nightmares. I know it was luck, every step of the way. When the whole business started, I was cursing you for going to Aunt Julia's."

"I? What had I to do with it?"

"If you were at the wedding, I reckoned you'd get the bride back to the groom and the minister in no time."

"Or I might have helped her go."

"That thought hadn't occurred to me."

"I doubt many thoughts occurred to you," she said.

"Be that as it may, luck was with me again. You were far away. But not with Aunt Julia."

"I was with her. For a time."

"And then the Drakeleys? Really?" His gaze went to Blackwood, who was on the other side of the room, dancing with Lady Charles. "Have you something to tell me?"

"No."

The dance was ending and Lady Charles was saying to Blackwood, "I should have thought you would have continued to the Drakeleys that day, and collected your wandering wife."

"Didn't know she needed collecting."

"I'm not surprised. Men usually don't know a blessed thing. I recommend you

507

dance with her."

"Dance with my own wife? What a shocking proposition."

"I thought you enjoyed shocking people. Ah, here is Lord Frederick."

The fair-haired gentleman bowed. "Lady Charles."

"Lord Frederick," she said crisply. "What do you think of men dancing with their own wives?"

"Stranger things have happened," said he. "Will you dance, Lady Charles?"

Lady Charles's eyebrows went up. "With you?"

He looked about. "I was not aware of asking on behalf of any other gentleman."

"Good heavens. Strange things, indeed."

But she let him lead her out.

Hours later, after their guests had gone, the Duke and Duchess of Ripley stood on the small balcony overlooking the garden and watched the sky lighten into the grey twilight that so often passes for dawn in London.

They were dressed for bed, but they were drinking champagne.

"That went off well, I thought, for my first do," Olympia said. "Not that I had much to do with it. I'm so glad I was practical and sensible enough to marry a man who likes to entertain, leaving me at leisure to rampage through his library." She looked up at him. "Though I fear the party might have been a little tame for your taste."

"Now that I'm an old, married man, my tastes have grown more subtle," he said. "I savor the fact that we threw the ton into an uproar. And you and Ashmont made a splendid show of flirting, tantalizing everybody with promises of complications, possibly deadly."

"Did we appear to be flirting?" she said. "I had no idea. I have so much to learn."

"I'd rather you didn't become an expert, but I fear you will. You made a good show, in any event. And you weren't the only ones. There was Blackwood looking daggers at Alice and vice versa." He sipped his champagne. "Been away for a year. Don't know whether this is a recent development or it's been going on for a good while. Wish I knew what that was about, but she tells me it's none of my bloody business."

"And you can't ask Blackwood."

Ripley gave her a shocked look. "Certainly not."

"It isn't done," she said, shaking her head. She'd noticed as well the way Blackwood and Alice watched each other, and the way they each contrived to do it when the other wasn't looking. She was vastly curious about them, too, but it was rather too early in her marriage, she felt, to try to get involved in her sister-in-law's private life. That didn't mean she'd never do it. She hoped they'd be like sisters, and get along at least as well as her mother and aunts did, and that if Alice wanted to talk or wanted help, she'd turn to Olympia. And vice versa.

But that was for the future.

"So there was Alice," he said. "And what else? Oh, yes. Aunt Julia and Ashmont's Uncle Fred. Talk of looking daggers."

"Yes, something between them," Olympia said. "One sensed it when he came to Camberley Place."

"I know I heard something, sometime," he said. "Some old story. Think I heard it from my mother. But I'm damned if I can remember the details."

Olympia remembered what Lady Charles had said to her.

Charles was not my first choice . . . I married him in resignation, if not despair.

"I believe there is a story," she said. "Your aunt hinted at it to me. But she did not offer details. I only know it happened before she married your uncle."

"That must be twenty-five years ago."

"Whatever the story is, I thought they danced well together, daggers or not."

"Not surprising," Ripley said. "They're diplomatists of the highest order. Not that one could tell, the way they went at each other that day, after you read Ashmont's letter and walked out."

"Fatal day. Fatal letter." Olympia leaned on the railing and closed her eyes. "I walked out of the house and on to my lovely ruination. What a pity one can be ruined only once."

"Not necessarily."

She turned and looked inquiringly up at him, forgetting the champagne glass in her hand. The drink spilled over the railing.

He took the glass from her. "I think you've had too little," he said. "Let's go inside and have some more, and I'll tell you my plan. One of those what-you-call-ems."

"I have no idea what you call them."

He gestured her toward the open doorway, which led to her apartments. She walked in ahead of him.

He set their glasses down. "Like charades or a tableau, but — no, like a vignette? Or a play. In this one, you've never been ruined before."

She straightened her spectacles. "Have I not?"

"No. In this one, I am the wicked seducer. I corner you in a dark part of the garden." He led her to a corner of the boudoir. "I twirl my mustachios and say, 'At last, fair maiden, I have you in my clutches,' and you say . . ." He waited.

She put up her hands in a theatrical gesture of terror. "Oh, no, somebody save me!"

"Nobody will save you. It's too late. You're mine." He pulled her into his arms.

Olympia pretended to fight him. "No, no, a thousand times no!"

"You can't fight me. I'm too strong."

"Oh, dear, it's true." She grasped his upper arm. "You are, indeed. Too big and strong. Such . . . muscles." She stroked his chest. "So manly. Wicked but manly."

"You'd better give in."

"Must I?"

"Of course you must. It would be the practical and sensible thing to do."

He kissed her, and being a practical and sensible girl, she did the practical and sensible thing, and let herself be ruined. Again. And again, that night, and on many, many other occasions thereafter.

AUTHOR'S NOTE

Pounds, shillings, pence, and other old money

Money equivalents: Until 1971, English money wasn't based on a decimal system. It went like this:

Twelve pence in a shilling (*bob,* in slang).
Twenty shillings in a pound or sovereign.
Twenty-one shillings in a guinea.

There were numerous smaller and larger units of these denominations, such as:

Ten shillings in a half sovereign.
Five shillings in a crown.

For more, please see Wikipedia's article on "Coins of the Pound Sterling," under "Pre-Decimal Coinage."

Attire

My characters' dress is derived mainly from early nineteenth-century ladies' magazines available online (with guidance from the Tailors, Milliners, and Mantua Makers of Colonial Williamsburg). Olympia's first bridal dress appeared in several publications of 1833, including the *Magazine of the Beau Monde,* where it was labeled an evening dress and colored yellow, though the lady holds a prayer book. However, it was common for magazines to plagiarize each other. In this case, the dress was copied from the *Petit Courrier des Dames.* The *Ladies' Cabinet* copied it, too. The original and the *Ladies' Cabinet* show it in white and label it a wedding dress. Given the number of different English publications in which it appears, it must have been a hit.

Contrary to popular belief, which gives Queen Victoria credit for starting the fashion for white wedding dresses, white was customary well before she married Prince Albert in 1840. By the 1820s at least, brides wore white, as fashion plates and other sources show.

Special License

Some of my British readers have written

to me about my various characters getting married in houses at odd times. As one reader pointed out, "weddings in England and Wales can only take place in authorized or licensed premises, so not in your own home. Following the Marriage Act of 1836 weddings could take place in a licensed 'Registry Office', but before that they could only be performed in places of worship."

True, unless you married by special license. This allowed a couple to wed wherever and whenever they wished. A special license was *very* expensive, and had to be obtained from Doctors' Commons. A great many members of the aristocracy married that way: In the Marriages listings in the various periodicals, we find the daughter or son of Lord This or That or Sir Thus & Such married at the family home.

In *The Law Dictionary* (1810 and later editions) we find this: "But by special licence or dispensation from the Archbishop of Canterbury, Marriages, especially of persons of quality, are frequently in their own houses, out of canonical hours, in the evening, and often solemnized by others in other churches than where one of the parties lives, and out of time of divine service, &c."

You can see an 1852 Special License in

The Etiquette of Courtship and Matrimony: with a Complete Guide to the Forms of a Wedding, which can be found online as part of the British Library's archives on Google Books.

On my website blog (http://www.lorettachase.com/blog) as well as at *Two Nerdy History Girls* (http://twonerdyhistorygirls.blogspot.com), where Susan Holloway Scott and I blog on historical fashion and other matters of social history, you can expect to find posts explaining many of the historical references in my stories.

When it comes to historical details, though, a picture can be worth a thousand words. This is why you might want to take a look at my Pinterest page (https://www.pinterest.com/lorettachase), which offers fashions as well as other illustrations for my books. If you want to *see* the difference between a hackney cab and a hackney coach or a landau and a curricle, that's the place to look.

If you encounter other historical puzzles in my story, please contact me via my website, www.LorettaChase.com. While my response time can be hideously slow, especially when I'm in the throes of a work-in-snail-like-progress, I do answer eventually, and some readers' questions have inspired blog posts and/or contributed to future stories.

ABOUT THE AUTHOR

Loretta Chase holds a B.A. from Clark University, where she majored in English and minored unofficially in visual art. Her job history includes clerical, administrative, and part-time teaching posts at Clark; stints with jewelry and clothing retailers; and a Dickensian six-month experience as a meter maid.

In the course of moonlighting as a corporate video scriptwriter, she fell under the spell of a producer who lured her into writing novels . . . and marrying him. The books resulting from this union have won a number of awards, including the Romance Writers of America's *Rita*.